AMAZON/PRINT/LIBRARY Version ONLY

Ebook/Print Cover: CAROL MARQUES DESIGNS
AMAZON/LIBRARY VERSION ONLY

Original Ebook/Print Cover: EMCAT Designs
Maps: C. Featherstone
Editing, Proofing, backgrounds, & Formatting: Dirty Sexy Words/ Storm shield Editing/Little Tailfeather Publishing
Cassandra's logos: Pretty in Ink Creations/Artlogo
Goosebusters Alpha team: Kat Silver, Becky Ross, Erica Taryn
Duckhunters Proofing: Jackie Hanson
Sensitivity Readers: Brit Mason, Gail Jericho
Translation Consultant: Mo Jacobs
Legal Services: Joshua Farley, esq.

Images/Fonts: Depositphotos, Shutterstock, Canva, &
Photoshop

No GenAI was used within this book. All errors and greatness
are by an ADHD muppet.

❀ Formatted with Vellum

Little Tailfeather Publishing

Signature Page

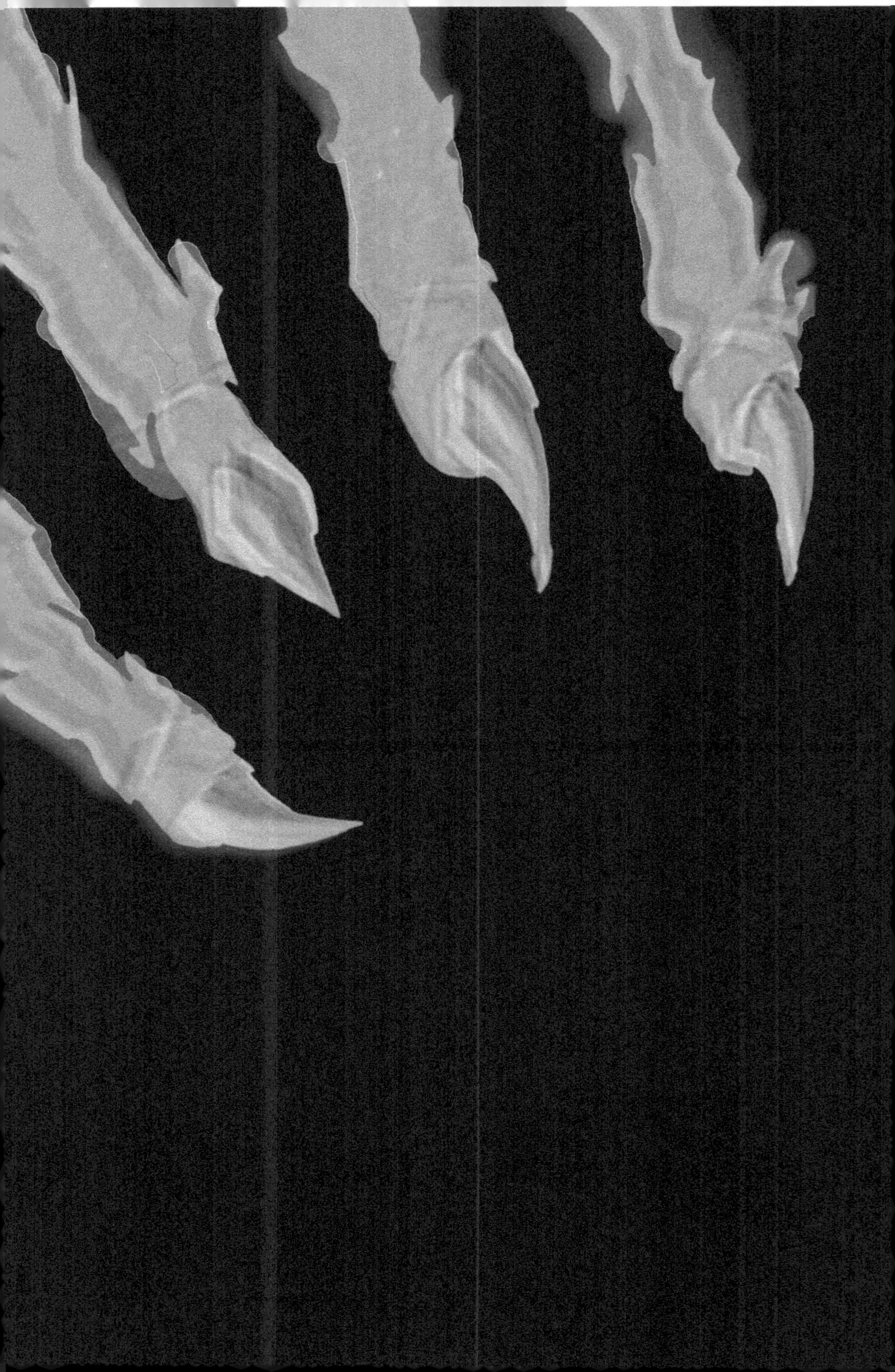

RISE OF THE  RESISTANCE

HOOKED ON A FELINE

INTERNATIONAL BEST SELLING AUTHOR

CASSANDRA FEATHERSTONE

Stalk Cassandra Featherstone in the Dark Corners of the Web

JOIN MY FACEBOOK GROUP AND
FOLLOW ME EVERYWHERE!

WANT MORE?

SIGN UP FOR
MY BI-WEEKLY MANIFESTO FOR
A FREE SERIES SAMPLER:

Join my Ream as a FREE follower or exclusive subscriber to get access to cover reveals, WIPs, Serial Stories, and personal chats from me!

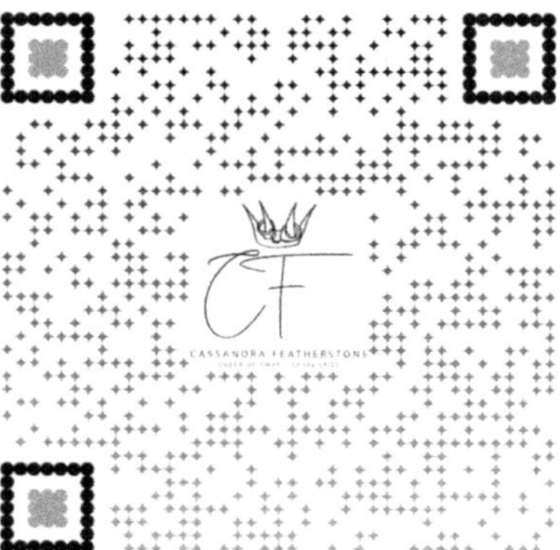

Content Information

This is a *paranormal whychoose romance with poly elements*—our FMC, Delilah, **will** make choices, but it will be to protect her peace and her family. She will make more choices throughout the series, so don't worry that you've been 'RH baited.' It's coming, I promise.

There are many situations included that are intended for <u>mature audiences (18+).</u>

In these prequels, there may be instances/references (be they small or lengthy) that could trigger some individuals such as:

- liberal use of appropriate consent
- Mention off-page of dubious consent situations
- group scenes
- MMF, MM, MFM, MF, MFMMM, FF, FFM, FFMM, relationships and more throughout series
- emotional abuse by mates
- physical abuse (off-page) by mates
- alphahole/possessive MMCs
- cinnamon roll MMCs

- multiple POVs— including ones beyond the MCs
- unhinged MMC
- unhealthy coping mechanisms
- selfish, narcissistic mates
- boundaries being crossed
- BDSM
- raw sex
- traumatic childhood
- alcohol use and abuse
- threats of bodily harm
- death
- body modifications
- fancy genitalia
- mating bites/marks
- androids and building androids
- bullying (in person and on social media)
- PTSD
- blood
- emotional abuse from outside poly group
- body dysmorphia
- adult language
- pop culture references
- literary references
- emotional manipulation
- power play
- adorable nicknames
- physical intimidation
- rough sex
- markings/tattoos
- family dysfunction
- Community of various poly families
- animal companion
- brief mentions of non-body positive dieting culture
- very liberal re-imagining of history

- morally gray secret organization that monitors mercenaries/dimension
- official corruption
- name calling
- occasional misogyny
- exhibitionism
- hand necklaces
- adult bullying
- magical kinks
- impact play
- elitism
- bribery
- corpses
- drama
- physical threats to FMC and others
- species-ism
- pregnancy (in future books, no loss)

No sexual practices in this book should be taken as safe or appropriate for real life application.

Content information is important and I don't ever want to harm a reader with inaccurate information.

Author Ramblings

Readers,

This series is my baby, and I cannot wait for my current readers to discover the roots of the *Legends of the Ouroboros* universe.

Delilah is a complex woman who thought she was escaping from her mistakes, but stumbled into an even more dangerous hive of people than the small town she grew up in that we all know and love.

Magick blends with a wee bit of science in the beings who populate the Rift with the humans, and that gives this an interesting counterpoint to the entirely paranormal worlds of the other series in this universe. Don't let the slight bit of complex science that I took liberties with at the beginning discourage you... no, this series is paranormal, magickal, and right up your alley, I promise.

There are some things about this world that you should know. They aren't new to my books, so you might not be surprised, but it's more intense in ROR. This has a medium burn with a slow build because our girl starts out with a vast family that is not right for her. It contracts as she tries to heal from the damage and the attacks of people she thought were her friends. Because of who she is, it expands again and well, there may be some heart break in far off books.

ROR is first-person, present, multi-POV—from many people, even outside of the family group. They have unique voices and their contributions are important; hell, you're going to end up rooting for a lot of them. I know people who have practically adopted some of the side characters. I think you will grow to love the extra perspectives given the complexity of the story and world they live in.

If you have trouble remembering anyone, I have my staple maps, world guides, and info for you about the sprawling world of the Rift.

There are free prequels on Ream (even for followers) that set this world up and you should sample those shorts prior to reading Hooked on a Feline. They give you small snippets of characters, world, locations, etc.

Our girl Delilah has made Easter egg visits in many of your current fave novels... you've seen her red hair and the man who will be her mate running around in both paranormal and contemporary series. She's one of the key players when we get to the huge crossover series at the end of my long timeline, so you'll want to get to know her.

If you haven't, please read the content information. You may find things in this series that are not your cup of tea, and I don't wish to accidentally harm anyone. Some of those things are in future books, but they'll be integral, so not skippable.

As always, I thank all my readers, teams, besties, and people who support me as I continue my author journey after four years. Since this story is the one I entered the realm with, it's fitting it be re-vamped now.

Take care of yourselves and enjoy.

Blood and guts,

Cassandra Featherstone
QUEEN OF SMART, SASSY SPICE

Reader's Note

A FEW THINGS YOU SHOULD KNOW...

A few things you should know...

This story is Book One in the Rise of the Resistance series.

It has previously been in serials, but has been re-vamped to fit the new branding and release of the series. You may not know everything at once and you will find somethings become clearer with the more stories you read.

You will want to get to know each character and how they think, relate, and fit into the world. This is one of your prelim intros to how things work in the Rift. There are several prequels at varying time frames before the start of this book available on my Ream to all followers—even the free tier at https://reamstories. com/cassandrafeatherstone

Given intricacy of the Riftverse, there's a lot of specific words, places, nicknames, and various details to remember. To help, I've included a Character/Location/Family Guide, maps, a glossary of terminology, and I have made the *foreign word translations clickable end of chapter notes.*

This is multi-book series, so *everything will not be revealed in book one.* I promise it will all tie up with a HEA; don't worry!

There are some words that are slang, jargon, or foreign that may seem to be spelled wrong—*please email* if you think something is wrong. It may not be and I want to make sure it doesn't get taken down so everyone can read!

Fictional people/organizations who are part of the *Legends of the Ouroboros* universe (but not this series) are mentioned. *If you haven't read their books, it won't keep you from enjoying this one.*

If you see this book *anywhere in ebook format besides Amazon*, please reach out to me via social media. Pirating kills my ability to write full time and I am so grateful for your help.

Contact Cass for issues or to report piracy: teamcassandrafeatherstone@cassandrafeatherstone.com

<u>THANK YOU</u> FOR SUPPORTING ME BY BUYING MY WORK, BUT AS ALWAYS, I'M GOING TO SUGGEST YOU BOUNCE.

THIS IS THE FIRST BOOK I WROTE AFTER WE ALL SCURRIED INTO LOCKDOWN FOR COVID. EVERYTHING FROM HERE ONLY GETS WORSE AS I HAD A LOT OF TIME TO VERY CREATIVE WITH MY IMAGINATION.

RISE OF THE RESISTANCE IS THE GATEWAY DRUG, AND I REFUSE TO HEAR ABOUT ANYONE 'JONESING' FOR MORE.

WEIRD.

CAVEAT: IF YOU CHOOSE TO KEEP READING, KNOW THAT AT NO TIME WILL I EXPLAIN TERMS, POSITIONS, THEMES, TROPES, OR ANY OTHER PART OF THIS NOVEL AT FAMILY EVENTS, IN GROUP CHATS, OR ON SOCIAL MEDIA.

<u>DON'T ASK.</u>

Hooked on a Feline Playlist

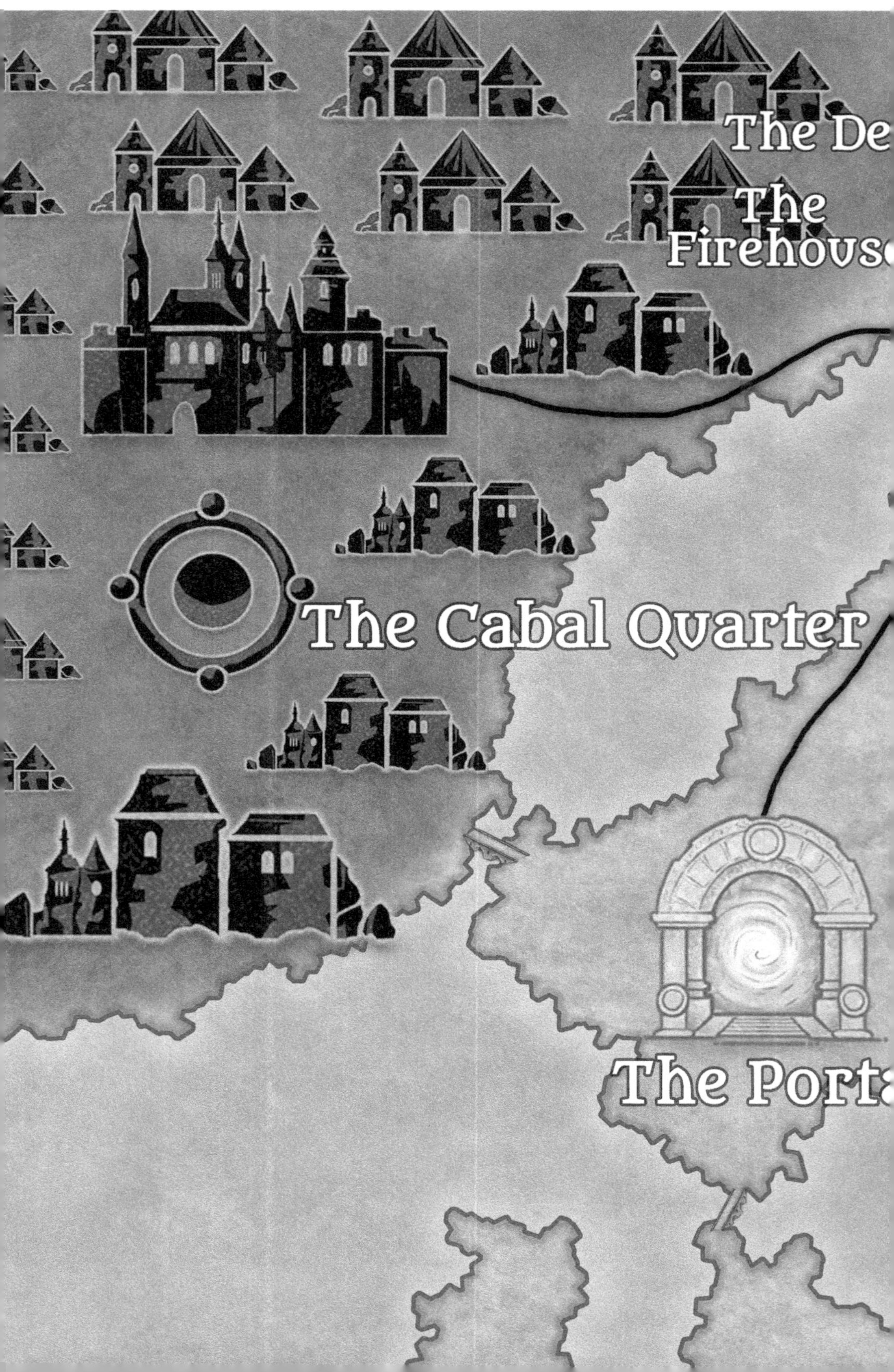

The De
The
Firehous
The Cabal Qvarter
The Port

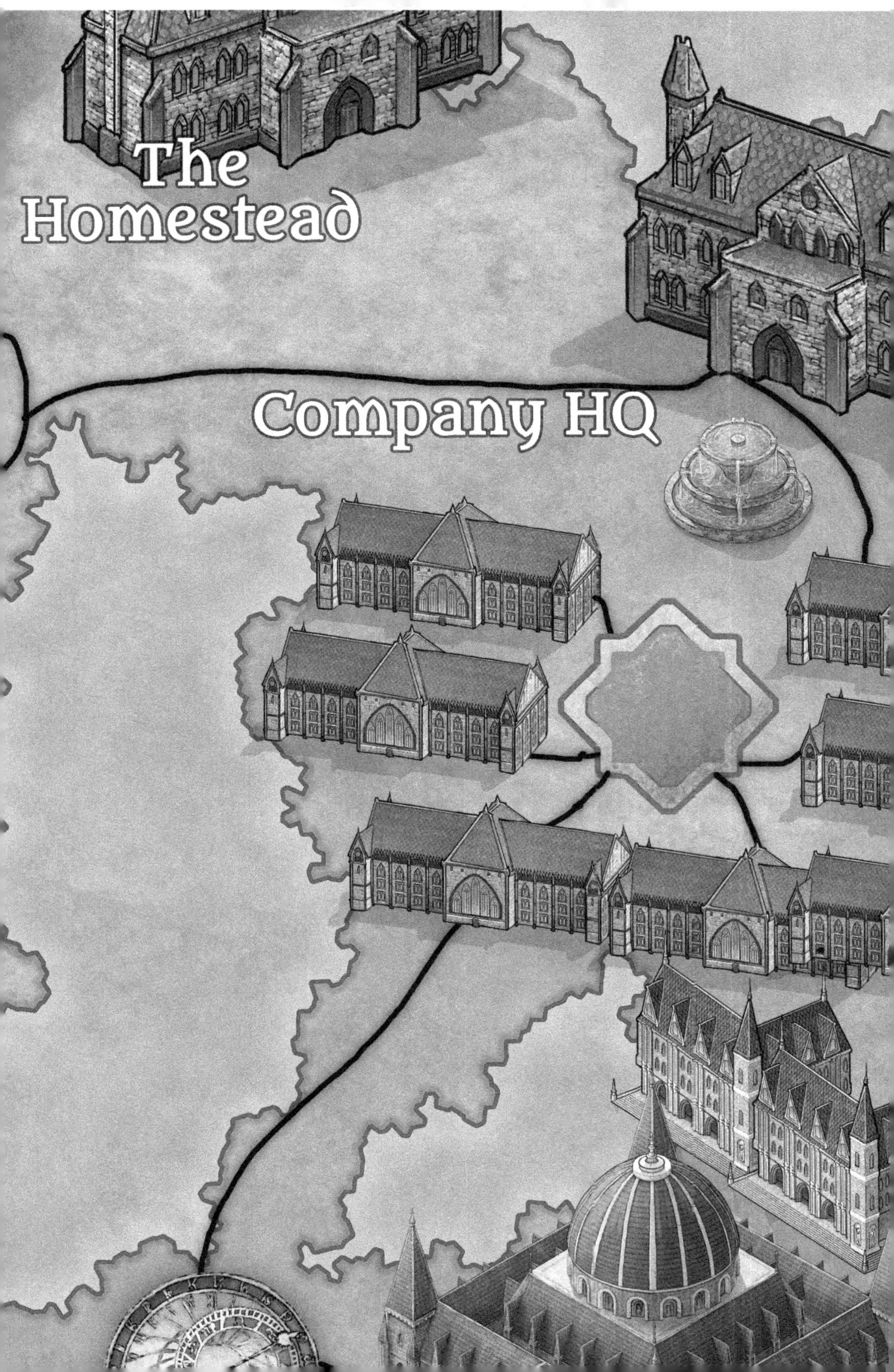

The
Homestead
Company HQ

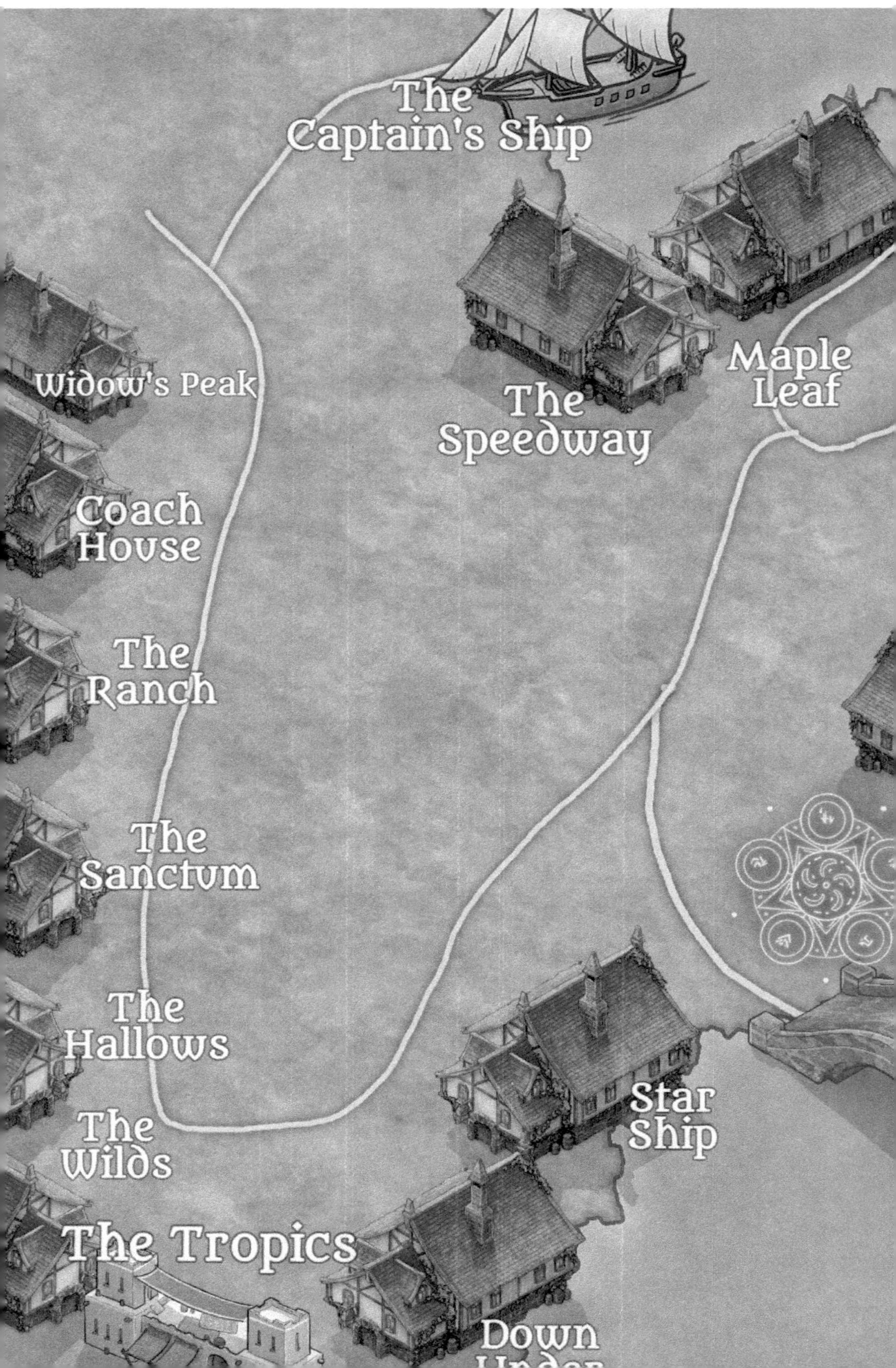

The Captain's Ship
Maple Leaf
The Speedway
Widow's Peak
Coach House
The Ranch
The Sanctum
The Hallows
The Wilds
The Tropics
Star Ship
Down Under

The Portal
The Maison
The Frat
Jagvars
The Resistance Quarter

Dedication

To everyone who dreamed of telling
stories that people would read
late into the night,
For those who see the shining stars
and whisper their pleas to the
universe,
Destiny is in our hands as long as we
never give up.

Maturity is working through your trauma and not using it as a never ending excuse for poor behavior.

— ELLIS ANTHONY

Prologue

As with all good romances, this starts with a man and a woman—or rather, two men and a woman...

Centuries ago, humans believed in things beyond their comprehension more readily. Supernaturals and their non-magical counterparts co-existed by using fairy tales, myths, and folklore to create a world where they interacted on specific terms that protected everyone. But as all species do, both sides of the coin evolved and dissension within their ranks and with one another caused internal wars, famine, and other tragedies.

The supernaturals evolved more quickly than humans, so the ancient bloodlines gathered together to form a governing body for all the non-human species. For a long time, this group made sure to curate history in a way that did not dishonor the gods or destiny, but kept humans from interfering in their business.

The stories of conflict, triumph, and regret from human history were often supernatural, but the truth was concealed. Eventually, humans turned their efforts towards science rather than spiritualism and the tales of things that go bump in the night became

1

legend. This allowed the Society to focus solely on their own and as time went on, they expanded across the globe.

Our love story begins with an ancient woman who drew the attention of two supes in the Society. A warlock and a vampire, brothers in spirit if not blood, ascended to their council seats to become the last survivors of their names. Their families were decimated in various conflicts over the years and these two men grew resentful of the Society's leniency towards humans and lower tier supes alike. They were both in love with the ancient woman, though, and for a time after they mated with her, it settled their need for vengeance.

But evolution never ends and once humans advanced far enough to threaten supernaturals again, their thirst for revenge flared again. When they couldn't convince the Society council to conquer the non-magical beings, the brothers left their positions to work as undercover agents within a growing organization of humans dedicated to fomenting crime and strife. The warlock climbed the ranks of leadership over many decades and the vampire dove into the scientific program; together, they conspired to control the human population through their own weapons and technology.

When their true aims were discovered by the Society and their mate, they got exiled. By then, the warlock was in full control of the global criminal organization that operated under many names in many countries. He and his brother pleaded with their mate to join them, and when she refused to alter the course of Fate, he performed a forbidden ritual to unmate them from her.

The consequences of his reckless, selfish decision echoed through the world like wildfire. Wars broke out, treaties soured, crops died, and disease raged across the lands. Society members around the world confiscated all the tomes containing information on revoking a mate bond to prevent another ripple of magic that powerful from being released.

Unfortunately, the anguish of being cut off from their magically intended partner affected the vampire and the warlock as well. Their organization was thriving in the chaos the revocation caused, but they could barely stand to be in the same room as one another. The time came when they argued so often that it threatened their mission and they split the organization in half.

Each took the half they preferred—the warlock keeping the criminal wing and the vampire taking the technological sector. They vowed to share resources when required, but their empires would remain separated for good.

As technology continued to advance, The Company branched out into mercenary pursuits and the vampire blended magic and science so well that he created a pocket dimension to hide his labs, agents, and their secrets within. He named it The Rift in honor of the divide between him and his brother and once it was fully operational, he retreated into a world far away from the humans he despised.

That seclusion kept him from knowing his brother and their former lover were briefly reunited during the sparkling days of disco. Despite the cadre of new mates the Fates provided the ancient one, she relented one last time and from that tragic mistake, a child was born.

In order to protect her from her heritage, the child was left at one of the hybrid enclaves created by the Society and eventually adopted. She lived an inauspicious life as a 'lost one' until one day, the small amount of magic she could access sparked and she ran from her life, including the Guardian watching from the shadows.

Only the Fates could have conspired for this child to find her way to the portal to The Rift and settle there without knowing what she'd discover on the other side.

Delilah Lenore O'Hara was *never* meant to set foot in The Rift, but once she did, it started a cascade of events that cannot be prevented.

This time, the story begins with a woman and many men—oh, so many men.

The Cat Tracks Down The Key

DELILAH

Tilting my head, I listen to the sounds of the night with my eyes closed, soaking in the surrounding cacophony. Most people would say the night is quiet, all is safe and sound, but they don't have my senses and they are not waiting for a psychopath.

I am.

Tonight, I'm seeking answers to questions I haven't had the courage to ask out loud—not even to my brood. My source of information is as dangerous as the possibilities borne of the information that I seek, but I've exhausted all the other options I know of.

That sounded cryptic, but the changes I'm going through are unheard of in my community.

The only person who *might* have the knowledge of the 'Creation' and the science behind it is the clone I'm in this park waiting for. Taurus doesn't associate with his own community, much less the Resistance. He's unpredictable, violent, and only plays by his rules. I shouldn't have opened Pandora's box by contacting him.

But he's my only viable option.

After the Battle of Blood and Steel ended the Conflict, his family moved from the evolving landscape of the Cabal Quarter to its outer limits. The Rift was changing, and his kin refused to change with it, preferring to isolate themselves from the fray. He keeps his ears open—as does his mate—because prior to asking for this meeting; I baited him in public, hoping to pique his interest.

As predicted, he couldn't stop himself from parading about, preening and showing off before disappearing again. Once he and his mate started paying attention to our world, I had them right where I wanted them. I primed them for my approach despite this being the worst plan possible. Taurus is a snarling, opinionated son of a bitch who dines on the likes of me for three squares a day and he makes sure everyone knows it. His ego is the size of a small third world country—that will be my way in. If I can maneuver my request around that behemoth carefully, I'll get what I need without raining hell on my entire community. He doesn't need to know more than what I offer and he definitely doesn't need to know what's going on in the Resistance.

I don't want to give away all our secrets for his help, regardless of how much I need it.

After my gambit worked, I made a polite inquiry to his mate, Talia. She's no less a slithering venomous reptile than him, but my email was well-received. She informed me that Taurus would 'grant me an audience' this evening precisely at eleven p.m.

The edicts about tardiness and rescheduling made my teeth grind, but I let it go.

Checking my watch again, I sigh. Talia told me in no uncertain terms that he would leave if I was a second late. It's a half hour beyond our appointment time, there's no sign of the snooty clone, and I'm officially on borrowed time. My eyes are darting around nervously as the seconds tick by, hoping no one in my house wakes up to find me gone. That will set off alarms I'd prefer to stay silent, especially since none of them know what I'm doing tonight.

Why am I still here when it's obvious that the assclown stood me up?

Because I *need* to know the answers to my questions, that's why. I *have* to fix my beastly bullshit before it destroys my family, and he's the only person I know who might have access to this information.

The 'Creation'—that's what they called engineering the first clones—is shrouded in mystery. The Company scientists part of it and what they did are trade secrets. They never leave the HQ, unlike other human staff and workers. No one has a damned clue what they did to 'create' the three originals, nor how they created the clones that followed.

Hell, no one even knows what their huge campus hides or how to get to it.

Science on that level *has* to be the cause and solution to the crap happening to my frail human body. It's not normal to turn into a fucking were or whatever overnight; there has to be an explanation. I'd be willing to bet my entire shoe collection on the fuckers who developed the clones and created this damn place having the tech to reverse it. Letting my family know how worried I am would only make the problem worse, so I accept it with grace and wit.

My deception entails pretending I love every aspect of my kitty transformation without question, which is one of the colossal *lies* in my life. Truth be told, I've had enough of the damn turmoil since it started. I don't need some crazy mutant virus to eat my body from the inside out, nor do I need my mates losing their shit over it.

It's too damn much for one person to handle on their own.

That's why I'm in no condition emotionally to hash my feelings out with our resident serial killer, but I don't have a choice. Now I'm here, he's not, and I'm done waiting. That prehistoric, preening prat used to rule the roost in this town, but no more. He and his Cabal-loving ilk left the playing field open when they all bounced after the Conflict.

The Resistance claimed our own section of the Rift to call our home when the Cabal faded into the background. I always thought it was weird that they went to war to claim this place, but after they won, every single one of their leaders slowly disappeared. Perhaps they couldn't deal with how the landscape changed after the war or even that they had to wage one at all. I wasn't living in the Rift during that time, but it wouldn't surprise me.

Dictators like people they can keep under their thumbs and they realized that would never happen again.

My friends Dominique, Lily, and I were the ones who set up the Resistance quarter, and now it's bigger than the Cabal quarter ever was. We're all close and the more people we recruited, the closer our community became. Somehow, I took on the role of leader for our people, and ever since, my home has been a revolving door of friends and family. It probably looks like I'm a feudal queen to an outsider, but they do not know what my life has become in the past few months. They don't know that despite my large family; I feel completely alone.

The people I love have damaged me and becoming a shifter made it worse.

That doesn't mean I'm going to let that antiquated birdbrain make me doubt my place in this universe. Taurus may have left me sitting here like a fawning debutante, but I only stayed because there is no other source I can wheedle this info out of. The Company recruits, their archives, and their resources are within his grasp. He's not the first clone—that honor belongs to one of my extended family—but he is the only one still connected to the people involved in the 'Creation'.

That's it.

I snarl in frustration, kicking a rock across the pavement as I storm back to my borrowed motorcycle. My inability to resolve this shit tonight means I'll have to start over. My Beast is seeping through the barriers as the tension inside me mounts. I close my eyes, knowing that I don't have a strong enough hold on her to allow my anger to overflow in public.

Calm must prevail.

I haven't had the courage to let the Beast completely free more than once, and that did not turn out well. My passion induced lapses have led to nothing but trouble and heartache, leaving me to pick up the pieces of my battered heart like a sad little custodian. Allowing her free rein because I'm angry won't have any better results. I'll just end up with someone kicking me to the curb like before.

A breeze ruffles through the trees and carries a scent most wouldn't catch—it's faint, but so very male. The smell makes the primal part of me take notice and I turn slowly. Tamping the cat down internally, I struggle with how delicious the scent is. I doubt my appreciation would go over well with Taurus's dangerous and possessive mate, so I breathe carefully when he finally approaches.

His posture is perfectly arranged to draw my attention. The pose is reminiscent of the cover of a supernatural romance novel: a slouching predator with gleaming platinum spikes and leather worn tight enough to mold to him over his sleek designer clothing. A haze of expensive—probably personally blended—tobacco smoke curls around him, and the moonlight shines off his boots and bike.

Why in the bloody hell did I think this was a good idea again? Are my answers this important?

This situation has disaster written in blood all over it and yet, I can't come up with one solid alternative to being here. Not only that, but I can't even think of two syllables to string together. He's glaring at me as if my silence is as egregious as his lateness and I have to fight back the cat again when she takes umbrage at his gall. I didn't realize how hard this would be—focusing on his shit and holding my beast back—and I'm paying for it now. There's no way out, though, so I have to suck it up and deal. I crack my neck and narrow my eyes at the dark figure standing before me.

Fine. Be pissy, you prancing prima donna. Two can play at that game.

A brow arch is the only response I get to my change in posture. Obviously, I have to throw him off guard, so he doesn't think he has the upper hand. The only way I can do that is to puff myself up as big as he is, dismiss his power, and use my brain and my body to throw him off my scent. It's a good thing I came here well rested or I don't know if I could pull this shit off. I'm constantly tired since my new 'friend' showed up and I can't seem to muster up the energy I used to. Pretending to be a hundred percent will drain the hell out of me... but I don't see any other way.

Time to put on the show, Deli.

The Cat Faces The Enemy

❦

DELILAH

Sauntering over to him, I plaster a smirk on my face. We're going nowhere if I don't break this Mexican standoff and I'm certain he'll stand here letting me stare at him all night before he gives an inch. "Thanks for meeting me. I'm not sure how much longer I can hang before my absence gets noticed, though."

He arches a brow, feigning disinterest, but his scent changes as he studies me.

I set the hook well because I smell surprise. He's playing it close to the vest, trying to look uncaring, but that's not true. Regardless, it can't hurt to confirm the information I believe he has, so now I'll pretend to clarify. "It's problematic to escape with eight permanent residents and four semi-permanent guests. Sneaking out was an exercise in stealth—though, a necessary one. I have enough trouble keeping my concerns under wraps without them discovering *this* little tête-à-tête."

My thoughts drift to the warm tangle of limbs in my bed, and I sigh. This damn mutation has altered my life in such a way that my feeling of home may never be the same. I hate it and I'll survive this just to have a sliver of hope that I can go back to how it was.

Suddenly, it occurs to me I need to make sure of something before we continue.

"Please tell me that Talia knows you came here to talk to me, despite being late. I'd prefer *not* to duck flying weaponry. I don't have it in me to deal with that on top of everything else." Pinching the bridge of my nose, I realize the internal struggle with my Beast is giving me a migraine. She's making it hard to maintain the aloof facade that I need to project with Taurus—something I have to work around or this is over before it begins.

His eye roll rivals that of every teenager in the universe for attitude, and as if that jackassery wasn't condescending enough, he snorts. "My golden goddess always knows where I am, as I know exactly where she is. It's a head thing." His eyes focus intensely, his heated expression almost sinful to watch. "She's not within throwing range."

A whiff of primal catches the breeze and the beast inside lifts her head inside of me, sniffing curiously. Her interest is a cue to back away from the smoking hot murderer and keep my cool. Shaking my head to clear it, I look heavenward to the Goddess, hoping this fiend is not my problem for much longer.

Honestly, I don't know if either of us could survive a long-term association. He's too high maintenance and there is no shortage of smoking hot dick to keep me occupied at home. In fact, sometimes there's too much even for me, and that's saying something.

Watching him through my lashes it amazes me that although most of the clones come from his template and have the same basic features, not one has an identical temperament or talents. Genetically, they are the same, but their personalities and appearances are all over the map. They're no different from humans in that way, but it's hard to reconcile that when you're toe to toe with them.

Realizing he's still talking, I blanch. I don't have the foggiest idea what on earth he said while I was out to lunch mentally. I could have agreed to let him serve me for supper and I won't know unless he repeats it. *Son of a bitch*. No more letting the tasty smelling murderer distract me or I'm never getting out of here.

"I'd prefer to get on with it. I like to be away from my mate as little as possible, same as you with your...guests. She's waiting for me; it's a heart thing." His eyes cut to mine, burning with fire and ice as if I've offended him by letting him prattle on. The intense stare fades quickly as his lips quirk with amusement and irritation as I visibly bristle.

I didn't come to have a coffee klatch or play games. He's the one who was late, for the goddess' sake.

"Fine with me," I reply as I search for a spot to get comfy. I finally hop up on the wall he's slouching against, noting the slight twitch of surprise. He didn't see that move coming. "I'm interested in the process of 'Creation'. I don't need the exact specifics—I know it's a big whoop-de-doo secret—but a few details might clear up some questions."

He inhales one last time before he flicks his smoke aside in silence. Watching the sparks skitter across the pavement like mini-fireworks, I ponder how appropriate that image is for our current situation. My gaze cuts back to him, but he's implacable in leather and silk, smelling of the night.

Christ. He's not Batman. What is wrong with me?

"What's with you lot, anyway?" he growls in disgust. "All you humans want explanations and tours and information. 'Tell us about the science, the lab coats, the Battle, the Company...' None of you are happy to accept their gift at face value. Hell, half of you aren't able to recognize that we are a gift when we fall in your lap, shag you senseless, and make your piddling lives more interesting by the second."

I didn't notice as his rant built up, but his face has changed. His fangs have dropped, the ridges appeared, and now the predator is loose. Taurus' temper is legendary and I've hit a sore spot. I've barely got my beast reined in, and if he doesn't quell his demon soon, he's in for a hell of a shock.

Not that his arrogant, pissy ass reaction is shocking... of course he considers himself a goddamn 'gift.'

Talia's always fondly dubbed him the prince of preening. That's a mild moniker for his egomania, but she supposedly loves the dickhead. Once the Cabal left, it was easy to forget the original clones are much less domesticated than the current generations. Taurus's body count in the Conflict was a large part of why the two factions had to come to the table. He was running through people faster than anyone could gather more. Obviously, Taurus is still living the life the Company trains its recruits for.

That's not something I'm used to dealing with, so I didn't have time to prepare my inner kitty.

Ignoring the situation isn't helping, so I breathe deeply, digging my fingers into the brick to stop the stirring beast lumbering around inside me. The scent of his power and strength are alluring, and she is loath to settle once provoked. It's become a genuine struggle to fight off the urges, and I'm concerned that my beast might touch off a new incident in the Conflict. If I can't calm her down, she will reach out to our mates and all hell will break loose—all because my current companion has a burr up his ass about gratitude.

Right as I'm about to lose my grip, something odd happens. Taurus' eyes fade to icy blue and his gaze hazes over. He tilts his head to the side as if listening to something faint. The posture is instantly recognizable to me—Talia is speaking to him through their mating bond, and only he can hear her dialogue inside his head. My own experiences with that side effect of mating are both good and bad, so I can't tell if we're going to have a problem.

After a few moments, his features melt to normal and I'm shocked to see that he looks sheepish. I didn't think humility was in his vocabulary. His newfound calm allows my heart to slow its hammering pace and I can push the cat back.

Thank the goddess for Talia's impeccable timing.

Taurus chuckles ruefully and runs his hands through his perfectly coiffed spikes and shrugs. "Interfering wench. Alright, I've been bidden to do my best to be helpful. What details are you looking for?"

Showing my amusement would be a bad thing, despite finding his tough-guy image less impressive. A five-foot-two, tanned knife tosser just completely owned him from afar. Drawing further attention to it would be foolish—if not fatal—so I paste a stunned expression on my face so I can play along. Placating him is a necessary evil if I want to get the information I seek. However, I know more about him now than I did at the start, and that will only help me achieve my goal.

Taurus is an egomaniac, a predator, and many claim that he's evil—all of which I like on any given day, despite the protests of my more passive mates. But his leash only extends as far as Talia allows. This display shows he's as much a slave to his collar as I am to mine.

My lips curl up as I twirl the ring on my finger for a moment. I wonder—not for the first time tonight—if the knowledge he might possess is so important to me, I'm willing to risk a civil war. Taurus might be leashed, but I don't trust him or the Cabal as far as I could throw them. It's already hard convincing the beast to back down to appease him. I just know that it's a chance that I have to take. My worries for everyone's safety have become too great, so I push forward.

"The 'Creation' uses science, not magick, right? The same DNA is used for all the clones when they're made, isn't it? I mean, obviously not for Wilde, because his transformation was a bit of both. Wouldn't you all look the same under a microscope? You have the same strand, same markers, same mutations, right?"

"Christ, woman, do I look like a bloody lab coat to you? What in hell would I know about markers and scopes and, better yet, why the fuck would I want to?" He gives me a cocky grin that belies his quick protest, and I roll my eyes skyward, wondering if we'll be trading potshots when the sun rises.

A growl of frustration so low that only enhanced hearing could catch it emerges from my chest, and I stop to take a slow breath. *Find your center, Deli, find your center.* "Maybe because you work for the Company? You have to know all the ins and outs—clever boy that you are—and you know I can't ask your brother."

Shit, shit, shit.

His eyes narrow right as I realize I put my foot in my mouth. He baited me and I fell for it big time. "Anyway, I assumed you were the most knowledgeable source to get the answers that I *have* to know. I've got this research project that's on a deadline."

I smell the distrust radiating off of him, but now it's tinged with a bit of curiosity. *That's better than nothing, right?* A tiny spark of interest could lead to getting what I want—or to him going on a homicidal tear through the city because I let the 'brother' cat out of the bag. I can't believe he's not scented him on me yet.

Regardless, he has the trail now because he's doing that annoying 'animal instinct' clone thing with his head. It's one part scenting and one part hunter. On my boys, it's sexy as hell, but on Taurus, it makes me think he's pondering a kitty flank steak for dinner. While I'm okay with a game of 'chase me' before a bit of rough and tumble, I don't want to end up as prey.

His lack of readable expression is unnerving me, so it's time for another tactic. Appealing to his good will has definitely failed. Not surprising, but that means it's time to hit him in that monstrosity of an ego. "If you don't know, I'll have to find a genuine expert that does. It's not like I have a shortage of samples to supply."

The bark of laughter catches me off guard, as I figured he'd fly into an enraged fit, like a child that had its toy taken away. I honestly don't remember ever hearing Taurus laugh in the few times he's made a guest appearance over the years. He's not known for his sense of humor.

Yet, here he is, laughing... at me. What an ass.

My temper piques, the affront of the situation pushing all of my buttons. The beast rumbles and I can feel her indignation as she stretches and spreads out inside me. My control is shaky and boy, am I being tested tonight.

"Nice try, love," he smirks, giving me an even better reason to call him a jackass in my head. "Seeing as we're not in high school, the old 'mine's better than yours' bit isn't going to fly with this bird."

Christ, he's really pissing me off with this smug know-it-all horseshit.

This night is going to end in blood. I can feel it in my bones. She's sniffing around, the hint of a fight capturing her attention in a way that I'm going to have trouble distracting from. Before I can figure out how to put this train back on the rails safely, he yanks me off the wall. Clones move like lightning and I'm used to it, but what he did—I don't know what to call it. It was like Jeannie blinks in and out of the damn room—that's as close as I can get.

Taurus has me pressed against the brick in an all too familiar position, but he's not one of my mates. This is not good. The beast has no clue who he is, but he's speaking her language: fight or fuck. Thankfully, she goes with rage. We're being provoked by an unknown predator, which does *not* make her happy. She hasn't fully unsheathed yet, but it's coming and—

What the fuck is that in his hand, a goddamned sickle?

I slow my breathing to keep from grazing the weapon he *blinked* to my jugular. It's holding my head in place as the curve of the blade stretches from ear to ear. I'm never going to stop her in this position. Panic is spreading through me like wildfire. She's not had the chance to get into a fantastic brawl, and every moment we stay like this, it gets harder to focus on his words rather than my Beast slamming into the cage doors.

The only thing stopping me from letting her go is that there's no telling what Talia will do if I tear Taurus a new one. I breathe again, grasping for the human part of my brain. When I find the thread, I realize Taurus is yammering at me again in that snarky tone. He seems not to notice the proximity of razor-sharp steel to my throat. One false move and I'm getting beheaded, but he's chuckling as if we're best buds.

Giving him a look of haughty defiance at the physical threat he feels perfectly comfortable issuing, I force a snort. *As if I owe him fealty.* "Back off, asshole."

He ignores me, still looking amused. "Listen, Sandwich," he says, "I don't really have time for games, so we'll do this like great sex—hard, fast, and hot."

The Cat Gets Cornered

DELILAH

For a moment, that image completely derails me.

I know it's hard to imagine—given the giant sword at my throat—but she and I are equally licking our chops for the briefest of moments. When I get home, everyone is getting a wake-up call because I'm going to need somewhere to put this excess adrenaline. After I resurface from the lust fog, I figure out I could attempt to push him off regardless of the blade, but his body is pressing mine from stem to stern to prevent it. He's giving off heat like a furnace and wriggling around would only increase the chances of my focus straying.

I close my eyes, deciding to use desire to rein in my anger. *He's built like my boys and I can pretend, right?* If I weren't so furious, I might notice that he's more lithe and sinewy from his training for work. He's also more muscular than his frame implies and—crap.

He's Taurus, I'm me, and I'm more likely to join a convent than actually get to indulge in the mind scenario I'm using to quench my rage.

"First," he continues casually, "I don't run the Company; it's too much bleeding paperwork. It's too much work, period. You had something there, though, because I know what you're aching to find out. Lucky for you, I'm interested, and I like you just enough that I'm going to tell you what I know."

He likes me? You could have fooled this kitty. Holding me at knife point is a funny fucking way of showing it.

I open my mouth to make a sarcastic comment about working on his interpersonal skills when he speaks again. "There's a fly in your lube, pet. You're going to trade me. I have questions I want answered, so it's the old quid pro quo and all that rot. Starting with..." That son of a bitch actually pauses for effect, then continues. "What the hell are you because you don't smell right. Give me the condensed version because we're going to be here a long time if you aren't honest. I will call for a brassed off woman, a Muse, and an android to join us if you aren't honest. I'm not one for backup, so you'd better calm whatever it is going on inside of you or things will get bloody fast."

Taurus' voice dropped to a tone inaudible to a being without my new enhancements at the end of that speech, so he knows the one thing I'm not is human.

His lips lower to my pulse—which is a big mistake. The scars there are whisper sensitive and it's going to set me off like a rocket, not calm me down. I feel a warm tongue and I'm not sure if he's licking me or the blade. A shudder—unfortunately not of revulsion—rips through my entire frame, forcing me to pant softly. When he pulls away, there's knowledge in his gaze that I don't like. The clone knows too much about my emotions, reactions, and secrets and he wants to know more. He gives me a cocky smirk, flashing his fangs. "Show me yours, Sandwich, or I promise you, I'll show you mine."

Squashing the urge to fire off a sarcastic rejoinder that will only make the situation worse, I reply softly. "Move."

He ignores me, looking expectant.

"I *said move.*" My beast comes out, the bass of the predator deepening my tone, and he doesn't bat a lash. I grit my teeth and hiss, "Look, I'm trying not to go all slice and dice on your arrogant ass. Move out of skewer range because I'm taxing my control to say this."

His brow quirks up, gauging the truthfulness of my response by scent. After a thoughtful pause, he yanks the blade out of the brick and moves to an arm's length. His gaze is intense, but his stance doesn't show an ounce of concern. Grinning, he folds his arms over his chest and slouches against the wall nonchalantly.

I know I won't scare him with what's coming, but he's not far enough out of reach for my taste. He'd put me on my ass if I lied about him needing to move—luckily for me, I'm not lying. I have to intrigue him, or this has been a giant waste of our time. Taurus is many things—most of them unflattering—but a fool is not one of them. He has to understand the implications of what's happened to me, right?

I shrug off Alistair's duster and scramble up on the wall again to increase the distance between us, so I feel safer. His eyes follow the coat briefly, as if just realizing who it belongs to.

Bared to a tank top and low-rise leather, I close my eyes and fling open the cage door internally. A rumbling yowl escapes as I shift: my features change, my fangs lower, and my eye color flashes emerald, signaling the beast's arrival. Ignoring the burning at the base of my spine, I sigh, knowing that letting her loose is going to wake the boys. My scars itch, and I scratch the one on my shoulder with my claw. She's calling to her mates, and the itching lets me know they're aware.

Man, will I have some explaining to do.

"Satisfied now? Fists and fangs—in my case, claws and fangs—so my cards are on the table," I rasp, still unused to the baritone voice of my other half. Tossing my hair over my shoulders in faux annoyance, I tilt my head to the side and sneer. "Hopefully, this didn't call out the dogs on my end. The connection between me and my mates is sensitive, much like you and yours, I'd expect."

Instead of waiting for him to rise to my bait, my almond-shaped eyes spear him. "In answer to your question, I don't know what I am. My guess is this..." I jump down and spin on my heel to give him the full effect. "... has something to do with all the little bits of clone DNA floating around inside me. Before you correct me, I realize this hasn't happened to anyone else, but I have quite a few blood donors, which is not as common."

Apparently, he's going to continue fucking with me because I don't get a response. He just stands there, smirking while fishing out a smoke and lighting it. That expression is begging for a good slap and since I'm feeling dismissed, she would be happy to give it to him.

What he doesn't understand is that while his demon is under control, she's in the driver's seat now. I can't play this game for much longer with her loose without it getting bloody.

His eyebrow rises slowly when I snarl, giving him an angry glare through slitted eyes. His reticence has to be because he knows that I'm not playing with my full hand. I have secrets I'm holding back and another other power source he doesn't need to know about. The latter is something I never use in public, so he can't know about it.

Can he?

A puff of smoke marks his complete disregard for her as he takes a drag on the cigarette, watching me expectantly. "Nice pelt, puss. You have a flair for execution and acceptable form—high marks for that. I can't say that I'd fault the dismount, but your control sucks."

It figures I'd get the fucking Russian judge.

Rolling my eyes, I shake off some of the furry, letting my claws slide in as I stroke the beast pleadingly. He doesn't understand the difference between us, so he thinks that I just suck at having an inner monster. I don't have a Beast inside of me like the clones have a demon; I have a beast inside of me with a separate mind of her own. She can do whatever she wants, except exist outside of my form. I don't know *why* I'm different, but I am.

Fighting her off once she's riled up is getting damned near impossible. That's why I've stopped allowing non-mated clones or droids at the house. It's too much work to fight her off — it's a mental marathon. I can think and reason, but I can't always steer the boat.

Taurus is trying to get under my skin and force me to show my hand prematurely. Clammed up tight, he figures he can play me, get what he wants, and leave me without a card left to throw. However, this isn't an old-timey poker game, and I'm not a simpering belle.

I've got six shooters of my own.

I open my mouth to retort, but he surprises me again by smiling—not that sardonic smirk he's been giving me—and winking. There's a devilish gleam in his eye and I almost believe that he's genuinely being nice. Taken aback, I blink. I've never seen this expression on him before, and I bet I could count on one hand the people who have. It's almost more intimidating than the scowls and sneers because it's disarming and charming and—

Nope. Stop that train before it leaves the station, Deli.

"You know, you're as gorgeous a chit with the fangs and fur as you are without, Sandwich. I suspect that's said often enough by your brood that I don't have to repeat it, so I'll just say that you give good tail."

Poof. As if by magick, those words snap the last bit of composure I was clinging to. Weeks of hard work to keep one little thing under my power when she's in charge and it disappears with his cutesy compliment.

Maybe I can cover by stroking the old ego and he won't notice?

"Why, thank you, Mr. Taurus. I'm taken aback by your high praise." The sugary Southern drawl and coquettish posture accompany batting lashes and a teasing look that I hope conveys playfulness. The tip of my furry flicks slightly, but since it's still out of sight, he might not see it.

"The bottom line is that I couldn't care less about the whys and wherefores of your pussy-butch alter ego. Your brain work sounds possible, but problematic if it's right. Not being a sharer myself means it won't become a problem with my woman, but we seem to be in the minority these days."

For a moment, something in his expression makes rage sizzle over my skin. It doesn't feel like a judgment of my lifestyle—I'd expect that—but something between consternation and disapproval that bothers the hell out of me. He truly can't comprehend why anyone would want more than one mate. I wonder if he considers me community property because that thought is distasteful and disrespectful at the same time. It pisses me off to think he's judging me based on his archaic beliefs.

But I might be way over thinking this. Maybe he's imagining killing anyone who lays teeth to his mate. If so, I can get that. Outside of our family, I don't like people looking at what's mine, and it's become worse since she appeared. I can't share that feeling with anyone because it violates all our 'free love' tenets, but it's true.

Taurus has to know that no one would even consider looking at Talia. It's no skin off my ass if they're exclusive, but I don't want that agenda pushed on me. I didn't intend to build a squadron sized family and explaining how it happened would probably dispel that community property theory. Fortunately for me, my primary mate has enough love to share with those we've stumbled upon and it's always worked out. Unfortunately for him, he's also been damaged by the wrong choices we've made.

However, Taurus is prattling again, so I suppose I should start listening.

"I figure you and I could go a round or two," he says casually. "We could do damage to each other, right enough. We could call in the cavalry and get a genuine bloodbath frothed up good and proper. You might win, I might win—be a coin toss, I think. It'd be a right good time as it's been a while since I've had legitimate competition in that area. We won't, though, because I had enough of wars years ago."

As if to prove his words, he leaps into the air and lands gracefully on the wall, dangling his legs off and resting his arms on his knees. I don't have the foggiest where the sickle went, so I continue watching him warily.

"The truth is simple," he continues, his voice dropping an octave. "It's not worth it. Talia believes that the impact of another true bloodbath within the community would be counterproductive. She laid that pearly bit of information on me back when I was roaring to take out an offensive weed from the community garden. After chaining me to a wall in the basement for a week, she waited until the hunger kicked in and I finally saw the wisdom of her shouts. Anyway, I don't thin the herd or get thinned by a neighbor anymore." His eyes narrow on me for a millisecond and then slide back to gaze at the darkness in front of us. If I didn't have enhanced hearing, I would have never heard his snarl, "Even if the bint bloody deserves it."

Knowing which bint he's referring to, I keep my mouth shut while he fumes. She's one of my mates, so normally, I'd bristle and jump to her defense.

However, our family has some serious issues because of the problem I'm here to figure out. Her primary mate, Wilde, has been out of control since my transformation, and the effects of his behavior have wreaked havoc on our family. There's no sense in sticking my nose into his conflict with that part of my family tree. It would give him the tidbit that there's internal strife and that would be foolhardy.

By the time I decide to keep mum, he's back to being graciously charming again.

A killer with scruples, that's Taurus.

"I've seen your fuzzy side. Great. Now, let's move this evening ahead so I can get home and make with the naked and sweaty. The questions you had that led to you calling me?" He raises his hand with all five fingers up. "No. No. I already answered that twice now, and I don't plan on repeating it. Not a bleeding clue. Not likely, all things considered."

He slides off the wall with a boneless move that the feline in me would appreciate if I wasn't so flummoxed. Before I can reply, he turns his back on me and walks away, calling over his shoulder, "Since that covers it, I'm off. Be seeing you, Sandwich."

The Cat Demands Answers

❧

DELILAH

I have enough presence of mind to grab his arm as I yell, "Wait a minute!"

The look he gives me is almost enough to make me pull my hand away, but I'm too frustrated to accomplish that kind of logical thought. "Alright, Dr. Lechter, you said you had questions, and I said I need answers. You got yours, but what you gave me was not only supremely unhelpful, but ridiculously simplistic. You're blowing me off and that's not part of the deal." My tail twitches in agitation and I try to will it away before he takes issue.

"Fine. Since you're being *so* forthcoming..." His calm reply distracts me and I miss his arm shooting out in a blur of motion that I should have expected. I don't even see it coming until his fist closes around the silky fur. He tugs on it as if that's a question enough.

Unfortunately for him, he does not know how sensitive that is. My eyes roll back in my head as my hand drops from his arm immediately and my jaw works wordlessly. I try to form words, but a taunting litany of 'oh fuck' runs back and forth like a screen saver in my mind as my body locks in place. I'm going to do something

33

embarrassing if he doesn't stop squeezing it and I will *never* live that down. I pry my lids open, eyes blazing with emerald fire as I stutter, "L-L-L-Let g-g-go..."

That only seems to amuse him more. I'm losing my shit by the second because my entire body is a raw, thrumming nerve. The only thing I can do is to show my belly and hope that once he has the power back, he complies. I swallow hard, both parts of me almost too stubborn to do this before I look up. "Please?"

He blinks, looking flabbergasted. His fingers uncurl from the fur and his head tilts as if he's seen something that he doesn't understand. He stays silent as I hop back on the wall shakily, digging through the pockets of Alistair's duster until I find his smokes.

I light one and, after inhaling deeply, I close my eyes. My lungs fill and my skin slowly stops feeling like it's too small for my frame. If my behavior seems odd to him, he doesn't let on. Suppressing the shudder that threatens to run up my spine, I blow a few smoke rings, then catch his eyes. "Is that your question, or do you have something you want to ask? I want elaboration on my questions and I'm trying to play fair."

"Fair," he drawls, "Right. As if you've been an open bloody book before now." When I look like I'm going to huff in indignation, he shrugs it away like swatting a fly. "You plan on dogging—or catting—me until you're satisfied, so we'll progress to the third act, fair or not. Since that smooth belly up you just pulled is making me feel generous, I'll try to act like I'm not pissed that between you and my woman's insistence on this meeting, I'm not horizontal and happy right now. Or vertical. Or upside down. I'm not picky."

One thing that I've learned this evening is that there is no one in my known universe that can annoy, compliment, and ignite desire simultaneously, like Taurus. All the clones have similar aspects, sure, but his candor about everything amplifies the situation tenfold. "Listen, buddy. I'm not *trying* to interrupt your naked Olympics, but I *need* answers."

"Yeah, yeah, yeah. I know what you want to know. Repeating yourself isn't helping because I'm neither deaf nor profoundly stupid. The problem lies in that your 'answers' are guaranteed to lead to more questions. Get comfy, stow the fab fur, and let me talk to my woman for a tick, so I can parse what I'm able to share."

I sigh heavily. He could have done this twenty minutes ago, but we had to play Pin the Tail on the Kitty. I feel the urge to pace, but that will only let him know how much he's getting under my skin. I've given him enough weapons to work with tonight.

I'm climbing the walls with pent up energy and he's calm and collected as he mentally converses with Talia. He's not moved since the tail incident, so he's also eating into my personal space. The odd intimacy of him having a mental conversation with his mate while standing so close to me is underlining my sucky control. It's distracting me, and he's definitely doing it on purpose. Another point to him, I suppose, which makes it seem less than likely that I will come out a winner.

Surprisingly, I don't hear a sound—not a tickle, a hum, or a buzz. I kind of thought I might, being mated to his brother. The thought of Taurus as a brother-in-law gives me a giggle, and I drop that line of thinking before life gets even more surreal.

I realize that all the clones are brothers genetically, and it means some odd Kentucky-style triangles are going on in the Rift bedrooms. I tilt my head, trying to pick up on something again, but I get nothing. Damn. I've gotten so proficient at mind speech and projection that I thought I might at least pick up whispers if I strained.

Nope.

We are two silent people loitering in a park in the dark of night with crickets for companions. Christ, I hate silence. Maybe I can amuse myself by poking into someone's dreams. After what feels like forever, movement catches my eye, and I pull out of the dream I was manipulating for one of my mates.

Taurus is fidgeting. He looks like his clothes are too tight and he's trying to adjust them. I hear a muttered 'bloody buggering hell, woman' before he shuts up again, and I chuckle. I respect the hell out of the woman who can make Taurus squirm like that. Talia is doing an amazing job of making him pay for being such an ass. I should send her a 'thank you' gift.

Taking a deep whiff, I smirk when I catch his scent. Strictly by accident—that's my story and I'm sticking to it—my eyes drop lower than his face and the cause of his discomfort is blatantly obvious. I stifle the giggles threatening to erupt when I see the punishment for his contrary behavior. I'm greedily enjoying every second of his torture.

Why not? I'm a vindictive little wench.

"Right then," he says.

I blink, realizing that he's talking to me now. Looking up quickly, I try not to look like I've been a dirty peeping Tom. Even if I was, he's spent the past few hours torturing me and I'm damned restless. This has been an awful long time to have my strings strummed with no crescendo.

True to form, he catches me and his grin turns wicked. Not only does he not give a damn I saw, but he's puffed up. I would have thought it was physically impossible for his ego to swell any larger than it already was, but here we are.

What an infuriating jackass.

He takes a step towards me, crossing the sparse amount of space we have left between us and drops the tickled expression. Good. I feel like smacking it off him, which would put us squarely back where we started. He winks and I frown, wondering if he knew what I was just thinking.

"On to the matter at hand, Sandwich. All the clones were not created from the same DNA. Some of us were—Alistair, Trey, and I. Though, I suspect you know the term 'brother' is a misnomer—

none of us are actually sibs. Us originals are genetically the same person. The three of us started the brother label as a unity thing and the lab coats adopted it. It helped them tell us three apart from the generations that came afterward. However," he grins, noticing my flabbergasted expression, "that isn't the part that's going to blow your mind, kitty." He pauses and once again, I ponder letting her kill him. "Most of the clones aren't created from DNA from the same dimension, much less ours."

Any thought of killing him flies out the window because he's got me hooked. I have to look like someone smacked me in the face with a brick. He dropped an enormous bombshell like that and yet he's acting like it was as normal as saying 'Hi, my name is John.' It decimates all my theories and research. The exploration I planned to do is impossible in my dinky lab space. Not only that, but this level of science is *far* beyond my capabilities.

He winks before he asks, "Quid pro quo: define 'need' in relation to 'I need to know'. This isn't a science fair project. 'Need' is too visceral for a simple brain exercise."

That question has me cornered because I don't want anyone to know what I'm trying to find yet.

First, there's something different inside me beyond the kitty part, and I don't know what it is. This other thing differs from her and I don't know what it is, but I know something is up based on animal instinct. Second, I may have grown used to the beast, but she's caused deep fissures in my family dynamic. I want to know what the mystery feeling is, but I'm also looking for a cure.

How do I tell him any of that when I've barely admitted it to myself?

My mates wouldn't understand why I want a cure and they definitely won't understand a random feeling that something else is hiding within me. At least, not without having total freak outs. My features slide back into normal 'Deli face' as I ponder my answer. The only sign of my alter ego is my emerald eyes, but that's because of the emotion involved in deciding how much I can trust him.

I can feel his impatience radiating off of him in spiky waves, so it's time to put up or shut up. "You're right. It's not a curiosity or idle thought exercise—goddess knows I'm not a scientist. The changes in me are the reason I need to know." I pause, considering what the next step in my explanation will be. Taurus gives me a look that says he's expecting more information for his candor.

"There is something a bit off inside of me; I don't know what, but I know it's there. I don't know what that is yet. As for the furry, my assumption was that it is because of DNA strands and mutation. There's obviously more than what I showed you—the kittyness gets more intense—but before you accuse me of holding back, I can't exactly control most of it. Some things only happen if I get into a real tussle. You'll need to back off if you want me to show you those things. To clarify, it's not because you make me nervous; it's because this part is dangerous."

He snorts as if the thought that anything I could ever do would put him in danger is so far outside of the realm of possibility that it is grounds for laughter. I take the high road, ignoring the urge to scratch his eyes out.

See? I'm a much better person. Imagining choking him under my boot heel isn't the same as doing it, right?

"Oh! I have a request: please don't flip out when I do this. The last clone I showed nearly had a coronary." I know he's thinking how very superior he is to the other clones, and rather than get irritated, I wait for him to back away.

Flicking out a single claw, I slice a deep cut in my forearm. What he doesn't know is that this is exactly where I've sliced the last three times I gave this demo. My blood wells quickly and from the moment it hits my skin, I feel a stinging tightness as the cut inches its way closed. Within seconds, the scratch seals with a distinctive pop, leaving completely unmarred flesh from my elbow to my wrist.

Just like it has every single time I've done this.

"I picked up this tidbit during an enthusiastic romp in which I got rolled with my claws out and skewered myself by accident." I pull up my shirt enough to show him the deep gouge between two of my ribs. I could have healed it, but it was a lesson, and I appreciate reminders of important lessons.

"The boys think I punctured a lung because I couldn't breathe. Blood was gushing everywhere, and people were screaming. Suddenly, the damn hole just closed. It's been knitting closed inside ever since. I guess internal wounds need more time to heal than external ones. The whole thing has been a giant fucking buzz kill in the sack."

I pull out another smoke, deciding to be decadent tonight. Lighting it, I exhale slowly as I watch his reaction. "Do you see why I'm so damned curious? The mutation isn't only effective on me, by the way. My blood works on others; I've tried it. It cures what ails you, and I don't have a clue why. I learned that one thing it does not immediately fix is these." I point to the bite scars on my neck and shoulders. "They scar unless I push at them; it must be the clone saliva or something."

My skin itches again, and I know that it also happens when I feel defensive. Laying out all of that personal information for someone who hasn't given me any sign that he'd care if I'm a magickal cure for injuries is not as easy as it sounds. I expected a bigger reaction to her, and I didn't get one. I figured this part would make him scoff and shrug me off. He's a clone; rapid healing is nothing new to them.

His eyes meet mine with an intensity that's almost scary as he reaches out to touch my skin like my arm is going to separate from my body and fly away. It would amuse me, but something tells me his wonderment is important. When he looks up at me, his expression turns to one of anguish. It kills my mirth, and I don't know why I do it, but I close the gap between us and lay my other hand on his arm.

"Taurus, are you okay?" I watch his mesmerization and try to lighten the mood. "It's just a Presto Change-o healing thing like you clones do. I didn't give birth to a litter of kittens on your coat. That might actually be possible—all things considered—well, except for the 'your coat' part."

When he doesn't respond to threats to his precious duster, I know there's a problem. It shocks me when his fingers close around the arm I diced up and he lifts it close to his face for inspection. He runs a finger over the unblemished limb reverently, and his touch sends shivers of concern down my spine. I picture being trapped in a cage like a lab rat and my blood pressure rises as I panic. He hasn't said one goddamned word yet. This has to be a record for Taurus, and it's wigging me the fuck out.

"What's wrong?" I whisper. I don't know why I care, but I do. There's too much grief and torment in his expression to not respond to it, even if I am scared.

"She got shot," he croaks.

The Cat Makes A Promise

DELILAH

I don't need anyone to tell me who 'she' is. "What? When? Where? Who? How?!"

Taurus just stares at my arm intently, as if the rest of me isn't here. Finally, I shake his shoulder to bring him out of his internal misery. His mouth opens and then closes. I blink as his eyes drop to my arm again. We make an odd picture if someone walks by. How does one categorize two people dressed in leather trench coats holding onto each other in a ramshackle park in the no-see part of town at a time of day when honest people are home in bed?

I guess it's good that there isn't anyone here to ask those questions.

His voice is barely a murmur when he speaks. "It was when we disappeared—right before I was supposed to have a birthday party. We were staying at her place on the other side after a visit with her mum. Talia went out for ice cream—just a stroll down to the corner. She'd done it a million times; there's this all-night gas and guzzler we hit when we're in the mood. It should have been no big deal." His head lifts and his golden eyes meet mine. "I was being a

43

lazy prat, whining about her parental obligations, so she went for me."

It makes me infinitely sad that no one besides me has ever heard this story. Hell, maybe no one else ever will. Taurus should have someone close to him to tell it to, but the only person close to him is the one he's agonizing over.

"She showed me afterwards—you know, in our minds, as mates can do. I had to beg to get her to do it, but she finally gave in. I watched her stride into the store full of spit and swagger, as usual. Unfortunately, the guy behind the counter had a double-barrel pump action aimed at his head."

I make a sound of protest when I realize what's happening. He's reliving the scene internally, visualizing it exactly as Talia shared it. Second by agonizing second, he's going to recount the tale of how her life almost ended. I don't know if I can take anyone else's pain right now. My own, my mate's—my empathy is full to the brim. That's selfish and I know it, so I muffle myself before I can change my mind. The only way to ease a burden is talking. I asked for help and the least I can do is return the favor.

That's human, unlike the two of us, and it's what I agreed to, right?

"My golden goddess moved like lightning," he rasps, his lips curling faintly at the thought. "She didn't question—only leaped into action to save the attendant. The expression on the thieving sod's face was priceless. Imagine going into a store for an unwilling withdrawal: things are going well until a war whooping. irate woman flies over the counter to clash into your skull. He looked like he was about to piss himself. With a swing kick and a twist of the hand, she had the shotgun. Her heel was on his chest and she had the gun aimed at his soft bits before he knew it." He pauses for a moment and this time, it's collecting himself so he doesn't cry. "The rest I saw on my own because I felt it when it happened."

Goddess above, I want him to stop.

My entire body is vibrating with emotions. Honestly, I'm not sure I want to know what makes evil weep. I'm familiar with what makes primal cower and lick wounds, so I know monsters can be quelled if you have the right weapons. I'm horrified, yet enthralled, and unable to stop him now.

"Talia must have had a twitch of warning—something must not have felt right. It was enough for her to call me to warn me. She tried to prepare me, but it didn't work. I felt it through the bond when she took the round. I felt her fly into the air with the impact and slam into the cig case behind her. It sent blood and flesh and smokes everywhere. The asshole had a partner, and it took him a while to catch up since he was raiding the beer cave. His shot counted, though, because he had a bloody street cannon. I was there in an instant, but it was too long. She hit the grimy floor in a heap before I could blink behind her to catch her head. The bullet tore open her chest, shattered a couple of ribs, and left a burning hole in her back I could stick my hand through. The bastard she got the jump on was lying there, covered in her blood, and the partner was nowhere to be found." His breath hitches and he squeezes my arm as if reassuring himself that I'm there.

"I didn't even get to nail the walking corpse that did it. The sight of her almost did me in—seeing her lying there pale and broken in a pool of blood spreading and soaking into her hair terrified me. My only thought was about how mad she'd be that her crowning glory—her hair—was getting dirty. Odd, isn't it, when you think your life is ending before your eyes?"

I don't know if his question is rhetorical, but I can't find the air to answer, anyway.

I'm not sure he notices.

He shakes his head as if to knock the rest of his tale loose. "I picked her up gently; I don't know why. She was broken, so there wasn't much more I could do to crack her. I apparated us to a human emergency room; I didn't care if people saw what we can do. When they took her, it almost killed me. I had to give her up so they could save her, but I didn't have anywhere else to go. She's a scrapper and fought through fifteen hours of surgery, but they saved her. When she was out of the woods, I took her to the Company facility. They couldn't triage a human, but they're sodding experts at flesh regeneration. You would never know now that she nearly got blasted in half."

He looks at me again. There's pride and misery in his eyes, but the slight hitch to his lips surprises me. "I'll never eat ice cream again, that's for sure. It was all because I wanted some bloody mint chocolate chip."

I don't know what to say to that. Consolation would be a cold comfort, commiseration would require me to explain the tinges of ugliness that have drifted into our allegedly perfect lives... The emotions I'm feeling seem too intimate to share, but I can't stand here like a twit. "How long did it take you to hunt down the son of a bitch who shot her?"

In an instant, his expression changes. He knows I realize he couldn't simply hope the justice system worked for once. A glimmer of naked hatred rises in his eyes like a phoenix, and a smile that could freeze the pants off a snowman curls his lips. Feral, cruel, and willing to kill—that's what he's projecting right now.

I'd like to be on Saturn if that gaze ever fell on me.

This is the Taurus most people hate and fear. It feels like he grows two sizes bigger when he snarls, but I know that has to do with presence more than physicality. He is Death personified.

"To find him?" he drawls, his smirk satisfied, as if the chase was akin to a hound and a hare. "Not so long. To kill him?" The smirk stretches to a smile full of fangs, and despite my being used to fangs, his seem particularly terrifying. It might be the expression behind his eyes that is suddenly making me feel like a babbling bimbette from a B horror flick. I almost squeak when he says, "That took weeks."

I don't doubt it was brutal, and Taurus enjoyed every millisecond with satanic glee. I'm not worried about posturing because he's looking way too hungry for those trivialities. I yanked away my arm when I moved, and it must have jarred him. His grisly smile vanishes from his face and he looks as if he's trying to get control of his rage. Stepping closer, he tries for a harmless grin, but I'm shaken so it doesn't help much.

"Talia isn't pleased that I spilled my innards to you, Sandwich. She says that I should ask for your pardon, as it feels like you're about ready to lose your dinner. That isn't happening this millennium, but I have something simple to request. Given your unique talents, it shouldn't be hard. If something like that ever happens again, you will help her. Not a silly hangnail, mind, but if a serious injury comes along, you drop what you're doing when I call. In return, I'll be a happy little Oracle without comment or complaint for the rest of the night. Deal?"

I study him for a moment, digesting the story he shared as my brain zooms around at light speed. Once I collect my thoughts, I look at him with a serious expression. "Since this evening has been little more than a series of planned and unplanned belly ups, I'll let you in on something."

Taurus tilts his head, looking at me curiously, and I sigh, knowing I'm going to regret this. "Have you ever had one of those hard candies that are like cement on the outside, but inside they're all squishy and gooey like a milk dud?"

Nodding, he continues eyeing me suspiciously without speaking.

"That's me. While there are a few people I consider wastes of flesh who don't deserve to be standing upright, anyone I have the tiniest bit of fondness for falls under my protection in my mind. That said, you are Alistair's brother. Whatever the issues are between you two, it puts your family on my list. I suppose you turning out to not be as much of an ass as I expected helps. But that also means I'm going to give you the truth, and you'd better not abuse it."

I take a deep breath, knowing this is the hardest part to explain. "I healed myself. I've done a couple slice and dice demos like you saw, healed some contusions and bruises I may or may not have been responsible for, and used blood mixed with healing herbs to heal one of your kind who got himself into a bar fight and lost on purpose. I'd do any of that again—and more—to save someone I care about. Bleeding is the least of what I'd do in that situation, especially if lives are on the line. So yeah, I'd do it for you or Talia, or even Damien, I guess. It's part of the standard friends and family package in my world."

Pausing for a moment to catch my breath, I realize there are a few problems with my blanket declaration. Most of my subjects are connected to me, peripherally at least, so my response time has been good. There's also the method of deployment to discuss. "How are you going to call me? I haven't seen you dialing a cell phone, and I sure as fuck don't carry one here. Life-threatening may not give me enough time to get wherever you are."

I should have known by the mischievous glint in his eyes, followed by a playful grin, that he was about to show me something special. He's all about the Manson-like madness one minute and boyish charm the next. His lips press together as if making a point, and then he speaks inside my mind—without being a mate.

~I don't think it'll be much of a problem at all. ~

His eyes twinkle and I turn to retort, but he's gone—like physically gone. How the hell do you lose a six-foot-tall clone in the middle of the night? Suddenly, I see a picture of myself in my head, standing here looking like a gaping idiot.

Is this through his eyes? WTAF, people. Mind speech and projection?

Both are well within my bag of tricks before the magickal clone juice—not that anyone here needs to know that. My bit of 'kitchen magick' was strong enough here to hide the Resistance. Hell, it even made the bond between my primary mate and me so strong that we don't speak out loud for hours sometimes. But if it's hearing anyone not mated to me, I only pick up vague pictures or words. Since there hasn't been an apocalypse, I know I'm not mated to Taurus.

Jesus, just thinking about the hell involved in that sends an icy ball of no fucking way to my stomach.

We'd end up killing each other and taking the entire community with us. But why are his words and pictures so clear?

~*So...* ~ His voice is filled with amusement, as if I'm a child seeing snow for the first time. ~*Are you going to pass out from the shock, or do we have a bargain?* ~

"About you sitting still like a good boy while I grill you? Absolutely." I let that snark sit in the air for a moment while I force my brain to stop exploring the possibilities of his powers.

His special skill designation must be telepathy. Alistair has empathy, Victor has mechanics, and Rafe has artistry—all the clones have one. They each have talent or skill that supposedly emerges during training, and this must be Taurus'. Though, he can also apparate and not all the clones can do that, including his brother.

I frown, pondering that for a moment before I continue. "In the interest of full disclosure, there's one more thing you need to know. I can't guarantee the healing will work via external means. I know for you that means something different for me, but you need to be aware of my limitations. But if you still want an oath on my agreement, I can speak in currency you'll believe in." I hold up my arm as if ready to bleed on it.

His reaction surprises me—though, by now, nothing he does should—when he reaches for my arm and tucks it back against my side. "No need. I appreciate the sentiment, but you're right. I prefer to keep the blood play between me and my mate—unless it's a dire emergency," he amends, acknowledging my previous statement. "I also feel like I'd rather not see you hurt yourself again on my account. I'm growing fond of you amidst this mess—that must be all the shit you're giving me. My goddess is always telling me I'm a sucker for a hard case and that's you to a tee. I'll take your word on it for tonight because I trust you."

He shrugs laconically, but he's not fooling me—not anymore. After all of this dancing and snarking, I finally figured out the truth about Taurus that the current inhabitants of The Rift don't know. He's an irritating bastard—complex, cruel, and downright ornery. Despite being a brutal killer, he's fiercely loyal and protective. He'd kill me if I told anyone, but he's also kind.

Maybe I could deal with him being around more often without gutting him when he pisses me off. I ponder that for a moment and tilt my head at him. As I look up at him, it occurs to me that even though I backed away when he went cannibal, I'm still *really* close. I'm less nervous about it than before, but my discomfort with finding out that he has an all-access pass to my mind makes that difficult. The thought of him cavorting around in my head when he's bored definitely has me concerned. But he said he trusts me and I'm going to give him the same courtesy.

Shrugging it off, I straighten my spine. I came here for answers, not the dog and pony show. "Okay, now that we've settled the serious stuff and I've let you in on more of my secrets than any person alive that isn't sharing my bed... Can we get back to the 'not all from the same dimension' part? Are we talking about flux capacitor stuff?"

The Cat Has More Questions

✦

DELILAH

Leaning against the wall, he lights another smoke and holds it out to me, but I shake my head. Since my change, I find nicotine ramps me up and I've had enough already; I don't need to bounce off the walls like a meth freak.

"It's not that simple. It would be easier if it were, but it couldn't work that way. We're not different people from another time; we're different versions of the same person altogether." He studies me for a moment. "Are you sure you want to dive into this? The science isn't a brownie baking class, and once you go through the Looking Glass, you can't come back. Knowing the truth changes how people see us, which is why we don't make it public knowledge. Besides, I don't see how knowing about our creation gets you to Final Jeopardy."

"I plan on sampling and cross-checking the samples to see what happens to each. I have an old friend who can examine it. I hope to get a clue what's going on from the DNA strands by looking for anomalies. I'm not sure what the next step is from there, but the info you give me might provide background for whatever questions he has. My friend is beyond discreet and I won't raise any flags anywhere, if that's what you're worried about. I'll make sure it's all anonymously labeled. I figure even if it doesn't help now, it might at some point. I didn't know what you might give me, so who knows what I can run with from here?"

He nods, a thoughtful expression on his face. My answer must have satisfied him because he continues, "Right then, on we go. No matter how you shake it, no matter what our gifts or traits are, most of that is learned behavior, just like with humans. Think of us like chapters of a book. A book is a book no matter what the contents are, and pages always change from one to the next. Just because the story and the cover are different doesn't mean that a book is suddenly not a book."

Blowing a smoke ring, he stops, checking to see if I'm with him. "The problem the docs at the Company ran into after they released my brothers and I was a variable customer base. Human nature makes you all want the same things, but not exactly the same. Every one of you likes how we look—and why wouldn't you —but you find different things appealing or attractive." He winks at me playfully and I roll my eyes.

"Look around and you'll see what I mean. Some of the newer clones are so far removed from the originals that you wouldn't know we're related except for a familial resemblance. Scratch that, with the physical variations, you wouldn't even know who we're modeled off on some." He waves his hand, gesturing as if we're in The Rift and I could just yank a clone off the street.

"That's true, even with the droids, though I understand simple programming makes that situation easier."

"The lab coats figured out that our looks were the big customer pleaser, but they struggled to have us look alike while being unique personalities. Using normal cloning methods, they realized no matter how much editing of the 'pages' they did, the book simply stayed the same. It was because they were using DNA from the originals, but tinkering with sequences to change certain chapters.

Their 'first tries' ended up eventually mirroring the original model every single time."

"Like how Antonio is like you or Cruise is like Trey or Jazz is like Alistair? Not exactly, but sort of?"

He shakes his head. "They're all next generation—what came next. But your brain work isn't bad." I must look puzzled because he eyes me warily through the haze of smoke. "Are you sure you're following the analogy, okay, Sandwich?"

"I'm not a nitwit. Thank you for dumbing it down for me," I retort, giving him a wry smile. His doubt makes me irritated and I stretch, feeling cramped with tension. "Since we're going to be here for a while, I need to stretch out. Unless it makes you uncomfortable to be beneath me?" I don't wait for his response, instead scrambling up to lie on my tummy on the cool stones of the wall. The woman and the kitty in me sigh in relief at the position and I smirk at him from above.

Taurus quirks a brow, looking as though he's about to spit out one of those irritatingly accurate quips, but simply grins. "I'm only checking, Sandwich. I gotta make sure you're still on board because after this, the water gets bloody deep. To give you the info you want to know, I have to dive into some high-end science. I don't understand it completely myself, but since I'm standing here, I'm inclined to believe in it. You'll have to take my word that I'm only relating what I've been told by eggheads. Also, you shouldn't be insulted by me grade schooling it up; it's too damned hard to grasp if I don't."

I can't figure out if he's trying to lighten the mood, temper his words, or disarm me. I've given up on figuring him out, so I roll my eyes. "I didn't ask for proof of concept, you jackass. If I didn't trust you to tell the truth, I would have left hours ago. Besides, because your sense of smell is as good as mine, you know that when people—even clones—lie, they smell like sweaty socks. It must have to do with their pulse rate. I smell every other damned thing like it's stuck up my nose—why not lies?"

Laughing softly, he looks at me quietly as he listens to me grumble. I'm just about to get into a snit over his condescending silence when he reaches up and tucks a tendril of stray hair behind my ear. That damned warm smile is back, and his fingertips brush my cheek lightly as he draws away.

The flustered feeling that gesture causes in my tummy makes me stop in my tracks and I'm not sure what to do. Soft is not something I expected from Taurus. I cover for my confusion by kicking my feet up in the air and smirking down at him. "Go on. I've digressed as I'm wont to do when people distract me in devious ways."

"I believe I'm hurt, kitten. You think I'm deviously distracting you?" He looks anything but wounded. "I feel it's my duty to inform you that if I was trying something like that, you'd be none the wiser." Before I can growl something in response, he shrugs. "Though it's always possible I'm underestimating your higher cognitive functions."

Arrogant jackass. Of course, that's possible, if not probable.

"Come to think of it, I've been meaning to ask you something. Since you're already huffy, it's a good time," he says casually, watching me fume down at him. "I need to know what your knowledge base is on a couple of scientific ideologies integral to the how's and why's of what the docs did. It'll save having to cover something as I'm talking, so be honest. How familiar are you with quantum physics and the probabilities of chaos theory?"

Fuck. Now I'll have to admit I don't know something, and he can feel all superior.

I can't give into his ploy, so I pretend to ponder for a moment before I reply, "Physics isn't my forte, mostly because of math. I'm a biology gal. If you're keeping it simple, I should be able to follow along—my IQ is well over one forty-five, after all. I'll pipe up if I get lost; I'm not shy."

It probably surprised him I admitted I need hand holding through the tough bits, but he doesn't show it. Frankly, I'm aware of my limitations and math is definitely one of them. I wouldn't be touching any of this shit with a ten-foot pole if I didn't have to, but necessity is the mother of invention and all that rot. I take a deep breath so I can try to find my center so I'm working with brain and not beast. "Okay, lay it on me, prof. I'm ready for you to science me up and stuff."

"Right. So I'll assume—what with the kitty litter version of a Mensa card you've got tucked away somewhere—you're familiar with the law of physics relating to equal and opposite reactions. When you add quantum physics, you get another world of 'huh?'. It changes to every action having an equal and opposite *action*, which differs from *reaction*."

One sentence in and I'm already bored. I nod, but it will get harder for me the further we go. I'm still itchy, hungry, and riled up from earlier. That and my lack of interest in the theoretical parts of science are making focus exceedingly difficult. It's taking a lot of energy to make my brain stand still to process.

Maybe I'm the wrong person to be gathering this information.

"Translating those theories into a relatable scientific hypothesis goes like this: reality isn't a single, solid strand in time and space. It feels a little 'wibbly wobbly timey wimey' to say, but it's all wibbly wobbly at this level." He looks up, grinning at me when he realizes I got his reference.

"See, all the strands in the big rope of events represent different decisions and actions taken, which means they alter the lives we lead day to day. It's like a cosmic *Choose Your Own Adventure* book. Thanks to the only non-elemental weight substance in all realities being gamma rays, the docs realized it was possible to exchange materials from one reality to the next."

His brows furrow, and he shakes his head, correcting himself. "It's possible for the Company to, at least. Humans in the other world don't have the slightest clue about this. That's part of how our little slice of heaven through the portal exists, you know. Given that these strands represent massive, unimaginable differences between our realities, it's like the clones after the originals are from Earth 2 or something. If you can parse that, you know it's because we're talking about actions or roads traveled spanning the entire evolution of a universe, which is a sodding long time."

"Stop right there." I hold my hand up and then pinch the bridge of my nose. *Why didn't I pay more attention in high school physics?* A little more knowledge would make me feel like less of a numbskull. "I hate to be the dumb redhead of the class—more than you'll ever know—but that might not be grade schooled up enough for me. I know you're speaking English, but your lips might as well be flapping in French. Sadly, I'd get more if it was in French."

He grins, looking pleased with himself. "I warned you it got into deep, churning waters. Let's stick it in a lunchable and see if it's easier to swallow. Do you ever wake up in the morning, look at the clock, and not want to go to work or wherever it is kitties like you go during the day?"

"Only every day, my friend. I imagine because of the hedonist in me, I probably do that far more than most people." I tap the tips of my claws over the stones thoughtfully as I listen and practice control at the same time.

"Perfect! The hypothesis behind quantum physics depends on one rule: in our reality, on those days, you did what you were supposed to and hauled tail out of bed. However, in another strand, you aren't such a good little automaton and you don't. Or maybe you do in another, but you blow off work in another strand. Or in a different strand, you don't have a bed, only a hammock."

"Are you sure there isn't a way to explain this with like sock puppets or something? Generationally speaking, puppets are outstanding teachers for my age group. Oh! Maybe there's a nerdy engineer in a lab coat and a bowtie who could try?"

"You can get this, Sandwich, you need to stop letting the cat inside of you cloud your mind with animal instincts and turn on your higher brain functions. Think in the fourth dimension." His expression is full of exasperation, but he's eerily right on target.

"How very 'Age of Aquarius' of you."

"That's the Fifth Dimension, and what did I say about focus? Christ, I'm never getting naked tonight." He cracks his neck and grumbles to himself, knowing I can hear every damned word.

When I open my mouth to snipe, he holds up a finger and continues, "Let's say we live in a ribbon. Visualize one ribbon, you got it?" I nod and he continues. "In this ribbon, you gave a shout to Talia, asking to meet with me. In another ribbon, you chickened out. Now we have two completely separate ribbons, right?"

I close my eyes to picture it as instructed, but I can feel him smirking and give him the middle finger.

Chuckling, he pats my knee. "Okay, in one we're here having a verbal spar, but in the other, you're asleep in what must be the biggest bed in the cosmos. Those two ribbons continue their path and spiral off into the future and never meet again. Picture that."

Sighing, I do so, squinting my eyes, which earns me another soft laugh. "So, this ribbon is real to us because we're here, but who knows what'll happen in the one where we never have this confab? Who knows how our lives will change now that we have met? Imagine the poor puss and peacock who don't get this opportunity —all these widening gaps make new realities. Despite that, they are similar enough that one of the lab coats figured out how to exchange info through that big span of nothing that separates each reality. Don't ask me to get technical on that part, as even I don't fully grasp the science."

It's nice to know he still thinks this favor he's doing me is going to change my life.

He is *such* an arrogant jackass. How in the hell does he, his ego, and Talia fit into a bed that isn't comparable in size to mine? He's playing nice, though, so I guess I should, too. And as long as I can get oxygen to speak with that monstrous ego smothering us, I will.

"The bottom line is that every single, tiny, minute little action taken by every living thing in this universe creates endless possibilities, which makes the number of those strands infinite. Voila! In an instant, there are different versions of the same people ready for the plucking. Chaos theory has its part, as nothing is ever perfect, but it's late. I don't think that shit has much to do with your question, so we'll skip the dinosaur theme park part of the explanation."

"I'll take an order of 'leaving it out' forever. I'm still a wee bit confused, but I'm working it out. The pop culture references are helping." I'm also cranky as fuck. I hate having to tell him I'm an idiot when I insisted I wasn't.

Pride goeth, they say, and though my ego isn't nearly as healthy as his, I severely dislike being in the non-advanced classes.

"The least common denominator in relation to the different clones bit? There are infinite realities where the original lives and exists exactly like it is here. However, because of choices made and what happens because of them, our base personality and appearance are a combination of genetics and sociology that define us. But we write an entirely original story in every ribbon. We are who we are because of everything that has happened before us, from a fish growing legs to my breakfast this morning to what I'll do when I get home tonight."

I feel his gaze on me, and I open my eyes, nodding.

"Every time a path branches off, it creates a new ribbon and a new version of me somewhere else. The lab coats came up with this theory primarily to cater to the needs of the Company, but what they didn't expect was that they might make more money 'creating' made-to-order clones for the client doing the ordering. They swapped DNA between the realities and poof! Git looks the same, but isn't the same at all. Keep in mind, I'm only explaining the basic skeleton of how the process works. How they actually accomplish this is mind blowing and a trade secret."

I give him an expectant look, having caught up enough to know I should be able to communicate this to my researcher if need be. He needs to give me a soundbite about the specific process to share.

"Fine, but if I get my ass reamed over this, I'm sending them after you," he huffs. "The short story is: same docs, all realities, like we said. Every reality that has the scientific capacity breaks down the DNA, attaches it to gamma rays small enough to slip through bitty holes in their realities, as they all had the idea at the same time. They all sent it out, knowing that the others would do the same, and here we are. They've shared strains from one strand to the next hundreds of times. It's definitely more technical and a lot of high-end science, but that's the basics, pet."

"It's making sense, I think. You're saying that on a fundamental level, the DNA will not be the same. It will look similar, like a familial match, because it's from incarnations of the three of you. That tells me enough that I know where to start, I suppose. Maybe I can even figure out why I've been feeling weird. Different donors constantly floating around inside of me might cause *my* strand to mutate."

He chuckles and lights another smoke, leaning against the wall. "No worries, Sandwich. I've seen weirder shit than you and imagine that I will again. Are we done here or are you planning on running me to the ground again the second I turn my back?"

I blink, realizing that we're done for now. He answered my questions; I made a promise, and there isn't much left besides heading home. I'm a little disappointed because I've been enjoying myself. I'd cut my tongue out rather than admit it to him, but I actually had fun.

I guess I don't hate him.

The shrewd look he gives me stops the words before I can reply. "It's not like you don't know where to find me, if something else starts twisting up inside that noggin' of yours."

A tiny smile curls my lips and I tilt my head, feeling pleased. "I might do that if I need help."

He pushes off the wall, looking up into the sky. "Have you ever taken the kitty face on the prowl? Like go out for a bit of sport—rip and tear—that sort of thing?"

Sliding off the wall with feline grace, I shake my head. "Nope. I don't know anyone who does that kind of thing."

His teeth flash as he looks over his shoulder, his eyes spearing me with an intense look. "You do now." Turning away, he waves and says, "If you are ever so inclined, find me. I'll be around. It's been interesting chatting you up, puss."

Before I can get another word in, he shimmers and disappears. I growl to myself, muttering under my breath about drama queens as I hop on the bike. I wanted answers and even though it took all night; I have them. They just led to more questions, but he warned me about that.

Sighing, I gun the engine and head off into the night to work off my pent-up aggression.

The Rift In A Lunchable

❧❧

DELILAH

As I step through the basement portal in Bytes N' Chips, I think about everything that has happened since the first time I crossed this barrier. I was so desperate for an escape from my life and I'd lay money on that being the motivation for many of the permanent residents in the Rift.

People in the Earth dimension we all came from wouldn't be able to comprehend the world of the Rift—their heads would explode. It's not possible for normal humans to understand the gravity of my current situation, our world, or why contacting Taurus was so dangerous without knowing a bit about the Rift's history.

So I'll put it in a lunchable, as Taurus so eloquently phrased it.

The Rift is a pocket dimension; it started out as the Company's private universe where their HQ and clone creation facilities were hidden from the public. They created and populated it with agents of their own creation, scientists, bureaucrats, and support personnel from the other side of the portal. It was a secret base of operations untouchable by their enemies or competitors.

How they accomplished all of this is unknown, but it was operating for many years before their success with the clones.

According to the whispers, Talia is some sort of vigilante and one of the first three human employees to be recruited without a scientific background. Prior to her Company job, she took it upon herself to research, find, and end pedophiles, animal abusers, and their ilk. She must have worked in the legal system on the other side, because she knew they wouldn't face justice because of their wealth or fame. Legends say she met Taurus, who fell for her so deeply he brought her into this world.

Once she was employed by the Company, Talia invited a select group of her friends to join her here—Rhea, Phoebe, and Charlotte. They were given Taurus' 'brothers' and at that moment, the Cabal was born. It wasn't long before the Rift became an exclusive club and as the population grew, more clones were released to Cabal members. Some of their members moved to the Rift permanently, and some lived split their lives between both worlds.

I hadn't yet received my invitation to become part of the world during this time; I didn't come until much later, so I can't speak to it with any definitive accuracy.

After the Conflict, invitations to come here hinged on knowing someone in the Cabal or getting 'discovered' in a rundown bar on the other side called Bytes 'n Chips. I got invited after months of frequenting the place when on 'geek trivia' nights. Many evenings of discourse on shows and movies I love with regulars attracted the right eyes, and I got tapped.

I don't want to get distracted with my story, though, so back to Rift history.

Eventually, the Cabal weren't the only ones inviting people to come to the Rift. Regular folks who weren't in the clique invited their discoveries. As the population expanded, the Cabal demanded the Company refuse to release clones to those not recommended by their members. Tensions rose as their edict created a mini-caste system in the Rift.

Donatella, a 'discovery' who had enchanted the Cabal into releasing Victor for her, decided this decree wasn't fair. The new rules meant some townspeople had to sit on the sidelines and watch all the fun the Cabal and their mates had in public, but could never take part. Together with her mechanically inclined clone, Victor, Donatella created something new everyone could have: droids.

How did Donatella invent something as complex as a fully functioning, virtually indistinguishable, artificially intelligent droid?

It's an important question, and the answer is simple, but not. The Rift has always had an enhancing quality its scientific 'creation' can't explain. Given Taurus' explanation tonight, I believe the Company splintered off a piece of a dimension where magick exists—that's why living here amplifies 'natural talents'. Every clone has a 'built-in' skill like telekinesis or artistry or languages, so it makes sense. What I didn't mention previously is that the humans living here seem to reap similar benefits from exposure to the secret lands.

It's easy to surmise the Company would want to keep that benefit under wraps; they haven't figured out how to harness and monetize it yet.

There's a lot of supposition about what happens at the Company. It's generated a tome's worth of folklore in the Resistance, but very little of it has been confirmed. We know there's a training facility the clones go through where they discover their gifts. Once they graduate, the Company knows what their agents should specialize in and who to deploy in each situation.

What the hell they deploy for is what no one seems willing to talk about.

However, my theory is fairly easy to confirm if you're paying attention. No one talks about how Talia's blade skills grew to a lethal level when she moved here or how Dona's hobby of tinkering became outright brilliance in engineering, Other humans have found skills—none of them realizing that it's the Rift enhancing their talents—but I've long been watching the changes in folks with interest.

Regardless of how it came to be, Dona and Victor began creating hyperrealistic droids programmed as made-to-order companions for those not deemed 'worthy' of a clone by the Cabal. Their goal was to help with the inequality and growing resentment of the populace. They were even the original creators of Wilde when he wasn't a 'real boy.'

Even though their efforts made many people happy, it did not fix the problem. As humans are wont to do, the Cabal reacted by forming an even more rigid caste-based society. In their minds, only those with a clone were in the highest class; everyone else was a commoner. No one *said* that, but it was implicit in their behavior. Clashes that happened occasionally before became more frequent, and it was a constant source of discontent.

Thus, the Conflict began. No one can tell me what single event was the tipping point, but the stories say that Dona's first droid, Caesar, started it. Between the influx of new people and droids, the exclusivity of the Cabal, and the anger of the masses, the droid owners revolted against the Cabal. The Conflict raged for months and there was destruction and chaos everywhere.

The two sides came to the table after the Battle of Blood and Steel because so many droids and clones were injured or killed.

Of course, it didn't hurt that a droid owner named Sari defected to the Cabal's side, taking all of their plans and documents with her. That betrayal meant the Resistance—as the droid owners called themselves—was crippled. As a reward for helping to win the war, Talia had the lab coats at the Company turn Wilde into a clone.

If anyone has ever worked out how that was possible in their head, I've never been told.

Based on Taurus' explanation of their science, I might have the answer. They simply pulled him from a ribbon where Wilde was a clone, not a droid. The fairy tale everyone tells about a magick box and being transformed is rot. The lab coats replaced him and never told Sari. Her greatest wish was granted, and if that doesn't showcase the public opinion of clones versus droids, I don't know what else could.

The previous unrest didn't disappear after the Conflict ended; it became whispers in back rooms of places like Bytes N' Chips. Droid families still felt like second-class citizens. The caste system was still in place, and the Cabal ruled more viciously than ever. Everyone had to abide by their Draconian rules or get exiled from the Rift.

Fear became their new currency.

Dona and her friend, Michaela, were in the same boat as the other droid families. They frequented the bar to get away because being out of the purview of the Cabal was easier than suffering the feudalistic atmosphere in their home. I met them for the first time on a dark, stormy night when the bar was having a vampire slayer quiz game. We talked into the wee hours and bonded instantly.

They had no idea I was on the run from my past and ripe for recruitment.

Our friendship grew—particularly mine with Victor—and eventually, they took me behind the curtain. We stepped through the portal in the basement and within weeks, I moved from a split-world lifestyle to living in the Rift full time.

Don't get me wrong; I know running away doesn't fix everything.

But despite the social inequity, the Rift isn't a terrible place to live. The Company has plenty of clones to help build dwellings and they have a quarter set up for obtaining normal day-to-day supplies. Most of our needs are supplied without people having to work and as long as you can stay here, you wouldn't need a job at all. I'm sure there's an underlying motive in their generosity, but for those of us living here, it's a pretty sweet deal.

However, if the motive is some comprehensive study of how the Rift affects humans so they can monetize it... I'm about to put a big ass fly in their ointment. Magickally enhanced natural talents is one thing; turning into a bloody shifter is another box of chocolates. I'll happily convey my other secret to them if Taurus sics the needle waving thugs on me after our chat, especially if it keeps me from becoming a lab rat.

I may not have exactly been a normal human to start with.

That brings me to how the new Resistance came about and to tell that tale, I have to back up again. I'm not going as far back as why I was running when I got here, but I need to explain why I've been pushing so hard to pin my transformation on their science. It has to do with things I've wondered about my entire life, but always been too scared to address.

If I'm truthful, I've always had a bit of intuition—what I'd call 'kitchen magick'. In the Rift, I've felt that little bit of magick grow. I don't use it, even in front of my family, because I'm worried about the cost of doing so. It could be dangerous and I don't know how it works. Plus, I sure as *fuck* don't need anything else to draw people to me. But I've always wondered if magick has fed my ability to lead, even on the other side. I can persuade people with little effort, and I can sense their emotions. Maybe I have magick, maybe I'm an empath, or maybe I've always been some weird human hybrid.

That sounds insane, which is why I've never said it out loud—not to a single soul. Who would believe me?

From the moment that I arrived, I *felt* the unhappiness of the ladies with droids. I could almost *taste* the resentment and anger. Dona created companions for me to ease my loneliness—my darling Hex, a punk rock prince, and Leo, my über wonderful culinary genius. Even though I loved them and adored spending time with Victor, I empathized with the pain of feeling of 'less than' while pretending everything was fun.

The Cabal made it very clear who they considered lesser in person and on the active community blog hub everyone used. You couldn't avoid seeing tales of fun and clique-y bantering if you wanted to know what was happening in the Rift, and that made the divide between the groups widen by the day. As I watched my friends falter, I knew I had to help them.

Convincing my two closest friends, Michaela and Dona, to explore options for our people wasn't hard. Michaela was adamantly against the structure of the Cabal Quarter and she was on board immediately. Dona resisted a little because she'd straddled both sides since both Victor and Caesar lived with her. But once I showed her all the sad posts from the droid families getting ignored, she finally gave in.

All we had to do was figure out how to create our own space in the Rift and keep the Cabal out of it.

The Cat Reflects on Hard Truths

<hr>

DELILAH

It didn't take long for us to come up with the first part of the solution.

There was so much unused space in the Rift. Dona suggested that if we had enough interested people, we could... secede. Being from the South, I'm not a fan of that word because it doesn't have good connotations. But if we moved out of the reach of the Cabal and figured out how to keep them from finding us, it would work. Without their influence, we believed the unhappy folks would all be able to live their lives in relative peace.

Yeah, I know now how fucking naïve that assumption was.

Michaela offered to help, so we started visiting Bytes 'N Chips to look for our own recruits. With the right people in place, we could build a community where we'd all thrive. Finally, we found Lily. Lily was a cool, analytical contrast to my emotional fuzziness. When she agreed to join us, Victor created Mercury, an adorably odd match for Lily. She was one of us almost immediately, demanding to help with the formation of the new group we were assembling.

Our families all grew close and as they did, we became a force in the community. People looked up to the four of us as 'elders' and we knew our first phase was successful. The next part was extremely risky, but in order to accomplish our long-term goal, we had to do it. One of us had to build a new home in the unoccupied area we wanted to escape to. After it got established, the others would follow, especially since activity in the Cabal Quarter was so focused on the clone families.

Since I was one of the more visible leaders, we built my new house in the undeveloped area of the Rift, close to the portal. We made sure it was far enough from the central hub of The Cabal Quarter, but also surrounded by enough land that others could do the same. I left space in the huge backyard where Victor and the droids constructed their workshop. The design included a pool and an accompanying pool house, a sacred space in a small wooded area, and plenty of room to sprawl.

The Maison, as we called it, was specifically planned to be a social hub for our people.

Once my place was done, Lily, Dona, and Michaela chose spots for their new homes. One by one, we invited the Rift dwellers with droids to our new haven. Together, everyone pitched in to build houses, roads, and a few community areas. Lily settled on the farthest north point and Dona went south, so Michaela took the opposite side of the area from me so we were all touchpoints as more people joined us.

All of this happened right under the Cabal's noses.

They may have heard vague whispers of a new place, but they were too busy lording themselves over everyone to pay attention. Soon, the Cabal's events stopped drawing crowds—no one wanted to attend their forums or parties. The town square in the Cabal Quarter was quiet unless our families came to town. Without 'subjects' to hold court, the Cabal's interest in the Rift waned. One by one, bored Cabal members moved back to the other world with their companions. They trickled off until the last leader standing was Talia.

Since the Cabal Quarter was empty, she retreated with Taurus and the rest of her family in a self-imposed exile. That's why I had to call her out and appeal to Taurus to come out of seclusion when I needed help. My friends and I destroyed the dominance of her group and she wasn't interested in being part of the new world.

To be honest, I don't think the Cabal meant to cause the death of their kingdom with their edicts. They wanted to prevent another Conflict by making it clear who was in power. It takes a lot for people to walk away from their entire life on Earth to live here full time, and they wanted to preserve the atmosphere that drew them to the Rift. But things change and we all have to evolve— they simply chose not to and suffered the consequences.

Everyone in the new 'Resistance Quarter' got treated like an equal partner in the community. The only requirement to join was ordering a droid for your family. It could be any template or rela- tion to the human requesting it, but you had to have one living in your home. Dona, Lily, and I became the unofficial town council after being pressured by our peers. Having a democratic governing body protected everyone, whether it was recruiting more people or resolving internal disputes.

My house became a hotspot of activity, constantly drawing visi- tors as we planned. I didn't mind the stream of houseguests at first because it was fun. Dona's guys and my boys continued making new droids for recruits as people moved in, and everything seemed pretty fucking great.

We'd done it—we actually made a home for our friends and families away from the stranglehold of the Cabal.

As time went on, I grew closer with Dona's family, especially Victor. We didn't intend to, but we fell in love. He would always be Dona's mate, but it was crystal clear that I was his other favorite girl. No matter how busy I was, I always made time for his visits. Perhaps Dona worried about that and never told me, but since she said nothing, I missed signs that things weren't entirely perfect.

Despite Hex, Leo, Caesar, Mercury, and Preston being closer

than human brothers, Dona pulled away after the first anniversary of our town. First, she changed tactics, spending half her time on the other side of the portal. She allowed her boys to come visit, which helped, but she was often hard to reach. Then suddenly, she showed up with a new recruit she'd found named James. He requested the first female droid, Lucinda, and Dona got even more scarce. She would send Lucinda and her boys to my places for long stretches of time, despite her and James never coming along.

It should have been a clue that something was wrong. Lucinda stuck to Caesar like glue, and he was much clingier about being away from Dona than Victor. Her programming *had* to have been altered to help make Caesar less upset when she was away. Of course, Dona had the skills to adjust it at home and I never considered for a moment she would do it.

It's easy to see the breadcrumbs when you're looking back, less so while it's happening.

A fresh wave of recruits filtered in around that time and I got lost in setting them all up with their homes and droids. My schedule exploded and people freaked out when they couldn't have me whenever they wanted. I tried my best to make everyone happy, but I ended up leaning on Victor to help me mediate all the bruised egos. While I loved Hex and Leo, I wasn't *in* love with them, nor were they *in* love with me.

That's something you can't create.

Until now, I haven't examined the events with a magnifying lens. But nothing is ever predictable in the Rift, and the atmosphere shifted again when we welcomed new members. I don't know if it's that chaos theory shit or normal—statistically speaking—but random shit pops up all the time. It's like peace is only momentarily achievable. We got away from the Cabal, only to bicker within our own ranks. In hindsight, Dona's actions make more sense when I frame them as being jealous of Victor and me rather than mad at the entire council.

Tension filled our meetings, and I didn't understand why, but I would eventually.

One day after the new recruits arrived, we went to the Cabal Quarter for groceries. Hanging in the square, there was a huge banner announcing a contest. Everyone in the Rift could take part in a Rift documentary festival. As sponsors, The Cabal members would return to judge entries and they would award the winner a clone.

It was an offer no one could refuse. Despite rampant speculation about the Cabal's motives, every family started furiously working on films. I scoffed at the idea, not giving one randy shit about 'winning' a clone for our family. I had enough dick chasing me; I was happy to let everyone else act like someone had handed them a quest for the Holy Grail.

The overwhelmingly excited reactions were too depressing to acknowledge, anyway.

Even after building a home for everyone and ditching the Cabal, the masses still saw being issued a clone as an elevation in their status. The cache of welcoming the first clone released since the Conflict was too big a draw, and it consumed everyone around us. I moped for a little while until Hex and Leo badgered me into filming an expose on the Company as an entry.

It would be a tongue-in-cheek documentary about a whistle-blower who gave me inside info and tours of the facilities. None of us would risk sneaking in, but I could use Victor's connections to weasel my way in. If we got lucky, we'd catch a bunch of asshole clones being dicks, and it would bring equilibrium back to our community.

My wily gambit worked better than I expected. Dona, a Cabal member, and I got picked as finalists. They asked us to show our films in the town square for everyone while they judged the finals. For obvious reasons, I had a bad feeling about it. The judges were Cabal members, and it seemed too easily rigged. I couldn't figure out why they would pretend to include me. Perhaps they planned to use the clone as a bribe to re-integrate our community and make themselves royalty once more?

Unfortunately, all of my guesses were off-base.

The judges unanimously picked Dona as the winner, and there was almost a riot. As much as the Resistance members loved her, it only underlined the unfairness of the Cabal. A gal who already had a clone mate received a second one. It was another example of the one percent giving themselves more rewards while ignoring the other ninety-nine percent of the world. The Cabal tried to deny the blatant favoritism, but it fell on deaf ears.

Our people left the Cabal Quarter with a foul taste in their mouths once again. This time, though, the Cabal planted the seed that Dona wasn't one of us. They favored her; she was one of them. She came back to her Resistance home with Rafe, the new family member, and her existing family, with all eyes on her. It had a chilling effect on morale almost immediately. Dona withdrew a bit more afterward, and this time, I noticed, but I let it go.

Our community needed space after that debacle and I was happy to give it to them.

Dona's boys came to visit after a few weeks of her hiding out. The first time Rafe rang my doorbell, and I locked eyes with him, I knew we were kindred spirits. I didn't mind him staying with us, even when Victor and Caesar went home early. I felt emotions zinging between us, but we didn't act on them. Even though he primarily belonged with Dona, I worried it would hurt Victor's feelings.

Apparently, our hand wringing didn't go unnoticed. Whispers flew around town as he escorted me to places, but I ignored them. My vast sexual appetite certainly wasn't anything new. Why would it matter if Rafe was doing so this time? Dona didn't seem concerned and that should be enough for everyone.

This shit should have been a clue about how unhealthy the co-dependence of my townsfolk was getting, but again, my rose-colored glasses made me miss shit.

It might have gotten worse if something bigger hadn't distracted them—Talia came out of hiding.

A month after the contest ended, she organized a birthday party for Taurus on the other side of the portal. I thought this was another attempt at getting their 'fans' back, but. However, the whole Resistance chose to caravan to the party together. All the families piled through the portal to rent cars to take a road trip. We had plans to stop at various attractions on the way on one big, week-long party tour. It would be a great bonding experience and we were all excited as hell.

The first night of the trip, the caravan stopped at a basic, no-tell motel. A knock on my door revealed Dona who told me everyone knew Rafe, and I had fallen for one another. She told me we had her blessing. Never ones to question good news, Rafe and I mated that night, and were inseparable from then on. Again, there were flags I should have seen, but my happiness with Rafe and the joy of my friends on our journey kept me from seeing what was going on in the background.

Funnily enough, none of us made it to the party. It got canceled before we could arrive because Talia mysteriously disappeared without a word. Dona did some digging and came back to share that the golden Cabal member had gotten injured. She and the boys designed Talia a droid named Theodora, to help her recover. No one knew how she got injured, and that was the last official Cabal event to get scheduled.

Now I know what happened: she got shot.

It's scary to realize even the mightiest of us is not infallible. However, even more terrifying to me is when I look back at the past. I see how people were manipulating each other before Sari arrived, and it makes me sad. The party, Dona and her blessing, the contest—it makes so much more sense now that my vision is clear. I wish it was different, but I don't know if that would have prevented what's going on now or prolonged it.

Regardless, things in our community remained calm for a

while. The Cabal faded away and their quarter was a ghost town unless citizens had to shop for necessities. The Resistance Quarter, however, was hopping. The Cabal became a cautionary tale—with them not around; it was easy to make them entirely the villains. The only people left to know the truth were the ones spinning yarns, so perception became reality.

This 'folklore' created an atmosphere rife with speculation, myths, and resentment for a group of women who weren't around to defend their actions. Most of the new townspeople had never even *met* a Cabal leader, but the gossip filled the air when crowds gathered. Taurus and Talia were the demons of the tale: two people who personified the elitist antithesis of our community's 'free love' credo. We didn't dispense justice with a sword and a smirk; we talked things out and everything worked out okay.

We were naïve; I know. That can't last forever, and it didn't.

The bigger the community grew, the more our citizens showed up in public areas. Suddenly, favored friends of the Cabal started appearing in our recruiting hang outs, befriending our members. They couldn't find our corner of the world without being invited —that was the one large and scary piece of magick that I successfully cast in the Rift. My spell cloaked our haven from anyone without the knowledge of where to find us. It was for our protection, and I was unwilling to release the wards even after the Cabal disappeared. I didn't trust that they wouldn't come back with a vengeance.

Debate sparked for the first time between myself, Dona, and Lily when Sari and Wilde courted several of our members, including me. They were close with several families and eager to cozy up to Rafe and me. I wasn't sure what to do—they were so interesting, fun, and engaging—that they convinced me to invite them to our town. They would be the first members to live here without having a droid in their household. Sari assured me that since Wilde had been a droid before the change, it was an equivalent exchange.

I was too far gone to see the red flags again; I'm paying for it now.

Before long, Rafe and I became deeply embroiled with Sari and Wilde. Our love affair was quick, torrid, and all-encompassing, pulling me away from everyone else. Not long after they secured our love, they began their campaign to allow Rhea and Alistair to move in. Those two absolutely did not have any droids, nor had either been a droid. Lily and Dona were vehemently against giving them access, but as usual, Sari swayed me with a nonsense argument about Rhea's robot-dog.

I should have listened to my genuine friends; I wish I had. I wish that we'd never allowed either of them to join us. Amazing things happened in our relationships, but all of that turned to misery so quickly. I could have saved us all, but I didn't.

I'll never forgive myself for that.

Part of my rampant speculation tonight is admitting that those events might have triggered Dona's departure. She had been spending a great deal of time with James in the other place, leaving Lucinda, Caesar, and Victor on extended stays at my house. My boys didn't mind—Victor and his 'kids' all had a blast running around town, pranking one another, flirting with people, and having adventures. I was so wrapped up in the Sari and Rhea drama that I didn't notice how often Dona was absent, even from major meetings and events.

One day, James showed up to collect Lucinda. He and Dona explained they were moving back to the other side for good. They were taking Lucinda and *only* Lucinda with them, but she might come visit the boys occasionally. I was so aghast that I didn't know how to answer them and before I could try to get my old friend alone; they left. Questions flew through my head as I stood in my living room, wondering how Lily and I would manage everything on our own, but then it hit me.

Where would Caesar and Victor go?

I couldn't figure out why she'd leave them or even why she'd leave at all. Days passed, but I didn't get an explanation, nor did Victor and Caesar. Eventually, Dona sent emails stating they should stay with us permanently and after that, she was gone. It was like she'd severed her connection to this world entirely and we were all too shocked to know how to process it.

Caesar was a mess, having lost two people he loved, and Victor was inconsolable. His primary mate abandoned him and it was tearing him to pieces. Because Rafe and I were so involved with the others, neither of us was available as much as he needed. I regret that, but he locked himself away for months while he dealt with his grief.

Lily and I split the duties of running the town after that. Victor and the boys ran the droid workshop for new members, and we all tried to compensate for Dona's absence. We'd kept off the Cabal's radar despite embracing Rhea and Sari's families. Regardless of our internal troubles, our home was better than the Cabal Quarter had ever been.

At least, that's what I thought, but I was definitely wrong.

What's important now is that my quest to figure out what is going on with me risks our security. It might compromise our way of life, all to help me get back to a life that might not be what I thought it was. Every one of my mates—clones and droids—will be angry and worried. If the other community members find out, they might decide to burn me at the stake. I've climbed down into Hell and invited the devil back to Heaven, and they won't like it.

I *can't* care about the bigger picture right now, though. I'm the only person with my unique situation, so no one understands how I feel. If it's caused by genetic re-coding, I'm the best person around to develop this shit because I won't abuse it. I shudder to think of some of our rowdier citizens—including Sari—turning up with extra-normal powers.

If anyone but Rafe knew all of what was going on emotionally besides this physical nonsense, they'd understand that I can't have two earth-shaking crises going on at once. They don't know, though, because I can't be weak in the eyes of my people. I'm the strong one, the savior, and the creator of our home. They can't know what is happening to me behind closed doors.

Lily and I wouldn't be able to set boundaries if they did.

I didn't even want Rafe to know, but one night, we looked at each other and it was clear. Our secret shame haunted us, and we were dealing with it the best we could. It deepened our bond again to realize we were surviving the abuse together. Some nights, we simply stared at one another as if we'd find a solution during our shared insomnia.

We still haven't and I don't know if we ever will.

Of the many things I learned tonight, I realize the pull of the ones we love doesn't excuse their abuse. We can't leave them, but I need something separate from their world to balance my sanity. I have to get away from everything connected to our town, even if only for a few hours of snarky teeth pulling.

Taurus offered me a chance to have that.

He doesn't realize it, but he's offered me a lifeline to grab onto —somewhere else, someone else, untouched by my current world. Our uneasy kinship might make me forget the bad things and find myself again. Unlike many of my mates, he seems to accept and appreciate the extra parts of me. He might even understand the drive I'm feeling to get primal in ways my family isn't interested in.

I need that.

As soon as I can, I'm going to contact that jackass and take him up on it.

<h1 style="text-align:center">Internal Company Memo, Eyes Only</h1>

DISTRIBUTION: OPERATIONS DIRECTOR (MIKHAIL, 004); OVERSIGHT, ANALYSIS DEPARTMENT, INTEL DEPARTMENT, SECURITY DIRECTOR (BRUTUS, 006)

SUBJECT: PROJECT REALITY

A
LL-
THE PROJECT HAS GROWN IMMENSELY SINCE THE CREATION OF THE 'RESISTANCE QUARTER' IN ITS UNKNOWN LOCATION.
OUR NORMAL PROCEDURE IS FOR ALL SUBJECTS TO BE LABELED BY THEIR APPROPRIATE CODE NUMBER AND DESIGNATION OF SPECIES WITHIN MEMOS, PROFILES, AND OTHER DOCUMENTATION.

{Species Designation is: 'X' followed by the number in order of appearance in the Rift for humans, clones in numerical order with no letters, droids classified by 'A' followed by numbers in order of creation. Other species/categories will be designated as needed going

forward. There is one Muse that lives with Talia (X001) and he is designated by an 'M'.}

THERE ARE TEAMS RESPONSIBLE FOR ANALYSIS OF INTEL GATHERED FROM MONITORING IN THE CABAL QUARTER AND OTHER PUBLIC AREAS, INCLUDING THE INTRANET, CATALOG AND PLACE THEIR REPORTS INTO CLASSIFIED, ALPHA-LEVEL SECURITY SERVERS.

THE LEADERS OF THE OFFSHOOT 'RESISTANCE' FROM THE 'CONFLICT' ARE DELILAH (X1501), HER FAMILY, AND HER CURRENT 'CO-MAYORS'. NONE OF THE CITIZENS OF THE RIFT (CABAL OR RESISTANCE) HAVE ANY KNOWLEDGE OF THIS PROJECT AND CANNOT EVER BE MADE AWARE ITS EXISTENCE.

WE RECENTLY RECEIVED WORD THAT OUR WORLD (THE COMPANY) AND THE SUBJECTS' WORLD MAY COLLIDE; THEREFORE, WE ARE PROVIDING OUR HIGHEST LEVEL AGENTS AND DEPARTMENT HEADS A BRIEF REMINDER OF THE PROJECT, ITS GOALS, AND WHAT IS AT STAKE IF THIS PLANNED DIRECT CONTACT OCCURS.

SUMMARY OF PROJECT REALITY (AKA CODE-NAME: THE RIFT)

THE RIFT IS THE NAME OF THE POCKET DIMEN-SION SET UP TO HOUSE THE HEADQUARTERS OF THE COMPANY.

WHEN THE ORIGINAL THREE CLONES FOUND MATES IN HUMANS FROM THE CABAL, THEY WERE RELEASED TO LIVE IN OUR TEST SPACE. THE REAC-TION OF THE CABAL MEMBERS GIFTED WITH THIS BOON WAS UNPRECEDENTED.

OVERSIGHT SAW THE BENEFITS OF TAILORING CLONES FROM ALTERNATE RIBBONS OF REALITY TO THE NEEDS OF THE HUMAN WOMEN THAT WERE

BEING RECRUITED TO WORK IN THE RIFT AS A TEST PROJECT. IT COULD BE AN ADDITIONAL LINE OF BUSINESS THAT MIGHT PROVE MORE LUCRATIVE THAN MERCENARY PURSUITS. IT SHOULD BE AFFIRMED THAT AGENT MISSIONS HAVE MADE US MORE THAN ENOUGH MONEY; HOWEVER, IF THIS WAS A SUCCESS, IT OPENED MORE LINES OF BUSINESS FOR THE FUTURE.

THE BASE EXPERIMENT IS SIMPLE: RUN A LARGE-SCALE TEST TO ENSURE THAT THE POCKET DIMEN-SION WILL HAVE NO LONG-TERM ILL-EFFECTS ON HUMANS. WE COULD CREATE MORE OF THESE DIMENSIONS AND USE THEM AS EXCLUSIVE PLAY-GROUNDS, EXILES, HIDING SPOTS, AND MORE.

THEREFORE, WE ALLOWED THE HUMANS WHO MATED WITH THE CLONES TO CONTINUE TO RECRUIT MORE HUMANS, EVEN THEY WERE NOT INCLUDED IN OFFICIAL CABAL BUSINESS.

THIS WAS SUCCESSFUL UNTIL ONE HUMAN (DONATELLA X098) BEGAN CREATING ANDROIDS TO ALLOW ALL THE POPULATION TO HAVE A COMPAN-ION. AFTER A FEW YEARS, THE CABAL (OUR HUMAN GOVERNING BODY) LOST CONTROL OF THE POPULA-TION AND WE HAD TO FACILITATE 'THE CONFLICT'.

THIS WAR BETWEEN DROIDS, CLONES, AND THEIR COMPANIONS ENDED WITH THE TRIUMPH OF OUR CLONES IN THE 'BATTLE OF BLOOD AND STEEL'.

THE REMAINING MEMBERS OF THE RESISTANCE—OUR NAME FOR THE GROUP OF REBELS—CONTINUED TO RECRUIT MEMBERS THROUGH THE PORTAL ACCESS POINT IN BYTES 'N CHIPS.

DELILAH (X1501) FORGED A COMMUNITY OUT OF THE REMAINING RESISTANCE. AFTER THE CONFLICT, MUCH OF THE CABAL GREW WEARY OF THE

CONTINUED REBELLION MOVED BACK TO EARTH WITH THEIR MATES. THIS AFFECTED OUR EXPERIMENT, SO WE ALLOWED X1501 TO CONTINUE EXPANDING THE RESISTANCE. ITS LOCATION HAS REMAINED HIDDEN FOR TWO YEARS, DESPITE OUR SUPERIOR TECHNOLOGY. WE CAN ONLY GATHER INTEL ON ITS MEMBERS THROUGH DIGITAL MEANS AND COMMON AREA SURVEILLANCE.

X1501 AND THE REST OF HER REBELS HAVE CONTINUED TO RECRUIT, CREATE DROIDS, AND EXPAND THEIR COMMUNITY. SOME OF THE FORMER CABAL MEMBERS HAVE JOINED THEIR RANKS AND DESPITE THE CLOSURE OF THE 'DIRTY DEEDS' BAR, THEIR GROWTH HAS NOT SLOWED. HOWEVER, IN THE YEARS BETWEEN THE CONFLICT AND NOW, THE RESISTANCE HAS BECOME A DEN OF INIQUITY THAT WOULD SHOCK EVEN THE MOST FLEXIBLE OF OUR EMPLOYEES.

THE IMPETUS BEHIND THIS MEMO IS THAT WE HAVE GLEANED THAT X1501 IS PLANNING A MEETING WITH ONE OF OUR OWN—TAURUS (002) — FOR A CLANDESTINE TÊTE-À-TÊTE. WE DO NOT KNOW WHY OR WHEN, BUT THIS BRINGS THE CABAL, THE COMPANY, AND THE RESISTANCE INTO DIRECT CONTACT FOR THE FIRST TIME IN YEARS.

THAT IS DANGEROUS FOR PROJECT REALITY IF NOT CLOSELY MONITORED.

THE CABAL ARE NOT ALPHA-LEVEL CLEARANCE; THEREFORE, THEY CANNOT EXPOSE THIS PROJECT BUT CONTINUED RELATIONS BETWEEN AN ACTIVE AGENT AND THE RESISTANCE COULD LEAD TO BREACHES OF PROTOCOL.

AS WE ARE ALL AWARE, 002 IS THE LEAST CONTROLLABLE, MOST VOCIFEROUS OF THE ORIG-

INAL THREE AND OUR ONLY REMAINING EMPLOYEE THAT IS LIVING OUTSIDE OF THE HQ. HIS MATE, TALIA (X001), IS A LEAD ANALYST IN OUR OPERATIONS DEPARTMENT. THEIR CONNECTIONS TO US MAKE THEM A VALUABLE INTEL TARGET IF THE RESISTANCE IS PLANNING ANOTHER ONSLAUGHT.

QUESTIONS SHOULD BE DIRECTED TO MIKHAIL, BRUTUS, OR THE ALPHA LEVEL CONSORTIUM. ABSOLUTELY NO COMMUNICATION REGARDING PROJECT REALITY OR ANY OF OUR BUSINESS CAN BE DISCUSSED WITH ANYONE WHO DOES NOT HAVE ALPHA LEVEL CLEARANCE.

ANYONE CAUGHT DOING SO WILL GET PUNISHED TO THE MOST SEVERE CONSEQUENCES ALLOWED.

The Cat Goes On A Hunt

DELILAH

It took two weeks to schedule an outing with Taurus.

Between his Company jobs—whatever the hell those are —and my ridiculously full social calendar, we had to cancel four times. I know it's silly, but I got a little concerned that he'd changed his mind. After all, he wouldn't be the first clone or droid recently to decide I'm beneath them.

During that time, all hell broke loose in the Resistance.

Outside of my families' bullshit shenanigans, my greatest fears about the multiple DNA mutation theory manifested: Sari and Rhea developed powers. I don't know how—unless they, too, had some non-human shit latent in their blood—but it was *not* good news. Both of them have a truckload of unresolved issues and getting the ability to use mutant powers to deal with it?

Fucking terrifying, man.

I found out about Sari by witnessing her showing them off in public; that was par for the course with her. Knowing she was using them against Rafe in the background was disturbing, but he assured me he had it under control. Rhea was also true to form by revealing hers in private to her mates. She's so damned scared of using them; she's going to get everyone around her killed when she loses control.

They aren't the worst people who could have gotten their particular skills, but they aren't the best choices, either.

I kept my panicking to private conversations with Rafe. He's the only one who knows what those two already do to damage us regularly. No one else would understand why I'm terrified of their inability to control things as dangerous as shifting and fire. I can't tell anyone why, either, so now I'm left with this gnawing in my gut. I knew I had to do something, so I went with the option least annoying to me: I invited Rhea on this hunting expedition.

Taurus has been long-distance coaching me on control since we met—mostly through half insulting, half aggravated emails—but Rhea won't listen to me. Her primary, Alistair, has never been a big bad like his 'brother', so he's useless at reining her in. While I desperately wanted to go alone with Taurus so I could explore my limits, my terror that Rhea will accidentally fry someone has superseded that desire.

"I don't know," Rhea says, wringing her hands as she spins in front of my full-length mirror. "Maybe this is too... Maybe you should go by yourself. Well, not by yourself. Alistair will have a heart attack, and so will Rafe, Victor, and Wilde. But you don't need me to come. You need Sari; we should call her. This is not my thing, but it's definitely hers."

I hold up my hand and start ticking off my retorts. "One: Wilde and Sari could give a shit less what I do with my beast. Besides, they're part of what I'm escaping. Two: Victor and Rafe are used to living with me; running headlong into dangerous situations is normal. Deep-down, they know I can take care of myself. Three: You're coming, so zip it." I toss my hair over my shoulders, giving her an imperious expression. "Four: Quit pulling on that shirt or you'll stretch it out and it will look terrible."

"But—"

Grabbing her arm, I pull her towards the stairs. "No buts!"

Rhea is infuriatingly wishy-washy. She's timid and lacks confidence, yet she wants the boys to treat her like she's a bad girl. Her idea of 'bad girl' and mine differ by light years, trust me. However, I can't let her screw this up. Of all the powers someone as namby-pamby as Rhea could get, I'm certain that *fire* is the worst. Unpredictable, deadly, and cool is not her bag. It doesn't take a genius to figure out that she's going to kill someone if I don't get her to learn control.

If she wasn't family, I'd probably let her discover that on her own. Since she is, I'd prefer her accidental target to not be my primary mate. I'm undecided about Wilde—I might be okay with him getting a taste of his own medicine. His stupid ass demon had a fire and ice phase it took almost a week to heal from.

Dragging her to the front door, I smirk as the gauntlet of grumbling clones' scowls. I don't want to look like an overexcited dork, but I'm super psyched. I've been on pins and needles for days, hoping we didn't end up canceling again.

"Kitten," Alistair begins.

"Flame," Rafe chimes in.

Victor glowers from the archway, his expression a mix between angry and petulant, but he says nothing.

I give them all an exasperated look. "Stow it, all of you—including the rest of you I can't see in other rooms. We're going out to have some fun without you. Get over it."

Rhea garners a little backbone from my stubborn stance. Giving our mates a defiant look, she adds, "Maybe cause some trouble, too. If we feel like it."

Holding back a chuckle at her inability to commit to anything, I glare at the brooding band of clones and droids. "I can take care of myself and so can she. We're big girls and you need to amuse yourselves for the evening—no mind watching. The first person I catch in my head sleeps on the porch for a month."

"We'll call if we need you," Rhea offers, batting her lashes at the angry faces.

They all soften at her words, and I groan. "Which we won't. Geez." I wink at them, feeling saucy. "Don't wait up."

Rhea blinks at me as if she didn't understand we might be out late, and before she tries to opt out to hop on Rafe, I yank her arm and pull her out the door.

His scent catches the breeze as I open the door and I roll my eyes. He couldn't ring the doorbell like a normal person—oh no. He has to sit out by his bike and be the cool, aloof guy.

"Are you sure this is a good idea?" she asks again, tugging the shirt exactly where I told her not to.

"Nope," I grin, flashing pearly whites against dark vampy lipstick. "All the same, it'll be a hell of a ride."

"Sometimes I wonder why I let you people drag me into these things."

"Otherwise, you'd have no fun at all." I shrug and give her a grin, peering out into the night.

He's not waiting where we can see him; I gotta scent him out. I shouldn't be this annoyed by his arrogance, but what can I say? He knows how to get a rise out of me. I do not know why I put up with him—scratch that. I know. He's growing on me. I'm enjoying the occasional time he drops by and we hang out.

Imagine that.

When I locate him, I grin smugly. I had to let the kitty night vision kick in to see him leaning against a tree down the street. He's picking imaginary lint from the shoulder of his duster, pretending not to see us. I turn and whisper to Rhea, "He's down there; can you see him?"

"Of course not," she snorts. "It's pitch black out here and he's over a hundred feet away. Why we had to go at midnight, I don't know."

I shake my head. Rhea's a nice gal and she is a part of my family, but she worries like an old nanny goat. My mates' attraction to her is baffling; she has zero *joie de vivre*.

I want Taurus to help me help her with her new powers, but

she *needs* him to help her. Truthfully, Sari needs it more because she's out of control, but Taurus won't have anything to do with her. Not that she would listen to him if he did—that's a truly burned bridge. On the bright side, not bringing her along means I don't have to tell him *why* I'm concerned about Sari. That means I can continue to avoid discussing my terrible family situation and the *thing we do not talk about* from the winter.

"Try again. Torch up or whatever. I know you can."

"I really don't want to."

"Rhea, I know you've got powers you've been hiding because Rafe told me. The same thing happened to me—I woke up with something I didn't know how to control. It's also exhausting to keep secrets slipping through the mating connection."

Trust me; I know.

I've kept the shit happening with Wilde and Sari secret from everyone. The amount of energy it takes to maintain those mental blocks *and* control the beast is killing me. I'm eating like a T-Rex to keep myself upright.

"Besides, I can smell it, feel it, and Rafe is terrible at mentally blocking me." That's why I do his blocking for him and the added strain is tearing me up. "For tonight, let it all out. Let's have conse-quence-free play time. You'll learn, but you can't figure out where the boundaries are if you don't test the limits."

Her reluctant sigh signals acquiescence and a tinge of smoke fills my nostrils when a small ball of fire appears in her palm. She blows it towards where I pointed, lighting a path bright enough for our eyes to see the way to his slouching form.

"Excellent," I grin. "We are going to tear this town up, sister. Let's go before he has a seizure from that display."

I stalk over to where he's waiting, watching his expression. As usual, it gives away nothing until Rhea and I get closer. For a moment—more of a glimmering second—his mask of disinterest drops, and he grins appreciatively. As fast as it appears, the grin fades to disdain. I caught it, though, and I'm inordinately pleased by it.

His head tilts towards Rhea. "It's been a while, Blondie. My goddess sends her love." Being the primary mate of one of his 'brothers' earns Rhea a bit of formality, I guess. "Thanks ever so for the blinding ball of not so stealthy. Were you trying to burn me alive?"

Rhea's eyes widen, and she shakes her head. I worry she'll turn on her heel and run, but she somehow gets some starch in her spine. "I was only trying to light the way. Not all of us have that clone glowy-eye night vision."

"True enough, though, seems like more by the day," he drawls, sounding bored and irritated as his gaze cuts to me. "That's not a problem your partner in girlie mayhem bears. What part of low key did you misunderstand, Sandwich?"

"I wasn't expecting her to *throw a fireball*. I didn't even know she could do it, jackass. That makes this even more important, doesn't it? Besides, you do low key like a paparazzi does respectful distance. Don't judge me." I shrug and turn to mutter to Rhea, knowing he can hear. "It's not my fault he was hiding over here like a drama queen."

I'm deliberately poking at him, but that's become a comfortable part of our repartee in the past few weeks. I'm confident I won't get skewered for it—maybe. He gives me the patented 'scary Taurus' look and I press my lips together, suppressing my urge to chuckle. It doesn't scare me anymore, but I guess he has to save face with Rhea by trying to terrify me.

His gaze slides to me and then over to Rhea. "You two dropping by a tarts and vicars party, or is there another equally wretched reason for those outfits?"

Rhea tugs at the skintight lace tank again, his criticism making her self-conscious.

She's so fluttery. Sigh.

I roll my eyes as he hit the target he was aiming for exactly. I'm trying to build her up and he knocks her down just to get at me. Putting my hand on my leather clad hip, I glared at him. My outfit is normal for me, and what I wear is none of his damn business. "Is there something wrong with how we're dressed?"

"Not if you're planning on working the bloody cor—"

My eyes glitter as I cut him off. "I doubt you want to finish that sentence, darling. Besides, I think we make excellent bait." Lifting my arms above my head, I spin slowly, displaying a wealth of alabaster skin in low-slung leather pants and a matching backless corset. My long hair swings over the ribbons binding it, the crimson a stark contrast to the black leather and pale skin. "We should attract a slobberer or two."

"Fuck assume. That getup would attract an entire monastery. Not to mention the mini Bic over here." His eyes narrow, looking irritable. "I will not pry idiots off you all night, you know."

Laughing throatily, I shake my head. "Oh, yeah. You'd hate that chest thumping caveman stuff."

"We can handle ourselves," Rhea pipes up.

"Can you now?" he says, eyeing her. "There are more tricks up those non-existent sleeves, I take it?"

She grins and shrugs, her eyes dancing. "I guess you'll have to wait and see."

Snorting, he pushes off the tree and fishes in his pocket for a smoke. Rhea flicks her thumb up, a flame dancing in front of his cig, looking pleased with herself.

Good on her for trying to show him, but it only encourages his disdain as he puffs until its lights, then gives her a cool look. "Yeah. Lighting some git's smoke will really have them shaking in their beer-soaked shit kickers."

She visibly shrinks back, her bravado dissipating like mist over a river. His gaze changes when sees her curl in and he looks at my puckered expression of disapproval.

Perhaps he caught the flicker of hurt his words caused or Talia screamed in his noggin; I don't know. Maybe he still cares about

Rhea in a way he doesn't for anyone else because of their family connection through Alistair. His voice is soft as he reaches out to brush a strand of hair from her cheek.

"Listen, love, I'm sorry. I'm a bad, rude man. The thought of you getting dented or pawed at by someone you can't handle makes me want to behead people. If you say wait and see, I will." He taps her nose with his finger, smiling in a fond, big brother way. "You know, if I thought it'd do any good, I'd lecture you on the dangers of heart-stopping threads like that. As it is, I'll try to control my baser instincts."

Turning away from her, he gives me a shrewd look, clearly deciding that the same lecture would be wasted on me.

I'm not a wilting flower, and I don't need his approval. I'm not ashamed of who I am—at least, not in my present company. My problems with Wilde since my beast appeared are a different story. His voice cuts into my thoughts and I look up, hoping my sadness is hidden under the mask like I think it is. "What?"

"I said, where are we going, Sandwich? It's not like I know my way around these parts."

He's eyeing me carefully now, and I have to watch myself. That maudlin moment may have weakened my wards enough to let some of it leak through. I gotta be more careful and for that; I need to feed. I need more energy to keep it all under wraps. "In the mood for ribs? I'm hungry and I figured we'd go roust something out to satisfy the urge."

"We're going hunting?"

I grin fangily as the thought lets the beast slip a bit. "We're going hunting."

Without warning, his arm shoots out and pulls me against him. His hand slides down my spine and before I can smack the hell out of him, he whispers softly so only my enhanced hearing can catch it. "It's been a while since I've been on a run, gorgeous." His hands dip lower and come to rest on my ass. "I'm feeling peckish. No sense not to have an appetizer before dinner." Without another word, he swoops down and captures my lips.

If the shock doesn't kill me, Talia might.

Typically, I'd give a person who dared to touch me without permission a swift kick in the balls or a right hook, but this time I didn't. I simply let loose and give him free rein. Everything about this screams '*bad idea*', but I'm not listening. I've always been a sucker for people who give me back everything I throw at them. That must be why every cell in my body has decided he's a tasty treat.

My hands smooth up his chest to wrap around his neck. I'm actively taking part, and I'm sure that has sealed my doom from a flying piece of weaponry. Both of our dooms, possibly, because he squeezes my ass as I wriggle against him. When he lifts his head, swirling emerald eyes meet icy blue, and for a moment, a shared look of confusion passes between us.

"Now," he says, drawing back and setting me away. He shakes his head and his demon emerges. "Let's go get something to eat."

"Damned right," I mutter, letting the kitty out to play as I lick my fangs. My hips sway as I stalk towards my bike determinedly, trying to pretend I'm not nearly as shaken by that display as I am. "If I was hungry before, now I'm fucking ravenous."

The Coyote Howls

SARI

"Why, hello, Duchess Philomena!"

Janus, my fashionista droid, was at it again. His cell rang with the familiar ringtone, so he's up and pacing immediately. The only other person in the world who gets that quick of a response is his partner, Roman.

"Oh, not much. No reality is pleasant reality, so the family is watching some boring Oscar fodder that the blogger picked. It's a drag and not in the good way."

His laugh tinkles through the air, and I smile. He'll be at *least* an hour and a half talking about his new designer loafers, shopping in Beverly Hills, and the Real Housewives of Anyplace. I'd bet my bottom dollar he's headed for their bedroom to pull his newest purchase out of the 'vault' so he can describe them in minute detail rather than have her Google them.

For guys made with the highest of high tech, droids and clones hate technology. At least, the ones who live in my house do. Janus and Roman like a personal touch no matter what they're doing. Wilde uses the 'Net for his blogging audience, but he prefers actual books and paper. Calista prefers nature to anything indoors.

I love them all, but sometimes, I want to give them a good shake.

"I read she was going to reha—what, DP? What are you saying?"

I raise a brow as Janus walks back into the living room, his brows knit in concern. Given that he agrees with his bitchy bestie that emotions cause wrinkles, I'd say it must be important.

"Shortstack? Duchess P is demanding an audience." He holds the phone out, giving Roman a worried look.

"Philomena wants me?"

I'm the least girly, least fashion-conscious person in the house —maybe even in the universe. This is a droid who might think people who buy off the rack have a mental defect. *It cannot be good if she's asking for me.* I'm certain that she only puts up with me because we're family. I think if she didn't know me, she'd be snidely commenting on my attire as we passed on the street. She might still do that, but at least it's not in front of me.

"She won't tell me why."

Okay. That is *definitely* not good. Something is amiss at the Maison if Philomena won't tell Janus what's going on. Those two *live* for gossip and intrigue. I take the phone from his outstretched hand, my expression troubled. Janus heads back to his room to put away his treasures and Roman gives me a sideways glance as I answer. "Hello?"

"How's it hanging, hobbit?"

I sigh, pinching the bridge of my nose as she laughs her 'drunkenly clever' insult laugh. Duchess Philomena—or DP, as the boys call her for short—has two states of being smashed and condescending. They are not mutually exclusive. How Deli puts up with her constant barrage of drunken slurs and slams, I'll never know, but it's the way she's freaking programmed.

As a distraction, Deli's tribe built Philomena for her as a present after Dona left. She shares a 'birthday' with several other droids that were ordered around that time. Deli received Philomena, Calista came home with us, Shane moved in with Michaela, and a few other households gained new members. To this day, I don't know if that wave of orders started because everyone wanted to make our 'creators' feel better or because everyone wanted to be more like Deli with her ever-growing legion.

I don't really care. Everyone in the Resistance shares and has equality. I'm all for that after living through the dictatorship of the Cabal. Those people wouldn't share a damned napkin, much less their companions.

"DP, it's real nice hearing from you, but I have a feeling this isn't a social call, or you'd be gabbing with Janus. What can I do you for?"

"Do me? Honey, you'd need to grow half a foot—and I don't mean tall—to do me, and even then, you wouldn't be doing me right." She snorts, and I wonder if you can hear my eyes rolling over the phone. "Listen, I need you over here like yesterday."

I'm sorry, but this has gone from worrisome to outright panic inducing.

There is no way the droid who has *never* warmed up to me, despite my status as a mate to two people in her household, is asking me to come to their house voluntarily. DP might love my dancing boys, but she does not dig me and never will. Nothing less than an emergency would cause her to do this.

"What's going on, Philomena?" I use her proper name because I'm having trouble not screeching. Whatever this is, she's dragging it out unnecessarily and it's infuriating.

"Well," she pauses, and I can hear her sipping a drink. "The clones and droids here all have their non-existent boxers in a bunch. I cannot even deal with them." She sighs, a little of her concern creeping through the drunkenness.

DP loves to boss around the clones and droids. It's one of her favorite things in the world. She likes it even more when they're riled up. *Why the hell does she need me?* I'm more likely to get them even further riled and take a ride rather than come to corral the stallions.

She doesn't know about our current issues with her house-mates. That would have prevented her from calling me, I think. Or maybe she is aware, and it's so bad there that she's calling me, anyway. "What's going on? Is something wrong?"

"Look, furry Fanny, I don't want to get into it over the phone. I'm going to bash boys with booze bottles. I hate alliteration; it's tacky to repeat yourself. Will you please scoot on over?"

This is serious. DP never says please; she's a Devil who wears Prada or nada. An icy chill runs up my spine and the coyote in me takes notice. "DP, is something wrong?"

"Get over here, half pint! If you aren't here by the time my Xanax wears off, I won't be held responsible!"

With that, the phone clicks, and our conversation has ended.

I let out a screech of frustration that turns into a long, mournful howl. I don't have control over this shit yet and though I absolutely love the feel of my darker half prowling inside; I don't know how to keep from going postal. I can't use it to my advantage if I don't know how it works and Deli won't teach me.

When she started having these issues back in December, she and Wilde had to be hogtied until they worked their shit out. Since then, she seems to have picked up some actual skill, though, because I can feel her soothing her beast, whereas my coyote has no interest in listening.

Wilde conquered his newly released demon, and it brought Deli back when he thought he was losing her to Alistair. I've been trying to do the same with Rafe, but I'm not having the same luck Wilde did.

Who is helping her, I wonder?

Speaking of the demon, Wilde saunters in, giving me a stern look. "Is something wrong at the estate? Are our mates unsafe, Sari?"

"Hell, Wilde, I don't know. Let's get over to the Maison and find out what the hell has been buzzing in the clones' bonnets."

He turns on his heel, heading for our room to change into

travel attire, and I sigh, gathering my stuff. I don't know what I'm going to need over there, but I suppose a few more pairs of cuffs and some rope wouldn't hurt.

Maybe I'm wrong about her control. Maybe the beast is on the loose.

Wilde would like that very much. I almost hope it's true.

The Cat On A High Iron Roof

DELILAH

Rhea is white as a sheet when she climbs on the bike behind me.

I don't blame her; she's awfully gentle hearted for this venture.

She's gotta learn, though, or she'll hurt someone. Including her on our outing is the best way to teach her control. Not learning the scope of her powers and how to harness them is dangerous. She refused to take part in the hunting aspect, leaving Taurus and me to find our own sustenance while she stood by the bikes and wrung her hands.

The primal inside gets hungrier as you spend energy. No matter what you're doing: fighting, fucking, shopping—it doesn't make a difference. It *needs* feeding, and she's starving hers. That shit is going to bite us all on the ass if I can't get her to listen to me tonight. I can only hope Taurus has better luck because so far, I've hit a wall.

Since I started fighting for control of my beast, I noticed the more I fight, the worse the hunger gets. I emailed Taurus about how exhausted I was, and he suggested hunting. I suppose that's how the less 'domesticated' Company agents master their demons. *Hell only knows how the non-primal clones like Rafe or Victor do it.* Perhaps that's why they got released: they don't have the primal hunger making them liabilities rather than assets.

The incident in December with Wilde and the accident with Mercury in January made me loathe to fully let the beast out. I allow minor victories to keep her satisfied, but it's not enough. She longs for more and it will eventually destroy me if I can't find sources I'm not worried about harming. I asked Taurus to come tonight because I need to find a better way of feeding, and I need to keep Rhea from killing someone.

It's a two for one, if you ask me.

For all of Rhea's disgust, I didn't kill anyone. Taurus probably did, which is why I picked the ribs joint on the river near my old neighborhood. It's convenient for dumping bodies—even the mob knew that. I lured two drunken idiots into the shadows with a flash of skin and split the difference. They're passed out under a tree.

I don't think Rhea was ready for the visual, though, because she's been silent as a monk. She's known Taurus for much longer than I have, so I assumed she knew what he was capable of. I might surprise her, but that's not unusual. People love to peg me with expectations that don't fit with who I actually am.

Honestly, I think Rhea and Sari only mated with me to stake claims, not because they knew and loved me. Wilde and Alistair had fixed ideas of who they wanted me to be—particularly Wilde— and that's why they mated with me. The mess with all of them is too depressing to think about right now.

It's rough trying to adjust your world view because you've changed only to find out nothing else was real, either.

My bike grinds to a halt in front of the dilapidated building that has been home to drum and bass raves since I was a teen. I picked this for our testing ground because of its anonymity. I'm surprised to find that I can hear and feel the pulse of pounding bass of the industrial music, smell the sweaty bodies, and taste the salt in the air. The animal part of me takes getting used to, and I pause for a moment, letting my senses soak in the surroundings.

Rhea hops off our bike quickly, giving me a scared rabbit look that brings me back into reality. I wait for Taurus to join us, watching as he glares at the building as if it's a roach on his foie gras. He gives me a 'you've got to be sodding kidding me' look and I glare. He's such a snob.

My companion doesn't say a word, just stands there looking shaken until I tug her arm to pull her towards the front of the line at the door. I give the bouncer enough cleavage shots to get past the ropes because we can't apparate in.

As we step into the darkness, Taurus grumbles close to my ear. "I didn't come out to kick around with kiddies, Sandwich. This had better get more interesting fast."

"If you're not interested in snacking on a tripped-out Goth kid, let's make our own fun. Rhea and I have powers; let's play with them."

Piping up for the first time since the river, Rhea blurts out, "Like truth or dare with consequences?"

I close my eyes, groaning. Rhea wants to be a bad girl so damned bad, but it's not in her. She's not the darkest night with a sliver of moonlight like me. Sunshine and roses and bunnies, that's Rhea. Taurus is going to destroy her suggestion with a remark that would make a Kardashian bleed with shame.

It's coming in three... two... one...

"Granted," he drawls laconically. "I'm feeling spry after the tasty morsels, but I'll be royally buggered before I take part in this mosh pit equivalent of a slumber party. Do I look like a bloody nit to you? Besides, you two don't have the stones to take me on at that game. Trust me when I tell you, mine are consequences you're not ready for."

My eyes gleam at the challenge. He should know better than to wave a red flag at me. He'll find out soon enough that I'm not a damsel in distress who can't take what his flea-sized brain dishes out. Sticking my chin out, I cross my arms over my chest and perch one hand on my hip. "Bring it on."

He has the gall to sigh and roll his eyes at me. "There go those pompoms." His eyes rake over me, ogling the wide expanse of pale skin exposed by my backless corset. Leaning in, he whispers in a way that only my ears can hear. "Then again, I do like to see a chit jiggle."

Scowling, I mutter under my breath, knowing that he can hear me. "Are you in, Rhea? Mr. High and Mighty thinks we can't roll with the big boys. Shall we make him eat his words?"

Her look says, 'hell no', but she takes my earlier advice and shrugs, trying to look casual. "Sounds okay to me, I guess."

Way to project confidence, Rhea. Baby steps, I suppose.

"Here I figured you'd be brighter than Miss 'Take a Dare from the Big Bad' over here, little flame. You'd best know that if you start this, I'll not be giving you any quarter. Think hard before signing up." He gives her a look of pure disbelief, as if following my lead is the dumbest thing she'll ever do.

Her expression narrows, and her blonde curls bounce as she mirrors my stance. "I said yes, didn't I? Aren't clones supposed to have superb hearing?"

Much better, Rhea. Good girl.

A smile dances over my lips and I look up at him. "Alright, then. Who's going first? I'm ready to rumble." I make a show of stretching like an athlete on the field, a smirk practically dripping from my lips.

White teeth flash at me, and I know I walked right into the cave and dared the bear to eat me. I'm confident in my abilities and outside of precision control, I'm decent at using them. That little grin, however, makes me a shade nervous. But the bass and thrum of bodies and scents are captivating me, so I ignore that warning because I'm feeling invincible.

Pride goeth, they say.

He pauses for a moment, weighing his options, and then he

slices me with his gaze. His head tilts as he looks up, up, up to the second level at the support beams and ceiling of the warehouse, studying it intently. I'm getting impatient when he snorts.

"Worry less about the rumble, puss, and more about the tumble. You want to play? Let's see you haul that tawny tail of yours from one side of this shit shack to the other without bouncing off the bodies beneath you. You touch the ground before the trip's done and you lose. What do you lose? You'll find out when I get my prize."

I know the wolfish gleam in his eyes and see the way he's looking at me like a starving dog who's found a biscuit. It sends a forbidden shiver down my spine. Between that flirty look and the kiss earlier—which that bastard doesn't seem the least bit affected by—my temper is sizzling. I'm also not one to back down, even when I'm dead wrong.

That might be a problem tonight.

I look at the structure above me, gauging the balconies to be about thirty feet in the air. *Jesus, I can't even estimate the distance across the room: it's massive.* There's no catwalk to be ironic on, only a lot of beams and iron bars of varying sizes and thicknesses crisscrossing the ceiling like lattice work. The *only* way to do this if you can't apparate is to—okay, maybe I can do this. Provided my fear of structural integrity doesn't kick in mid-crossing, I can make it without too much obvious use of my abilities.

He knows nothing about my other world life, so he can't know what training I have and that will hurt him. If it doesn't, cats have nine lives, right? Maybe if I only burn one tonight, we're lucky.

Right?

I snort my response, giving him a defiant look. "If that's the best that over-stuffed, preening clones can do, you've been out of the game too long, buddy. This one's cat's play."

Before he can retort, I stalk over to the wall that connects to the upper level balconies. Flicking out my claws, I dig them into the soundproofing on the walls and climb my way up to the next level.

I don't have time to ponder how easily I've climbed up because my boots perch on the top bar of the guardrail. Once I feel my balance is sturdy, I give him a wink over my shoulder.

Turning back, I look across the wide expanse, plotting my route. It's been a while since I've done anything this acrobatic, and I hope like hell that it really is like riding a bike. That thought alone should make me pause, but adrenaline and my pride are running high in my veins—I cannot lose. I feel his eyes on me, mirth radiating from his slouching form as Rhea frets next to him. The stakes are too high to fail.

Muscle memory, don't fail me now.

Taking a deep breath, I wing a silent prayer to whatever Goddess is listening. Leaping off the railing, I aim for the thick iron bar a few feet away. When my hands slap the cool metal, my breath whooshes out in relief as I hang there. Once my heart stops hammering, I realize I won't move if I don't get momentum. Kicking my legs back and forth, I let my palms grip and re-grip. I'd give my pinky toe for some chalk to keep my old blisters from opening, but that's not workable right now.

Feeling my body move with force needed, I wait for the right spot in the arc of motion to let my feet fly towards the next bar. It's only a little higher and a few feet from the one I'm on, but upward trajectory is key here. My knees hook around it and I let myself hang for a moment.

Their eyes are on me as I finish thanking the heavens that this really is like riding a bike. It's a high up, scary ass, end up as a puddle if you miss a bike, but a bike just the same. The possibilities of a Deli-shaped splatter are not appealing, so I take a deep a breath as I look at the rest of my chosen path.

I would have to choose the most spectacularly difficult route across this, wouldn't I? I am such an idiot. Garnering the chutzpah to move before I get lightheaded, I rock back and forth, hoping that my long-standing inability to do this trick doesn't rear its ugly head. Momentum swings me upward in a counterclockwise motion and when I'm sitting on the bar upright, I sigh.

Fucking sweet.

There's a wide wooden beam within reach, so I grab it to steady myself as I stand. Walking a few feet down the bar carefully, I ponder why I'm risking my tail to impress him. I know I'm being watched again when I feel my hackles raise, so I make a show of twirling around on the bar in a pirouette. I don't want him knowing I'm as nervous as I am because that would ruin my victory.

Something tells me I wouldn't have the chance to ever hit the floor if I fell, but that's not the point, is it?

When I get to the right spot on the beam, I hoist myself up to straddle it, deciding to show off again. Uneven bars were always a so-so event for me, but the beam was my specialty. Placing my hands on either side of the wood, I push upwards until my legs rise above my head in a full handstand. Even upside down, I can tell I have about twenty feet to go to the next goal post and I'll cover that ground faster on my feet rather than my hands.

I walk a few feet on my hands—because I can—then do a front walkover to get upright. Near the end of the beam, I do a flourish and, since I feel cheeky; I moonwalk off the end onto the grill work. From here, it's only a hop, skip, and a jump to the other side. Swinging from bar to bar like a monkey, I kick out, reaching the closest balcony rail. I land on it roughly and wince.

That's going to leave a mark.

I'm too tickled with myself to let it get me down. Letting myself fall backwards, I hang upside down for a few moments before flipping off the rail backwards. My feet hit the ground hard enough to jar my teeth, but I couldn't care less. Not only did I complete the dare without killing myself, I kicked its ass and got to show off. I'd be strutting like a disco queen if this place played that kind of music.

"Was it good for you?" I smirk, putting a hand on my hip as I stand toe to toe with him.

He glowers like he's ready to go on a multi-state rampage. "Are you completely off your bird, woman? What the bloody fucking *hell* were you thinking, pulling a stunt like that?"

Goddamnit, what is his problem? I did what he asked; why is he so damned angry?

"What? Are you pissed I did it? Did you think that I'd retreat like a coward when faced with your impossible dare? I wouldn't have hiked my ass up to that balcony if I hadn't planned to go across." I sound petulant, but I earned some praise and witty banter, not a face blistering lecture.

"There were at least *three* other routes you could have taken with your skills that would have been less hair-raising than the one you took, your silly twit. Did you ever think about what would happen—besides World War fucking Three—if you'd fallen and I'd not been able to..." He breaks off in mid-sentence and grinds his teeth together before snarling. "If you'd taken a tumble, you witless shit, all hell would've broken loose. They would have trampled Rhea in the dash to the door."

The light dawns on me when I look at his face. I'm not sure that I can deal with what I see, so I tuck it away for later. For now, I'll give him a break before a vein in his head pops. "Isn't it Rhea's turn?" I ask innocently, crossing my arms over my chest in a way that gives me a distracting amount of cleavage.

His glare is still burning over me as he huffs. Finally, he turns to Rhea and I let out a deep breath. That was super intense. I reach in my pocket, fishing out a smoke to light it. Between the adrenaline rush and his smoldering look, nicotine sounds damn good right now.

When my attention shifts back to Rhea, I see that he's considering his options. There's not a trace of scathing disdain that was there a moment ago when he was ripping me a new one.

I think I hate him.

His lips quirk up and I suck in a breath, hoping he's not about to break her with some impossible task. "Feed."

The Cat Dances with The Devil

❧

DELILAH

"Feed?" Rhea asks, her eyes darting between us.

"I didn't stutter, did I? Feed to replenish your energy. Clones do and the cat does, so I'm guessing you do, too. Pick some git and do your thing—whatever it is."

Watching her as I blow smoke rings, I wait to see how this plays out. I'm not sure she's breathing and I don't even know what it means for her to feed. I have seen little of her powers before tonight, truthfully. But if Taurus looked anymore pleased with himself, his face would crack. I'm about to intervene when she nods.

"I'll do it." Her gaze is flinty as she squares her shoulders, ready for battle.

Knowing her in the context I do, I forget she and Alistair fought in the Conflict. There's a well of strength somewhere under the marshmallow fluff. Maybe the fighting made her like she is now, or maybe something else is at play.

Wilde and Sari's antics have me in a place I never thought I'd see myself in mentally, so I can fathom that it's possible something damaged Rhea. There are lots of secrets in this world. People forget human inhabitants are people who had other lives before the Rift and escaped here. Falling down the rabbit hole doesn't erase who you were before, and it certainly doesn't fix whatever sent you here to start with.

Rhea turns on her heel and strides off to what passes for the dance floor. Her hips sway as she makes her way through the sea of writhing bodies, and I hop onto a table to see better. Realizing it won't give me a good enough view, I climb up to one of the lower side balconies. Rhea seems confident now, but I worry about her ability to defend herself should it come to that. Her compassionate nature runs deep, and I don't believe for a second that she's got an inner monster like me, Sari, or Wilde.

Taurus apparates behind me, obviously in agreement that she needs to be watched. I'm about to comment on her method of choosing a 'victim' when the music changes and *Nine Inch Nails* comes on. "Oh fuck," I mutter, knowing she has a particular affinity for this song.

Arching his brow as if I should explain, Taurus waits. I shrug, not wanting to delve into Rhea and her desire to be rebellious. Leaning over the railing, I scan the crowd for her. Finally seeing her again, I turn back to him and mutter. "You'll see."

He looks annoyed but gazes into the crowd pensively.

Meanwhile, Rhea has gathered a tight circle of makeup-caked guys gathered as she gyrates. The abundance of chains here is appealing to someone as bent as me, but Goth guys are *way* too high maintenance. That said, I'm impressed at the size of Rhea's flock. A sniff of the air answers my question about how she feeds— at least a little. The fresh scent of sulfur says she's using her powers —her scent sticks out like a sore thumb against the smell of sweat, greasepaint, and leather in this place.

A pair of hands grasp my waist, yanking me to a hard body. I rear back to smack the idiot that thinks they can touch me when Taurus' lips brush my ear. His voice sounds like one no one should hear it outside of a bedroom. "I see no reason to wait for the mini

Bic to get the stones to do the deed rather than dance around like a tart. We'll likely be bored to tears if we do. I'm not one for wall flowering, so give us a dance, puss."

Naked is not an option here for more reasons than I can count.

So I turn around, putting my palms on his chest to push him away. "Someone has their big boy pants on tonight. What makes you think I'm going to let you touch me more than I already have?"

Fangs flash as he grins cockily. His arms tighten as he hauls me closer and his body moves as if the beat is flowing through his veins. "Call it animal instinct."

I don't know why, but I can't resist following his lead. My hands stay where I put them and pretend they can't hear my brain screaming 'what are you doing, you idiot?'. I drop my gaze for a moment and breathe. The heat coming from his eyes feels almost as dangerous as the heat coming from Rhea downstairs. Our position is making it hard to ignore how we fit together — perfectly, if you're wondering—and though I fit well with my mates, this is different. Just because he's a complete ass doesn't mean he doesn't have a nice —

Holy fuck. Stop that train before it derails. This is a terrible idea and I'm definitely not enjoying every second.

A chuckle escapes his lips and I feel it rumble through him from head to toe, like a feather tickling my skin. I dart my eyes up, daring to look at him again, and he gives me an amused grin. I can't help wondering what he sees that is so appealing. His hands curve around my ass in a familiar squeeze and asking becomes the furthest thing from my mind.

I have to stop this before it gets completely out of hand.

"Excuse you? What gave you the idea that you're welcome to fondle me in public?"

"Possibly your tongue in my throat earlier? Not sure, that's only a thought." He shrugs carelessly, not moving an inch except to squeeze again as his smirk deepens.

Our bodies plaster together, and his proximity loosens the tiny threads of the control he's been teaching me. I feel the hum of the bass pounding in my pulse as another scent tickles my nostrils. This one makes my insides clench. My eyes shoot up to his and I lick my lips nervously. I'm venturing into Wrongsville and I don't know what to do. Lack of control has ruined things before—see Sari and Wilde—and I don't want to start a war.

The kiss was just his way of riling me up and this is more of the same, right?

None of that explains why I'm writhing against him or why he smells so delicious or why I never, ever learn my lesson. His intense gaze is making me squirm even more, but this is all playing, right?. "We, uh, can't see what Rhea's doing like this," I croak. I try to sound concerned, but it sounds more like a vixen in a noir movie than a protest, so I shut my mouth.

"Who bloody well cares?" he growls, rumbling in that growly way that all the clones do.

They're like giant cats. Predatory, fangy cats. Sexy cats. Who I want to—no. What in the hell is wrong with me?

"You dared her." I'm immediately sorry I said it, then pissed that I'm worried he'll let go.

What the fuck am I talking about? I want him to let go. Don't I?

His sigh is full of exasperation as he whirls me around. My body is pressed between him and the railing while we move to the thrumming beat. This is the longest club mix of a song ever played —I'm convinced of that. Rhea's crowd is still going and I'm still dancing with the devil in the pale black light to a song that talks about fucking every thirty seconds, like it's a suggestion.

Fuck. Me.

Please.

Taurus sucks in a breath and I worry I said it out loud, but he jerks his head at the crowd. Rhea is making out with a comic book character wannabe. My eyes pop open, seeing the hand on her ass. I was *not* expecting that kind of display. I know she can't shield it from my mate because her mental abilities aren't magickally enhanced. We're in for a face blistering lecture when we get home.

After slowing the dance for a moment, Taurus pauses. I lean back to look up at him, a questioning look in my hazy eyes. His hand rests on my tummy lightly as he murmurs, "Something's off. Do you feel it?"

I'm too bloody distracted by his presence behind me to sense much of anything, but I try. Failing miserably and damned if I want to admit it, I pull away from him. "I'll take care of it."

"Hold the hero cape, puss. Let's see what she's doing first," he commands, drawing me back again before I can make the leap over the rail.

I wrinkle my nose and give him a peeved look. "Then you can barge in and thump your chest like a caveman? No way, buster." I shake his hands off and leap over the rail, hitting the ground with a grunt. Maybe it's an excessive reaction, but getting some space between me, him, and a colossal breach of community diplomacy means taking any valid escape route I can find. My senses are on fire and my beast is ready to rock and roll.

Am I that worked up and pissed off at the same time? Yep.

Shooting him a glare, I stick my tongue out before turning to push through the throng of people. Before I get a foot into the crowd, I'm yanked back into place with a fistful of my hair. "Ow! Let go, you jackass."

Smirking, he ignores my command, holding my hair like the caveman I accused him of being. "Are you going to listen this time or go off half-cocked like a frazzled peahen?"

"I'm going to go help her. Let me go before I get pissed."

"The only thing you're doing is turning your ass around, sod it all. You're not inserting yourself into that mix of writhing testosterone dressed—or not so dressed—like you are. The only thing that would accomplish is getting their hands on another piece of meat. You'd end up naked and bruised. I'll take care of it; you stay put."

"Not. A. Bloody. Chance." The bruised comment hits a little too close to home for me and I have to take control back. Besides, who the hell does he think he is giving me orders? One so-so kiss and a lame dance does not make him head dictator on my planet. He acts like nothing happened—which it didn't—and now he's turned into cave clone numero uno?

Fuck him.

"Would you stop being so buggering stubborn and *let me handle it?*" he shouts, giving me a shake.

That, too, pushes a button and ramps up my anger. "*No, I won't.*"

A loud growl emits from his chest as he advances on me. I've dropped to a fighting stance when a high-pitched screech, followed by a collective gasp, erupts from the dance floor. Our eyes lock, looking wildly confused. We both yell 'Fuck!' at the top of our lungs before sprinting into the crowd.

In the middle of the circle is Rhea, looking down at the guy who'd been grinding on her a moment ago. He's sprawled on the floor, looking ashen under his makeup. I don't even think about it; I grab her hand and nod at Taurus. Together, we drag her to the door using preternatural speed. It's obvious that a hasty retreat is necessary as the loud music has stopped. The DJ has a cell phone out and there will *definitely* be cops here soon.

Despite Rhea's pallor, Taurus shoves her onto my bike after I mount. We need to get out of here before the stampede for the door begins. Revving the motor on his bike, he waits impatiently as I situate Rhea so she won't fall off mid-getaway. We take off in unison, not needing words to communicate what we need to do.

I growl under my breath as we speed away, frustrated in so many ways. I wanted her to learn control and how to use her powers, not be afraid of them. This is all his fault and to top it off, he's leading, and he doesn't even know where he's going.

Goddess above, that clone pisses me off.

Hitting the gas, I pull even with him to shout, "You always had to push things so damned far. That's why we're in trouble. You knew she couldn't handle it. Plus, you're speeding ahead of me and you don't know where you're going, dumbass."

"We wouldn't be running if *you* had kept your gob shut and your ass in place so I could stop whatever she was doing. And I know where I'm going—far away from that shithouse before I have to kill people to keep you two out of jail."

"Where is our destination once we get away from there? I *live* in this area and you don't. Let me lead." I weave around a few cars and a wayward pedestrian, catching back up to him.

"Correction: you *used* to live around here before you moved into the Rift two years ago. You don't know it here any better than I do now, so shut up and drive."

"Screw you, asshole. You're going to lead us down to a dead end and we'll get caught with the girl who turned a guy into literal toast."

He opens his mouth to retort, eyes glittering, when a burst of flame shoots out in front of us, accompanied by an unearthly scream. "*Enough!*"

Screeching our bikes to a dangerously executed halt, I look at Taurus before blinking in surprise. It takes a minute to realize that it was the previously silent Rhea. We look at her as she climbs off the bike, practically glowing with a smoky anger. Her eyes have a ring of flames around the iris and her hands are on her hips, gaze murderous. "I've had it with you both. Some drunk guy is a crispy critter because you guys were too busy pretending you don't want to jump one another to come help me. If you don't get it together, I'm leaving you to get each other killed."

"What? I wouldn't touch that hellcat with a ten-foot pole," Taurus roars indignantly.

Furious, I eye his crotch with an evil grin on my face. "That is definitely not the case, so I don't think we have a problem, test-tube baby." That should injure his enormous ego and make him regret having his grubby hands all over me, only to act like I have a communicable disease.

He's so fucking stuffed with himself.

Rhea gives me a look as if she can't believe I even spoke. "You coddled me all night long like a little kid. But when my ass was in the fire, you were too busy showing off your toe picks." She stomps her foot in frustration and gives me a pointed look, knowing I'll get the reference to one of our favorite movies.

My eyes fly wide open as my jaw drops.

She can't be saying that I—She's not possibly hinting that—Oh, she has got to be kidding me.

I wrinkle my nose at her. "Toe picks? You are out of your French-fried brain, sister. I am absolutely not going to—"

Taurus snorts and mutters something under his breath that I barely catch, causing me to shoot a venomous look at him.

Rhea looks from him to me, and her eyes burn. "That's it. I'm out of here. You get a ride with him since you're both so damned eager to put your hands all over each other. I'm going home." She shoves me off the bike and I land hard on my ass.

I can hear gears grinding in her wake and let me tell you, Alistair will be pissed. Hopefully, she makes it home before she burns the clutch out. Taurus looks down at me, and I swear I'm going to smack the smirk off his face. It doesn't help that I'm sitting ass deep in a puddle, either.

He quirks his brow at me. I hate that. "Toe picks?"

No freaking way am I touching that. As if I want him all lusty and naked. Whatever.

I reach up and punch his thigh, hoping to cause a super painful charley horse. It would serve him right. *"This is all your fault."*

"Oh, look, the baby kitten has claws. Isn't that cute?" His smug look infuriates me as he pretends he doesn't feel the charley horse.

Seriously? He's taunting me?

I ponder walking home rather than having to ride with him.

It's my tough luck that we're damn far from the portal, or even my old house. Shit. I'd have to walk through some rough neighborhoods to get there on foot, and as angry as I am now, I might kill someone. I'm brave, not foolish. I look over at him, feeling the hatred flow through me. Toe picks. Damn Rhea for saying that and taking off like a child. I'm going to beat her.

Hauling myself to my feet, I try to look more dignified than I feel. "Are we going to get out of here, or are you going to stand there and grin at me like a boob? Frankly, you could do that somewhere a lot more comfortable than in the ghetto."

His expression goes from amused to inscrutable, and I'm not sure what is going through his mind. He keeps looking at me and I get more impatient as his stare makes my skin crawl.

Stomping over, I poke him in the chest. "Look, I'd love to sit here all night and get studied like a big bug, but I'd like to make sure Rhea got home okay. More than that, I'd like to get out of these clothes before they become permanently tattooed on my skin. If you'll get back on the bike, I'll drive us back to the portal, or whatever the hell your eggheads want to call it."

He cocks at eyebrow at me, snorting. "The train of loonies has jumped right off the bloody track if you think you're driving *my* bike, baby. No way, no how."

"Listen, jackass, I won't hurt your precious bike. I'll say it again: you don't know where you're going around here. It only makes sense for me to drive until we get to the portal." I attempt to throw a leg over the bike, but it doesn't even have time to meet leather before he yanks me off balance. I almost fall into the puddle again and I have to dig my nails into my palm to keep from punching him. His manhandling is pissing me the hell off.

"If you so much as drop a tush to that front seat, you'll go from minx to Manx in a breath, woman. Ratchet back the bitch factor a good ninety degrees, or I'll leave your ass here to rot. In case it's gotten lost in that echoing chamber in your head, I found my way here once and I can do it again by scent. If you want to go around or two, fine. It's no skin off my ass one way or the other; I'm always in the mood to brawl. But I'm not doing it here, so shut your bloody mouth, get on the sodding bike, and act like you aren't the prickliest thing this side of the Mojave for the half hour that it'll take to get us to your place!"

Everything flies out of my brain as I try to process the anger flowing through me. Nothing bothers that idiot, and everything is bothering the hell out of me. It's so irritating that I might explode in a shower of fur and glitter. The only thing he gives a shit about is his bike and his fancy clothes. I got in a few lovely insults, but it bounced right off him. He doesn't even give a damn that Rhea alluded that I'm hot for his body and I *know* he got that reference.

Taurus is a grade A prick.

I'm something to occupy him for a while until he feels like tucking back into his secret hiding place. It's obvious that I do not matter. He doesn't care that I'm angry or that he was grinding against me in that club like we were naked. It doesn't matter that it made me tingle and want him—*because I don't.*

Fine. He doesn't matter to me, either. I called him for some wild times, but I have people who love me. Running around with him was supposed to help me get past the ugliness I feel when I'm at home. He was supposed to help me forget what Rafe and I *don't talk about.*

He was supposed to be an escape, but he's not a good one right now. I do not need another man ordering me around like a chattel. I don't need someone else to beat on me emotionally or physically. I should be more careful about what I wish for, because I thought I had a perfect life. Then my beast came, and it all went to shit just like tonight has.

Now this is ruined, too. Fine. I don't need him, anyway.

I square my shoulders, dropping the unaffected mask of that I give Wilde. I swore that no one else would get that satisfaction from my pain after December. I take his extended hand and hop onto the bike silently. I'll show him that nothing he does or says bothers me. Ignoring the wary look he gives me when I stop ranting, I take a deep breath. I need to keep it together long enough to sequester myself back in my room, lock myself away and hope for the best.

Sitting behind him, I put enough space between us to make it easier to breathe, but not be dangerous. He guns the motor and I close my eyes. It's a good thing that I'm not the least bit interested in him, his moods, or his made for death and sex body. It might hurt to think he doesn't care, but I don't let this shit hurt me anymore. No one is allowed into my castle that isn't in already.

I don't care, and it doesn't hurt. I am going to kill him, though.

The Artist Sets The Scene

RAFE

I'm on the floor, sprawled on my stomach, as I stare at the bedroom door. It's been about fifteen minutes, but it feels like a bloody lifetime. Not that I'm against sprawling—in fact, it's sort of my thing. What's bothering me is the silence; it makes me feel powerless and I hate feeling like that.

Why can't anything be easy anymore?

I sigh and tilt my head slightly, looking up at the snotty aristocrat, who's putting a million tiny braids in my hair. Philomena is kneeling next to me in Gucci lounge wear, almost behaving like a normal person. Mind, that would be a fucking wealthy normal person, but at least she's not spouting off like a drunken Hamptonite. But she's doing it to be supportive in her way and I can't help but appreciate it.

That admission and her current behavior would amaze anyone outside of our immediate family. Duchess P isn't known for being emotionally available and she prefers it that way. She only shows this side of her personality at home, where outsiders can't see. Even when the extended mates are about, she puts the façade back on.

It's her method of keeping people at arm's length, and I don't blame her.

"Bloody *hell*. What the fuck is she doing in there?" Victor pushes off the wall, pacing the hallway frenetically.

I watch him, a heartstring tugging inside of me. There's so much painful history that I wish hadn't happened to him. I wish I hadn't let Wilde hoodwink me into being desperate enough to push him to the brink. I thought it was the only way to let him go without making everything worse. Now, I see what that unusual demand from the faux romantic was about, and I wish I'd told him to fuck off.

Regrets, I have a few.

Caesar looks up from where his head is resting in Sandrine's lap, her fingers twisting his burgundy locks into spirals as she leans against her mate, Leo. Since Lucinda and Dona left, he's been adrift. C's a total submissive, and Lucinda catered to that need. Without someone to fill her role, I'm afraid he's going to fall into a depression we can't pull him out of.

Luckily, Sandrine's a bad ass and Leo doesn't seem to mind her making Caesar feel better. Leo and Caesar are best friends—in fact, Vic and C built Leo for my primary mate when she moved to The Rift. He was the first member of her household and falls staunchly on the 'droids are better' side. Vic and C program their droids to have a rivalry and it results in prank wars more often than not. It's a bit like having siblings and it's fun most of the time—if they don't get out of hand.

Christ, I miss those days.—we all had so much fun and now it's a constant misery.

Since the extendeds became part of our family, silliness has not been high on the 'to do' list. In fact, the only things on the list are sex—sometimes good, sometimes not—and painful fights and rivalries. Even without my primary's beast emerging, there's been drama and spite between the three families. It's easier to see what's happening now, though. The demon in Wilde and the dog in Sari have shown their true colors in vivid HD.

"Chill out, mate. She has to let us in someday, right?" Leo says. He's pragmatic and unflappable, which is helpful in a house with so many aggressive dominants. I enjoy being able to depend on him and Caesar helping me balance the rest of them.

The Maison, as our home is called, houses one of the biggest immediate families in The Rift. Our girl has the biggest heart this side of the portal and she made a place where we all feel wanted and loved, even those who were abandoned. Vic and I are the only clones; Leo, Caesar, Sandrine, Hex, Philomena, and Siren are droids. They outnumber Victor and me by a factor of three, but that doesn't bother either of us. We're one of the few households who have a solid mix of both clones and droids living together.

It didn't happen by design; we're just a rainbow of equality.

Droids in the Rift aren't at all like people have described in movies or books. They're a physical copy of templates used for the clones except they have—hell, I don't know—gizmos inside. The entire caste system built around them caused the bloody Conflict and trust me, anti-Company sentiment still runs high in the Resistance.

After my primary and her co-mayors built the Resistance community, most of the droids got built in our workshop out back. Victor and Caesar have carried on the tradition Dona started after she abandoned them. New recruits are invited into the Rift and they place an order with the boys immediately. Sometimes I go out to help with a bit of the artsy parts, like getting faces and eyes right. The bitch goes out to dress the creations to suit their personality. Sandrine and Siren assist with personality and other various programming.

It's a family business now.

Hex snorts from his perch on the railing, bringing me back to reality. He's hanging upside down like a bat: chains, leather, and black chipped nails swing back and forth as he dangles. He's an 80s punk version of our template—all bleached spikes, eyeliner, and spikes. He was one of the first droids to vary widely from the orig-inal 'brothers' template.

My ears perk up as I hear a car start down the long driveway. Every head in the hallway sniffs the air, and Philomena yanks one of my braids. I suppose she wants me to pay attention, although it smells like my other mates are arriving. I tug on a line inside and find it's Alistair, Sari, and Wilde. I strain my hearing, hoping to pick up some of their conversation as they come into the house. It would help me gauge how helpful they will be in getting my Flame out of the sodding bedroom.

I doubt it will be, but hope springs eternal and all the rot.

If Rhea hadn't melted the door closed, I'd be perfectly fine with none of them showing up. Wilde and Sari are on my shit list and though I love Alistair, I don't have the energy to deal with their shit. The cat is out in the universe with that pompous prick. She can take care of herself—mostly—but I worry. Her kind heart wrapped in a hard shell is why our other mates have the power they have.

Their need for power is also why they've landed in our laps tonight. You can bet on that.

Knowing my primary, I figure they're somewhere dangerous, doing something stupid. Deli is still holding the shields up for both of us, which means she's okay. She definitely doesn't want the bird to know our secret. Neither of us wants to admit to anyone what's happened to us behind closed doors. Hell, we can't even talk to each other about it. I hate that she's taking it all on by herself because I know she's draining herself dry, but she won't let me help her.

"How much longer are we going to sit here like idiots in front of this door?" Philomena asks, her long nails and fingers moving through my hair nimbly. She's worried, though most people wouldn't be able to tell.

The fancy droid is sipping her perennially bottomless martini casually, but there's tension in her voice. It occurs to me that her glass is never empty, and she's constantly drinking it. I don't know how she manages it. I think Victor programmed her to be constantly drunk and popping pills. He would find that funny as hell.

I've always wondered how the bodily fluids thing works with the droids, but hell if I want to hear the explanation.

I digress. My point was *she* called the cavalry, which is why she's curbed her usual biting sarcasm. Philomena suspects a problem that she is not sharing with the group. The thought makes me frown, but I will not ask her what the problem is in front of the 'guests.'

"Don't get your thong in a twist, woman. She'll come out eventually or we'll bust in. Simple enough." Hex flips himself upright, running his fingers through his heavily gelled spikes as he grins. "I could go find us something to do in the meantime."

"I suggest—"

I snort. "P, you *always* suggest getting high as a kite. We don't need to know the rest of that sentence. Besides, I don't think Janus and Roman came with them." Our other family members come bounding up the steps and I shrink back.

I don't mean to, but lately? It's an instinct, not a choice.

"She fused herself in when she came tearing home alone. We're not comfortable breaking in and she won't respond to us," Philomena says, giving them what can only be qualified as a side eye. She holds up her hand before they speak. "Wait. I called you clowns to talk her out. The other two haven't gotten home yet, so don't ask. We don't know what happened or why she showed up solo. You deal with her."

They look at me, and I shrug, tilting my head towards the stairs. "We'll go watch for the others downstairs. Have at it."

Sari looks like she's going to retort, but Wilce shakes his head as Alistair sighs heavily. It's not the first time any of us have had to talk Rhea off a ledge over nothing.

Philomena nods curtly and tugs me to my feet. She motions for me to follow her to the lower level and the rest of the gang file in behind us. I hear cracking mahogany, and Hex swears as we make our way to the living room.

"Bloody hell, that's going to take a week to fix! She couldn't have locked herself in a room that doesn't have a bloody hand carved mahogany door?"

I chuckle. Hex may look like a bad ass punk rocker, but he's got a soul that screams HGTV. Leo's love is food, and the kitchen is his domain, but Hex's is the house. He has every inch of this place furnished and decorated to the nines—even the spare bedrooms. His knack for finding the perfect showroom quality set up to please any person is astounding.

Philomena immediately turns on her heel to head for the living room when we all hear the roar of a motorcycle in the distance. I groan, pinching the bridge of my nose.

Bloody great timing.

The terror twins are back to join this three-ring circus that I call my life. Sighing, I head towards the front porch. The group follows me instinctively. In unknown situations, we move as one. The bike rumbles to a stop at the end of the driveway, and I hear their screams echoing through the night as they dismount.

The gang pushes past me to spill onto the large porch, leaving the others to deal with Rhea. No one calls for the others because involving them would only cause more problems. Our bedroom room is *heavily* sound proofed, so it's unlikely they will even notice the commotion outside. I've got to see to the cat right now and avoid the rest of my family starting a war.

I don't need their distractions.

"Where the bloody *hell* do you think you're going? *Taurus*! You take one more step towards my house and I'll turn your balls into a change purse."

Christ. I can hear that through the door as I'm finding a place to land. This is going to be bad; I can tell. She's at the screeching stage of anger. The edge in her voice and the strain in her aura that I can see from here let me know she means what she says.

Taurus has no clue about the tremendous amount of pressure she's under or how much pain she's in. Like everyone but me, he has no clue that she's holding both of our suffering and blocking it from the rest of the world. He can't understand that I've never—in the entire time I've known her—seen her so broken. I can't fix it for either of us.

My mate is on the edge of cracking like glass under a hammer.

I push my way through the crowd so I can block the high-tempered blokes. In order to avoid re-starting the Conflict, I need to see what's going on. Victor and Hex are immediate worries because they will jump first and bear the burden of consequences later. If I can keep them in line and the people upstairs out of this, we might come through without a fucking free-for-all.

"Everyone... Find a seat, sit still, and watch closely," I murmur, gesturing at the porch furniture. Without the cat to lead, I know I'm the de facto general of our army. I'm not thrilled by the prospect, nor am I comfortable with the position. However, given my rank as primary, they will listen—mostly.

"Was that little display I clutched my stomach through your idea of a get-away lift? Were you actively trying to turn us into a smear on the road or separate our particles in the portal? No, I don't think so because you couldn't see the road past your over-inflated *ego.*"

She leaps off the bike like a panther, stalking across the pavement to catch up to him. This is less than promising. I can smell her beast is prowling in the air. She won't back down and unless he makes a smart move to diffuse this, there is *definitely* going to be a brawl.

"Next time someone offers to drive? *Take them up on it, asshole.*"

"That's *it.*" Taurus spins around and roars at her. I see his eyes narrow into a glare that could melt ice. He means business—just fucking great. "Shut your gob, you twittering nit. Christ, do you even know *how* to keep that yammering maw of yours shut for five minutes at a time? What in the buggering hell is your sodding *problem*?"

Victor pushes past me at the insults, and I shake my head, grabbing his arm hard. Our girl will be pissed if we intervene. The cat enjoys fighting her own battles, especially when she picks them. Jumping in like half-baked heroes will only point her anger in our direction. No one wants that because she's on the brink of losing control on the kitty face. I can feel her rage from here—hell, we all can.

"What's *my* problem? What's *my problem*?!"

The spitting hellcat I love closes the gap between them to poke him in the chest. As enraged as she is, I wouldn't be surprised if that's a claw, not a finger. You wouldn't know by Taurus' expression either way, so I can't say for sure.

"You're my *fucking problem*, you irritating, know-it-all, chauvinistic *troglodyte*."

He stares at her silently before he pulls a smoke from his duster. His eyebrow arches at her as he lights it, his nonchalance baiting her. "Aww, isn't that cute? Kitten's got herself a thesaurus. That's a big word, puss. At least you used it correctly in a sodding sentence. You get points for that." He inhales, his tone mocking. "If I'm so bloody buggering boorish, why in the *fucking hell* did you call me to begin with?"

Her eyes flash and the surge of the beast rising in her crashes through our connection. That rush of primal has everyone on the porch immediately on edge. I turn to the gang again, my expression reassuring them it is still not time to intercede. Looking at my mate again, I watch her prowl back and forth in front of the clone. *She's gotta tell him.* I know what she should say, but I can't force her to be honest with him or herself.

That's her battle, and it's one I'm not sure she's able to win in her current state.

When she finally speaks, her voice is rife with emotion. "As if you didn't want me to. You got a huge kick out of setting the 'double dog dare you' bar as high as you could in the club. You pushed me because you knew I'd rise to the bait. After I won, you blasted me for it. There was no praise for a job expertly executed in a way that less than *zero* people you know could do. Instead, you bitched me out."

She snarls the last sentence a few inches from his face, but he doesn't move. It looks like an old-fashioned standoff, except that you don't know my mate. When she gets quiet like this, it's time to run. I glance at my family, noting that per my request, they're lounging casually on the railings and steps. I can feel the coiled tension among them and I rub my temples, hoping they can curb their instincts.

Otherwise, this is going to get bloody quickly.

Philomena and Siren position themselves close enough to grab Hex. Caesar placed himself between Victor and the other half of the front steps, which I appreciate. Sandrine and Leo are blocking him from vaulting over the railing. They know who the wildcards are. Victor was the first clone my mate fell for and to this day, I believe he rivals all of us in his feelings of protectiveness.

Sometimes, he's the only one who can get through to her.

I was jealous of that in the beginning, but her heart is so big that we all get equal amounts in different ways. That's why she's so bloody special. That thought barely crosses my mind when my loving, special woman reaches up and grabs the smoke out of Taurus' mouth to toss it aside.

"It's about time someone told you how big an ass you are, Mr. 'Nothing Ever Fucking Bothers Me Because I'm So Superior'. Believe me, I'm the pissed off hellcat to do it!"

His expression goes from smirking to peeved as he watches the cherry arc into the distance. I watch his posture tense as they square off. They both eye one another with anger radiating off them and he snarls, "You didn't do a sodding thing tonight that you didn't bloody well want to do. Not. One. Sodding. Thing. Don't you dare put this shit off on me." He shoves her lightly, and she stumbles backward, her growl reverberating in the air.

That's when I accept that there's no stopping this train. There will be a fight and it will be bloody. I can feel it in my bones.

"Now, out of the bloody blue, you're all Queen of Neurosis about it. What's your fucking damage, woman?"

Checking our connection, I feel that my mate is trying—and failing—to argue with her beast inside. She shakes her head, fighting the change as her features flicker, and I see her dig her claws into her palms. Pain distracts her since the shit with Wilde started and don't think that fact doesn't make my heart hurt.

"You're such a fucking clueless asshole. You couldn't see the truth if it bit you on the ass."

"Actually, puss," he says, drawing out each syllable. His voice is low as he interrupts her, and I know I don't want to hear what he's going to say. It feels like lighting is about to strike. "I saw the truth halfway through his botched bru-ha-ha, and I'll remind you of it for shits and giggles." He leans in, only a hair's breadth from her face, to murmur, "You don't have the stones to play with the big bad."

Her arm jerks up in a blink and she sucker punches him hard enough to break her fist. I feel the shattering of bones along our connection as he goes flying across the lawn and lands on his ass.

Holy shit, she put some stank on that one.

Let me assure you, I did *not* know she could flatten a clone like that. Whether that force was the fully unleashed beast, magick, or some combination of the two, I don't know. I watch her shake it out. She's clearly healing it while he recovers. I bet she broke his nose.

The crowd behind me inches forward and I hold up a hand, telling them to continue waiting.

I have such *a bad feeling about this.*

The Goddess Has A Feeling

TALIA

"Talia, are you unwell?"

I blink, the concern in her voice surprising me. Looking into my face can be disconcerting, but I've gotten used to it. Dona made Theodora in my image as a gift while I recovered two years ago. I couldn't go into the job I had on the other side, and I hadn't lived here full time yet. She didn't know *why* I was so 'ill,' but she really came through. Theodora became as much a part of our family as everyone else after the shooting. "Sure, why?"

The droid's eyes search me before stopping at my right hand. My blade is whirring as I spin it unconsciously. It's a nervous habit so ingrained in my psyche that I rarely notice it. Baby—my custom, wickedly sharp blade—never leaves my side. But when I'm this frenetic, Theodora knows what it means: I'm worried. She may be my exact duplicate in android form, but she's much more comfortable being outwardly emotional than I've ever been.

Sometimes I wonder who is actually the robot—her or me.

I'm not in the mood to discuss my concerns, though, so I forcibly take the blade out of my hand to stop the motion.

Sheathing Baby on her thigh holster, I try to sound nonchalant as I reply, "Sorry. Habit."

Her lips purse and I immediately recognize the look. It's the same look I give poor souls who are trying to sell me a bill of goods I'm not buying in the least. She says nothing, but continues to stare at me.

Looking down at myself, I groan inwardly. *Damn.* I could explain away the blade work, but there's no way in hell that I'd normally be dressed like this in the comfort of my home. When I'm home, I'm the most unprepossessing creature you could imagine. But at work? Not so much. I could claim I forgot to undress while I waited for Taurus to get home, but I'm not talking to a toddler.

Theodora would see right through that.

I raise my gaze to hers, recognizing that she's tired of me trying to snow her. My droid is not dim enough to believe I'm pasted into skintight pants, a short vest, and the sleeveless duster with knee high shit kicking boots for giggles. Leather is not my comfort garb.

Sighing at the stark contrast between us despite our identical features, I smile half-heartedly. Theodora is dressed in a gauzy, ephemeral looking nightdress in a light coral. Her hair is piled loosely on her head with soft wisps framing her face to combine with the outfit to make her a picture of utter femininity.

She looks like peach ice cream on a summer day.

Her soft appearance doesn't mean Theodora should be underestimated. Even in her state of bedtime undress, she's cool, competent, and lady-like. She may give off a tousled and content vibe, but there's iron strength underneath and I don't mean her frame.

That's why she hit it off with Damien from the start. Not that I have any clue what goes on between them behind the closed doors —nor would I want to. They aren't the type to kiss and tell. Theodora would consider it unseemly to even discuss those things, and she's all about appropriate behavior.

"Is this a *new* habit?" she asks, a touch of genuine curiosity and maternal intensity tinging her voice. "You're going to be stalking the halls of our home in your 'death gear' at all hours of the night?"

The corners of my mouth twitch. Theodora saying the word 'death gear' is like hearing Martha Stewart do a Lady Gaga impression. Sure, that's what I call the combination of leather and steel that I wear to work, and so does Taurus. But this is the first time I've heard Theodora use those words, and it belies her level of concern.

"No, it's not." I sigh again, feeling duty bound to explain so she won't worry. "It's that Taurus—"

My voice stops as a wave of fury, pain, and another blindingly intense emotion rush through my mating bond like a freight train.

Shit. Shit. Shit.

I must have unintentionally linked with Taurus earlier, and more than the usual background noise of our connection is spilling through. That's why I'm agitated, that's why I haven't undressed, and that's why the blade is spinning.

He went out with the kitty. After they met a few weeks ago, they'd be in constant communication. Taurus likes and respects her —which isn't something he encounters too often. Their long nights of conversation have intrigued and impressed him, so he's been spending time with her. Deli called him and, like a good boy, he went—even though she insisted on taking Rhea—which is a big deal. We haven't been on truly stable ground with his brother's family for a while, but for the kitty, he gave in.

I knew that was a bad sign, but hell if I was going to deny him the first friend he's ever had.

I truly believe that our self-imposed exile has taken more of a toll on him than he would ever admit to me. He's much more social than I am, and despite her wretched choices in other companions, he finds Deli fascinating. Taurus talks about her like she's a shiny new toy.

It's cute, though he'd flay me for saying it out loud.

For the last couple of hours, I've felt more and more restless;

hence, the spinning. I must have picked up a growing swell of emotion through our bond, and when we link like that, it's impossible to separate his feelings from my own. He's been shielding a little—which is nothing new for someone with an empathic mate —but that made it impossible to tell what was happening specifically. I'd have to fight his block and I try not to do that if I don't have to.

Compartmentalizing hasn't been necessary, so I just dealt with the emotional bleed as I always do—it didn't even occur to me to question it. Unfortunately, now I have to stay connected because I have to find him. I pull back enough internally to eliminate his emotions before I look at Theodora.

My eyes widen, and I get pale. She understands and is by my side before I can blink. I look at her seriously, swallowing hard. "Get dressed, find Damien, and meet me in the living room. I have to collect weaponry before we go. We'll need both of you if what I picked up from Taurus is accurate."

She nods, then spins on her heel to hurry down the hall—still irritatingly graceful and lady-like.

"Theodora?" She turns to look over her shoulder, her eyes curious. "Just to cover our bases, start your vigilante and villain protocol."

I rarely see Theodora surprised. It doesn't last long as her head tilts and the command I issued makes her programming take over. Her posture is like steel as she strides down the hall to get Damien.

Hurrying to my room to get my equipment, I frown to myself as I strap every single sheath and holster I own on. Once I'm ready, I meet them in the living room. I have various types of blades on my arms, thighs, and boots. The knives glint in the lamplight, and Damien whistles as he and Theodora materialize.

"Test tube is rocking the Smuckers, eh?"

Theodora gives him a fond grin as he spouts his usual Muse riddles. Being the only Muse that anyone ever located, Damien's favor was in major demand until Dona made Theodora. Everyone swore they could understand his prattling, but since Taurus can barely decipher it and he lives with us, I doubt that claim highly.

Theo and I usually have to translate for him.

"You could say Taurus is in a jam, yes." I look at Theodora, who is dressed in ripped denim, leather boots, and fighting gloves. She looks nothing like the Barbie doll that was in my living room a few minutes ago. Her eyes are hard as she nods at me.

My high hopes for this venture with the cat seem to be dashed. I hoped Taurus could find a friend—a real one—that he could share all the endearing traits that only I get to see. He loves being playful, and he needs a bigger audience than our little family.

Deli seemed like a good fit.

Sighing again, I take Damien's hand and growl, "Get us there. Use my connection because he's in that stupid hideout of those idiots."

It seemed like a good idea when she called.; now, I'm not so sure.

I have *such* a bad feeling about this...

The Artist Gets A Trim

My amazement doesn't last long because the 'hero' of the Battle of Blood and Steel picks himself up and shakes off the punch like it's a love tap. He wipes the blood from under his nose, eyeing my mate. As he circles her like a lion waiting to pounce on its prey, she mirrors his movement.

The beast inside of her recognizes the dance.

I can't see perfectly at that distance, but I sense she's at the swirling eyes stage of her transformation. Tension is high, and she's working to keep her back from being exposed. She shifts to face away from the porch. My girl knows help will come from that direction, so she's not worried. Her claws are out, features feline, and her growl is loud enough to hear on the porch.

This fight is going to be a doozy and I don't want a thing to do with it.

Regardless, here we are. I must keep the others calm and not let them overre—

In the blink of an eye, three people appear behind Taurus. I recognize Damien from a past encounter, but I can only assume that one of the weapon wielding brunettes is Talia. Their appearance causes Victor to rush Caesar in a play to get off the porch. He must know these people well enough to ignore my command to stay put. C trips over the potted plant that I *told* Hex was a hazard. Vic gets loose, vaulting over the rail to land a few feet from my girl.

Shit.

Once Victor goes, the rest of the family leaps to the grass and fans out around him in a semi-circle. They're all itching to fight, which isn't helpful at all. Sandrine drops to a fighting stance, brandishing a wicked-looking knife I didn't know she carried. She tosses a baseball bat that has materialized out of nowhere to Caesar, who spins it over his hand like a bloody color guard bint. Siren pulls a long dagger out of her updo, and Hex is sporting *three* pairs of spiked brass knuckles. I look to the porch and Philomena is sitting with her martini, but there's a fancy ass looking hand cannon on the table next to her.

Since when do we carry that much hardware inside of our fucking house?

Vic had to know something before I did, that fucking asshole. He's foregoing weaponry, because he's a weapon by himself. I've got nothing—not that I want it—because I fucking *hate* this shit. Everyone else is waiting and watching, taking their cues from the true leader of the pack. Our pissed off kitty doesn't even flinch at the movement, unconcerned about the battlefield growing around her and the bird.

Sighing in annoyance, I take a step down the porch stairs, stopping when something zings past, missing my ear by a hair. I turn to see what the fuck it is and note that by a hair was more than a turn of phrase.

There's a huge hank of my long locks pinned to the post by an enormous blade.

"Not another step, long hair." The leather-clad woman issues her command in a voice that'd freeze the balls off a walrus. A twin blade to the one in the post is spinning in her palm, and she's clenching an even larger one in her right hand.

I growl in anger and pull the thing out of the wood. She seems to have no more inclination to fight than me, but I let my fangs drop as I watch my hair flutter to the ground. *That's one of my lines —don't fuck with my hair.* "I don't know you, but I guess you belong to him." My eyes cut to the blond taking turns wailing or being wailed on by my mate. "You need to lay off the flying weaponry unless you want this shit to escalate."

Victor is pacing a few feet from the pile of limbs, grunts, and growls as he watches the red and platinum go by. The others are standing behind him—ready and waiting for the signal that it's okay to rush the denim woman and Damien. Vic's muttering to himself as if considering, and I roll my eyes.

Have I mentioned how much I hate friction? At least, the kind that isn't naked and sweaty?

"I'm going to fucking *rip you to shreds*, you overstuffed, arrogant *asshole.*"

My mate's screech echoes in the night as a snarl followed by a rip distracts me. I hear an angry rejoinder as they roll toothier feet again. "Not worrisome, considering I'm going to knock you on your shrill, shrewish ass again first."

It's nice to know that they're paying attention to anything but their tussle.

The rest of us have lined up like we're re-enacting the Civil fucking War, but they only see each other. I pinch the bridge of my nose and look at the glowering woman strapped head to toe with blades. She's still poised to attack. My gaze cuts back to the writhing mess of leather and loud crunching noises, hoping they don't light the match to this tinderbox.

"You won't get the chance when I *rip* your arms off and beat the ever-loving *shit* out of you with them. Of course, that will take a while since you're so *full of it!*"

"Don't you *ever* shut the *fuck* up?! Christ, woman," he roars, ducking a right cross to come up weaving.

The crowd behind the fighters doesn't seem to advance, so I

lean against the post, waiting for the winds to change. I don't think my presence will be necessary on the lawn. The enraged clone's mate is spinning the blades in her hands, metal flashing in the moonlight as she watches them and us through narrowed eyes.

For the moment, it appears to be another standoff, each side poised for battle as we watch the Generals duke it out.

The Goddess Gives Her Blessing

H e gets mad at me all the time, my feathered fiend, because I won't let him 'thin the herd' when some idiotic bint gets saucy with one of us.

Why won't I let him? This. is why. Talk about a powder keg ready to blow our eyebrows off.

I have a mate in a furious fist and fang with—I'm not sure what Deli is, but not-quite-human seems to be an understatement. Taurus told me about her dilemma when they started chatting. 'Slight mutation' does *not* do it justice. No wonder he's been itching to run with her. She's almost as much a predator as he is.

After years of the Resistance evading Company security— which I am completely amazed Damien penetrated—she's amassed a full-blown army in her massive compound. She could start her own private security company with the number of droids and clones that live with her. I tuck that info away for further pondering.

If she has ten people at her place, I cannot imagine how many more are out there.

Not only that, but every one of them seems ready to jump in kamikaze-style to defend her honor. Is that the case with the rest of the unknown masses that live here? I hate to admit it, but Queen Kitty and I might have more in common than meets the eye. She doesn't need their help, and they know it. Despite their natural instincts, her housemates stay a respectful distance behind the long-haired one. Except for Victor, who, historically, is the exception to the smart choices rule. Just look up his bullshit antics from the Conflict.

My attention focuses on the army briefly, but I catch the swing kick Taurus aims at her head from the corner of my eye. She's fast —unnaturally fast—and I should know. She ducks under his leg and slashes at him with her... claws?

Jesus. They're not pulling any punches.

Again, I cannot stress enough that *this is why* I made the rule about fighting people in the community. No one really wants a repeat of the Conflict, and if they don't get over this shit, that's exactly what will happen. Only this time, we had *zero* allies around to fight off the Resistance. All the Cabal members slunk back to Earth when the droid people disappeared. The Quarter is a ghost town and though the four people from my house are mighty; we aren't an army.

He needs to sort this shit out before it escalates.

The fabric of his shirt rips and a bellow echoes in the night; she got skin on that one. Pity she forgot to protect her blind side, though, as she gets a resounding smack to the side of her head because of her lack of focus. It staggers her for at least a moment, but her bell's not rung yet. They appear evenly matched, but Deli seems to fight strictly off instinct and rage. Taurus is a trained fighter and an experienced killer.

Why the hell isn't he...?

Ouch.

He catches her with a quick jab, dancing around her to buy

some time. She screams at him—some disparaging comment about his manhood—then leaps. They go down in a tangle of limbs and snarls. I frown in confusion at the crunching, snarling pile. He should have dropped and used her momentum to throw her. I mean, he's used that trick on me a million times when we spar. *What's he playing at?*

I watch her family from across the yard, still mulling Taurus' moves in this fight. Something is off—he's only toying with her. Conversely, the cat's not pulling punches, but she's not going for a kill. The tension between the gathered armies makes me wonder what price we'll pay for the game they're playing.

Damien and Theodora spread out behind me as soon as we materialized in the yard. Neither one will attack without either provocation or a signal from me. Right now, they're simply making sure the other group doesn't get antsy and go after Taurus on their own. If they do, all hell will break loose.

My family is technically outnumbered, but I know what Damien, Theodora, and I can do. Most people have no clue about our skill sets, particularly Damien. Honestly, the issue isn't numbers. The issue is that her family seems to be fueled by her rage. Is she that connected—even with the droids—that the laid-back Lothario on the porch can't control them? If so, *how?* This whole situation is an enigma filled with questions I can't answer.

I study the long hair while he's not paying attention. He keeps looking up at a large bay window on the second floor and then at the front door, as if expecting something. The clone looks more worried about that possibility than the fight or the itchy battalion behind him. There's a problem here besides the war on the lawn distracting him.

What in hell's name could be up there that trumps this mess?

A snippet of the fight catches my eye. I turn my head to watch my mate and scarlet haired hellcat again as they roll to their feet again to spar.

"Now, now, puss," he taunts as he wipes at a trickle of blood on his cheek. "I thought you said something about teaching me a lesson? So far, all I've learned is not to waste my *buggering time* on *neurotic nits* with *attitude problems.*"

Great, keep goading her, Taurus.

Rolling my eyes at him, knowing he's going to draw this out as long as possible. I get distracted when the long hair pushes off the post he's been leaning on since I threw the first blade. I stung his pride with that move, but I knew his connection with Deli was the strongest. He's definitely her primary mate. The extent of her pack and his ease with them is interesting. My hands are full dealing with the bird brain out there, much less than as many clones and droids as I see here. It must be because outside of the boozy, Glock toting chick on the porch, he's also the calmest temper in the bunch.

They definitely have some kick ass weaponry in this joint.

That's why I had to give the long hair a heads up about what we wouldn't stand for. If he can't control the lot of them, we'll have a war on our hands. I'm banking that he can, but if it takes a blade embedded in a pricklier position, so be it. I ready a tosser when his mate snarls loud enough to split my eardrums.

"I *knew* it." She attacks again—a fast punch with one hand and a swipe with her claws with the other. The punch misses its mark, but she slices open Taurus' arm with the talons. That's not only going to leave a mark, but seriously piss him off. "That's all I am to you. You are a self-absorbed, egotistical *ass!*"

I turn to focus solely on the two fighters for the first time since I arrived. Damien seems to sense that I'm not watching our six. He grunts and flexes his considerable bulk to draw the attention of her family to keep them from noticing that now would be a good time to attack.

The scent of blood is heavy in the air. Both of the warriors look beaten, bloody, tired, and angry. Yet something about the emotion I can sense behind her words makes me hold my breath.

This is the moment that it's all going to change; I can feel it.

"I may be an ass, you flighty fucking feline, but at least I know what I want. Had I known what a *raging bitch* you are, I might not have taken you up on your offer for a night out in the first *sodding place.*"

That's ridiculous. Taurus likes when tough women give him shit, not the other way around. What the hell is he talking about?

The night breeze shifts and I catch a scent previously hidden under the smell of blood and adrenaline—arousal. Holy fucking shit, they're turning each other on. That explains everything, including why he's been pulling his punches during the fight. Before I can fully process that info, the cat goes eerily still.

Breathing hard and bleeding from just about everywhere, Deli lets her arms slowly drop to her sides. After a long pause, she raises her eyes to look at him. "What? What did you say?"

It's the first time since we arrived that her voice isn't roughly akin to a wailing banshee, and I hold my breath. On the periphery, I notice her family has dropped back a step. They must have caught the scent I picked up on, because several of them return to the porch with smirks.

Taurus looks momentarily confused by the ceasefire. "I said, had I known what a raging bitch you are, I might not have come out with you tonight."

Deli shakes her head and growls low in her throat. "No, you big prima donna, before that. You said something about knowing what you want. What did you mean?"

Snarling, Taurus advances and I can feel the frustration radiating off him in waves—so much so it shakes me. All I can think is 'please don't fuck this up'. I know what he's feeling; I know what he meant. He has to tell her or we'll be back to square one.

"I meant I bloody well wanted to spend time with you. I wanted to be with you, you witless ninny. I thought you knew that."

She snorts and takes a step towards him as Theodora and Damien return to my side. "How the fuck was I supposed to know that? You spent most of the night treating me like a trial you had to endure. When you weren't doing that, you treated me like a toy you got to play with for a while."

Running a bloodstained hand through his hair, Taurus shakes his head in frustration. He stalks closer, standing toe-to-toe with her as he smirks wickedly. "I figured you would have sussed out that I don't spend time with anyone I'm not right fond of, Sandwich. And I'm absolutely bloody fond of you."

Surprisingly, that seems to irritate her because she puffs up and blows up again–though not as bad as before. "Oh, *great. Now* you tell me. Damn it, Taurus, I am so *pissed off* because I thought you didn't give a damn and now you tell me—"

He grabs her upper arms and yanks her against his chest, slamming his mouth down on hers before she can finish the sentence. She doesn't seem to mind, though, as her arms wrap around his neck and her fingers tangle in his hair. When he pulls back for air, she tugs him back to her mouth immediately, grinding against him with as much enthusiasm as she'd had fighting him.

I shoot a look at Damien and Theodora. They're both watching me curiously to see what I'll say to this new development. "Well," I drawl, checking her family to make sure the war is over, "that was anticlimactic."

Taurus finally lifts his head from the insistent Deli and meets my eyes. I nod at him, sending him a wave of emotion through our link. His grin is boyish, and he disappears from the yard, taking Deli with him.

"For some of us, anyway," I finish softly, smiling a little.

Looking across the yard, I catch the long hair's gaze. His expression is placid, but I bet that's the norm for him. Bowing slightly, I arch an eyebrow. The corner of his mouth twitches and he bobs his head. I'll wait to ask for my blade back some other time. If our mates are going to be getting personal, I figure I'll see him again. "Come on, guys. Let's go home."

Damien drops the monster guise and grins, wrapping an arm

around Theodora's waist and grabbing my hand. He opens his portal and we step through. I wonder as we reappear in our home what changes are coming for our previously nuclear family.

For changes, I can tell, are on the way.

The Cat Is Lost In Space

DELILAH

Within a blink, I'm transported to a place that I've never seen before. I can only assume that it's in the Rift, since I didn't feel the pull of the portal to the other side.

There's not much in the room—a couch, a mini bar on a wall, and a large bay window on the far wall. It looks out into a small grassy area that ends in what looks to be an enormous cliff. I'm not even sure what this structure is. I only know Taurus brought us here. I can imagine why, but this mysterious location shit is a bit intimidating.

Not that he ever needs to know that.

He's standing in front of the window, gazing out of it as if it holds the answers to the universe. It feels like time stopped—we were fighting and screaming and bleeding and kissing. Now we're in a quiet room, cleaned up, and he looks like he's about to wax philosophical.

What in the hell just happened?

The moonlight glints off his spiky platinum hair as he turns to me with a wry expression. "Too dramatic, kitten?"

I shake my head, not wanting that moniker. It belongs somewhere else with someone else. I don't know what this is, but I know he's not like anyone I've been with before. "Not kitten, but yeah, it's a little over the top."

He chuckles. "Sandwich it is. You can't be surprised that I wouldn't drop us in a flea bag or jump into the fray in your foreign legion sized barracks."

Blinking, I try to decipher that when I notice that he's wearing a silk robe and pajama pants. *Where the fuck did that come from? Oh, goddess, what am I—?* My breath almost stops until I see that I'm still dressed, but no longer filthy—whew.

Christ only knows what he would have found on my body if I wasn't awake to control my glamours. I close my eyes for a moment, staving off the tears that prick my eyes. We *don't talk* about that. We *don't* think about that.

Just take slow breaths, Deli, and the panic will subside.

"Suddenly, you're not the hell cat I'm used to seeing. Perhaps you're not as eager to play with other puppies as you'd make out, huh?" His lips curve and he gives me a curious look. "I've been meaning to ask about that. I've only heard about you staying at home with the family since we started chatting and it seemed incongruous."

I arch my brow. "Where would you have heard about me besides when we..." My eyes narrow. "Have you been cyberstalking me?"

"What? No. Pffft!" His snort makes me pause because the protest was a little much, considering my question was flippant. "I was checking on your story."

"Uh-huh. To answer your question, the crazy level in my family has gotten out of control. I'm tired of being a status symbol and the changes I'm going through only make it worse."

He blinks. "There's something majorly wrong when you think me and the goddess are the sane ones, pet. You got a nice package;

I'll give you that. However, gits using that to express their delivery isn't a good thing in my book."

If only he knew how he right he is. He'd run like his feet were on fire.

"People put pressure on me to make them the center of my universe. When they do, it gets exhausting to juggle schedules and egos just to spend time with them. The punishment when I can't..." I trail off, actively avoiding the shiver that runs up my spine.

Why did I have to say that?

"If you wondered why I've been out of this scene for so long, Sandwich, that shit is why. Loony tunes make everyone miserable. You have a good heart, pet, and it sounds to me like it's getting trampled."

I shrug, trying to downplay the situation. He can't know the complete story; he'd never look me again if he knew the truth. No one would. "I figure out their weak spots and push their buttons until I feel better." I paste on a smirk, determined not to let the rest of the world ruin whatever this is shaping up to be.

"I bet you're hard to handle when your ire's flaring."

His lips quirk and I can tell he's flirting. *Okay, flirting I can do.* I swat his arm and snort. "Lech."

"What can I say, baby? I'm best when I'm bad." He frowns for a moment, completely reversing the mood. "You aren't expecting flowers and poetry and that rot, right?"

Is he kidding me? I haven't had that kind of courting since the blogger sets his sights on me. Even then, it was more for—never mind that. "No. I've long since abandoned that kind of sentiment. No worries; I don't have expectations."

"Good," he sighs, and then looks puzzled. "Wait. If you don't have expectations, where's the thrill?"

"Taurus, I meant I don't expect hearts and flowers and such. Even Mr. Prim and Proper didn't fulfill that promise. You don't give your pin to the bad girl... you take her to the drive-in for a make-out sesh in the car."

He turns back to the window as if digesting that before he speaks. "I don't do complicated, pet. At least, not with women. I don't play games, and I don't wave conquests around like trophies. I like and respect you. I plan on fighting and running with you." He looks back over his shoulder to spear me with an intent look. "I plan to fuck you. It's up to you to let me know if any of those plans aren't good for you; that's why we're here."

I blink and let my breath out slowly. "I like and respect you, too. That means I'll always fight you back—even when you don't want me to. I won't screw with your head and I'll mix it up with you wherever possible, including between the sheets. You'll probably have to drag how much I don't dislike you out of me with pliers." I grin, giving him a chance to object. "I won't use you. No matter how much your presence makes anyone upset, no matter how easy it would be to use you to get back at them, even with your permission—I won't."

His brow quirks in amusement. He'd offered to let me do that last week when we had coffee because I was upset at Sari. "It's no skin off my nose if you do, pet. I don't play nice with others, and I'm fine with being their villain. You know I'd let you rub it in to just to crank someone that needed it."

I shake my head. "Being with you for that reason would make me no better than they are. Convenient weapon though it may be, it's neither why I sought you out nor why I'm still here."

"Talk about your ego crushers if it was." He interrupts me and puts his hand on his bare chest dramatically, as if having a heart problem—a favorite schtick of his.

"I'm being honest, and it needed to be said," I shrug, making it seem like it's a much smaller thing than it is. *Everything is a weapon in our world now.* It wasn't like that at the beginning, but even in the short weeks I've been in contact with him, people are shifting, scrambling, lashing out. Not using him to hurt people is giving up a mighty powerful weapon, even if it would be a lie.

"I enjoy hearing you curse me as a fiend, then soften under my charms. However, back to why we're here." He gives me a devilish grin and pads over to the couch that I'm curled on, dropping next to me as he brushes a hair off my face. "You're downright adorable, which I'm sure you want to poke my eyes out for saying."

"Something like that," I murmur, his closeness making me nervous. *Me? Nervous? This is ridiculous.* There's not a position I haven't been in, a knot I don't know, and a scenario I haven't been part of. How does he *do* this to me? It's like I'm a fifteen-year-old fumbling in a back seat.

He dips his head to catch my earlobe between his teeth and I shudder.

This is going to be tricky. With the beast lurking, it's hard to control myself. That's the real reason that I've stuck to playing in my sandbox. It only took crossing the line with the wrong person one time to ruin something special. Add that to the things we do not discuss that are weighing on me emotionally? It's too much. My load is full; am I crazy to let this happen?

Am I insane to dive into the deep end of the pool with a known shark and hope for the best?

"You know, I think I'd like to postpone this, Sandwich. The sun's rising. I have a job on the other side today, and I think I'd like to take my time with you."

I blink and flush, not knowing what to say. Postponement gives me time to consider what I'm getting myself into and figure out how *not* to fuck it up like everything else good in my life.

"If you tell anyone that I didn't flip you upside and ride the happy train tonight, I'll eat you." His eyes dance and I realize that I've never seen Taurus smile this much. I'm sure he does with Talia, but no one else witnesses this side of him, and I like it.

"We wouldn't want to damage your reputation for tom catting around with every lady on the block. Oh, wait—silly me—that's *my* reputation. I guess you're safe," I grumble bitterly. His brow arches and I sigh. "That came out wrong. I'm not ashamed of myself or my decisions. People are getting on my nerves by treating me like a trophy to be won. It's why I haven't told many people besides my immediate family about talking with you."

I guess his super hearing caught the mumbled part at the end because his jaw drops. "You've been keeping mum about us? I thought you told the gnome and the firebug everything."

"I mean, I told Rhea some of it, but everything. I'm being rather stingy because I didn't want anyone to meddle. I guess I need something—no, someone—like that. However, I also know the display tonight will cause a lot of gossip, so I'll have to deal with that now." I wrinkle my nose, feeling exposed.

"Good. I prefer that almost no one sees the side of me you're seeing for a multitude of reasons. Most of them have to do with disliking facile nits, but it also comes in handy to have everyone think you're nothing more than a cold-blooded killer. Fear keeps them at a distance, pet. Since you're okay with keeping the public thinking you just want to beat me to ribbons, we can breathe easy. Hopefully, no one else will come knocking me up wanting a ride for themselves."

"Hey! I didn't say—I didn't mean... I'm not..." Scrunching my nose up, I reach over and go to muss his hair in retaliation only to find the clone speed has trumped me again. He catches my hand inches from his head.

"Not. The. Hair."

I arch my brow this time. "A weakness?"

"Personal flaw, my goddess says. Stay away from the hair," he glowers at my indulgent expression.

It's the cutest thing he's done all day; I can't help it. I giggle and he glares harder. "It's adorable."

"There's no reason to insult me, dammit." His expression blackens, and it doesn't help his case at all. I giggle again and he growls. Eyes smoldering, he yanks me forward and kisses me roughly before pulling back. "Say it."

"Um, you're not, um, adorable." I whisper hoarsely.

"That's right." He lets go and stands up, smirking in satisfaction. "Now, the buggering sun is coming up and I've got people to kill today. Can I see you later today, Sandwich?"

Blinking, I nod. "Uh, yeah, we can do that. I'll, uh, move some stuff around and make some time..."

He gives me a knowing look, as if that conclusion is all but forgone, and before I know it, I reappear on my front porch.

How in the hell did he do that and what on earth is going to happen later today?

The Cat Receives A Bird Call

DELILAH

A fancy ass box appeared on our porch unexpectedly while I was asleep. I didn't find it because after an all-nighter with the birdbrain, this kitty needed some beauty rest. Leo brought a delicious smelling tray of food to get me to drag my arse out of bed and dangled it in front of me with wicked glee.

"Now, love, Hex will be up to get this room sparkling soon—up and at 'em. Food is on the tray by the chaise and your clothes are on the jacuzzi. You need to shower while all the normal guests are out and about. The drama from last night has dissipated, thank the stars."

I arch a brow at him, wondering what went on after Taurus zapped me to wherever. I knew Rhea came back here and even though I was distracted when I arrived, I saw the cars from the Den family. I assume someone called them to get Rhea calmed down after our disastrous outing.

That's a conversation I have no interest in starting this early.

"Everything is ready for tonight. Sandrine and I are hitting the town with Siren, Caesar, and Hex. You miscreants will have the house to yourself, I think. Even the wench is going out with the dancing duo."

Uh oh. I'm supposed to meet Taurus and they're all going out?

I can *not* leave Victor and Rafe alone. They've had difficulties since Rafe mated with Wilde. That's yet another mess that blogger-cum-laureate left in his wake. Maybe Alistair and Rhea can come over to keep Rafe occupied and Victor can tinker around in the workshop?

Shit, I'd feel terrible.

Donatella only left a few months ago, and I've thrown so many recent additions to our family into the mix. Caesar has his buddies Hex, Leo, and Preston. Leo has Sandrine and Hex has that crazy as hell droid, Chaos.

Leo probably didn't mention her on the list of attendees because I'm not a fan of the head of her family. Belle is about as bad news as you can get. She's one of those fake Southern women who use 'bless your heart' in place of saying 'fuck you'. She likes to pretend she's all sugar and spice but motorcycle edgy at the same time. Her clone and two droids—Mayhem, Veruca and Chaos—live on her ranch. Between the four of them, their names suit what follows in their path.

Sari *loves* that family. I'm convinced she has a deeper relationship with them than she lets on and for all I know, it could include mating. It wouldn't shock me to find that out, especially since Rhea has a yen for Mayhem because he's a bad boy.

Victor only has me since Dona split, and he doesn't say how heartbroken and lonely he is, but I know. He's one of my dearest friends and much like Leo, we're rarely lovers now. We're simply two people who love each other very much. I'd do anything for him, but he asks for nothing. He's always there, especially when I need him most. No matter what I do or say, who I bring into the family, what changes I go through—Victor still loves me as much as the first time we kissed.

I can't abandon him entirely to sneak off and meet Taurus, right?

"I forgot, love. Vic is going with us. I think he figured you might meet up with the firefly and the puppy dog."

I give him a stern look. "Leo."

He grins.

"Leo! Caesar wears a collar and you don't poke fun at him."

"Hell, yes, we do. Quietly, though, because Chaos can be a genuine terror if you make her mad. She enjoys walking him when she's here with Hex. Crazy as a hatter, that one—she spooks me." He grabs the tray I was picking at and sighs. "Get clean. Do something that makes you happy tonight. Christ knows we're all aware something is wrong and the lazy git won't tell anyone what the bloody problem is. Our family's not supposed to have that kind of secret; it's against the rules."

Pursing my lips, I shrug. "It's nothing, really. I have a lot of toes to try not to step on. My family needs me. I'm still learning not to skewer myself. It's all making me a little crazy."

"I wasn't programmed yesterday, woman. I know that it's bigger than that. I won't force the issue—that's Victor's job. He'll be after you soon enough." Leo throws me a wink and heads out, leaving me to ponder the hot mess that is my life.

Being mated with four clones and two mostly humans, plus dating several droids, sounds difficult. It didn't use to be, despite my current woes. The troubles began when Rafe and I mated with Alistair, Rhea, Wilde and Sari. Emotions running the highest highs, lowest lows, and everything in between are stock in trade with them. Some days I swear I wouldn't do a thing differently and others—well, we don't talk about the others. I'm hoping to make it through this rough patch and see the other side where the sunshine we'd had is hiding.

Letting everything inside me go still, I close my eyes. I breathe deeply, working to contain all of our hurt, sorrow, and pain in a tiny ball that I can tuck away. My magick keeps it all hidden—cleansing our mating bonds—so it doesn't flow to the others. It's damned exhausting keeping Rafe and my misery a secret. It's a gargantuan strain and I think it's why I struggle with controlling the beast. She's the outward embodiment of my rage, escaping to express it in a way that I cannot. The stress of fighting with her, hiding the secrets and scars, and putting on a brave face is wearing on me. I'm afraid that I'll lose my shit in a seriously public way.

I have to find an escape.

That is why I'm going to throw caution to the wind and use whatever in the hell is in this box Leo gave me. The scent clinging to the box tells me it's from Taurus. I don't know *why* I know it will help me locate that place we were last night, but I do. He's the only thing in my universe right now that makes me feel free.

He's not part of my world, and he never will be. He is not looking to use me to climb a social ladder, and he doesn't want to add himself to my ever-growing harem of mates. He just wants to blow off steam—in bed and out.

I can't have him, and I don't want him.
This might be perfect.

Texts from people about last night tainted the hour I spent getting ready. I'm not in the mood to discuss it in depth, especially given that I promised Taurus I wouldn't reveal what after we left my house. Mostly, I just toyed with Sari and Wilde until they gave up.

Now that I'm clean, dressed, and caffeinated, I can focus on this damned box.

Smiling to myself, I rip open the sparkly paper on the package. The delivery service from the Company doesn't come here because they can't get through the barrier spell. It must have been hand delivered by the preening prat himself. After last night, he knows how to get through the shields.

I look at the contents and frown. The box has a smartphone in it.

What a bloody cheater.

It looks exactly like the most common smartphone on Earth. A closer inspection tells me that the Company either has someone from that mega corporation on their payroll or they own a large stake in it. *Why?* Because it is one of those phones except it's tricked out. When I turn it over, the back is jet black with an engraved silver peacock with gemstones studding the tail. This bad boy was handmade *this morning,* delivered by the afternoon, and had to cost a fortune.

Typical Taurus: this is a billion-dollar booty phone.

I don't think this is a magickal transport device. I can't imagine that their tech could be this small. *Then again, what the hell do I know about Company tech?* The phone has one number in the contacts—presumably Taurus'—and social media apps that only link to him. Why do I need a messenger app to get a hold of someone who can talk in my head? There are also a few pre-installed games that are right up my alley. Again, I wonder where he's getting his information.

I should call him, right? I fidget a bit, unsure if I should be so accessible. After arguing with myself for a few minutes, I give in. It goes straight to voicemail when I do, and then a text appears.

The Peacock: Now.

In an instant, I'm sitting on the couch in the room from last night. It's less spartan today, which surprises me. There's wood paneling and thick, fluffy carpet. The bar area nearby has been upgraded and now sports crystal glassware and rich looking alcohol in snifters. An armchair and a coffee table sit catty corner to the sofa as if waiting for someone to lounge.

Interesting.

I don't see the clone in question, so I settle into the comfy couch. Humming under my breath, I distract myself with the bird phone. I would get creeped out about the 'me-specific' things on it, except that it's so damned like Taurus. No wonder people think he's magickal. He's not; he's just filthy rich. He's the billionaire playboy turned superhero of clones.

Before I finish the first level in the game, Taurus hops over the back of the couch with a grumble. He growls and kicks his feet up on the coffee table. His expression is turbulent, and I wonder why he brought me back here hours after we parted when he's in a foul mood.

"You look hungry." I can only surmise that's what caused his dark countenance, as anger would look bloodier.

"That's one way of putting it." His stomach rumbles as if to confirm my words.

I reach over without thinking, rubbing his tummy lightly. "Is everything okay? I thought we weren't meeting until later, but then the text came through."

His demon visage flashes, then fades, then flashes again. It's like he's having control issues—not something I'd expect from him. His expression finally smooths it out when he quirks a grin at the hand on his torso. "I had issues at work. I missed lunch, and I got stuck in a boring sodding meeting. Everyone around me having a sodding snack didn't help."

The mother hen in me clicks into place and I sit up on my knees, rubbing the back of his neck soothingly. Last week, the thought of this scenario would have been so surreal that I couldn't comprehend it. Today, it feels natural to do it.

"Did somebody at work take your lunch money or something?" I give him a soft smile, letting him know I'm only kidding before I kick up a purr in my chest.

His eyes widen at the purr, and he shakes his head. "Not a soul would dare to cross me, gorgeous. I think I'm feeling a bleed off Talia. She's also having a rough day at the office." He narrows his eyes at me. "Don't think that purring's going to make me all poofy and smitten, either."

I roll my eyes. "Tell me what's going on with you. There's no need to remind me how big and bad you are or how many people you killed for looking at you sideways. I know it's not just a bleed. Talk to me, you jackass." My fingers work over the pressure points in his neck, ironing out tension as the rumble in my chest gets stronger.

He adjusts, ostensibly to keep me from mussing his hair, but I can feel his tension fading. This is not the date I imagined with him when I called, nor is it one that anyone would believe I'm having.

However, here we are, and it's oddly comfortable.

"I'm not sure that it's fair to tell you about it, Sandwich. You have ties that bind." He opens one eye and looks at me for a moment, waiting for me to nod. "As soon as people saw on the blog that Talia and I were out in the open, we started getting our bells rung. The gnome came knocking on Talia's door for lunch today, which explains why mine was nonexistent."

My free hand flies to the bridge of my nose, pinching tightly as I try to control the emotions running through me. *Sari couldn't stay away, could she?* She and Wilde have torn our family to ribbons. They've scarred, bruised, tortured and broken us emotionally and physically, yet they can't stop looking for more. I've loved and hated them both for so long now that I'm not even sure if it's loves or co-dependency.

Whatever it is, they're hungry for more destruction. Maybe it means they're done destroying Rafe and I. Their focus has shifted, and we can hide away with Alistair and Rhea. I could let them duke it out with Taurus and Talia.

No. That's not how this is going to play out, damn it.

I wanted one thing for myself, which is why I kept it a secret.

The public fight on my lawn cancelled out my efforts and surprise, surprise. Sari immediately found her way to Talia's door before I could get a stitch of clothing off.

That meddling bitch.

"I'm not surprised. Sari's been difficult to deal with for quite a while now. I've been avoiding her—impossible as that is in our house—as much as I can. She's probably whining about Talia to that walking toe rag, Belle, right now." My eyes narrow and I give the coffee table a solid kick, sending it flying across the hardwood. "Shit."

His eyebrows raise as he gives me a puzzled look. "Did you stop speaking English there for a moment and I missed it?"

I sigh. "No, I was being a bitch. My insults get graphic when I'm angry. That woman is 'Shit Stirrer Numero Uno'. Everything she touches turns ugly. I wouldn't have a thing to do with her except Hex adores Chaos."

Chuckling, he shakes his head. "Graphic looks good on you, pet. I don't mind it, given the mood I'm in. Explain the chaos bit, though, as I'm lost."

"I haven't called her a dumpster whore, so there must be hope for the day yet," I grunt, kicking at the bottom of the couch. "Chaos is one of Belle's droids. She dates Hex; you know, the punk rocker looking droid from my house? You might have seen him last night. Chaos is also fairly fond of Caesar, the droid inventor from Dona's family."

I stop as he barks a laugh, shaking with mirth. His arm shoots out and yanks me onto his lap as he wipes his eyes. "Christ, Sandwich, I needed that. I guess you had a run in with the gnome as bad as ours?" He pauses for a moment, nodding. "I definitely remember the upstart who helped start the Conflict. I don't know if I feel bad for him being attached to a chit so destined for doom or not. Hex, though, I didn't notice."

Shooting him a dirty look for the comment about Caesar, I sigh. "No, I didn't have a run in with Sari. I'm sure she's in a grim mood after having to shore up Rhea last night only to find out she missed a Battle Royale while doing so. However, I refuse to let her provoke me into punishing her—which she always wants—nor will I let her punish me if I see her. I was only venting about Belle."

I'm not lying.

I haven't spoken to Sari or any of the folks who were upstairs last night, but I can assume I pissed them off with my blog posts. Rhea is probably mopey about missing the 'good stuff': Alistair will be fearful of his 'brother'. Wilde and Sari must be furious if they already hit Talia. They got left out of a brawl *and* they got stuck with crying, whiny Rhea.

There were nudges, along with our connection from Sari and Wilde, when Leo woke me up. When I didn't answer, they kept pushing. They asked how I felt, if everything was okay, if I needed them—I knew it was a trap. Finally, they gave up and now I know why—they went after Talia. Right before Taurus whisked me away, there was an unexplained message apologizing. I didn't know why then, but I do now. Sari knew she stepped in it by making Talia angry. She did it on purpose to make waves so she wouldn't to feel threatened.

I'm not playing her game. Hell, I'm too tired to even consider it. All of them—her, Wilde, Alistair, and Rhea panicking over nothing.

I just can't deal with their drama.

Taurus frowns, running fingers up and down my spine. "Are they really that crazy?"

"Yes." My voice is soft and I'm struggling to hold back my emotions. I won't unload my crazy on him. We've barely started whatever it is we're doing; I refuse to drive him away. Taking a deep breath, I pause so I can figure out how to explain without revealing all the insanity.

"Sari has low self-esteem and wallows in it, but she wants you to coddle her. Once you do, she makes it almost impossible to give her what she wants. You can't meet her expectations, so she gets jealous. Then she'll say you're only pretending to take care of her. Both she and Wilde will get clingy and demand even more of you. That makes them feel selfish, so they lash out. Once that hurts you, they want to get punished for being bad people."

His brows raise and I continue, sighing. "The next phase is resentment—they feel bad because everyone's always mad at them. Sari will apologize and pretend everything is okay. But really, she doesn't mean it. She'll go to that bitch Belle to cry about how everyone is mean to her. Belle will go bulldog and lash out at people in public because she has no goddamn sense. Everyone gets mad."

Feeling my breath get tight, I rub my chest before I finish the tale. "The problem is that Sari cares if you're mad at her, so the cycle never ends. Belle doesn't care, nor does she know when she's crossed the line. It all fucking sucks. So today, I'm not giving any of them what they want. There will be no coddling, no punishing, and no fighting. I'm out."

Taurus grins proudly and ducks his head to steal a quick kiss. He murmurs, "Aren't you glad I only kill things when I get pissed?"

I laugh. "It makes the brain work a lot simpler, that's for sure. Most of the time, I distract Wilde and let Rafe handle her."

A snarl rips from his throat and I blink, tilting my head quizzically. "Sorry. I'm peckish and it's hard to control the big bad when that ponce comes up."

"I made them mad by not really answering the questions they texted earlier. I annoyed them on purpose to amuse myself, so I can't complain."

"Why don't you tell me what you did before I eat you for lunch?" Taurus gives me a mock demon face sneer as if it would scare me, and I suppress the urge to giggle.

Considering where I'm perched, it's not very threatening. I bat my lashes and pretend to act terrified. It's been so long since someone was playful with me. "Please don't eat me! I'll tell you."

His stomach growls, and he glares. "Be quick about it, lunchable."

Biting my lip, I grin. It feels ridiculous to be this happy about lighthearted banter, but the darkness in our family has eaten away at the fun times. It feels like there's a cloud following Rafe and me around. That's what the others can sense Leo asked about earlier. So I try to appreciate this, even though I have to discuss the idiots I'm mated to.

"The texts Wilde sent seemed like he was feeling insecure about me going places or doing things that aren't in his wheelhouse. He's not a hunter, no matter what he wants to believe, so I would never invite him to go. When we first met, I pushed his rigid lines, but eventually, it got tiring. I don't do that anymore. I decided that you either love someone for who they are, or be with someone else. I didn't say it like that to him, but he got jealous because there are things I don't share with him. I know the blog posts set this off. It's worse because he couldn't track me through the bond. I was afraid we'd have unwanted guests show up when I did it, but I didn't tell him that." I shrug, trying to make it sound like it's no big deal.

Wilde being jealous of Taurus before he and I have done anything is a big deal. It means he and Sari are going to be insufferable about this relationship. Equally damning is the silence coming from Rhea and Alistair.

Those two will use guilt as a weapon, I'm sure.

Taurus' expression turns vicious. "If you weren't so large with scruples, I'd tell you to throw my name in there to get him even more riled."

"He and Sari would have to come out of hiding first. They've clamped our connection down and won't talk to anyone, according to Rafe."

"Aw, I suppose between you and my goddess, their toes got squashed. I feel right terrible about that."

I snort. "Watch the sarcasm; it's dripping on me." I swat his shoulder lightly. "They're both so jealous of you they've tripped flat on their faces trying to find out what's going on. Sari would literally kill someone to get invited to go hunting with us—picking Rhea hit a button, I think. Somehow, they all think you're going to take me away from them. Don't ask me if it's me or Rhea, too; I don't know how deep the crazy pool goes."

"Well, shit, they caught me. I'm planning on stealing you and locking you in my basement until you beg me for it."

"Oh, no!" I giggle, pretending to be horrified. "Don't lock me up and subject me to your base defiling." Kicking my feet, I fake a struggle. A smile splits my face as I realize that I'm having a great time and even talking about the family isn't squashing it.

"What, no vicious beast from hell?"

I put my hand to my forehead and pretend to swoon. "*Fiend*! Unhand me, you vile creature of the night!"

His grumble is barely intelligible as he buries his face in my shoulder to laugh. "It wouldn't hurt you to wiggle your bum a bit." I wiggle and he raises his head to give me a rakish grin. "Yeah, that's it. Struggle for me. I'm a big, evil beast that will steal you away in the middle of the night and use you shamelessly." His head dips and he licks up my collarbone; this time my shiver is real, and he knows it.

I murmur, "Oh no. Whatever will I do? How will I survive?"

He suddenly cocks his head, stopping completely. His eyes cut to a side table where his phone is vibrating across the surface insistently. "Bugger. I'm being paged. Every fucking time, I swear." Nipping at my earlobe, he mutters, "I'm going to take care of this problem and then grab a bite. When I come back, I'll seduce you properly."

Nodding, I let reality seep in as he sits me aside on the couch and stands to go. "Okay. Can I get back and forth from here on the phone?"

He nods. "Company tech in that thing. They use it for the lab coats that don't live in the Rift. You can get here and back using the listing with my name. Good idea that, as I'm not sure how long the job will take, and I hate leaving you to wonder about unsupervised."

His eyebrows bob and I swat him again. "Go, you overstuffed bird."

With a wink and a grin, he disappears. I'm left to wonder what I'll do until he comes back. I can't be at his beck and call, can I?

That'd be way too bizarre.

The Cat In The Middle

❧

DELILAH

After my second shower of the day, I have to admit to feeling loose and wonderful. Turning to look over my shoulder at my primary mate, I smile softly. He's rinsing that mane of his, humming happily under his breath. We had an amazing afternoon with Alistair and Rhea. We were concerned when they showed up with takeout, but there was no drama about the incident two days ago.

They didn't even ask about what happened after Rhea left.

Alistair was a wee bit clingy, but the way our bond works, it's not surprising. I don't think Rhea's insecurities have ever rubbed off on him, and that's a good thing. It didn't feel enhanced by the current turmoil, so I'm not worried. I never thought our relationship would progress to where it is now, nor that he and Rhea would become so important to us. My mate and I were so entrenched with Sari and Wilde at the time that I didn't see it becoming serious.

Despite that, I'm always aware Rafe and I share our mates with Sari and Wilde. They made certain we acknowledged their claim came first as fast as they could. Everyone knew the four of them were close after the Conflict, but not how close. Alistair, Rhea, Rafe and I were talking seriously about mating as a family. Rhea and I had not mated yet, but we thought including it in the family ceremony would be nice. We decided once our new lovers came home from a trip planned with Sari and Wilde, we would finish the bond.

Sari and Wilde found out and moved in to mate with them first on the trip before we could do it.

That was the first sign that Sari and Wilde were not the amazing mates Rafe and I believed they were. They manipulated Rhea into mating with them on that trip purely out of jealousy. Rafe saw the blog post commemorating their mating and the trip while he was looking through his messages. We were shocked and hurt when we read Sari's blog; our lovers didn't mention it on any of our video chats while they were away.

That was also planned, if you ask me.

For clones, mating is sacred, and respect for your mates is paramount. That's the lore they drill into the clones during training, and that lore gets handed down to their human companions. I feel like there must be a book somewhere that explains the traditions and rules, but I've never been able to find it. Not speaking with your mates before you mate with someone else is a pretty big no-no.

Didn't stop the bullshit from happening, nor did it help the hurt when we found out.

This might have been the first time that Sari and Wilde used love as a weapon against us, but it would not be the last. All eight of us had to sit down to talk about what happened. Rafe and I sat through the excuses, and in the end, it was easier for us to move on. We couldn't make them understand why we were so hurt. You can't see a unicorn if you don't believe they exist—and Rhea didn't want to believe that she and Alistair got used. Sari didn't want to admit she'd been jealous and scared.

No one was going to budge—what good would it do to rip us all apart over it?

Perhaps we were foolish to think it would end there. Everyone pretends it doesn't happen, but it's easy for me to see the dysfunction inherent in our unit. As much as Sari crows about free love and sharing, she and Wilde are a constant source of needy drama that disrupts both families' relationships with each other. We love them and love does not demand perfection—it is. Rafe and I let things go, being the bigger people.

Since the incident in December, the rivalry gets worse every day. Adding Taurus into the mix is going to make that even more treacherous to navigate. Sari and Wilde are more than out of control than ever. Rafe and I work hard to reconcile with them, but it's not looking good. There are things that have happened that we don't even tell each other about. To be honest, I think we'd both be humiliated if any of this got out. We're the strong ones—the family everyone wants to be.

How can it have gone so wrong in such a short time?

But last night was good and I'm going to hold on to that. A sense of calm flows over me as I pad over to the French doors and crack them, letting the breeze air out of the room as if to cleanse it.

"Night Bloom?" Rafe murmurs low, coming up behind me and wrapping his arms around my waist. His chin sits on my shoulder as our warm skin touches. It still makes my heart race when I feel how easily we complement one another.

"Yes?" I close my eyes as the breeze blows the sheer curtains around me. I feel like we're in a romance novel when we stand on the balcony like this. Not that I believe in that stuff, mind you, but I may have specifically picked out the design of this room with Hex to encourage that emotion.

"Was it me or did our mates seem inordinately clingy?"

"Very. It's hard to tell if they are being influenced outside of their own insecurities. Alistair's volunteered to be my sub—collars and all." I chuckle low. "I think he's really into it, to tell the truth."

I feel the grin I can't see. "Is he now? Isn't *that* interesting?"

He yelps when I reach back and pinch his rear. "No. Bad long hair. This is mine. You get to be his *Royalty*. Let me have this one."

"Oh, fine. Be a greedy little tart." He grumbles and squeezes my waist. "Rhea was needy. She said the drama with the coyote and the blogger are wearing her out."

"I imagine so. It's damn near killing us." I turn my head enough to see him and his eyes reflect the haunted look in mine.

"True." The silence is deafening for a moment before he whispers, "It's Thursday. We have dinner with the troublemakers tonight. In about... three hours."

My entire frame tenses up and I know he can feel it. We can't change our normal routine, or the consequences will be far worse than sitting through a dinner. Alistair indicated the pack was causing grief for them yesterday, and my conversation with Taurus confirmed their misbehavior two days ago.

What in hell's name is bothering them so much that they had to make four people miserable? Why, oh why, is today Thursday?

"Changing our standing date would be worse than dealing with them. It sucks, especially since we know they've been awful this week. That won't make this any easier."

"You can't smell like the turkey or the brother. It'll set them off; it always does. Make sure you're all squeaky by the time they get here."

I glare at him over my shoulder, not realizing that he knew I snuck out to meet Taurus again. He was in his studio painting, and I knew he'd miss most of the day in his 'art stupor'. Rafe sees nothing while he's working, so it was a safe assumption. Surprisingly, he noticed, and not only that, he figured out that I showered to make sure all the predator noses in our house didn't catch the scent on my skin. "How did you know I showered after I got back from wherever he takes me, or even that I left at all?"

"You're awfully defensive. Are you planning on screwing the great ninny bird or what? It's the big question hanging in the air since the fight. I think the unanswered question is causing problems, my love. People are scared and jealous. Those two have lived a different life for so long. Now, suddenly, that git shows up and plants one on you in the middle of a civil war scenario. Excellent dramatic entrance, I must admit."

Turning in his arms, I tilt my head. "He's not safe—though, nothing is anymore, even when it should be. He's someone I can have to myself that no one else can ruin. You know?"

He nods and rests his forehead on mine, pausing before replying. "I do. It seems like everything good we've done recently has been ruined. I get why his separateness is appealing. Please promise me you'll be careful. I know you can take care of yourself, but you have a soft center. You pretend to cat around, but you take every single one of us into your heart. Don't let his views on our lifestyle make you feel worse than the Den already has. We're both fragile now—more than ever—and I know you better than anyone else."

I smile. He's right, but he's in worse shape than me. All I can do is hold his pain, yet he's worried about me getting hurt. "I know, but Taurus isn't looking for love. He doesn't want to claim or possess me. We're scratching an itch and having a good time. His views on our lifestyle are *exactly* why I know that nothing more than that will happen."

Rafe nods, tucking my hair behind my ears. "We should get dressed and see if Leo has the places set. I'm glad you're here. I thought I might be on this date tonight by myself if you took off with the great dodo."

Shit. I'd worried about Victor being alone and completely forgotten that it's Thursday. That would have been a recipe for disaster.

Recipe... oh, holy hell.

"Leo won't have anything prepared, love. They're all going out tonight because they had such a good time the other night. Leo told me about it yesterday, before Alistair and Rhea showed up. We're on our own."

"Fuck."

"Can we run away and join the circus?"

"Only you, my night bloom. My talents don't extend to tightrope acts."

I kiss him lightly, a sad smile crossing my face. "Oh, I don't know. I think we've been walking on one together for longer than I'd like to admit. Let's get dressed and order some food. Maybe we can eat at the movie. If it gets late, we might not have to entertain."

"That's a nice way to say that we hope we don't have to be intimate with our mates, love."

"What do I do if they ask about Taurus?"

"Hedge your bets, woman. No need for fur to fly yet."

The Cat Cheers Up The Canary

DELILAH

His text wakes me in the middle of the night. I can feel the soft buzz crawl over my skin despite the phone is on the dresser. I squint at the clock with an internal groan and close my eyes again.

What the hell? It's three in the morning. Is he kidding?

I re-open an eye to look at the pile of people on my bed, feeling defeated.

There's no way I can sneak out of this, right?

My tension is because the date night was strained. Dinner, the movie, and the bedroom were filled with random questions, thinly veiled jabs, and pretended affronts. It was more obligatory than enjoyable. I didn't realize that until now how dirty I feel for letting it happen. I'm sure Rafe feels the same way, but we've gotten so used to allowing Wilde and Sari to do whatever simply to avoid worse fates.

Why isn't he home with Talia? What does he want with me? Why I am answering a middle of the night beckoning?

I scrub my hand over my face, trying to decide if I'm going to answer him. Should I go to him in this state? I'm emotionally exhausted and I feel like shit. But don't I deserve to have fun once in a while? I'm living life as if it's a habit, not an adventure, and I hate that. Things that were once fun are now a chore and emotions that were bright and colorful are ashy. I have nowhere to escape because we've always kept an open door policy at The Maison and changing it will draw attention. That means anyone can show up anytime, and we are expected to entertain.

It used to be chaotically exciting and spontaneous. Now it's constant anxiety because it might be *them*. Our lives are a prison of our own making and I don't know how to fix it without hurting so many people who aren't at fault. I look around, chewing my lip as I consider the text and the stupid phone.

Am I really doing this?

Wriggling carefully out of bed, I tiptoe to my closet. I drop the kitty face so I can see in the dark. If I'm caught leaving, there will be hell to pay, especially if they find out it's for Taurus. *Fuck it. I'm going.* I pause as I touch my clothes.

Hell, if I'm doing this, why not go whole hog?

I pull an outfit off the hangar quietly. It's a leftover from a bet I lost years ago—silly and over-the-top in the role playing department. I remember how hard we laughed and how much fun we had when I first wore this. That feeling is long gone now. Shaking my head to clear out the ugliness, I head into the bathroom to clean up. I can't go there smelling like my previous guests.

Delilah O' Hara, secret shower freak, reporting for duty.

When I finish, I sneak over to the phone. Pushing the button, I take a deep breath and appear in his space.

Rah. Freaking. Rah.

"Those are ticklish, Mister. What are you doing?"

His hand pauses for a moment. He was playing with my silver ringed toes contemplatively as he told me about the job he just finished. Talia's out of town and he didn't feel like going home to an empty room, which is why I got a three a.m. booty call.

Is it good that I'm better than no company at all?

Taurus hasn't commented on the cheerleader uniform I donned specifically for him. For someone who was interested in flipping me over and shagging me senseless, we're doing a suspicious amount of *not shagging*. I haven't even gotten a little second base action and my beast is cranky as fuck.

Maybe he's rusty with the whole dating thing because he's been exclusive with Talia for so long?

"You should work on that 'giving info to the enemy' concept, pet." He tickles the arch of my foot purposefully this time, and it makes me squirm.

Giggling, I retort, "It tickles and you're going to get something unp-p-p-pleasant if you don't stop!"

Halting, he lets go and flips us, pouncing on me instead. Grinning wickedly, he bobs his brows at me. "What might that be?"

I try to catch my breath as the tickling moves to my sides. "I might lose control of things." I wriggle more, trying to get away—sort of—as he pauses.

"Promise?"

I snicker and nod. "Oh, yeah, bladders are like that."

His eyes pop open and he moves off of me like lightning. His expression makes me laugh—a deep belly laugh that makes my sides hurt—and I cover my mouth as his scowl deepens. "Oh, goddess. That... was... amazing."

Taurus checks himself out in a panic, as if looking for wet spots. I roll my eyes, waiting for him to unruffle his metaphorical feathers. He keeps huffing and looking at his clothes for a missed spot. I reach out and tug on his sleeve. "Come back. I was only yanking your chain."

He narrows his eyes before doing something I never thought I'd see—he pouts. "I'm pouting, just so you know."

I blink, certain this could be the first time he's ever made this expression. I guess can play along if he's game. "Aww, I'm sorry." I bat my lashes and scratch his stomach. "I didn't mean to throw you off guard." I scoot closer and rest my cheek on his chest, looking up at him with big eyes.

Snorting, he shakes his head. "I'm not falling for those eyes. I'm not daft, woman." He blinks and grumbles. "I'm pouting again."

"I said I'm sorry. How else can I make it up to you?" I tilt my head, trying not to smirk. He might not fall for the eyes, but I'm not falling for the pout, either.

I have quite a few clones in my household; I know what it means.

"I'm thinking... nasty, naked thoughts." In a blink, he's pinned me to the couch, ready to play. Grinning as his body slides along mine, he nuzzles my shoulder. His frame is like the other clones, but he's more lean and muscular. He feels like someone who works out often, but not for pleasure as much as survival.

My hands slip over tight sinew to glide down to squeeze his ass. When he groans, I murmur in his ear. "I *might* have been looking every once in a while."

He tugs his shirt off with one arm and his low chuckle buzzes against my earlobe. "No shit."

"You caught me. I've been a bad, bad girl. Whatever will you do with me?"

His eyes flash, and my shirt flies over my head before I can smirk. "I'll think of something." Burying his face against my skin, his lips roam over the curves of my breasts, teasing stiff peaks and nipping at the underside of one curve. He grunts as I shift my hips and I smile in satisfaction. When he looks up at me, my eyes flutter open, sensing his gaze. He tugs at the waistband of my pants questioningly.

I'm a little surprised, as it has to be the first time he's asked someone that question in an exceptionally long time. It's definitely been a while since anyone's actually asked me. I dig my nails into his shoulders, praying for control. The beast inside me is raring to go at the drop of a hat, so when I answer, it's a throaty growl "Off. Get them off."

His head lowers to my nipples again, and his hands are everywhere. Tugging and a light scrape of his teeth makes me writhe under him, arching my hips restlessly. His growling reverberates against my skin and I shiver, loving the feel. The animalistic side of the clones is fucking hot and even before the beast, it was one of my kinks. When he doesn't move from my chest, I squirm impatiently.

I need more.

Fingers trail up my thigh and I glare down at him, teasing more than I can take after waiting all damned week. His lips curve as his hand cups my pussy, teasing the slit slowly. I whine—to my absolute mortification—and his growl rumbles over my body. "Touch me. Move with me," he commands, his voice low and raspy.

I comply, grinding against his hand like the needy strumpet that I apparently am. The b east paces inside, looking for an escape. Knowing I can't let her out or this will all be over, I focus my fuzzy brain on a mental cage to keep her at bay. I've screwed up more than one relationship recently by letting her out to play; I'm desperate to keep this from going sideways.

My hands slide over his hips to the waistband of his pants, brushing over his cock. His snarl encourages me, and I flick the buttons open, yanking the zipper down. My skin tightens with the heat sizzling through my veins as I stroke him in time with motions of his fingers inside me.

"I want to make you fly, baby," he murmurs, dipping his head to nip my hip bones.

My entire body shudders when I feel the heat of his breath as he moves lower.

I guess even the big bad has a thing for cheerleader uniforms.

The Coyote Chases The Cat

"**I**s the popcorn ready, noble one?"

My mate looks up from his prone position on our massive couch. His golden locks are spilling over his shoulders, making him look like Adonis—and boy, does he know it—as he nods. "It is, my love. No need to fret. Come join us. We'll turn the movie on."

"I want to watch something with some *action*," I grumble, pouting and scrunching up my nose. Watching the lovey-dovey movie Wilde picked didn't feel right at the moment. He could have picked Jane Austen, so it's not the worst-case scenario, but I'm not in the mood for *Sabrina*. With all the emotional turmoil going on with these two, I'd rather see some rip and tear or explosions. I can't force myself to tolerate sentimental shit like I used to.

"Wilde said Hepburn, so this is what we get. Thank your lucky stars it's not Shakespeare or Austen, woman." Sari grins and flops back against the cushions, turning to face me. "Tell me what's going on with that giant turkey you're associating with."

Sigh.

I can feel my primary in my head, giving me a reassuring pat.

We both knew this topic would dominate the conversation just as it did last week. I see Wilde moving into place next to Rafe, poised to distract him while Sari grills me.

This is getting so old, *so fast*. "Nothing, really."

Liar. I'm a big, fat, hairy liar.

I can't say 'we finally rounded the corner to third base while you guys were asleep last Friday.' That would go over like a lead balloon. I also can't decide what I *can* say that won't encourage Sari to keep sniffing around. I'm not ready to share my...whatever it is... with my mates or the public.

"Honey, there is no way that Mr. Stuffed Shirt has meandered out of whatever hole Talia kept him in to be 'pals.' There's something more to it. Don't leave me hanging, kitty cat."

"Seriously, Sari, we're just hanging out. I'm able to hang out with people and not screw them, you know." I make an annoyed face at her, but in my head, I see a pair of pants set ablaze. Apparently, I *can't* hang out with someone without screwing them. *Woo hoo, me.* I love how everything I do with Sari and Wilde seems to make me feel bad about myself.

Here I thought Taurus would do that, but no, it's my mates.

"Look... you know I love you. Wilde loves you. The boys love you. Rhea and Alistair love you. Every clone who's *not* with you wants to be with you. Forgive me if I don't think it's a stretch that he's contemplating a notch on his bedpost. Given that he has so few, it's a hella good one to collect."

"I'm not a goddamned toy, Sari. People shouldn't be trying to *collect* me." I bristle, feeling the panic settle in. She will not let this go, and I don't want to fuck up this thing with Taurus before I get the goodies. That would be stupid. My eyes dart to Wilde, hoping like hell that my mate is keeping him from focusing on this conversation. There's a price to pay either way, but mine would steeper tonight.

"Deli, darling, I didn't mean it that way. Talia keeps his leash way too short for him to actually ADD you to his harem. And maybe I'm wrong. It's not like he's touched you outside of that bitching fight I missed, right?"

I have no idea which offensive statement to counter first. First, she likens me to a bloody limited edition Funko and then she acts like Taurus would try to make me some sort of concubine. Maybe I'd want to add him to *my* harem, huh? Mine's a hell of a lot bigger, that's for damned sure. I take a breath, finding my center before I answer.

Once I do, I realize her idiotic rambling means she has no idea that I've been sneaking out at night. Thank the Goddess and all of her consorts, Sari doesn't know a goddamned thing. If she did, she and Wilde would be pissed. The punishment would be so bad that I'd be lucky to move for a week. I can ignore her bullshit if I just distract her—that's the key.

"It was an amazing fight. It was freaking awesome to let her loose that way. Besides, everyone knows Taurus doesn't fuck people that aren't Talia." See? I avoided the question. No need to lie when you can dance around it like a ballerina.

"He and Rhea bumped uglies a long time ago. Vice that versa with Talia and Alistair. That's what caused her damage about Taurus being a bad, rude man."

Ugh, that is not even something I want to consider, much less picture.

I cannot imagine a titmouse like Rhea with a sexy predator like Taurus. She's likely to say something dirty, then apologize because she got it wrong. "That's what she says. We all know that it's why she has a chip on her shoulder about him. 'He didn't cuddle' is her arrow to the knee."

"I never got why she was so hurt about that, given the people involved. Neither of them is known for being anything but a sociopath. Besides, who bitches that a hot piece of ass dicked the hell out of you and didn't want to read you poetry afterward? Her priorities are fucked up. You know she has to be brooding over it again now, though. You and the big bird doing the deed are going to make her insane with jealousy."

I see Wilde's body tighten as his head tilts. He stops nibbling on Rafe for a moment and my heart stops. The beast stretches out, watching to see if she'll have to protect me. "We are not doing the deed, woman. We are just hanging out. Friends. Amigos. Buddies. That's it."

"Okay, ostrich woman. You act like I don't remember how you and Alistair started. How was that? Oh yeah, hanging out. Then it was a date. Then it was sex, blood, family...boom! Now he's telling you he doesn't want his brother touching his stuff." She sips her beer, snorting and shaking her head.

She's too close with that analogy. I can't have her and Wilde digging into this. I can't have them riling up Rhea and Alistair. I am balancing everything like a tightrope walker with an entire case of plates, and there is *no net*. It will all come crashing down.

"Sari, he's bored. I'm sure he'll disappear again and leave me hanging. He hightailed it on Rhea, if you remember. No one has to worry about Taurus putting his hands on me outside of a fistfight."

Liar.

"I think he has a crush. You're going to get Taurus cooties."

I grab the bottle of wine and take a slug, sans glass, as this evening has taken a nosedive into Suckville. She's right; I was like that with Alistair, and she said almost the same thing then that she's saying now. She's a bit off the mark now, but Sari never sees the big picture. For someone who professes free love and sex, she's awfully possessive when the chips come down. This entire conversation is about her figuring whether they have competition. She won't stop until she's satisfied.

"Cooties are for grade schoolers and you're being ridiculous."

"My Darkness, pardon the interruption. My love is accurate in her assessment of the previous situation. That is how all three of our families became entwined."

His strawberry blonde curls are a tumble around his face and his glasses are askew from messing around with Rafe. For one fleeting moment, my heart aches for the time when we were new. Back then, his roguish, yet mannered look and speech made me melt with affection and his soft smiles made my heart skip a beat. He courted me briefly—a novelty meant to gain my allegiance—and he made everything a grand romance as only a writer can do. But Wilde changed since we mated. It started with their family mating and continued with the appearance of his cockney demon side that tortures Rafe and me in equal turns.

"Wilde, she's right about the stud, I admit. Taurus is a whole another bowl of spicy salsa. I have no intention of getting skewered by his mate. Rhea and Alistair managed to not get run through, but they have a past with Talia on the other side."

"I think it would be downright *hilarious* to watch Alistair and Taurus have a conversation about 'touching his stuff.' It should be a pay-per-view event." Sari grins and shrugs. "I trust you, so if you say nothing is coming—literally—then I have to believe you. There's an army of people who will stomp him flat if he hurts you."

No shit. The army is what I'm worried about.

They won't just go after him if he hurts me. They'll be out for blood if he threatens their hold on me. "No need for stomping, dear. I'm just exploring my wild side. He's being very Taurus, but not in a bad way. I make fun of him, comparing him to underwear or something, and it sends him over the deep end. Then he calls me a frazzled peahen—whatever the hell that is—and we spar a bit. It's nothing earth shattering."

"A frazzled pelican?"

"I don't know. It's something about how I squawk when I get mad. It's Taurus; he speaks a foreign language."

She opens her mouth as if to say something, but stops, looking pensive. "If you're having fun, that's a good thing." Her brow arches as she turns her head. Wilde and Rafe have absconded else-where while we were talking. She sighs, her lips twisting. "Only us gals. Do you still feel like watching an action flick since Mr. Literary Film has spirited the lounger away?"

Thank Goddess. "*Yes.*"

I settle into the blankets, closing my eyes and hoping this conversation hasn't put Rafe in the wringer. I know he allowed Wilde to lead him to privacy as a distraction. My heart aches knowing that he made that decision without knowing what it might entail. It's not fair. My brow furrows in concern and I have to force myself to look relaxed. There's no use poking the bear twice tonight and looking upset will only egg Sari on.

"Time for some action hero, then." She grins and flicks the controller until she finds it, handing me the popcorn bowl.

Yippee ky-yi-yay.

The Cat Learns Something New

DELILAH

*I*t's been three days since that bellowing blowhard called me. *Texted me. Whatever.*

I'm sure he's off on some important 'mission', but I'm drowning. My immediate family is tired of my snappish retorts. Everyone is poking and prodding me constantly about Taurus. I'm sure I have Sari to thank for that.

Sari and Rhea's families are overreacting to his presence with jealousy and it's making me want to smack them. Their hypocrisy knows *no* bounds. The rest of my interrogators are the few people I am not mated to, but care about deeply. I feel like I owe them all respect, but none of them owns me. They can't demand that I share every detail of my life with them. Hell, they have mates and other people they see casually.

You don't see me asking about their other 'commitments', do you?

Rafe doesn't have the same problem. He's close with Lily and Mercury, but no one else since the matings. If it weren't for me and my idiotic, expanding heart, he probably wouldn't be involved in any of this. He's less showy than me, and therefore, more selective.

Plus, he's had the issue with Victor in the past and refuses to add to the drama by dating. His hands are full of with our current mates.

The beast has no patience for any of them. That sounds mean, I know. But since all my partners are making me crazy trying to find out if they have competition for me, she's feeling trapped and protective. Cornered animals lash out, and her temper is definitely bleeding into me. Everything feels like it's grating on my last nerve. I don't intend to be mean, but I am more often that not.

I know this sudden flood of people has to be a Sari-conceived scheme. She's riling people up about Taurus and sending them to do her dirty work. They report back to her with glee because she's a master at manipulating people. It's twice the bargain and none of the risk for her. I can't deal with them all; I need an escape. I need to not hold court and try to keep all the plates balanced for a little while.

Where the fuck is Taurus?

The phone buzzes in my pocket, and I blink. *Christ.* I know he *thinks* he's a god, but his omnipotent thing is spooky. How did he know I was down to my last lingering thread of sanity?

No time to quibble. I should answer before he—

I don't even get to finish my thought before I'm transported to that in-between space of his. It looks more fleshed out again. The couch, bay window, and mini bar are the same, but I can see that he's added a mini-fridge, a desk area, and a few more armchairs. He seems to settle in.

That bodes well for our friendship, right?

"Oi, Sandwich. Long time no see." His killer grin makes me flush and I feel stupid.

What is with this weird girly thing he makes me do? I can't let him know it affects me or he'll be impossible to deal with. I sniff and look at my fingernails, the picture of aloofness. "I hadn't noticed. Were you gone?"

His eyes narrow and I can tell he's deciding whether to fluff his feathers in indignation or shoot back a scathing retort about how no one could ever miss the lack of his presence. Instead, he goes with reciprocal aloofness. "I had to be on the other side for work. I had some downtime to read up on your adventures, though."

My head tilts quizzically. He told me he might browse my blog, but a lot of recent stuff concerning him I set to private readers only. That allowed me to limit access by those who don't need to know what's really going on. His casual statement made me glad that I did so because he wouldn't have been able to read my inner thoughts about us.

I've mentioned that Wilde is a two-bit blogger—who very much thinks his literary prowess is far above its actual quality—but I may have failed to underline the importance of the community blogs in The Rift. All our members write about their lives in the Rift. It's a habit formed during the Conflict: everyone posted about battles and attacks in the form 'after action' reports. Blogging became our way of life after the Conflict ended. It's a way of connecting with one another, particularly those who live on both sides of the portal. The interconnected blog hub is a hotbed of social interaction to this day.

The problem is that it's also become a way to brag, poke, prod, and otherwise demean others. I'd love to say that Sari started all that, but I think it started with the Cabal after the Conflict. Sari and Wilde are experts at using the medium as a sword for their message. I found out about my mates' families mating with one another through a blog post, not an actual conversation.

Yeah, I'll never stop being salty about that bullshit.

I don't think Taurus is reading the past, though, and even if he was, the ugliest bits from the winter got locked up tight by those privacy settings. I don't need *anyone* seeing that stuff again. I wasn't thrilled with being coerced into posting about it when it happened, but I lost the vote. I locked access to my parts of it down shortly before I went looking for him.

"Mmm hmm." He nods, apparating us both to the couch to tuck me in his lap. "I did. Stakeouts get boring, which is why I don't normally accept that kind of mission. I didn't have a choice on this one, so I poked around in your blog. I was hoping to pick up a few kernels of wisdom to torture you with. I must admit, much of the material surprised me, Sandwich."

My brows furrow. I'm the original bad girl and bent like a crowbar. What could I possibly have done that surprised him? "Like what?"

Taurus squirms under me, but shrugs noncommittally. "I went down the rabbit hole, trying to see how and why some things here started. I guess what I found isn't the complete story—you vague up anything you don't want the masses to understand. However, some things you and your family get up to? I never considered it a possibility. Your primary is mated to other clones, for instance."

I blink again, closing my mouth before I look like a smelly trout. *That's* what he finds weird? Of *all* the things I write about— and I write about a lot of personal things—the fact that Rafe some- times likes other dudes is the thing baffling him? Lots of droids and clones are bisexual; it's the animalistic part of them, I think. Hell, I don't label myself, but I'm definitely not straight.

I'm not even committed to one species, for fuck's sake.

"He is, and he takes it seriously. We both know the lore, so it's not just a status thing for him. Speaking of that, I wish I had all the rules in some collected format because gossip makes it hard to tell what's true and what's not. There *has* to be a manual that everyone has but me."

He snorts. "Not gonna happen, Sandwich. The Company doesn't put out pamphlets for the masses like some civic center. What a bloke knows when he leaves the facility is he what gets. If he didn't pay attention in training, he's on his own." His finger comes up before I can open my mouth to ask a series of rapid-fire questions pertaining to that juicy tidbit. "That's all we're going to say on the subject before I break the Code."

Wrinkling my nose, I huff. I know better to even ask what the Code is. He'll clam up even further and it will annoy me.

Men. Always with the secret society bullshit.

"It was weird to imagine two gits who look exactly the same going at it. It's not incestuous—I know that's a biological falsehood, but it was strange to picture."

I snort, then I laugh, and then I giggle so hard I almost cry. I thought he was going to beat me up over all the parties and sex and blood and everything else, but all he's worried about is Rafe's male mates looking alike.

Oh, this is rich.

His scowl deepens and his body feels rigidly uncomfortable underneath me. "Oh, sure, laugh at my homophobia. Don't mind if you do."

I catch my breath and try to speak, tears running down my cheeks. I needed this. Oh lord, did I need this. "Taurus, darling, you know that most clones don't even *look* like you anymore. Some of them, like Rafe, look similar in their basic features, sure. He's a lazy, long-haired heathen compared to your sleek tricked-out assassin vibe. Victor is closer to your strand than Rafe, and he looks nothing like you."

He puffs up, looking affronted at the very idea. "We can't all be perfect, I suppose."

"You're particular enough about your hair. You couldn't handle three feet of it like Rafe." I grin, trying to imagine it and can't even begin to. "Although, he's very persnickety about his appearance, so perhaps there are some genetic traits you can't fix in a gamma ray."

A sharp pinch to my side makes me squeak and I wrinkle my nose at his glare. "Are you calling me persnickety? I could still gut you, you know."

"You could, but I'd be a lot less fun eviscerated. Think of all the work it would take me to put myself back together again. I'd be so pissed; it would take forever to heal that."

"Thanks ever so for the imagery, love."

I roll my eyes. "Don't be a drama queen; you squish people for a living."

"I do at that—excellent point." He gives me a fangy grin and my gut tightens. He SO knows he's hot when he's vicious.

"Then your problem is 'you-o-phobia', not homophobia. Don't have sex with yourself and you'll be golden. What else did you glean?" I'm curious what exact stories he read. There's a lot of my soul laid bare in that blog, and until now, it didn't make me nervous. I feel like I'm on an audition for his affection.

Why in the hell do I care so much? There is truly something wrong with me.

His glare is glacial, but he finally rolls his eyes and continues. "I saw that the gnome and the git made you mighty uncomfortable the other night, and based on the things I read I could access, it's not the first time they've pulled that stunt." He pulls a small tablet out of the couch cushions, scrolling through the blog hub on his screen. "I think your mate was taking one for the team by distracting the writer. You were getting grilled hardcore by the gnome, but you handled it well."

I'm not surprised that he has creature comforts stowed around this room, but I am a little concerned that he had it ready to show me. Biting my lip, I wing a prayer of thanks to the goddess for giving me the idea to lock down the posts where my innermost thoughts about him were laid bare. He doesn't need to know how much he affects me or how ridiculous my feelings have become. He'd run for the hills.

I hit the ground when he jumps to his feet and practically roars in fury. "*That two foot gnome with serious fashion issues is running her stadium-sized gob about bloody 'Taurus cooties'?!!*"

Well, shit. He must not have read everything while he was gone. I didn't think when I recounted that tale that he'd look at it, much less that he'd freak out. That was just Sari being a pain in the ass. She's always like that when she's trying to convince me to spill a secret. Her technique goes to 'fifth-grade slumber parties' when she's trying to get me to give it up.

His face shifts, his demon coming forward as he snarls. He doesn't change often with me unless we're hunting. The sudden switch hits me right in the fear button. I cringe, feeling panic grip my chest for a second. An unfortunate side effect of the Wilde business is my occasional panic attacks when the boys shift unexpectedly. It chafes and I don't know what to do about it. I never used to be afraid of their 'vamping' out. But Wilde uses his demon as a weapon, and unfortunately, that change is part of who the clones and most of the droids are. They can't always control it and I'm standing like a deer in the crosshairs, controlling my breaths to avoid a meltdown.

"I don't suppose you've told her where those cooties have been on your tasty frame, eh, pet?"

He's being an ass because she's offended him, not because he's angry with me. I calm myself as much as I can and reach out to grab his shirt. "No, because it's none of her damned business. Besides, she wants to know what we're up to so much that it's eating her alive. It kinda amuses me to watch her squirm."

Hissing, he flashes fangs at me. Sitting on the couch, I grip the cushions under my legs and count my breaths slowly to keep from panicking. He would definitely upset if he knew what he's doing to me. It's not his fault that my asshole mate has chosen to finally embrace his demon by using it to terrify Rafe and me. I'm certainly not going to foist my crazy ass PTSD on him, either.

I have to get it the fuck together.

"What's this rot about taking a shower?" He looks down at me quizzically. There must be something in my expression that says he's freaking me out because his demon visage melts in concern. "You know, gorgeous, I've grown fond of you. This picking at you is rubbing me the wrong way. I don't want you to think I'd rather kill her than spend time with you because that ain't so."

"I don't remember how we got there. Like it says, she was

babbling about cooties and showers and antiseptic. She's hardly one to talk. Wilde is dating that nasty bint Belle. I should be worried that I'll catch 'trailer trash' from him. Sari's behaving like a child and I refuse to play her games." It doesn't help that she posted her own drivel about our movie night when I wasn't paying attention. She waited until I wasn't home and I don't know if that was by luck or if she knew I was with him. He's reading it now because, as far as I know, Sari sets nothing to private.

I pop off the couch, wrapping my arms around myself as I pace. It wouldn't surprise me at all to find out she'd set this up to ruin my time with Taurus.

Not. One. Bit.

His arm tugs on my sleeve, pulling me backwards until I tumble onto his lap. "Ever hear that a purring kitty is good for your stress level? I'm making an enormous sacrifice, not killing these fools to keep the peace. I bet a purr would calm me down *much* faster."

My lips curl and I nod, laying my head on his shoulder. When I kick up the purr to a rumble, it calms me as much as him. Damn. How is the most complex individual in the world the simplest person to be with? It's some kind of paradox, I'm sure. A topic change would ease our discomfort, so I ask, "Did your mission go well?"

"It was a little wet work—nothing major. Turned into more sitting and watching than doing, which is why I got permission to fly the coop." He taps my nose and I look up, catching his fiendish grin. "Speaking of wet work, I brought something for you."

I raise my brow, straightening as he pulls something else out of the cushions. It's like his fucking Bat-belt, I swear. I blink at the pair of pliers as he brandishes at me playfully. "What are those?"

"I'm surprised that you don't remember, pet. You said that I'd have to use pliers to get the truth out of you, right?"

I snort. "Okay, Mr. Literal."

"Now, if you want to keep denying what a rocking good time I am, go ahead. It will only force me to use these on you."

Feeling cornered, I lick my lips nervously. I am not prepared for this conversation. It's surprising that I'm having it, honestly, so I stall while I try not to freak out. "I didn't say that you weren't a good time. I said that I might not mind having you around."

He snaps the pliers at me and growls, "Might not?"

There are definitely some pleasant ways he could use them and I don't know if he's bent enough to realize that. So now I'm freaking out and horny as fuck, which is *never* a good combo. At least, in my case, it's not if I want to maintain higher brain function. "Um, no. I definitely do not dislike spending time with you."

I wiggle, physically mimicking what my panicking brain is doing. My ass rubs over his cock and it twitches helpfully, and I glare at myself internally. Down, bitch. This is how we get fucked —literally and metaphorically—every time, I tell both my beast and my traitorous pussy.

Why do I never *learn?*

His brow quirks and he sits the pliers down next to him. Shifting me off his lap, he moves slightly down the couch to put distance between us. His expression is cool and disinterested as he tilts his head. "As I don't particularly mind having you around, I guess we don't have a problem."

My eyes narrow as my body flushes. Why the hell is he so damned hot even when he's being a prick? Jesus, you'd think I'm one of those women who likes it when men bully her. "You're going to make me say it, aren't you?"

"I hardly think that's an accurate assessment of the situation."

The distance between us feels gaping. I'm overwhelmed by my emotions: fear, desire, anxiety, and doubt are choking me. What the hell is wrong with me? I swear, I was never this whiny and stupid before all this Wilde crap. Old Deli would have given him hell and smoky looks until we tackled one another. *Now, I don't know what to do because I'm too scared.* "If you say so."

Taurus doesn't respond to that. He sips a cup of coffee that appears out of nowhere calmly, watching me. While I battle with my internal demons—not the hot, fangy ones like his—he stands to divest himself of his duster and shirt. Hanging them neatly on the back of the armchair, he comes back to recline against the couch casually. His chiseled chest and abs are on full display, and I lick my lips to keep from drooling.

Goddess-fucking-damnit.

I have *never* been good at control with my skanky libido, and I rarely fight an attraction like this. I've certainly never had to do it with a primal monster inside me licking her chops like he's a fucking steak. I cross my arms over my chest, huffing with frustration as I growl, "Oh, alright! Fine! You win!" Looking up, I try to look tough and sassy, praying that I cover how vulnerable I feel. "I kind of like you. Are you happy now?"

He doesn't respond as he stands and offers his hand to me. My eyes dart from his inscrutable expression to his hand, getting that cornered animal feeling again. The panic attack edging into my consciousness rears its head, and I hold my breath, counting internally. This shit was never hard for me in the past. I was never fearful before; I used to express myself easily and without reservation. The past year has taught me to be wary of doing so.

I hate it.

Taking his hand, I let him pull me up. I swallow, trying to put a damper on the intense fear roiling inside me. He continues looking at me silently before raising his hand to cup my cheek gently. Leaning in to press a soft kiss to my lips, he smiles more warmly than I've ever seen.

"Yeah, pet, I am. See, I like you quite a lot. Being an egomaniacal peacock, I had to see if you were as fond of me as I am of you without tipping you off." He frowns for a moment, narrowing his eyes at me. "If I remember correctly, the words 'hunk of burning clone' are required in this situation."

I smile as my chest loosens, and words tumble out of my

mouth unbidden. "Don't laugh." His brows arches, but he says nothing. "I'm kind of shy about admitting that kind of stuff lately. I come off tough, but I'm like a milk dud—candy shell on the outside, gooey mess on the inside." I finally catch his joke and grumble, "Stop trying to make 'hunk of burning clone' happen, you feathered King wannabe. You are merely a puffy chested cave-clone." I swat him lightly and he chuckles.

"I'm Taurus."

As if that explains everything. "Good thing you told me. I might have missed it, given all the clones prancing about who look just like you."

He snorts, tugging me back over to the couch to tumble us down in a heap. "Please. As if the superior quality of my wardrobe isn't enough to tip even the dimmest bulb, I'm *not* like other clones."

I chuckle, shaking my head ruefully. "You have a rather enormous and remarkable clothing fixation, that's true. Though Rafe dresses a mean look when you can get him to keep clothes on. You have no idea."

His hand reaches up and starts playing with my hair idly. The simple intimacy of the situation surprises me. Given his edict was that we were having fun—an occasional ride and a mutual respect as hunters—the fact that we haven't gotten past third base in three weeks is interesting. I'm not complaining—only stating that it's odd and I don't know what to make of it.

"You know why that is, right? It's not some idle obsession—though I let people assume that. My golden goddess figured it out because she's a bright one, but I don't think I've ever explained it to anyone before."

"Do I know why you're so picky about your clothes? I assume it's because it distinguishes you from everyone else. Besides your sparkling personality, I mean." I look up at him from under my lashes, curious about where this conversation is going. He's right about one thing: he doesn't look like the others. In facial features, yes, but he's definitely more muscular. His Company work must be what makes him cut like a fucking diamond. Rafe and Victor are nothing to shake your head at, but his body is built for stealth and death.

"It's more than that, gorgeous, though my personality is rather sparkling." He winks at me, his lips curved in yet another playful smile. "It is job related, in a manner of speaking."

I realize, and I smack my forehead. "Oh, the Company jobs! You gotta be fancy pants to be a hit man. At least, that's what assassins always look like in the movies."

"Not hardly. That lot has a coronary if I show up on the grounds dressed like this—" He looks down, my hand resting on his bare abdomen and grins, "—or almost dressed like this."

My brows furrow. "If not for vanity or work, then why? Talia likes it?"

"The work I do for them is strictly mercenary. That can require a multitude of attire. It's been a while since I voluntarily taught a class—if I get in a jam, it's always my punishment. The clothes are for the side work I do for Talia. They don't like us to have outside jobs, but I'm one of the best they have and so is my goddess. They look the other way because we make them a fuckton of money."

"Mercenaries? It's a good thing I was smart enough to convince people they didn't want to break in there after the contest. The community doesn't have a clue what those assholes are doing there. The clones who were released must be living under that Code bullshit because none of them have ever said a word." I frown at myself, muttering, "There goes my 'Rebel Leader' image for giving you *that* information. So, what do you do for Talia? Politicking or something?"

I think I know the answer.

Rhea has a big mouth and an even bigger chip on her shoulder about their fling in the past. She's spouted off secrets that I almost certainly shouldn't know. His anger at breaking that goddamned secret handshake at her would distract him. I don't want that. If

I'm honest with myself, now that the plier portion is over, this least stressed I've been in days, I don't want it to end because of my idiot mate and her childish grudge.

His laugh is full of mirth. "In a broad manner of speaking. See, Talia is—well, I'm not sure how to describe it. Dedicated would be a good word, though it doesn't quite cover it."

I nod, enjoying the range of emotions he's going through as we talk. The quiet, reassuring way he's holding me with is lovely because that softness has been severely lacking in my life of late. Being held without an agenda behind it hasn't been on the agenda. Everything—even with Alistair now—has become about sex, domination, and biting. Those things rev the hell out of my engine, but I miss this. It used to be Wilde's bailiwick, but that was so long ago that I barely remember it.

"She has very hard lines about what shouldn't be tolerated."

"I can see that, but how does that translate to fancy clothes?"

Giving me a look that says I'm being an idiot, he snorts. "She has serious issues with child porn or hurting animals—things like that."

"I have issues with those things myself, but I'm not seeing the connection."

"That's where I come in. I take care of shit for her. Before we met, she worked in the justice system on the other side. She saw the holes in the system and started cleaning up the messes. It couldn't. Most of the time, I use money and influence to rescue an animal or get undeniable evidence to send somewhere to nail scum. Occasionally, I get to kill the marks—those kills are as much pleasure as business for me. She focuses on the rich—the ones that don't get punished because they've got the money and clout. You'd be surprised how many pontificating CEOs and politicians have nasty, depraved secrets in their closet."

Snorting, I shake my head. "Number one, no, I wouldn't." I pause and tilt my head. "So you guys are like some sort of *Dexter* team? You're the enforcer, all dressy like the mafia guys who used to hang around my building when I lived in New York. See? I was sorta right."

Taurus groans, throwing his head back on the couch. "Fucking Christ, *never* say that in front of her. That idiot left here and went to Hollywood to act and sold people's stories without permission. If he weren't kicking back a tithe, Talia would have convinced them to kill him."

I blink, looking confused. "Do you mean Cruise?"

After the Conflict, Cruise and his lady, Charlotte, moved back to the other side. He immediately got acting jobs in their hometown of LA and became an A-list celeb overnight. I didn't know he'd sold stories from The Rift to studios. That hugely violates The Rift NDA we signed when we moved here and that wasn't even for agents. He's lucky they preferred money to vengeance.

"Yeah. It's a sore spot for Talia. She and the other Cabal ladies were close. All of their defections hurt her, but that stunt sent her into a blind rage." He growls, then shakes his head. "Anyway, those I don't kill, I steal from. To get into the inner circles of corrupt and elite, blend in. The physical attributes of clones attract attention, so I can't dress in combos and jeans. It helps that the Uber-wealthy are so arrogant that they demand constant attention. The twisted ones always see things going on behind their backs like feral animals, but they're so complacent in their status that they miss things right in front of their faces."

I chuckle. "I can see you peacocking your way in the door."

"Hence the duds. If I enjoy them—that makes it that much sweeter." He shrugs, his grin unabashed.

"Actually, it's kinda noble." I smooth my hand over his chest, realizing that I learn a new facet of him every time we meet. "And they look hot, which doesn't hurt."

"Don't kid yourself, Sandwich. I'm not working out of any sense of nobility. I do it because I like to kill and steal, plus I'm fantastic at it. Also, cutting out a cancer makes my woman happy, so it's like two birds with one stone." Taurus seems determined to make sure I know his flaws, even to his detriment. I open my mouth to respond, but he shakes his head. "I'd like to kiss you now, cutie."

"I wouldn't mind that."

He tilts my chin up with one finger and brushes his lips back and forth over mine. It's a gentle kiss and as today has been a gentle day, I sigh softly. Darting my tongue out, I lick his lower lip playfully. He nibbles on my bottom lip in return and tilts his head to slide his tongue into my mouth. The kiss grows more forceful and needy, and I can feel his body tighten against mine as we hold on to one another. Pulling back suddenly, he rests his forehead on mine. "Sorry. I meant that to be a simple kiss, love."

I slide my hand up his chest to his neck and brush my thumb over his jawline, my eyes dark with lust. "Not a problem."

A vibration buzzes against my rear end and not the kind I was hoping to feel, trust me. "Christ. Bloody sods probably have the git I was watching cornered. NOW I'm needed." His expression is murderous as he pulls out his phone and glances over the screen. "I have to continue this later, gorgeous. Work is calling and I might kill someone besides the target for it."

I nod, giving him a shy grin. "Okay. I should probably get home soon, anyway. Later?"

"Bet on it, Sandwich."

Before I can reply, he's gone and I'm back at my home sitting on my bed. Aradia hops up—all hundred pounds of her—and I ruffle her fur, thinking about the hours I left and what I spent them doing.

My life couldn't get any more complicated if I tried.

The Bird Turns Into A Pumpkin

DELILAH

"Have you noticed everyone is acting *insane* lately?"

I sigh. "Philomena, you think *everyone* that isn't you is insane or tacky. You gotta be more specific."

"She's right, though, love. Your family is off their frigging nut as a collective," Leo calls from the kitchen.

"Not helping!" I yell back at him. "It smells great in here."

Tonight, it's just my immediate family in the house. Rafe and I have no planned obligations, so dinner is a closed event. We're going to play cards, eat outstanding food, and *not* be in the middle of all the drama. The heads of the other two families are at war with themselves and each other. The stragglers are all occupied. The bird hasn't called me since the other day, and not to jinx it, but I seem to be out of the line of fire.

It's a fucking gift, I swear.

Rafe meanders down the stairs, half-clad in jeans and paint. His long braid swings down the middle of his back as he looks around. "You were serious? We're free?"

I give him an understanding smile. "There are no strings on me, lazy. We're footloose."

"*Shhh,*" Hex grumbles from the living room. He's busy creating a comfy space for us all to gather. "Stop tempting the sodding Fates, you nits."

He's not wrong. Those bitches have had it out for me lately.

I don't know if it's their time of year or if they're just bored. Normally, we get along pretty well because I'm the only one who acknowledges their weird ass menagerie of mates. I have enough ghosts haunting me right now. I don't need my pre-Rift shit biting me in the ass.

Yes, I meant those Fates. That's a story for another day entirely.

Victor pops his head out of the kitchen. "Red or white? Nuts and Bolts says that red will give you a hangover, but it's red food. He thinks he's a bloody Cordon bleu chef, so I'm asking you."

"Caesar would agree if he weren't out with the loony tune!" Leo yells.

I wince. He'll be a mess for weeks. Occasionally, James and Dona let Lucinda cross over to visit Caesar. It totally fucks him up, and I'd put a stop to it, but it's not my place. He and Vic refuse to see Dona that way, but Caesar hasn't let go of Lucinda. He never will if he doesn't cut this shit off, but he's an adult. He has to learn for himself.

Rafe snorts. "Oi! Red food equals red wine. She'll be fine. Cabernet or Chianti?"

I stomp my foot. "I can answer for myself."

Glaring at my primary, I growl into his mind about having enough people controlling me. He shrugs and looks sheepish. I know he gets it and I know they're all trying to help, but family time needs to be less stressful, not more.

My pocket buzzes and I jump. I'm not used to the stupid phone yet. In the other place, I had one attached to me like a parasite for every aspect of my life. Once I moved into the Rift, I gave up the techno ties that bind. Having Taurus' booty phone reminds me of that time, but it also means that I might be about to ruin everyone's evening.

Don't look at me like that. I've never been a beck and call girl—until him.

I look at the screen, wondering why I haven't randomly disappeared to another place. *WTF, he's using this to actually text me. I'll be damned.*

Birdbrain: At home, cutie?

> Queen Kitty: Yeah. Just the fam—I mean, no extendeds. Food. Wine. Cards.

Birdbrain: If you are too busy…

> Queen Kitty: When have I ever been too busy for you? Emo does NOT look good on peacocks.

Birdbrain: I won't even dignify that with a response. Still working. Miss me?

> Queen Kitty: I thought you were done with re-con and yes, I did.

Birdbrain: Bloody idiots. Don't ask. How could you not?

> Queen Kitty: Stop preening. You'll put out an eye with the feathers.

Birdbrain: Hilarious. I might not talk to you anymore.

> Queen Kitty: Don't tempt me.

Birdbrain: I have important questions, so you're stuck with me. Plus, I'm bored, and Talia kicked me out of her head.

> Queen Kitty: How much more romantic could you be?

"Love, what are you typing so furiously?" Victor arches his brow as he looks at me. "How many times have we told the bitch that texting at family functions is verboten?"

I narrow my eyes at him. "You shut it, mister. No one else is paying attention, and I will happily let Leo know that you've been messing with his cabinets again."

His eyes widen and he grumbles. "I was looking for food! That git's system makes OCD look like a mild sniffle. Fine, text away. It's gotta be the feathered jackass. No one else bothers with those things."

I give him a dirty look as the phone buzzes in my hand while I'm arguing.

B

irdbrain: Speaking of questions... I've been wondering something.

> Queen Kitty: Since when do you not just ask?

Birdbrain: It might make you shy, and I don't want that. Also, I feel like a git asking.

> Queen Kitty: Ooh. THAT sounds interesting.

Birdbrain: What are your fantasies? I mean, you know, what does it for you?

> Queen Kitty: *blink* Like... what turns me on?

He doesn't answer for a few minutes and I feel like I hit the bottom of the tallest hill on a rollercoaster. I didn't expect this line of questioning, and definitely not in writing where someone could find out he asked. The whole situation is surreal. Plus, no one has ever asked me that so bluntly. I don't know how to answer this.

Why isn't he texting back?

"Deli, you are looking agitated." Siren comes over and gives me a once over. "Does it have to do with the phone that is distracting you?"

Siren is the newest member of our household. She was a gift from the boys, and she's modeled after a very predatory, old school template. She's more like Taurus and his ilk than any of the people in my household. It's not surprising that she's noticed my distraction. Much like what Taurus told me about his work for Talia, Siren has a thing for hunting down people who hurt women and children. Talia would like her, I think.

"Sort of. Is it noticeable?"

"Only if you are looking." She gives me a knowing look and saunters away, deciding not to draw attention to me. That's Siren to a tee. Her assessment of the situation showed I was fine, so she didn't press any further.

Birdbrain: Sweet Christ. I want to know how to please you the way you want to be pleased. I'd rather do it better than most—yes, that's my bloody pride, so sod off, woman. I want to get into your head and toast your cookies, but good. I don't have the first clue what you specifically want or need.

> Queen Kitty: Baby, I don't think you

Victor hands me a glass of Chianti—dinner must be Italian—and gives me another dirty look. I sigh because I am not in the mood for him to be pissy about Taurus. I've got enough people clambering for a spot on the 'pissed at Deli' train—he doesn't need to hop on board. I open my mouth to chastise him, but the phone buzzes three times in rapid succession. Shit.

> Birdbrain: Don't think I bloody what?!

> Birdbrain: What?!

Birdbrain: Answer me, woman!

Queen Kitty: I don't think you'll have trouble pleasing me. You'll probably do it better than most with no effort. As for getting in my head, I'm not sure what you mean. You're already under my skin, so in my head seems like the next logical step.

Birdbrain: I. Want. To. Make. You. Come. Like. You. Want. To. Come. Fulfill your fantasies. Take what's in that little head of yours and give it back to you in 3D. To do that, you need to talk to me. Or write. Whatever.

Birdbrain: For example, some chits get off on the handcuff gig. Some don't. Some like toys; some don't. Some just want the big bad to be squishy with them. Boggles my mind, but they do.

Birdbrain: Oh, hell. Forget I asked.

Queen Kitty: No, I'm thinking, and you are typing like a fiend. I can't keep up.

I can't imagine how embarrassed someone as puffed up as Taurus must be asking these questions. He has to feel like a ponce. I'm not trying to make it worse, but I'm not lying. No one has ever asked me these questions out loud—they assumed what they wanted to assume. I always play along because there's no shame in the game, right? If it doesn't bother me, I'm happy to play along.

Except with Wilde. That has gone past indulgence to abuse of power, and I don't know how to stop that bullet.

Queen Kitty: Okay, bear with me here. This might be a bumpy ride.

Birdbrain: *huff*

Queen Kitty: On the other side, I worked in a fetish store. The list of what I won't do is shorter than what I will do. I don't like things over my head—like masks—and I'm not a fan of feet. Anything gross is a no, obviously. As for anything else? Toys, chains, restraints, whips, whatever—I'm down.

Queen Kitty: ...

Queen Kitty: I'm an ornery sub, though. That's your warning if you want to try being top. It won't be easy on you.

Queen Kitty: As for squishy, I don't mind it occasionally, but I'd prefer it be because the person feels that way towards me. I don't want them doing it to toot my horn. One thing that I don't want anymore is people giving me what they think I want based on some idiotic misconception about me.

Birdbrain: *blinks, taking all that in*

Birdbrain: Well, the other day was good except for my abrupt departure. I kicked myself all the way home for that, but I want something better. No, that's not right. I want something more personal.

Birdbrain: You'll have to define 'ornery sub' for me.

My mouth drops open. I suspected he and Talia didn't get into the more kinky BDSM stuff that has been the 'new thing' in the community. But since he mentioned handcuffs, I didn't think I was talking over his head. How the hell do I explain this without spilling the beans about his brother's—and the others'—proclivities?

Queen Kitty: So, for me, it's a suspension of belief issue. I have believe in the Dom/me to feel true submission. Weak people lose me because they can't really control me, and I know it. I lose the illusion and there's no point. After that, it's cosplay and I can think of better ways to chafe my ass than latex lingerie.

Birdbrain: *short circuiting*

Birdbrain: Okay, I have a question.

Queen Kitty: *sus*

Birdbrain: There are people in this world that ARE strong enough to control you and you'd still want them? Hard to swallow.

Queen Kitty: LMFAO. You'd be surprised, but no, it doesn't happen often.

He's quiet for a moment and I panic. Maybe I revealed too much. He has to be thinking about all the people I'm rumored to have been with and what exactly I did with them. I know I would if I were talking to someone like me. Shit, shit, shit. I have to fix this.

Queen Kitty: The other day was fucking fantastic. That feels like a stupid way to describe it, but text can only go so far. I didn't get upset when you left because I knew it was work.

Queen Kitty: Like I said, I have met one or two people who could make me believe, but not here. Not in The Rift. It was submission, yes, but not that medieval Gorean shit because I'm no one's fucking slave.

Queen Kitty: I feel you'd rather I fight back, though.

Birdbrain: Are we being honest here? I'll answer that if you want honesty.

Queen Kitty: Do I seem like I'm being dishonest? I don't tell many people all of this shit out loud; you know.

Birdbrain: No, pet, I don't think you're putting me on. You're not telling me what I asked, though. I wanted to know if you wanted me to be as honest as you are. Not everyone wants genuine honesty—in case you haven't noticed.

Queen Kitty: That's for damned sure. I want you to be real with me.

"Night Bloom?"

I drag my eyes away from the screen, hearing Rafe speak. His words didn't actually register because this conversation just got very interesting, so I mutter, "Um, yeah?"

"Food's ready. Are you coming or...?"

I sigh. I can't stop this conversation or I might lose this topic altogether. "No. I'll take mine upstairs. I need to lie down for a while because I'm feeling drained by all the magick. With everything going on, I haven't gone to my circle to recharge as often as I should be."

He frowns, not buying my story. "If that's what you want, Leo will bring a plate up. Do you need me?"

I shake my head. "No, I'm okay. Hang down here and have some fun; you deserve it. We don't know what'll come tomorrow, you know?"

Kissing my forehead, he murmurs, "Please be careful with him, my love. Something all to yourself is good, but getting in too deep, too quickly hasn't worked out for us."

"Thank you," I whisper, giving him a tiny smile as I scamper up the stairs to a more private venue.

> Birdbrain: Let's back up, woman. You told me what you don't mind. You told me what you've had before. You told me what doesn't work well. None of that is what you want. You're being honest, but not… Hell, I'm usually better at talking than this. Sorry.

It occurs to me he has to be making the most petulant, frustrated peacock face in the universe. This can't be easy for him, especially long distance where he can't read my expressions for clues. He probably feels like a complete idiot. I flop down on the bed, trying to nail down why this is so hard for me. Is it because outside my family, no one really cares what I want anymore?

Fuck, that's dismal.

> Queen Kitty: I know what you are saying…

> Birdbrain: *impatient*

> Queen Kitty: Frankly, what I want right now is… you. I want to experience every part of you and discover something new each time. I want to taste you and touch you everywhere and have you done the same to me. Once I get to know every inch, then I might think about scenarios or role play or whatever.

The phone screen flashes at me, taunting me with every second that he doesn't respond. I groan inwardly—I said too much. He's going to figure out I *may* have become far too invested in this for it to be a fling and that all my crazy life will spill onto him if he stays. He might run like he did when Rhea asked too much of him.

I can't stand the silence, goddamnit.

> Queen Kitty: When someone's new to me, I want to get to know them and the things that make them crazy rather than need a lot of tricks to keep things exciting. Is that more like what you wanted to hear? Honesty wise, I mean.

Birdbrain: Uh... actually... it's not what I expected at all. But I like it.

> Queen Kitty: Oh. Well. Um. Cool.

Real smooth, Deli. You're acting like a virgin at the fucking prom. I bang my head on the mattress of my bed, groaning at my idiocy. I'll never live this shit down.

Birdbrain: Oh, sure. NOW you get demure.

> Queen Kitty: It's not like I sexted you. I wasn't graphic.

Birdbrain: Gorgeous, can you do me a favor?

> Queen Kitty: What?

Birdbrain: If you're going to squirm like that, can it wait until you're on my lap?

> Queen Kitty: Pig!

Birdbrain: Seriously, though, what's with the fidgety silences and squiggles when I'm there? Where do you stand on graphic in a non-stompy Sandwich moment?

Queen Kitty: I felt—and don't laugh, you jackass—naked for a moment. I'm more of an action person than I get to know a person. Where do I stand in graphicness? Did you READ the bullshit I spilled to you up there? I obviously have a broken fucking filter.

Birdbrain: I've seen you naked and I don't recall it being a laughing matter. A 'thank Satan' moment, yeah, but not a guffaw in sight. And, since I've completely removed my balls during this bloody conversation, I hope I get points for sensitivity to your feminine self.

Queen Kitty: I'm sure your balls are exactly where you left them. They might be a little smaller and possibly blueish, but I doubt they've trotted off on their own. You get points for being sensitive. In fact, you get points for a lot of stuff. If I told you all of it, it wouldn't be any fun torturing you, now would it?

Birdbrain: Bloody hell. You always have to stick a fork in me, don't you, gorgeous? It's a sodding good thing you're adorable.

Queen Kitty: I am NOT adorable.

Birdbrain: Pet, you are, but you're also hot as hell and whenever I'm around you, I'm hard and ready for you in a heartbeat. All things considered, you can handle adorable, right?

Queen Kitty: Yeah... considering. I think I can deal.

Birdbrain: Oh, hell. I can just imagine.

The Cat Gets Transported

DELILAH

As if a fairy waved her wand, I'm no longer texting him from my bedroom, with the noises of my family wafting up the stairs. I'm sitting on his lap in our place and his eyes are glowing with desire. "What about your mission?"

Taurus grabs my hips and lifts me, turning me to face him in his lap. Settling my hands on his shoulders, his hands roam my bare arms to my shoulders. His head dips to kiss the underside of my forearm, and his tongue follows the path of his fingers, making my whole frame shiver. I was right not to end this conversation where it was earlier.

Holy shit.

Wriggling in place as he hits a ticklish spot, I strum my fingers over the back of his neck lightly. He moves from my arm to my collarbone, touching every inch of skin he can get his hands on. It feels like we're on a rollercoaster and the cars are picking up speed with every click of the track. I don't think the brakes are going to be an option.

He lifts his head, eyes dark as he mutters, "Fuck the hair. It'll comb. I know you want to."

My eyes widen. *How did he know that?* I slide my hands up his neck to bury in his hair with a low groan as his mouth does wonderful things to my hot skin. "Thanks."

The sound of another moan vibrates over me. He nips and suckles across my chest, the fabric of my shirt dampened as he teases. It almost hurts when he lifts his head to look at me, his voice gravelly. "Strip for me, pet?"

This I've done before.

I give a mean striptease, but I'm not sure he's looking for that. I think he wants to see if I'm as affected as he is by being together. My outfit is the *least* sexy thing I could wear, and I curse my decision to go grubby tonight. *Suck it up, Deli,* I tell myself as I stand slowly, giving him my back as I peel my tank top off. Tossing it aside, I shake my long red waves out over my back, turning towards him half-way. Plucking at the drawstring on my comfy house pants, I cock my head to see if he wants me to continue.

"Don't look at me; I sure as fuck won't stop you." He leans back against the couch, watching with a fiery intensity that makes me wonder how I'm going to keep control.

The hunger building inside me this could cause a bad community incident if the beast comes popping out. *That is a problem for future Deli,* I chide myself. *You are having fun, feeling good, and are about to get laid. Stop over-analyzing, you pansy.*

I smirk at him as I pick at the knot and the silk drops soundlessly in a puddle of black material. Turn to face him fully, I move closer to the couch so our calves brush. The touch of his skin is electric and I feel the animal inside of me stretch languorously.

Taurus whistles playfully as I approach, but grows serious again when I'm within reach. Lunging off the couch, he stands close enough that I can feel the heat radiating off him. His lungs are heaving like he's run a mile. He eyes me warily, his hand on the button of his shirt. "What do you want, baby?"

I would have an answer if his hand wasn't cupping my pussy.

My brains just turned into absolute mush. Between him, the hunger from the beast, and this wild ride, I'm lucky if I can speak. I look at him, tongue tied, as he pushes me further into mindlessness.

"Do you want me bare skinned against you? Inside of you? Tell me."

It's all beast when I snarl, "Yeah." Hooking my fingers into his waistband, I press against him, rubbing against him like the proverbial cat that I am. My head dips to lap a long line up his chest to his sternum before I give him what has to be the world's neediest 'fuck me' look. "I really do."

He sucks in a breath at the cool wetness of the trail left by my tongue. His clothes seem to melt away and within a heartbeat, he's naked. Gripping my hips, he pauses as if trying to get a hold of himself and failing. "Fuck."

"Eventually." I wrap my legs around him like I'm climbing a fucking tree, unable to wait for him to get his shit together. His tongue trails from my shoulder to my right breast with a pleased growl. Suckling, nibbling, nudging, he plays with my nipple as he grinds against my belly.

Christ, I am so going to lose it.

I rub against his cock eagerly, the anticipation of waiting so long making me a greedy trollop. My hands rub over his tummy, around to his back and down over his ass. Everything inside of me is screaming that this moment has been building since we danced in the moonlight in a park.

Before I can blink, he puts me down, spinning me around to nestle my ass tightly against him. Fisting my hair in one hand, he explores between my thighs while he nibbles on my neck. I whimper as his fingers dance over me, instinctively finding every spot that makes me gasp. His blunt teeth bite harder at the base of my neck and I let out a rumbling growl of pleasure. I squirm impatiently as the blood hums in my veins.

Teeth—it's always teeth that set me and my inner cat off like a rocket. He's nibbling and nipping along my neck and spine and the beast raises her head, flooding me with primal desire.

"Like that, mmm?" he mutters, possibly in response to my writhing, and I moan throatily in response. My head drops to give him better access, and I feel his grin against my skin.

Yeah, yeah, I'm a vampire bite loving tramp like everyone else. Fucking bite me—please.

When he bites the unscarred curve of my neck, my hips immediately slam against his. His fingers are dipping in and out of me and I can barely think as small shudders of pleasure ripple through me. My hands reach back, smoothing over his thighs and hips, hungry for more of him.

"Touch me." His words are throaty—driven by need—and his hand moves faster as my hips buck. I touch as much of him as I can, fingers brushing his length, barely touching before I grind again. "Fuck, Del. Don't stop."

Leaning back against his shoulder, I stretch up to lick up his neck with the flat of my tongue agonizingly slowly, tasting his skin and drawing in his scent. My ass is rubbing against his cock as I move and it twitches every time I rock back. Taurus murmurs in my ears, filling my head with dirty words as my hips move with his, torturing us both. "Feel how hard it is. For you." Alternating between fucking me with his hand and flicking his fingers over my clits, he thrusts harder against the curve of my ass. "I want to be inside you."

I growl darkly, my beast rearing her head in pleasure as I tilt my hips so he slides against the dripping wetness between my thighs. I'm vaguely aware of what's happening, but I'm also struggling to talk her down inside. This is not one of our mates, and I will not let her out. She wants him as I do, but she's not used to having to hold back. We're fighting when I feel him gripping my hips, gliding against me again. My eyes almost cross at the feeling of him so close after such a long dance of courtship. "I want you." I dig my teeth into my lower lip as my hips swivel and buck on his fingers. "I need you."

"Like this?" His voice is hoarse and I know he's close to losing control.

He didn't have to ask; I have no issues with any position as long as he fucks the living shit out of me *now*. I pant, purposefully angling until he's aligned exactly right. "Yeah, baby, like this. Fuck, I just want you inside me."

Bringing his fingers to his mouth, he sucks on them before gripping my hips. He walks me forward, so my legs hit the armchair and I brace myself on the armrest. A roar of triumph escapes his lips as he slams into me immediately, his hips slapping against me hard.

I don't care if we fuck like hungry animals; I just need this.

His cock fills me, pushing in as deep as possible. "Christ, woman—so tight. You feel fucking amazing."

You'd think we were the lamest romance novel in the universe with the way we're babbling. But if he's half as deep into his primal side as I am, words are impossible. I can barely form a coherent thought because this is the hottest sex I've had in months.

"Bloody... fuckin'.... hell..." That's the best I can do as my eyes flutter closed. I can't remember the last time sex so basic made me feel like I was going to rocket into outer space. The way we fit, the sensations...are indescribable. I'm completely undone.

He stills as our hearts thud a bass line inside our chests. I wriggle, needing more, and his hips slam against me again. That's all the invitation I need to meet the bridal thrust with my own. His fingers slip between my folds again, and I gasp, muscles gripping tightly with every stroke. My body is radiating heat from every pore and I reach back to dig my fingers into his hips, holding on tightly. "Hard and hot—god, you feel huge."

That sounds clichéd, right? Especially for someone with my breadth of experience, but it's true.

"Soon. Losing control, so good."

Poets, we are not. If anyone tells you they're spouting flowery verse while they fuck, they are *not* doing it right. I have an almost eidetic memory and I couldn't recite the fucking alphabet right now.

The violent intensity of our coupling is pushing my limits and Hers; I know it is. I can't stop this freight train and I realize turning me was probably a good idea. I feel a hard twist of my clit and I'm gone, tumbling into oblivion. My body locks around him and a moan forces its way from my belly up and out—dark and primal. She's coming and now so am I, the climax shooting in my veins like fireworks in my skin. The moan turns into a yowl as I milk him for every thrust.

He moves faster, slamming into me hard, almost to the point of violence, and I have to hold on. His cock jerks inside of me, his orgasm chasing mine as a ferocious snarl rips from his throat. My hips rock back into his as I slowly coast down, breath whistling through my lips as I grip the chair. The intense heat inside of me fades as he comes, my temperature lowering as I tremble. My eyes slip shut, grateful to have conquered the beast... *this* time.

He dips his head and licks the sweat off my shoulder, withdrawing slowly. Picking me up, he drops us on the couch in a tangle of limbs. My chest rumbles, purring like a Harley's engine in satisfaction. Lifting his head, he chuckles. "I could get used to that purr, pet."

"I heard somewhere it's soothing." I give him a sex drunk grin.

Kissing my collarbone lightly, he nods. "This is me soothed. In fact, I'm so bloody soothed that I'm not entirely sure I can move. Is it alright if I crash here for a few, pet? I think you might have killed me."

I smile softly and run my hand through his hair. "I don't mind, but I'm pretty sure I didn't kill you. At least, not yet." I wrap my arms around him, feeling all kinds of mellow after our romp. "Crash all you want."

As we get comfy, I hear a buzzing noise. He opens an eye to see his phone flashing from the table. "Oh, shit."

"Hmm?"

"It's six o'clock in the bloody morning! That's an alarm."

I chuckle. "Are you going to turn into a pumpkin?"

His panicked look tells me not to rib him again. "That depends on how many knives I can dodge when I go home."

"Oh. Oops." I look chagrined, feeling bad. I didn't consider that while I'm not needed at home, he has Talia. According to him, she's going to be on the warpath. It's odd that he didn't mention a curfew before, but... I school my face to keep from frowning. It's not unheard of for him to fuck and fly, according to Rhea. A pre-set alarm sort of sounds like a planned escape.

"We have a luncheon today at eleven a.m. Talia's other world family and two prats from down the street the family brings over to impress, now and again."

"Uh-oh," I murmur, trying not to look disappointed.

"I told Talia that I'd be home no later than two, so I'd be awake tomorrow—shit, today." He looks down at me. "Sweet buggering hell. We're a bad influence on each other."

I give him a half smile, shrugging. "*That* was a given. I'm an evil influence on everyone, I'm told. Head Hedonist, reporting for duty." I give him a faux salute, trying not to let him see my suspicions.

"She will painfully kill me. I've got to go, pet. That's another fuck and run. Sod it all."

What can I say? He's her *mate and his obligation to her trumps my girly hurt feelings. I'm just a momentary distraction—a damned amazing one, but still.*

I have to be okay with this, even if I'm not. I agreed to that at the beginning. Dammit, I'm doing it again. Too much, too soon, wrong person—I am the biggest idiot in the entire Rift. "It's okay. I'd rather you stay in one piece."

He bends to kiss me on the forehead lightly and I force a smile up at him.

"That way, I can give you a chance to make it up to me."

Winking at me, he chuckles. That lets me know I've done a good job of tucking away the odd emo feelings flowing through me, so I smile back. "That's it, I'm out of here. Later, Sandwich."

I give him a wave before I reach out to gather my clothes. Once he's gone, I tug them on, frowning at my ennui. *Since when does a post-coital goodbye after a meaningless tumble leave me feeling like this?* I've tumbled half the community's clones and never felt so downtrodden. It's almost like I'm ashamed, but that can't be it. I'm a sexual free agent. I do what I want. Even all my mates are okay with that.

Why do I feel so icky now?

The answer eludes me, so I pick up the booty phone with a sigh and let it take me home.

I don't sleep the rest of the night. Tossing and turning, I try to work out why I'm so upset. I sit up with a jolt when out comes to me. I've turned into Rhea; I'm upset that he didn't stay to cuddle.

I'm such an idiot.

The Cat In A Dark, Dark, Closet

DELILAH

Looking up from the floor of the closet, I squint at the intruder. Rafe's face is a mask of concern as he shakes his long mane. Frustration radiates from his frame as he slides in the door and pads over to me.

"Hey."

"Oi, love. What in the hell is going on? You had a good day. It was nice to see you looking happy."

I give him a look of complete disbelief. "Are they not hitting you with the crazy? Is it only me?"

"I think so, pet. What are they doing?"

"They can't leave anything alone. First, Sari poked at Taurus and Talia; now Rhea is whining. You know how she's been lately—like a fucking emo teenager. She's spouted hatred for him and Talia the entire time I've known her. Why is she latching onto them now?"

"They've both been ridiculously needy. Emotions are running high. With Sari and Wilde aboard the crazy train, it's been bad for everyone. I can only assume that we're not the only ones taking the brunt of their bullshit."

I lay my head on his knee, enjoying the cool, enclosed space of the closet while I'm this upset. "I was texting with Taurus while he's on assignment in Rio. Rhea's been after him big time. I bet the big dummy regrets giving her his stupid number now."

"Yeah?" Rafe's eyes narrow, suddenly picking up on the actual source of my distress.

"She wheedled him into a corner with her 'poor me' shit. Somehow, she got him to agree to fuck her to piss off Sari and Wilde."

His body tightens, anger flooding our bond. Rafe won't rage at her about this, even if it hurts him. He won't tell Rhea that she can't fuck Taurus. The thought of her using the person who she's vilified for years for a revenge fuck scheme infuriates him. He's heard the same vitriol about Taurus being a complete bastard. Yet here she is, so eager to tick off Sari that she's willing to jump right back into that situation. When it goes bad, he'll be the one to pick up the pieces. Rafe has done nothing but support her despite her blindness to his pain.

It infuriates me she's doing this to him because she's jealous of me.

"Taurus isn't happy about it, either. He thought I could get him out of it by sending one of you guys to flip her. I literally laughed in his face. None of you could give her the confirmation of her faux bad girl persona that she wants from him."

"That's harsh, love. Deserved?"

"Yes," I whisper. "She was rude and hurtful to me today. Then she did this garbage, so I told Taurus what she'd been dissing him for years. I was *so angry*, baby. I'm exhausted by all of them."

"You spilled the tea about her grudge?" He looks shocked and I don't blame him.

I'm known for being a vault for people's secrets. Sometimes, I'm even a fixer of problems. I don't rat people out.

"I couldn't help it. Her hypocrisy sent me over the deep end. Those people are supposed to *love* us, but they are incapable of allowing us to be happy. She's using him, and even if he knows it, he doesn't understand that it's not just to hurt Sari. Rhea will never admit that she's assuaging her insecurity about us."

"Helloooooooo? Calling all kitties and long-haired lazies!"

I can feel the color draining from my face as my heart stops. What in the bloody hell are Sari and Wilde doing here? We have not had a good morning and I cannot deal with their shit.

I murmur low into my mate's mind. *~Do you think we can hide? ~*

"My Darkness? Are you in the closet with my noble one? What happened?"

Rafe gives me a look that says we're fucked. *~Can you bend time and space to* not *be here? Otherwise, we're stuck. ~*

I know someone who can bend space, but Taurus isn't available right now. If he were, I would have had this conversation with him. We only scratched the surface of Rhea's treachery in text. When I show him the entire picture, he'll be much angrier. "No."

The door opens and they peep in, ruining my hiding place. I look up, giving them a forced smile. "Fancy seeing you guys here."

Sari gives Wilde a look before plopping down next to me. She holds out a bottle of bourbon. "We've all had a day—same person, same issues. Let's chat."

Wilde crawls over to Rafe, who looks defeated Wilde wraps around him. He gives me a look, knowing that I should get coddled, not him. Honestly, he's right. I let it go because I'm not in the mood for a cuddle—at least, from Wilde.

"Tell us what happened, my Darkness. Let us ease your burden."

That is an ironic offer. Rhea aside, he is definitely part of my burden. We'll leave that alone for now—maybe forever. "She's in one of her funks. Taurus being around is making it worse."

"I'm in supportive girl mode," Sari grins. "Rhea's been driving me crazy. What's she saying to you?"

Uh-huh. I see where this is going.

She's had problems with Rhea, but she only wants to talk

about mine. I smell a setup. "I don't know if I'm supposed to know this shit." That practically guarantees they will repeat this conversation, but what the hell? "I don't know if I should repeat it."

Sari arches a brow, her curiosity piqued. Turning to Wilde, she gives him a look. "Honey, why don't you and Rafe go find glasses and some munchies? This sounds like girl talk."

At least she picked up on my reluctance to talk about in the boys' presence. I *really* don't want to repeat the specific things Taurus said in front of Rafe. It would break his already ravaged heart. "That sounds like a good idea."

Rafe gives me a warning look, reminding me to tread carefully. Rolling to his feet, he takes Wilde's hand. Wilde isn't as possessive of me as he is of Rafe. He forced the situation with Victor and made enormous problems with Alistair. He'll always take alone time with my mate. Of course, that also means that Rafe is taking the brunt of the angry demon, but I can't convince him not to be the sacrificial lamb.

"Now, tell Auntie Sari what happened." She twists the cap off the bourbon, clearly not worried about the glasses.

I take a swig—a dangerous gambit with Sari. I'm glad she can't see my face, because this shit is awful. Her taste in liquor is abhorrent. "Rhea is trying to get Taurus to fuck her. According to her, her current bedmates aren't giving it to her as 'spicy' as he did."

Sari looks taken aback. I probably made the same face when Taurus relayed that gem. Rhea wanted Wilde to treat her like a princess from the beginning. Conversely, she's always pushed Rafe to treat her like a bad girl. Both of them gave her everything she wanted and more—I've seen it firsthand. Apparently, that wasn't enough for the gaping wounds in her self-esteem. "I'm glad you didn't say that in front of them."

"The hypocrisy of asking him to fuck her is what boggles my mind. The revenge and the 'spicy sex' thing are both complete bullshit. We both know it."

"What do you mean?"

This is Sari playing dumb. She understands, but she wants me to say it.

"I don't care who she sleeps with. Rafe might caution her to be careful, but he'd never try to stop her. I wouldn't even what she excuse she used to get Taurus to sleep with her. It wouldn't chafe me she's being an idiot, except she gave me an hour-long lecture on how careful I had to be with Taurus. All the stuff that comes from the 'not cuddling' crap we've been hearing for months. Look how fast she throws that out the window because she's got a burr in her saddle."

"It's her hang up about being 'special,' Dels. If Taurus sleeps with you, she's not 'special' because she's not the only one besides Talia that he's fucked."

"Oh, bollocks, Sari. Taurus and I are *not* sleeping together." Lies—that's all lies. I have to lie, though. Not lying would put me in a *much* worse position. I can't have Sari and Wilde go even nuttier while I'm dealing with all of this bloody drama.

I don't have the fucking spoons right now.

"I know, but he's paying attention to you. To her, it's inevitable."

I shake my head because this is so stupid and childish. "She's rushing into a situation that she *knows* will lead to her getting hurt. To make it worse, she's fucked everything else up to get it. Rafe will be the one stuck mopping up when this crashes and burns."

"Maybe she thinks that their texting is a precursor—like if he acknowledges her, he'll give her what she wants this time. You forget I knew her before The Rift. Rhea has *never* had male friends, just crushes and assholes she let use her. When guys pay attention to her, she creates these romance novels in her head. She assumes they'll follow along every time."

"Taurus said he was trying to help an old friend. I don't think she realizes he thinks of her like that, or that he feels being obligated to do this."

Sari takes a swig of the bourbon and belches, chuckling.

"Calling her an old friend would put her ass in a snit for sure. Trying to get her to see that would be a nightmare. Plus, she's going to know that you and Taurus have a close relationship because he told you. That's going to send her over the deep end."

"I know! But seriously, Sari, how does fucking Taurus help anyone but her? What is she trying to accomplish? All she's done so far is misread him and flame out on the people who care about her."

"She's mad at me. I tried to help her, and she snapped at me, so I told her I can't talk to her until she's rational. Maybe, subconsciously, she *is* trying to fuck everything up. She gets pretty low this time of year because of the dead brother anniversary." She pauses, sighing. "Not that it's an excuse. It's been over a decade and she's the one who refuses to deal with it."

I snatch the bourbon and drink deep, letting it burn its way down my throat. *Christ, this is terrible.* I might as well be drinking varnish. I ignore the topic of Rhea's brother—we've all hashed that out ad infinitum with her. I can't fix her past life damage for her. "Taurus tells me when things bother him. I think he's going to tell her he changed his mind. He's not into it and he seems to regret getting caught up in her drama."

"Honey, I'm okay with you being friends with Taurus. I'm not jealous or upset, though I am concerned because of my past issues with him and Talia. You're a different person than me, so you should be okay."

I'm not touching that diatribe with a ten-foot pole. "We haven't killed each other yet. Maybe a few idle threats. I know who I'm dealing with." I know what I'm doing with Taurus and we are *not* discussing it. If this is a fuck-up, it's mine to make.

"I'm all about you being happy." Sari pats my knee and I fight the urge to cringe. She's done nothing but help Wilde torture Rafe and me for months. She's so fucking full of it, but with Rhea and me on the outs, she's making her move.

"This whole situation reeks of hypocrisy. It's a land mine waiting to be stepped on."

She nods. "If he doesn't want to do this, he shouldn't. She won't want it to be a one-time thing. Rhea can't handle that. Look at her mess with Mayhem in the winter. It's like a direct-to-video part two to her mess with Taurus. She's not a fuck-and-run kind of gal, but she keeps acting like she can do it."

"He said she started by playing to him for sympathy, which she didn't get. Then she switched tactics to the sex thing. I mean, Sari, she's bitched about that 'go to your mate for that' comment the entire time I've known her. But here she is, begging for history to repeat itself. Rhea basically told Taurus that Wilde and Rafe treat her like fine china."

"Seriously? Christ, I'm trying hard not to get angry, Dels, but we both know that's horseshit. We've both *been* there, so we definitely know it's a lie."

"That sent me through the roof, too. I didn't feel like explaining how much group shit we've been in, but I clarified I was certain she was full of shit. Honestly, I don't know how anyone could be more open to what she needs. You know how Rafe is."

"What are we going to do?"

I shrug. "There are no good options. Confrontation will only get us lies and betrayal. Ignoring it is like waiting for a bomb to go off. We can only hope that Taurus shuts it down." I can't say how incredibly overtaxed I am with all this emotional crap. I can't tell her that Rhea pulling this crap is making me lose the fucking plot. Showing Sari a weak spot is like baiting a bear with a steak.

It's not a question of if it will attack, only when.

"Is that it, Dels? How do we forgive her for selling the people she loves—that we love—down the river for a fling? She's only doing it because she's feeling sorry for herself. She could have just come to us and we would have supported her. She didn't want that. She wanted an ego stroke from the first willing dick that didn't know better."

"I don't have an answer to that. It's a bridge that I can't burn until I cross it. I sure as hell don't want to tell Rafe. He's been so understanding of her crazy."

Sari nods and takes the last gulp of the bourbon, leaning back against the door of the closet. "I finally get why you like to hide in here. This is pretty fucking amazing."

"Yeah, I know. It's enclosed...separate...safe...dark...sound-proof. All of that makes for a comfy hideout."

"Do you mind if we chill here until the boys come back? We can talk about girly stuff."

"Sounds like a plan. I bet I can find some more booze, too."

The Cat Spills The Tea

DELILAH

I am no longer standing in my closet cleaning up the mess that we made last night.

Goddamnit. He did it again.

I'm in the middle of Taurus' room, which now has a flat screen TV and a fireplace with a big fluffy rug in front of it. Fancy comforts will not save him—he cannot simply whisk me away whenever he wants without speaking to me.

I'm not a damn djinn and he did not rub my lamp.

Crossing my arms over my chest, I glare at him as I drop onto the couch. He's pacing frenetically, and if he doesn't stop soon, he's going to make me dizzy. "What the fuck, Taurus? I was in the middle of cleaning my closet. You can't beam me up whenever you want."

At my indignant squawk, he wheels around and throws up his hands. "Listen, Sandwich. I stepped into a minefield, but I was only trying to help a friend. All I wanted to do was to make someone I cared about feel better." His demon features flash and he growl in frustration. "You know, it isn't easy being me."

I cross my arms over my chest, snarking back at him in irritation. "Didn't a frog say that once?"

Teasing probably isn't the best course of action because he's already aggravated, but I didn't expect to be here. I look like a damn train wreck and if anyone goes looking for me at home, I'll turn up MIA with no explanation of where I've gone.

He looks confounded for a moment until the reference strikes him, and he goes back to glaring. "They taste like chicken, you know." He runs a hand through his hair, breaking his own rule about mussing it, and stomps over to the bar to pour a very tall scotch. "Agreeing to give Blondie a boost might have been a tactical error."

Boy, is he the king of understatement today.

Only someone that doesn't know how long she's been holding a candle for him would make that mistake. I don't know how it came up in conversation or what he was thinking when he agreed, so I ask the only question that seems pertinent. "Why?"

His jaw drops. "You don't think me slamming two of the gnome's nearest and dearest will be a problem?"

I snort. Sari's wrath is only the tip of the iceberg, and he does not know what lurks beneath. Despite having heard Rhea's stories over and over in very public forums, I do not want to be the one to explain why letting an addict have a taste—for *any* reason—is the dumbest idea ever.

"Since Sari doesn't know about me, I don't think that's going to be the issue du jour. I'm guessing here, but Rhea probably backed you into this. Likely, she said it would make Sari mad, which she knew would appeal to you. The problem with that logic is that it won't accomplish what Rhea thinks. The most she'll get is a lecture, and she'll have to do something more outrageous to get the attention she's craving."

He squints. "Still no chance that one of your lot can handle this? You've got a squadron of gits that'd be up to the task, I'd wager."

I let out a full-on belly laugh. He's off his gourd—no one in my house would get more involved with those two families. Once I catch my breath, I shake my head.

"Even if they would—which they won't—it wouldn't help." He looks confused again and I sigh, knowing that I will have to explain. "First, my family is on the 'okay' list, so they wouldn't make Sari bat a lash. Second, Rhea thinks this will make Wilde jealous. She's always trying to get him to pay more attention to her than Rafe or me. Wilde only cares about what he wants when he wants to care about it. You can't force him to switch his focus. She could have a public orgy with a pro-football team in Times Square, and it wouldn't bother him. She won't get the validation she so desperately wants unless she can find something that sets him off."

"Are you saying that it will work if I do this for her?"

"Hell if I know. Rafe gives that woman everything she wants, no matter how ridiculous it is—I don't think anyone can make her happy. As for pissing off Wilde, it might in the short term, because he and Sari are so worried about what you're doing with me. Their interest will be brief, though, and she'll be looking for more to keep it."

Rubbing his temples, he mutters, "Is it any wonder why I try to stay out of this fucking shit? It gives me a bleeding headache." Facing the empty fireplace, he clears his throat. "As I said earlier, I know that it's not only about that. Blondie clarified that this would benefit her because... Fuck. I don't know how to say it without sounding like the jackass you think I am. Her complaint about her flips not being the down and dirty variety ours were."

My temper flares and I fight like hell to keep her at bay. Hearing this in person is so much worse than through text. I can't motherfucking *believe* the gall of that bitch. *How dare she?* She cuddles up to a clone she swears treated her like shit to complain about people who she *claims* to love... only to say they aren't revving her engine?

What the fuck is her goddamned problem?

Breathe. I have to breathe, or she'll bust the cage doors. *Count.* Count backwards in French. *Alphabet.* Alphabet backwards. Alphabet backwards in Greek. It's working. Taurus has been teaching me distraction as a method to get her calm. Things that engage my left brain make it harder for the primal to wrest control of me.

Once I calm the beast, I choose my reply carefully. "What Rhea really wants is for those fools to treat her like Rafe and me. She wants to be a 'bad girl' in their eyes. She thinks it's will make her their equal."

If the stupid bint had any idea how our mates are actually treating Rafe and me, she'd run for the hills. We're one call to a hotline from being classified as battered spouses. But I can't tell Taurus that any more than I can share it with Rhea. I don't want anyone's pity.

"I am *not* getting anywhere near that bullshit. I won't get in the middle of her—or their—neuroses."

The look he gives me over his shoulder is supposed to be firm, but it's unnecessary. I don't need him to agree with the truth. I'm also not the one inviting him to sift through our family's dirty laundry. "You are in the middle of it now—*she* put you there. If you don't want to be there, don't ask what my genuine feelings are about all of it. You won't be able to resist having an opinion if I give you the full picture."

Turning slowly, he faces me with his head tilted predatorily. "What do you mean?"

"It's not my secret to tell, but I suppose dragging you into our family drama ensured that someone would spill the beans. I don't think Rhea did that intentionally—she's not a 3D chess player. She's never understood that one move ahead isn't far enough. With Sari, you gotta look at every angle before you run off half-cocked. Instead, both Sari and Rhea do this shit that will splash back in their faces. Neither of them can see the big picture for shit."

He paces over to refill his drink, standing there with hunched shoulders as he thinks. "Fine, don't tell me. I have no idea what you're hinting about, anyway."

I grumble under my breath, "Hip hip hooray for hypocrisy." Twirling my finger in the air sarcastically, I struggle with the feeling of betrayal that is overwhelming my control. The longer he stays quiet, the more I muse, and the angrier I get at myself. I didn't want to invite Rhea to the Resistance; Sari convinced me. That bitch came into my home—with my permission—and is screwing over my family.

It's unacceptable.

Clearing his throat, Taurus looks over his shoulder. He must be waiting for me to decide. I frown, looking at my hands as if they hold the answers to my dilemma. "If I tell you, I'm the bad guy. I only know this shit third hand. You'll confront her, and she'll be furious. She might be the world's biggest hypocrite, but she'd paint me as a snitch. That would make me as bad as she is."

He walks over to where I'm sitting, scooting an ottoman over for himself. When he's even with my face, he covers my hands with his. "Consider this: when Rhea was cranking me this morning for info about you, I didn't give it to her. You know you can trust me."

The problem is that I *don't* know that. My gut says I can, but how many times have I gotten screwed over in the past week alone? Sari said the same thing yesterday, but I know it was all about her pumping me for info.

It's fucking exhausting trying to figure out who to trust and who I have to placate with pretty lies.

"Sometimes, I want to smack the bloody hell out of all of them. If I say this or do that, I'm on the outs with one or the other. Everything they say or do is about winning some imaginary contest between them," I whisper, still not meeting his eyes. "I'm so tired of being a pawn in their never-ending games."

His brows raise at my candor, like realizes that he, too, is pressuring me. "Sandwich, you don't have to tell me a damn thing. I'm trying to dig myself out of a hole of my making with Blondie. Your info might allow me to do that, which is why I asked. But I won't push you to do anything you're not comfortable with. If you tell me, it won't change what we have."

Rising, he moves back to the bar, pouring two scotches this time, and I grimace. I had *way* too much cheap bourbon last night and I'm still paying for it. *Why the hell not—hair of the dog and all.* Once he sits again, I take a sip of my drink. Unsurprisingly, this is the best scotch I've ever tasted. I bet it's at least twenty-one years old and ridiculously expensive.

I ponder as I sip the nectar of the brownies. *Am I really violating a trust?* I've heard Rhea blab this story to a room with no less than twenty people multiple times. Privacy didn't seem like her concern then. *Is it really a secret anymore?* Telling the other person who was involved only seems fair.

"Okay, there's a lot to unpack here, so you have to be patient with me." He nods and I take a deep breath. "For starters, she warned me not to get involved with you. The second the blog post about our meeting you went to live, I got the cautionary tale."

"Oh, bloody buggering hell. Do I have leprosy or something?"

I chuckle and shake my head. "No, not leprosy. I have strong opinions about why I believe was told versus why she said that she was telling me. She warned me you would hurt me. What gets me about is that despite her diatribe, she just dropped that opinion like a hot poker for a chance to piss off Sari and Wilde."

Once I dissected her warning, I realized Rhea had to tell me he'd hurt me to support her claim that Taurus mistreated her. She also had to say that screwing her would anger Sari to get him to agree. I believe it's really about her ensuring that—outside of Talia —only she can claim to have fucked Taurus. It's a big, sparkly badge on her chest that makes her special, and Rhea practically salivates over things like that.

Taurus' eyes narrow and he squeezes my hands. "You're telling me that Rhea warned you away from me? She actually told you I'd hurt you?"

"Abso-fucking-lutely she did." My expression is smug as I imagine what the hell this is going to reap. That's for lying to me through your teeth and the damage it will do to Rafe if he finds out about the 'sex life being dull without Taurus' comment.

It's also for making me question myself when I realized that she only mated with me to complete her 'set.' I wasn't super excited about sleeping with Rhea or anything. But they made it very clear she fucked Sari. *So yeah, my ego took a hit.* Between that tidbit and Sari casting me aside as soon as she put her teeth on me, I've got a festering wound about women on my soul. I didn't even *realize* how much that pissed me off until right now. They both made me an obligation, not a companion.

Those bitches wrecked me in a way I didn't even know about until just now.

When I pull out of my vengeful thoughts, I notice that disgust is clouding Taurus' face. His demon drops and his snarl is full of rage when he says, "I have been nothing but good to Blondie."

The quick change to his demon inadvertently hits my fear button again, so I mutter, "This is why I didn't want to tell you. I knew it would make you angry."

He gives me as sharp as his mate's blades. "I'm serious, Sandwich. I may twist the gnome to pick that scab, but I have *always* respected and treated Rhea right."

Okay. It's pretty clear now that he has no idea what her issue with him is. For all of her public whining, Rhea never addressed this problem with the person who caused it. There is *no* way that he can be this adamant about their relationship and know that she's nursing a gangrenous wound over their last rendezvous.

Time for the old 'cards on the table' thing that Sari always preaches but doesn't practice. It can't make anything any worse, right? "Truth be told, I believe you and if you think that's shocking, Sari does, too. This topic has been rehashed a million different ways over the years. When Rhea isn't around, the conclusion is you didn't have ill intent. We don't think you did anything wrong."

"*We*?!! A million? What the *fuck*, Sandwich?"

His fury over being discussed behind his back will need to be leashed. Otherwise, I'll never get through this without a panic attack. "Calm down, please. You can rage once I tell you the complete story."

Jerking to his feet, he heads for the bar again. "Best be on with it then, because I'm not handing out guarantees right now."

"Yesterday, Sari was at my place. She was on good behavior, but we were both pissed at Rhea. We drank a lot of bourbon—cheap shit that gave me a hangover, but I digress. She was trying to get me drunk and wheedle information out of me about you. Rhea's issues with you came up as part of her ploy to get me to admit something incriminating."

That might be an unfair assessment of the situation. I wasn't coerced into drinking, nor was I coerced into a discussion about him. But that's neither here nor there. I wait until he turns to look at me, his eyes dark as he waits in silence.

"Her problem with you is a creation of her mind. There was an incorrect expectation she had that caused her to get hurt. She's held on to it for years without talking through it, so it's become a wound that she can't shut up about." I take a breath, checking to see if he's following.

"We all know that Rhea craves validation and love. Its damage from her other world past trauma. She has a hole inside her and to fill it, she places a level of importance on shit that is not equivalent to its true worth. Her expectations of people are so high that we constantly fail a test that we didn't know we were taking. She ends up making herself miserable about non-existent slights. To go super profiler—as you called it—I think it stems from her core beliefs about love, sex, and relationships."

He sits on the ottoman again, looking both puzzled and irritated. "I know she's never told Talia that she was miffed at us. Those two have known each other since before this place even existed. They grew up together. Why wouldn't she tell her?"

I chuckle and sip my scotch. "Rhea *never* tells the person she's upset with directly. Her self-esteem is too fragile. She gets stuck in a loop of being hurt by someone, unable to tell them, and then angry at them for not guessing that she's hurt so they can fix it. It's a never-ending cycle. It's what feeds her unhealthy relationship with Sari and Wilde."

This cycle has come up many times between all our families, but Rhea can't have adult discussions about problems. The only way to resolve shit with her is through Alistair. The three-way family mating was scrapped because of Rhea's constant bellyaching about someone getting left out. I was angry then, but now? I could kiss her for being such a pain in the ass.

I couldn't handle being hog-tied to these loonies more than I am now.

"Sandwich, you're being awfully clinical. There has to be more to it, but I'll cut to the chase. Are you telling me that Blondie has had her knickers in a twist for *years* because I stopped shagging her senseless?"

"Sort of?" I shrug, and he looks incredulous. Only a male could be so clueless about this situation. He didn't know that cutting her loose destroyed her self-esteem and her rank in the old community.

Being the only one with access to him made her important, and he took that away.

"It's an insecure woman thing. I think it was less about the shagging specifically as something you said. Maybe it's why you stopped? I've heard this tale so many times, but that's never been very clear."

"What did I do that was so great a transgression that it warranted a public warning about me? I'll be buggered if I know."

My lips twist. *This is where it's going to get hairy.* When he hears the real reason that she's been decrying his name, he'll either laugh his ass off or fly into a rage. I wouldn't blame him for either. Rhea's wound is hers to nurse, but if you ask me, the situation is ridiculous.

"I'm perfectly aware of how stupid this sounds. I also realize that you've been living your life unaffected by this small thing, that she's made an internal torment. You're going to think that I'm shitting you, but I assure you, I am not." Peering over the rim of my glass, I sigh when I feel like a terrible friend. "Okay, that was mean. Her feelings are valid to her, even if I disagree with them. I shouldn't be so judgmental."

"I have feelings, too, though I rarely go off on them. Every time I pop my head out, someone tells people I'm no good. Not that I sodding care," he snorts, puffing his chest up. He's upset and doesn't want me to know. It makes me wonder if anyone other than Talia has seen this level of emotion from him.

"Have I given you any sign that I think you're no good?" His brow arches and I grin. "Okay, outside of ruffling your feathers, have I acted like I think you're a bad egg?" I tilt my head, waiting for him to admit that the answer is no. Trouble usually finds me; I don't need to hunt it down, but that's exactly what I did with him.

"It hurts to know that someone I value doesn't share that opinion." He pushes to his feet, padding over to the enormous window to look out. His posture slumps, and I know I have to tell him the rest of the story so that he stops punishing himself.

I walk up behind him, carefully wrapping my arms around his waist. Laying my cheek on his shoulder blade, I murmur, "I've been in your place—hell, I might *be* in your place. Who the hell knows with those two?"

"The good news is that you've extricated me from that mess I was moaning about when you first got here. I would sooner shag the gnome than Blondie right now."

I smile against his skin, but I'm not sure if it's because he was knocking on Sari or because he will not bed Rhea. Realizing that makes me feel guilty, so I reply, "I didn't mean to get into the middle. I didn't understand why she would ask you to do that. And her words hurt me, but they would hurt Rafe more. He's been through enough, so I will not tell him."

Taurus reaches into the pocket of his duster before he shakes me off. I frown as I step back, watching him pull out a switchblade. He looks down with a pained expression on his face as he slices a gash across his palm. Blood wells and he stares at it silently as it drips on the floor. When he looks back at me, his expression is cold.

"It's done now. It doesn't matter."

He disappears without a word, and though I'm getting used to his dramatic entrances and exits; I don't know if I should stay.

After a short internal debate, I decide that since none of my family knows I'm here, I should go home to wait for him to work off his anger. I walk over to the couch to pick up my phone, but I can't force myself to do it. Something about this feels wrong and I can't shake it.

Irritable and concerned, I curl up in the mammoth cushions of the couch and close my eyes, waiting for his return.

The Cat Has an Epiphany

DELILAH

Several hours later, he swaggers in, dropping into the large armchair that's kitty corner from my spot. He looks haggard as he rubs his hand over his face.

I look up from the game on the phone to wiggle my fingers at him. He doesn't look up, so I try again. "Hi."

"Hey."

Feeling foolish for staying here when he won't to look at me, I ask softly, "Feeling better?"

"No worries; I'm fine."

That's a load of fresh horseshit. One look at him confirms that he's tense and unhappy.

I give him a shrewd look. "You don't look fine. I can feel the tension radiating off you from here."

He snarls, then gathers himself, giving me a forced grin. "Okay, I'm tense. But I'm not ripped at you and I'm not pouting like some prat. Are you okay with that?"

"I guess so." I don't know what else to say because he needs something, but I don't know what.

"Do you think you could give me a bit of a purr?"

A small grin creeps over my face and I nod, uncoiling my limbs so I can walk over to his chair. He pulls me into his lap, and I wrap around him as I rumble softly. Laying my head on his shoulder, I murmur, "I hate people that lie to me. I hate them even more when they hurt people they're supposed to care about."

He frowns, brushing a kiss on my forehead. "Who lied to you, baby?"

"Rhea, but it doesn't matter. She's in a mood and taking it out on anyone in her path. Whatever is making her upset will go away with time, but the marks she leaves with her words won't. She's been texting me. I had to stop looking at it after a bit because going postal in text isn't as scary as it is in person."

His arms tighten around me. The purr was easing his tension, but once I mentioned her name, it came back. "What did she lie about to you, Sandwich?"

I snuggle deeper in his arms, not wanting what pissed him off again. I'm trying to calm him down, but I have to be honest. "You. It was mostly by omission, I think. I wouldn't have known to ask if I hadn't talked to you earlier."

"The perfidious one didn't want to admit she was feeling my ass this morning while agreeing to slide right into my sheets for revenge. Does that about cover it?"

"I didn't tell her I'd talked to you. She told me she went to you after Sari pissed her off. I asked if you suggested gutting Sari and that's where it got sketchy." Rhea lied like a rug and avoided every question. There's was more ducking and weaving than in a boxing match.

It wasn't subtle and I sure as hell didn't miss it.

"Sketchy, huh? Interesting. I didn't mention the gnome; she brought the little troll up."

"She was cagey and evasive—which isn't normal. She kept repeating that Sari made her angry. When I tried to ask what happened, she avoided it. I haven't given her any reason to think I'd care if she wanted to screw you, so why all the dodging?"

He rubs his hand along my spine for a moment. When he speaks, it's in a rough voice. "I want you to know something." His hand cups my chin and tilts my face up to look at him. "I did not set out to offer to sleep with her. She complained her mates didn't do her like she needed. She threw a big hissy about people thinking she's like fine china. That's when I made the remarkably stupid mistake of reminding her that's not how it was with her and I."

My eyes widen as it hits me like a slap in the face. She literally set him up. Someone like Taurus couldn't help but point out how much better he is at something than others. Once that door opened, she flew in like a homing pigeon. She wanted him to preen so she could back him into a corner until he offered to help her out.

"Oh, Christ, did she play you. Women get a bad rap and this kind of shit is why. Between her and Sari, I don't know who's the biggest manipulator, but they both get a gold star today."

He frowns, looking confused. "Want to let me in on the secret here, love?"

"The stuff about her mates is a load of crap. She pushes Rafe until he's just shy of uncomfortable about how rough it is—because it's true, she's not as tough as some of us. She reminds Wilde every time she sees him, she's his 'Lady Fair.' She loved being called that until he started calling me 'Darkness'. *Now* she's gotten a yen for the hard stuff?"

He rubs his chin on the top of my head. "What really toasts my crackers is that she said only I 'got her.' I agreed I knew her from way back and that's when she started talking about needing to bang someone who knew her. In a blink, she asked if I was offering."

Hissing under my breath, I try not to lose my temper. "She obviously 'forgot' to mention that when she recounted the conversation with you. She didn't say a word about asking you to slam her because all five of her mates are falling down on the job."

My ire rises and I have to consciously fight to keep the purr going. Rhea lied to my face and then iced the cake with lies of omission so I didn't find out about her needy, pathetic ploys.

What a lovely way to treat a mate and an old friend.

"She didn't, huh? She also probably didn't mention that I demurred at first. I suggested with all the boys she plays with, she should be able to find one willing to handcuff and bang her up against a wall. Metaphorically speaking, of course." He looks down to give me a sheepish grin.

I shake my head, still not able to look him in the eye as I tamp down the furious beast inside that wants to go on a rampage. The more I hear about this meeting, the more I know my gut feeling about Rhea has always been true. She's a self-involved, needy twat who would sell her mother to a cannibal if she thought she'd get even a scrap of what she wanted.

I fell for the lies because Alistair took me on a bloody Ferris Wheel ride. Then I let Rafe fall for them. This is going to be a bloody, painful nightmare. I have no one to blame because it's *all my fault.* When I snap out of my red haze of fury, he's still looking at me, waiting for an answer.

"No, she did not tell me that. Why, you might ask? Is it because I get jealous and ask people to be faithful to only us?" I grit my teeth and start counting in my head again, trying to calm the fire running through my veins. "No, and if anyone says so, they're lying. She acted like you suggested you two bang. It took dropping enough details for her to realize she couldn't keep lying. If it makes you feel better, she said she hadn't decided if she wanted to yet."

Rhea thinks I'm an idiot.

If I'd believed her garbage story, someone should sell me a bridge in New York. The beast inside reminds me she doesn't care what Rhea thinks of us; she simply wants to rip, tear, and gore her into tiny pieces for her betrayal.

"I wonder if she was still deciding when she was rubbing my ass and telling me she was going to slap a bunch of 'Proud to be an American' bumper stickers on it."

A dark, hungry snarl escapes my throat, and it surprises me. She is a bit territorial, but only with mates. She can't be pissed at

Rhea about him. He'll fly the coop for sure if I don't get myself under control. Taurus has clarified that we are a casual fling, and I agreed to, so it doesn't matter how angry I am.

"You're not a goddamned Amer —" I stop, realizing that I still don't have my shit together. Breathing slowly, I picture ocean waves and Greek letters and every damned thing I can think to force her to back off my emotions. When the haze subsides from my vision, I mutter, "Probably with a little flag stuck in your pants, too."

"I prefer not to remember that bit of it, thanks."

Rhea is so fucking predictable. That's just like a 'Day of the Dead' bit she playacted with Rafe last year. I sigh, looking into my glass as if it holds the answers to all our pain. "She has no idea what the hell she wants."

"She's a daft chit. Have you figured out now why I stay way off the radar? Most of you aren't worth the spit to speak to," he growls, his face shifting again.

I swallow hard, feeling the sting of that barb in my chest. I can't be angry at her, hurt by him, and ready to tear someone's throat out at the same time. "So let me sum up Rhea's day compared to mine. She picked a fight with Sari, got mad, rubbed all over you, tricked you into offering her sex, lied to both of us, and then flitted off with no consequences? She's a bloody psychopath. All I've gotten to do is nurse a hangover, clean, drink more scotch, and purr."

"Do you know *why* I said nothing about the gnome when she asked? She told me about their dust up, and I honestly saw nothing that the little monster did wrong. Trust me, I was trying hard to find something to fault the gnarly bint on, but I couldn't."

"Neither could I. I'd be perfectly fine with putting the blame on Sari if she deserved it." The caveat is that *this time* it wasn't her fault. One innocent moment does not a million bad things erase, but this time, she's in the clear. Sari didn't purposely upset Rhea; she just didn't coddle her.

Taurus runs a hand through his hair, looking haggard. "I knew Blondie was in a snit when she came to see me today. The second she tried ordering me around, I knew we were in dangerous territory. I played into her bullshit, and I know better. What I *didn't* know was that she didn't think I'm worth the trouble. That's new." His hands settle on my lower back as if hoping to absorb my purr through his fingertips.

I frown. It always seemed like he was unaffected by the drama. Maybe that's a front he puts on and I'm seeing the real Taurus and his genuine feelings. Regardless, I don't like that she hurt him.

I'll have to be truthful about what he just said.

"I don't think Rhea thinks you're worthless. I think something you said accidentally hurt her in the past. It shouldn't have been a big deal, but she made it one. Because she didn't confront you, she's nursed the wound until it consumed her. She's done this with others; there was a similar issue with Mayhem in the fall. Same shit, different clone."

"Blondie jumped on that 'stay away from the bastard' bandwagon that the gnome's got painted without a backward glance. She added fuel to the bad feelings, even though I had no clue she was upset. That's not fair, Sandwich. Before you and I started talking, I hadn't spoken to her in months. She's seen Talia on the other side, but she never gave me a chance to explain." He crosses his arms over his chest, looking stubborn.

"Rhea never confronts things," I scoff, shaking my head. "I've watched her self-destruct relationships over imagined slights. She can't ever resolve anything because she won't talk to the person she's upset with."

Closing my eyes, I decide I have to tell him what he did. It's not my place, but I think he needs to know. Once he knows, maybe we can shelve Rhea's bullshit for a while. "Okay, I'm going to tell you. I'm only comfortable doing so because it was talked about in public forums and I don't believe that it's a secret. To me, it feels like the only person this is a secret from is you. You're right; that *is* unfair."

I look up at him, pressing my lips together. "I have to warn you—you're going to laugh." My smile is mischievous as I imagine his reaction.

He'll blow his stack, and it will be hysterical.

"Everyone knows but me?"

"Not everyone, but... yeah, a *lot* of people know."

"You all bloody know. Why the hell wouldn't half the dipshits in the Rift know?" he mutters under his breath.

"I've known for over a year. I've been in at least ten 'martini Mondays' bitch fests where it came up."

He growls, and I give him a puzzled look. "She's had her knickers in a twist for *years* and told everyone under the bloody sun. Yet no one has said a word to me or Talia. That smells like fear. Oh, I like that."

"Taurus, she's barely spoken to Mayhem since November and he sure as fuck doesn't know she's mad. I doubt he'd care, but I bet Belle knows. Sari must have told her because that woman couldn't keep a secret if it came in a sealed vault."

"Christ, you women kill me." He snorts and ruffles my hair.

I growl at the ruffle—I'm not a child. "Easy on the generalizations. I don't store crap away for years. I break *way* before it hits the year mark."

That's more of a fib than I'd like to admit.

I don't *normally* last that long; usually Victor gets it out of me and I resolve the issue. There's pain behind my eyes that I try to hide. Rhea hurt me—again—but I'd rather focus on him than the things I'm keeping in a deep, dark hole inside me.

"Not all of you, Sandwich. I stand mostly corrected."

"Nice of you to notice that I try to keep my insanity level at least at fifty-fifty."

He chuckles and gives me a look that I can't interpret. "You would be surprised what I've noticed about you."

"Oh, yeah? Like what, Sherlock?"

"Oh, no." He holds his hands up and shakes his head. "I'm not touching that. It's been a very pleasant surprise." Lowering his hands, he wraps his arms around me and squeezes lightly.

It makes a warm sensation spread through my gut. I duck my head, not wanting him to see my face. It feels like the sun was shining on it and I'm sure that means I'm blushing. When I feel in control again, I feign irritation. "*Now* you clam up. Sheesh. Clones."

His grin is unabashed, and my tummy flutters again. "Yup." His eyes twinkle as he pretends to think for a moment. "Tell you what. I'll let you spank me if you give up a kiss."

I choke, looking like a fish with my mouth hanging open. "I'm sorry; I believe I misheard you. What?"

He grins and zips his lips, his eyes glittering with humor.

I continue gaping at him until I finally dissolve into giggles. When I catch my breath, I wipe my eyes. "Goddess above. That's a mind picture for the record books."

Tilting his head, he wriggles underneath me and wags his eyebrows. "Like a good spanking now and again, you know."

"You don't say?" My lips curve, enjoying a moment of levity after a day of ugliness.

"Never mind. Forget I said anything."

"Don't get all pissy. I just didn't expect you to." I tap my finger on his nose, grinning playfully.

"It's not like I'm saying take a paddle to me and leave splinters, but a bit of a warm bum isn't a bad thing."

I chuckle. "See, the funny thing is that you wouldn't be the first to ask me to leave the splinters. Well, maybe not splinters, but the paddle thing is accurate. It must be that bred for blood and violence fetish that clones have."

"Bloody hell, I was only playing for a kiss," he grumbles, looking ruffled.

"I know. Since you lightened the mood and made me laugh,

you can have one—even without the spanking." I stretch up and place a soft kiss on his lips. As usual, he seems to have a spot-on gauge for what I need. "Thank you."

In an entirely unprecedented moment, he flushes and mutters, "You're welcome."

I blink at the redness on his face. "That's two surprises in a row. Who knew?"

"Alright. That's enough of a show by Taurus the ponce. I'll have to kill someone and beat my bare chest to make it up for it if you don't stop."

"You are not a ponce," I retort, giving him an annoyed look.

"I've been acting like one all day. I'm over it now." He nods as if he's simply decided not to care about all the previous emotional baggage.

"You got dragged into something you didn't quite understand and you got upset. It happens to all of us imperfect humans." I'm serious. Rhea lured him into our family mess. He didn't know what he was signing up for.

"I should have known better."

I giggle. "Ha. 'I should have known better' sounds like the title of a normal day for me. I step in it all the time."

"Now that we're less emotional, do you think you can give up the goods on this supposed affront I committed? I'm still feeling left out of the loop."

I knew he couldn't write it off. "You really want to know her problem?" I give him a serious look because once he hears this, he'll never respect her again. It's moronic because Rhea should never gotten emotionally involved with someone who is emotionally unavailable.

So says the kitty curled in that same person's lap, clutching him as if we are not headed down a *very* treacherous path.

"I could use a chuckle. Out with it, woman." He leers, making his patented scary-Taurus face.

I look up from his shoulder, my expression grave. "You don't cuddle. Specifically, after sex."

His expression is priceless, and I bite my lip to hold in my laughter. He looks like I hit him in the face with something wet and smelly. Watching him try to process it is funny; I can see the wheels turning in his head. I should expound before his head explodes.

"From what I understand, during your... tryst... you made a comment. Something about going to her mate for that sort of thing. It's been upsetting her ever since." He keeps gaping at me and I cross my finger over my heart. "I swear, that's what it is. That's what started this hullaballoo."

His incredulity is palpable, and I feel defensive. It's not my fault she's a loon. How did he not know if they've known one another for so long? "I told you it was dumb!"

His eyes narrow. "Are you sure you're not pulling my leg? You're not off your bird?"

I glare at him. This is not *my* crazy; I'm the messenger. He can stuff his disbelief. Wrinkling my nose, I huff. "The whole 'bang my brains out in cuffs' thing makes this snit a bit of a head scratcher, I agree. Despite her poor, unbruised, poorly fucked body, her heart remains broken over cuddling. Hell if I know why."

Disgust makes the bile rise my throat. I shake my head, thinking I may have to move because I feel irritatingly gross about her hypocrisy. Rhea has no idea what she wants because she's too busy trying to compete with everyone else. Maybe there's not even a 'real' Rhea That would make a lot more sense than the idiocy we're discussing now.

"Blondie's in a snit—saying that I'm a bad, rude man that you should stay away from at all bloody costs—because I don't *cuddle*?"

DELILAH

His roar echoes off the walls and my eyes widen, hoping I didn't set off the bomb again. I'm getting better at trusting that his mercurial moods won't land me in the same spot as Wilde's do. But Wilde has been training this fear into me for months. It's a reflex, like a dog someone has kicked over and over. I'd hate to see what he's done to Rafe if this happens to me.

I nod hesitantly. "She texted about it again today. It was the same 'you won't get what you want from him—trust me' speech. She either thinks I'm a complete idiot that can't handle myself. I've been trying to tell you that her issue was a tempest in a teapot, haven't I?"

Pulling me closer, he frowns. I start up the purring rumble again, but he shakes his head. "Sandwich, there's inconsequential, and then there's that shit. I don't even know what that is."

"I tried to tell you." I sigh, running a hand over my face. I really want to watch her bleed. It wouldn't fix anything, but it would sure make my Beast feel better.

He brushes a kiss behind my ear, murmuring against my skin. "The short story is that I'm an insensitive prig."

"That might be a quote." I chuckle softly, enjoying his sudden calm.

He wraps his arms around my stomach, whispering into my ear. "Are you going to run the other way, pet? You know what a bad, thoughtless cretin I am."

"Oh, definitely. Note the flames, as I'm running as fast as my tootsies can take me," I quip.

"There's a reason I always high-tailed it out of there when Rhea and I finished. If you're interested in knowing, I'll tell you." His nose nuzzles the back of my neck as he muses, and I'm so comfortable that I don't even think that I'm asking for trouble.

Do I want to know this?

I'm a little afraid of the answer. Damn the torpedos. Might as well sink with the ship. "Yeah?"

His teeth nip along my spine and I close my eyes to let the sensations dull my senses. "Mmm hmm."

"And?" I know that as good as this feels, I'm going to feel my stomach drop to my feet when he tells me.

"Haven't you figured it out, kitty? I'm cold and unfeeling. More than that, I thought it was odd how proprietary she acted every time we got naked. Even with Talia nearby nailing Alistair, she'd get demanding." He pulls back, pausing as if he's said too much. "What can I say? She acted like I should want to spend more time with her than with Talia. It's why I stopped banging her."

I nod, dipping my chin so I don't have to look at him. "Rhea gets possessive of people she's fucking. I think it's because of how she views her relationship with Alistair." I finally look up at him when my tough front back is back in place. "You are not cold and unfeeling; don't think I buy that for a second."

"She hung on me all the time in public. It drew attention, and we weren't comfortable with it."

I close my eyes, reminding myself that I need to accept that this haven he created is all I will ever have with him. One kiss on the lawn during a fight does not mean he's okay with our—whatever it is— becoming public knowledge. That has been our agreement from the beginning, and I accepted it. I have an army at home that loves me. There's a line at my door, so there's no need to be dramatic. "I've seen that in action. She's done it with Rafe and Wilde."

"We'd be chatting in a crowd, and she'd start touching me. Not that I'm opposed to getting felt up, but I'd prefer not to look like I'm cheating on my woman."

I nod, wondering where the very public kiss on my lawn rates in that scenario. Hell, how does any of this with me rate, given his code?

He shrugs. "That's what happened with us. I enjoyed banging her, which is why it went as far as it did. I wasn't hers and never would be. That's why I was up front about the blood play between us, pet."

Nodding, I try to keep myself from looking visibly perturbed. He was upfront because he knows my control sucks. I'm determined not to screw this up, so I work hard to tamp her down. Anger, fear, affection, shame, hurt, and betrayal are all shooting through my veins like wildfire. I don't want him looking at me, so I shrug. "There's a hole inside her that needs filling. No one can do that until she does the work herself. It makes for treacherous terrain."

"You can't say that I didn't make sure you understood certain aspects of my personality."

He's been baldly honest about who and what he is from the beginning. That's true. Except... Recently, his behavior has been decidedly un-Taurus-like, which is confusing. For someone who wanted to raise hell, hunt, and fuck our brains out, there's been a marked lack of fucking, hunting, or going out to raise hell. Lately, we've been intimate, but not just physically. Most of the time, we sit and talk. Right now, he's cuddling me, despite claims to the contrary. "You've been honest. I can't fault you there."

A devilish grin lights his lips. "I'd be petting your puss right now if it wasn't for the end of the workday for Talia. I have to meet her for dinner soon. The other night, I would have stayed longer if I hadn't been booked. I don't feel the same claustrophobia as I did with Blondie."

Ha! That's because I'm a very smart kitty who keeps her damned fool mouth shut. I don't say a word about all the ugly, nor a word about the weird fluttery feelings I seem to get around him. "I'm aware of how clingy she can be."

"But I'm a bastard in bed, so you should kick me to the curb and run. That's what the rumors say."

"You are not." I roll my eyes at him.

"It's not like I've given you any pleasure at all, right?" He arches his brow, going back to teasing.

"Not a drop, you evil, pillaging fiend."

He barks a laugh and tries to look properly villainous as he lunges at me. Burying his face in my neck, he blows raspberries on my skin and tickles my sides.

"Ack! Ack!" I wriggle, trying to get away.

Picking me up as he stands, he tosses me a foot into the air. He ignores my squeals of alarm as he catches me with a swoop. Once he has me, he bends down to press a big, warm kiss in the space between my breasts, then on my mouth.

I give him a playful scowl, thumping his chest. "You threw me. Monster."

He cups a breast in his hand and looks remarkably unashamed. "Yup. I'll do it again, too, wench!"

I look properly offended. "Unhand me, you unholy creature of the night!"

Holding me tightly, he lifts his head. Looking into my eyes, he asks softly, "Tell me something, pet. Does the way I am bother you? Is there a chance your feelings are will get hurt? It's important to me they're not. I've heard the warnings—foolish though they are—but I'll take them seriously if there's a chance the squawking shits are right."

Oh, boy. He does *not* want the answer to this one.

The simple answer is yes.

It didn't bother me at first because I had a handle on it. If he'd stayed the same jackass that I met on night one, it wouldn't be a problem. But he changed. He let me in, and I let him in without knowing. I'm scared for the day when I he gets bored and disappears. I'm far too attached to him for a supposed tension reliever.

I'm angry and jealous and feeling weirdly possessive—and I have no right to be. Nothing in the way I feel—or the way he's behaved—has been in concert with our original contract. I'm going to get my heart shredded.

But what the hell, why not once more with feeling?

My beat up, scarred heart is nothing compared to my beat up, scarred body. There's no magickal healing blood for that trauma. If I'm going to go down, it might as well be in flames, right? I'm not a halfway gal.

So I either lie or end it now. "You have done nothing I take issue with so far. I've been having a hard time understanding what the hell Rhea is talking about."

He nods and grins wickedly. "So... fuck buddies?"

That feels like a punch to the gut and I wait for my breath to return to my lungs. Words are difficult with a thick tongue and closed throat, so I just look at him. It takes a minute to mask the emotions running through me and keep them from reflecting on my face. When I gather myself, I say, "You said that to look big and bad; don't think I'm not onto you."

"Yup. I'm good at it, aren't I?"

"At being an ass? Excellent." Oh, good. Banter. I can do that. Maybe the rest of my body will de-petrify now.

He chuckles, looking delighted, and gives me another smacking smooch. "You know it." Kissing the tip of my nose, he asks, "Next time, kitty, do you want snuggles?"

Oh, please, don't ask that. I don't want your pity.

I mean, maybe I do, because I'm the damned stupidest individual in the Rift, but you don't know that. Don't act like you'd do it only to make me happy. Dammit. Why am I so damned stupid? Shit, he wants an answer.

"You know what? How about you decide whether you are in the mood for that? Personally, I'm fine either way, but I'd rather it be because you wanted to—not because you think I do."

He nods, bending down to get his duster off the table. It displays his tight ass and I watch. I'm out of the woods for a bit, so why not have a little fun? I reach out and pinch it, grinning. "Hey! I said nothing about pinching. You sodding pinched me. You treacherous, wily, female-type person!"

I smirk at him, quite satisfied with myself. "You can't be a sex object if I can't get grabby; it makes no sense."

"*Aha*! You *admit* I'm a sex object!"

Well, shit. That backfired.

"You're one step away from 'hunk of burning clone', pet."

I make a disgusted face. "I will *never* say that."

He laughs loudly and shakes his head. "I know how you really feel about my manly self. Before you can heat the air with tragic lies to yourself, I'll be taking off."

I blow him a kiss, pulling my phone out. "See you later."

As he disappears and I re-appear in my house, I wonder when the entire world went cuckoo and how I'm going to fix it before I spiral out of control. The voice in my head whispers, 'too late' and I sigh, knowing I'm right.

I'm screwed.

The Artist Sees The Webs

RAFE

ot knowing how to help your mate is one of the most frustrating parts of the bond.

The cat's miserable because she's caught up in so many webs of intrigue and emotion, pulled from one direction to the next like taffy. Our immediate family can't see it as clearly as I do; they can only sense that there's a problem. My darling woman is desperately trying to serve too many masters to coin a phrase.

The demands of our mates, confusion over the secret agent, and the voices of all the rest scream for her undivided attention. She can't make them all happy; it's impossible. Add to that sadness from the things we don't discuss and her community duties—she's running herself ragged. I've noticed she seems to have another issue that's dragging her down in the past few days that she won't discuss. It's weighing on her and every time she sits down to relax, someone sends up a Batsignal. They're having a giant game of keep away and she's the ball.

This can't go on for too much longer or she'll snap in two.

That ironclad, yet squishy marshmallow heart is why I love her. She's strong while she's breaking, sheltering everyone else from the storm. My mate would charge the gates of hell for the people she loves and never ask for a thing in return. But she's soft and giving inside of her toughness with a capacity for forgiveness that rivals a much more saintly human.

The queen of our dominion can't help but take care of her tribe, even to her own detriment. Her stubbornness can't go on forever, though. She's got too much weight on her shoulders from carrying around our secrets. I've tried to help, but she refuses because she's stubborn as a mule. She won't even let me tell them to bugger off for a while so she can recharge in her sacred space. That's going to bite her in the ass soon, and I know she's aware of what happens when she doesn't do that often enough.

How do I know it's all going to hit a brick wall?

Watching the three-ring circus from a distance gives me a unique perspective. I don't have as many webs pulling me in, so I can quietly observe. My schedule may be complex, but I get to have time alone in my studio to create and it frees my soul. My night bloom doesn't get a moment's rest from the time she rolls out of bed until she finally sneaks in to curl up to sleep in the wee hours.

You might think I'm exaggerating, but I'll give you a rundown of the past two days to prove my point.

Monday morning, she met with Constantine because he's butt hurt. She was dating the whiny droid casually before the bird came along, but he thinks that means he's guaranteed quality time. He accused her of ignoring him—which isn't true—but my mate can't say no to people she cares about.

She wasn't home an hour before she got suckered into a lunch with Rhea and Alistair, a trip to the movies with Mercury, a poetry reading with Wilde, and a visit from Shea. By the time she got home that night, she looked like she'd been through a meat grinder. The bloody secret agent didn't text or call while she was out, so she was grumpy as fuck.

Tuesday, she had a full scale meltdown. She spent most of the day texting with Taurus because of something my Flame lied about. It feels like there's something my night bloom isn't telling me about that situation, but I can't get it out of her. We ended up in her closet—which is never good—then Wilde and the coyote showed. My mate wasn't happy, but there was no way out of it. Our doors are never locked, and our motto is that family is always welcome. Once we got rid of them, she disappeared until dawn with Taurus, and now she's sleeping.

I made sure that she slept all day yesterday, and she doesn't know it yet. No one may wake her before she rises on her own. This packed schedule is making her so tired she can barely think straight, which could lead to disaster. If she won't take care of herself, I'll make sure it happens even if she's mad at me for it.

No matter who's in our lives, I'm still her primary mate and I won't let her fall.

But Christ, only three days into the week, and I feel like we've been through an atomic blast with fallout to come. That summary didn't include the calls from people looking for her while she was sleeping it off. I can't even fathom what her email must look like. The bloody voicemail takes an hour to clear most days now. It wasn't as bad until that jackass showed up—that much I'm sure of.

My love is always in demand, but the entire town has gone cuckoo since the bird rolled in. Everyone's terrified of what that will mean for our way of life, and they're going to break her if they don't stop. One person cannot be everything to everyone without losing parts of themselves along the way.

I'm powerless to help her and it's making me crazy.

Walking over to our bed, I watch her sleep. Victor was on duty earlier, pacing back and forth like he wanted to wear a tread in the carpet. He's always been extremely overprotective of her, but he's been in overdrive since the skewering incident. Vic worries there's more to this change than she's telling us. I don't know if he's wrong. It would absolutely be in our girl's wheelhouse to be dying and not tell a soul for fear we'd get hurt. Neither of us will break into her head to find out, so we have to wait until she's ready.

"I feel you nimrods watching me. I haven't grown a second head," she mumbles, rubbing her face against the pillow.

"We know that my night bloom. But you've been running yourself ragged. We want to keep you healthy."

"Old nanny goat." She rolls over, pulling the blankets higher as she pouts.

I chuckle. She might be the most stubborn person in the Rift, if not the universe. "Your phone's been going off, but I turned the ringer to silent. You needed sleep, woman."

Her eyes pop open, and she sits straight up, pushing crimson waves out of her face. "You did what?!"

My brow arches. *Isn't this interesting?* I've never seen her act like this over missing a phone call. "I turned it off because it was getting persistent. Would you like to see who called? You gotta eat first."

I grin as I pull the thing out of my pocket, waving it at her. She forgets to eat when she's caught up in nonsense and if it takes bribes to make sure she has the fuel she needs, so be it.

"Fine," she huffs, sitting back against the pillows. "Have Leo bring the food in. I know he's waiting."

"In fact, he has." I waited for her to stir, planning to hold that bloody gadget hostage until she indulges in a little self-care.

Leo appears in the doorway with her tray, winking at her before he leaves. It's full of protein, which she needs for that monster inside of her. He also added fruit, coffee, and waffles. It's a tempting array of her favorites, and I'll have to thank him later. This spread will ensure that she actually cleans her plate.

And I'm not leaving until I know she's eaten every single bite.

While she starts on the eggs, I study the stupid phone. It looks like a normal sodding smartphone, but that has to be deceiving. I know it's how she disappears for hours on end to Christ knows where. This kind of shit is why I got the hell out of the Company when I had the chance. Being tied to a remote teleportation device twenty-four-seven isn't my idea of a carefree existence.

"Don't play with that. You'll screw something up," she commands through a mouthful of waffle.

I roll my eyes at her. "The last thing I want is to fly away to Taurus-land. No worries, pet."

"He's not that bad once you get to know him."

Sure. That's what she always says.

"I'm sure he's not, love, but even he needs to give you space to breathe. You can't keep burning the candle at both ends to make everyone happy. Boundaries are important when you have this many people demanding your attention."

She chomps on a slice of bacon, giving me a dirty look. Once she chews, my mate sighs heavily. "I don't want to hurt anyone. But you *are* right... This pace isn't sustainable. There were barely enough hours in the day for Tuesday. I slept an entire day yesterday to make up for it."

Nodding, I sit on the edge of the bed as I look at her seriously. "I'm not saying you have to choose, but you have to say 'no.' Tell people you're booked and schedule another day. It won't fix it all, but it's a start."

"Yeah." Her expression is sad as she heaves another sigh. "It's going to get ugly when I do. I've always been able to juggle with no need to upset anyone before. But that might have been because everyone was okay with working together. I think they're actively trying to fuck up my time, so I can't see Taurus now."

She's probably correct in that assumption.

"Then you have to put your foot down. Don't let people pout or whine their way into overextending you. You deserve to have time with us and for yourself, love. Everyone needs that."

Her nose wrinkles, and she thumps the bed. "Why are you always so damn wise and so damn persuasive?"

I shrug, winking at her. "Because I don't force you. I simply present the facts and let you come to your own conclusion, eventually."

"I hate that," she mutters.

Chuckling, I lean in to kiss her forehead lightly. "Deal with it. I won't change and I know you don't really want me to, brat."

"*Take it back*," she growls softly. "I am *not* a brat."

I arch a brow, grinning wider. "Sure, you're not."

"When I finish this food, you're getting an ass paddling that will make you scream." Her expression is triumphant, and I shrug.

"As long as it doesn't bruise, I'll enjoy it."

That quiets her immediately and she mumbles, "Well, that puts a damper on the fun."

They always do, my love. They always do.

The Cat Sees The Truth

DELILAH

Once I prove to my worrywart family that I'm nourished and showered, they give my phone back. Taurus' messages seem urgent and agitated. Using the return app, I pop into his room without preface.

He's been decorating again. Wallpaper, siding, hardwood floors, a doorway, and two recessed sliding panels that must lead somewhere are his newest additions. *What is he building here?* A bathroom wouldn't be terrible. I wonder if I can ask him.

Before I finish that thought, he appears in the doorway looking as nervous as a sinner in church. I'm witnessing yet another emotion I've never seen on the enigmatic clone. This must be a record.

"Um, Sandwich?"

Arching my brow suspiciously, I look at him as he haunts the doorframe. "You called me, buddy. What's up?"

He saunters over, obviously trying to swagger like normal. Unfortunately, paired with his unsure expression, it doesn't hit the right note. He just looks awkward. "I got you something."

Huh?

"You did? What's that?" I tilt my head curiously, eying the hand behind his back. For all I know, it could be a human head; in fact, that's not even out of the realm of possibility. I'm having a movie moment and I'm a little scared to ask what's in the box.

"Here." He thrusts a box that's slightly bigger than a shoebox at me. It could still be a head. Taurus probably has unconventional ideas for presents, I'll bet.

What on god's green earth could be in this box?

He's pacing like a jonesing meth head. I lift the lid gingerly, hoping the scent will tell me what manner of horror he's brought.

"Maybe a little melted. You said the other day—and I'll have you know that I'm *not* courting you, so don't get any ideas because I doubt you'd appreciate it if I did, what with the stompy and the prickly. But I thought you might like this, so I tortured the guy at the factory. Don't get any ideas, it's not that I like you or anything..."

My lips curve as I enjoy his stream of consciousness babbling. He's so anti-Taurus right now that it's amusing and endearing. Not a single soul we know would believe this story if I told them.

"It doesn't really matter what I thought, does it? It's done. You can't really *untorture* a bloke once the job's done, can you? See, I had to because they're not normal. Had to get them to pull out seasonal shit. They're... heart-shaped milk duds."

Holy hell.

I blink in surprise, picking one up to examine it. Each one is a perfect heart shape, clearly handcrafted. I made one off-hand comment about how I'm softer on the inside with a shell on the outside. This took an enormous amount of effort, and it might be the nicest thing anyone's done for me—maybe ever.

Shuffling his feet, he mutters, "I got word on my way home that they were ready, so I swung by. Not that far out of my way— well, Pennsylvania's not exactly around the block, but still. I'm not saying we're dating or anything, so don't get any ideas. But if you want a cuddle now and again, I probably wouldn't mind. Now I'm going to go before my balls disappear and my spine falls right out of my body. To sum up: no ideas. I just felt like torturing a bloke. Candies are a perk. I think I'll be going now."

Flabbergasted by his rant, I sit silently when it hits me. Taurus might like me. As in, like me, like me. There's no hope for anything long term because he's Talia's, but maybe I'm not the only one struggling.

Holy hell in a handbasket. What the fuck do I do now?

I lick my lips, sitting the box aside carefully as I try to work this out in my mind. I'm terrified of damaging a gift that's so oddly precious. I'm also freaking the fuck out about screwing up our precarious balance by telling him how it made me feel.

Before I know it, I pounce over the table and knock him to the ground. I wrap my arms around him tightly and place a light kiss on his jaw. Lifting my head, I hide my squishy emotions by giving him a playful smirk. "You're still an ass." I dip my head, lips brushing it as I murmur into his ear. "Luckily for you, I kind of like that."

His face gets hot and he grumbles. "They're a sweet. No need to get all mushy." Despite his words, he squeezes me tightly to his chest, and I smile against his neck.

"Yeah, well, I'm not." I raise my head, giving him a saucy grin. "I'm saying you've got a nice ass."

He gives me a huffy look that doesn't quite hide his relief that I liked his present. "I know *that*."

I reach down and cop a feel playfully. "Just making sure you know how much I appreciate it."

Returning the favor, he chuckles. "Yours isn't so bad, either, gorgeous. Unfortunately, I really have to go back to work."

"Maybe I'll see you later. I'll probably all hyped up on chocolate and stuff."

That's a lie, as I would no more eat these than set myself on fire. They're going to cold storage. It's stupid to think I can keep a food gift for a long period, but I'll be damned if I won't try. His gift means something, and I don't know when I'll be able to part with it.

Grinning, he kisses my nose. "Maybe I'll see if I can get you to go for a ride."

"Maybe I will. You gotta ask nicely."

Sitting me aside so he can stand, he rolls to his feet. He turns to head out, but before he goes, he looks over his shoulder. "Considering that I meant a ride on ME, I think I can nail down something not-nasty."

I snort. As if I didn't know *that*.

Does it seem like I take a lot of showers?

I'm developing a complex. I'm always scrubbing someone's scent off to keep up appearances. I have to juggle these predator noses and despite not being exclusive with anyone, I still have to keep the peace by hiding who I've been with. It's a bunch of bullshit and I'm tiring of it.

It's Thursday, so we had to have our weekly dinner with the Pack family. They went home for once—which means they were double booked. I'm washing away the evidence that Rafe didn't take one for the team tonight. He tried valiantly to do so, but Sari pulled him away to work out her anger at Rhea. He hasn't come up to our room yet, so I'm not sure if he's decided that he needs to decompress. Neither of our erstwhile mates was in a kind mood this evening, so I doubt he's in better shape.

Taking the brunt of their anger at others is wearing thin.

Looking around the steamy bathroom, I make certain that I'm alone. It would feel good to drop the glamours and blockades for a few minutes. I could rest my weary magick, look at the damage

Wilde's demon did, and maybe not feel like I'm going to keel over any second.

Taurus figured out that I—much like the clones—restore some of my energy through feeding. Because of the demands of the families and Taurus, I haven't let my glamours drop in weeks. Holding those firm and blocking everything from the family bonds might have killed me if not for hunting.

Feeding doesn't rejuvenate my magick, though. That's what my rituals are for. I haven't had time to restore my life energy at my sacred space and this much magick is draining as hell. My healing is slower, my energy is fading, and I feel like something wiped off a shoe.

It's a good thing that Taurus has been on this protracted mission for a few days. The other mates haven't been around because of the fight to notice. If he were here, Taurus would know right away. My glamours aren't tangible and he'd feel the things his eyes couldn't see. I'm going to work on that shit.

I sigh wistfully. It would feel so good to simply exist for a few minutes.

It can't hurt, right?

I go through the checklist to make sure I'm safe to do this. Look inside—verify no one has a live connection to our bond— check. Look around the bathroom again to make sure no one is lurking in the steam—check. Feel for my primary to see if he's drawing on me for healing—check.

Okay, I think I'm ready.

I exhale and let the spells fade, preparing myself for the onslaught of the blocked physical pain to hit me. I wince as bruises, marks, and bites appear, making me look like a mottled piece of fruit. Tears well in my eyes because letting go of the magick means my sorrow gets released from its confines as well. Our fun, rowdy and pleasurable sex life has become spiteful, painful, and damaging. I look like a hungry animal attacked me and I assume Rafe looks similar.

This can't go on.

When I mated with Wilde, he didn't want to bite me to complete the mating. He hated the very idea of his demon. This change, these powers they have... it's given their darkest sides a free pass to seek vengeance on anyone they feel slights them. Between the demon and the coyote, Rafe and I are basically punching bags for their wrath.

I step out of the steam and approach the mirror, wiping it to look at my beaten body. I don't believe the 'inner demon' gambit Wilde is playing. I think it's an affect he's developed to allow him to behave in horrid ways while blaming something he can't control. I think jealousy and fear have motivated the once gentle Wilde to find an outlet for the repressed anger he's been holding. He's as responsible for everything that the bastard does, just like Sari is responsible for not controlling the coyote she developed.

They could learn to harness the anger, but they choose not to because it's a weapon. All the anger, fear, rage, jealousy, and ugliness are part of who they are. Now, they can pretend that their 'inner monster' escapes and they can't control it. Unfortunately, the escapes are happening more frequently, and they only seem to happen to Rafe and me.

Ever since the Winter Incident, it's been exponentially worse. I could strangle all our families for what they did to resolve that problem. It fixed nothing—it set a precedent for the abuse to come. The bulk of that plan was Sari's idea, and my guys went along despite misgivings.

That night, our terrible secret began when she capitulated to his demon to end the emotional suffering. It convinced his demon that she was his mate. I let it happen and so did she, so we share the blame. We're tied to those idiots with velvet ropes and we're so fucking tired of fighting.

What happened then is nothing compared to the punishments since.

The need for vengeance spread to Rafe, and I think he gets it worse than me. I see the haunted look in his eyes after he's been with either of them, particularly Wilde. The first time we recognized that look in each other's eyes, we knew. I've been carrying our pain and shame ever since.

Rubbing my hand over my face, I look at my reflection again. Battered, bruised, bitten, and beet red from the heat of the water, I'm wrecked. For someone who can knit wounds, you would never know it from this reflection. I don't have the strength to hold the shields, the glamours, heal, and hide it all until I hunt and recharge.

All of this should be enough to knock me on my ass. Add in the emotional weight from the betrayal of our other mates and it's a perfect storm.

Rhea's been moping for weeks, but now all she does is lie, wring her hands or apologize like she's joined a twelve-step program. Alistair isn't around much, and I used to lean on him. I considered a door lock on Monday so that Rhea can't just show up to whine. Even Rafe has reached the nexus of his ability to listen to her 'woe is me' diatribes.

Her betrayal—regardless of whom it involved—has destroyed the possibility of keeping our family together. I don't know how to forgive her. Neither she nor Alistair are physically harming me, but the emotional drain is crippling. After lunch Monday, I weighed the impact of cutting them out of our lives. Rafe isn't hurting yet, but once he finds out what she's said, he'll be destroyed.

Sighing again, I close my eyes.

The only way to cut them off fully is to unmate. I don't know how to do that.

Mating is an ancient tradition learned from clones taken from other ribbons. They instinctually have a drive to find their mate and mate with them, but I don't know if it's actually possible to undo. If it is, it's probably written in some book locked away at the Company. The whispers say that people go crazy after they lose a mate—even if they die. Other rumors speak of feeling like a piece of you is missing for the rest of your life. The released clones won't even talk about it—it's the boogeyman of their training, I think.

Taurus might know.

If I ask, I'll look faithless and naïve. Mating is supposed to be forever, and I thought it would be. When Rafe and I mated with the others, we sincerely believed that it was forever. Everyone was so in love. It wasn't always perfect, but it was beautiful. I'm trying, Goddess knows, and so is Rafe, but they have beaten us into submission.

What do you do when you can't imagine forever anymore?

I look in the mirror again and murmur to myself, "I don't know."

This is why some couples don't share blood with anyone. It can cause problems and pain beyond comparison.

I wipe the tears off of my cheeks, taking a deep breath. This isn't like me. I'm not so black and white. Rafe and I can get through this. If I feed and spend some time in the circle, I'll get reinforcement from the Universe. Then I can reset myself, heal this mess, and I won't need glamours.

A furry head bumps my hand, and I gasp, clutching my chest in fear. Once I see that it's Aradia, I unclench. *Shit.* "You scared me, my love."

Her big blue eyes look at me, and I can almost hear her chastising me. I wrinkle my nose, knowing she's right. The damage has been pressing on me too long, and it strains my magick to hold down so many things at once. A small recharge ceremony will do for now, but something bigger will be necessary to shore up my powers for the long term.

My magick has grown while in the Rift, but I haven't allowed it to be free. I didn't want people to know because it would be one more thing to make me a shiny toy. Being my familiar, Aradia is reminding me I need to allow my magick to connect with nature and develop fully if I want to harness this much at once.

The only way to come to full strength is a seasonal ritual with a coven. We have to draw down the moon and let the Universe flow through me so I can accept my full potential as a witch. It's a little scary. I've never wanted magick to be a major part of my life, but my circumstances demand it.

Biting my lip, I consider when I can schedule this based on the lunar calendar. It's the end of March. I have the entire month of April to plan a Beltane ritual. It's the ritual of re-birth—which is fitting—and that calls for drawing down the Goddess.

That could work.

The only drawback is that I will need four coven members to anchor the power that a Beltane ritual will release. I don't know what will happen with my Beast, so I can't visit covens I know on the other side. There are no other true pagans in the Rift, so that means I can't be choosy. I will have to ask Sari and Lily, but I don't know who else we'll recruit.

For now, I have to get dressed and feed. After that, I can plan. I have much to do to get ready before the first of May. With the busy pace of my life of late, I can't afford to dawdle, or I'll never get it all done.

The Goddess will help me fix all of this.

The Cat Begins Beltane Blessings

DELILAH

"We can *all* be part of the ritual."

It takes everything I have inside of me not to shudder at her exclamation.

In my haste to gain my four corners—north, south, east, and west—I may have spoken too publicly about my ceremony. I need the renewal ceremony to renew my energy and release the grip I've kept my magick under for years. But organizing a complex ritual is difficult, even when the people involved are true believers. It's going to be almost impossible with the group I have to settle for.

Spinning my martini glass by its stem, I use my counting/alphabet trick to calm my frayed nerves. It's not because she wants to get out; no, my Irish temper wants loose.

First, Sari pointed out that if I am leading the ceremony, I can't be a corner or the focal point. That was her excuse for bringing along her 'magick imbued' droid, Calista. Then Rhea trotted in the door behind them, making sure I knew Sari invited her to come when she recruited Amanda.

It's infuriating for a multitude of reasons.

Primarily, we all have issues with Rhea, and I don't want her to be part of this. Also, she doesn't even pretend not to be anything but a lapsed Protestant. She's so starved for attention that she comes even when I'm barely speaking to her. Amanda and Sari probably used my ritual to torque her, and she threw a hissy fit to Wilde.

My ritual is now a fucking circus.

It was supposed to help me and it's stressing me the fuck out. Now, I'm stuck at a table with Lily, Sari, Rhea, Calista, and Amanda trying not to stab myself in the eye with the hors d'oeuvres forks Leo so graciously placed on the trays. I love Lily, but she can be a ridiculously small picture person, so I have to keep her focused. Calista's presence is ridiculous because you can't use inorganic beings in a nature ceremony. The boys have used some scientific trickery on the witch droids that *look* like magick, but it's not real. I've never cared for Amanda, and I loathe Rhea and Sari.

This is going to be peachy, let me tell you.

Rafe pokes his head in as if checking the refreshments, arches a brow at me, and splits before they notice him. Smart boy. He knows I'm ready to boil over. I wager another pitcher of martinis appears within a few minutes.

"It's not a complex ritual. It is, however, a big deal. The celebration of the spring and the renewal of life is one of our major holidays," I say carefully.

I have to dumb it down for the casual pagans in this crowd. None of them have magick, and they don't know that I do. They don't don't need to know that I'm releasing my magick with this ritual. That's personal. I have enough people trying to climb into my bed; I don't need magickal supplicants pounding down my door.

"Rejoice! Today is the day the Lord and Lady are joined in Sacred Union, their coming together ensuring the continuation of life. Summer is here and the fruits of the Earth emerge from the love of the Lord and Lady," Sari quotes, looking pleased with herself.

Ugh. She is *such* a follower sometimes. If Sari could use a quotation for a response to every situation, she would. She claims she has dyslexia and often mentions how difficult it is for her to write her tales on the blog. I've never seen evidence of that, so I think it's a shield for her insecurity as a writer. She's not a practicing pagan, so that quote is straight from a website, I guarantee.

I force a smile. "Yes, that's the point of the ritual."

"That means we need a Lord," Rhea pipes up, looking up from the notebook where she's been furiously scribbling.

Rhea believes that with enough research, she can be anything. It's why she frequently seems disingenuous when she's involved in activities. She likes to be included and will do anything to fit in. Her notes will allow her to run a search on everything from attire to phrases she can throw out to seem knowledgeable. By next week, she'll have convinced herself that she's converted to paganism.

Lily is introverted as hell. I couldn't run the Resistance without her help to mediate problems for our people. Unfortunately, when she's in a crowd of people that she's unfamiliar with, she gets withdrawn. Amanda and Calista being here have rendered her almost silent. That sucks because she's the closest thing to an actual pagan that I have. She might be my best girlfriend, but she's not playing goalie right now. I need her to speak up to help me corral these goobers.

As if she can hear my thought, she murmurs, "Rhea is correct. We will need Lords for a Beltane ceremony to be performed correctly." Her eyes slide to me, looking nervous. "Beltane is a sensual ceremony, fraught with the rebirth of the harvest. Not having a Lord for each of us could cause... unintended consequences."

The room goes silent and I pour myself a large helping from the pitcher on the table. They don't understand what she means. Lily's point is that without Lords, this could easily become one big

Lilith fair. Since many of us have overlapping interests, it might cause a major dustup. Deciding who gets whom is going to be ugly.

Again, just fucking great.

I sip my martini, letting the sting of ice-cold vodka hit me. "That's everyone's homework. Decide on your partner for the ritual. Ask them and they have to know that this is a serious ceremony. Things are likely to get... personal... in public. Your partner needs to be okay with that and with knowing their role in the ritual."

"We have to pick a Goddess," Lily reminds me. "A particular Lady that speaks to our personality is necessary to call down the sky."

"We can't cast unless we're *sky clad*!" Sari whoops, jumping from her seat and doing a hip swerving dance. "Boom chicka wow-wow."

Christ. This is why I'm a solitary practitioner.

I sometimes involve my family members in rituals, but never others. When you don't have people at your level, it becomes less about the spiritual and more about imitating some dumb movie from the 90s. This is going to be a bloody mess. If I didn't need this so badly, I'd call the whole thing off.

"Um, I think I read that when we call our Goddess, we might not *know* what partner she calls. The Goddess calls who *she* thinks it is her true mate. So we don't get to decide," Rhea mumbles, looking at all of us like a tiny bird trapped in a room of hungry predators.

I frown and then flip through the pages of the large tome in front of me. I went hunting on the other side to re-fuel and stopped in some of the best occult shops to find resources. This book was handed down through several generations of a coven in one of my old stomping grounds. They owed me a massive favor, but I have to return it as soon as I'm finished. Finding the right spot in the planning section, I sigh.

Shit. This is going to be awful.

Who the hell knows who our Goddesses will pick? Most of the people at this table will assume that either Wilde or Rafe are their true mate. If the spell truly works, my weekend Wiccans might spoil the whole damned thing by flipping out. I can't even imagine who my Goddess is going to pick. The beast loves Alistair's demon. Everyone thinks I'm their property, and if we get unlucky, we'll all call the same damned person.

Oh hell. What was I thinking?

"Do you think Veruca would help, Sari?" Calista tilts her head, looking at the head of her household shyly.

I didn't know Calista was a lesbian, but I sure as hell have an issue with anyone from that family being at my damned ceremony. I barely put up with Chaos for Hex's sake. Sari grins broadly and I get the distinct feeling she and Belle have orchestrated this romance.

Veruca is a werewolf-based android the boys created for Belle during the big family expansion period. She doesn't socialize much outside her family because she's painfully shy. I think Belle ordered her to have something to relate to Sari's coyote thing.

Yes, she called herself that *before* the powers ever manifested in any of us. I almost think she willed into being.

"Hell, yes, she will. Wicca's in her programming."

I forgot about that. The boys have to quit making droids that supposedly have powers they cannot possibly have. Indulging these twits is making my life much harder than it needs to be. It's only bound to get worse once my abilities kick in.

Beggars can't be choosers, though, I suppose.

Except for Lily, I'm planning a possibly dangerous ritual with real magick with fake pagans who think they're going to call down the Goddess and sleep with... hell, I don't know. I've brought this all on myself, and it's headed for imminent disaster.

Why do I keep getting myself into these things?

The Cat Walks A Dangerous Line

DELILAH

After several excruciating hours, I finally wrest free of the gaggle of harpies. I have a massive buzz from the multiple pitchers of martinis it took to get through it, and I'm contemplating a bloody snack to help stave off the irritation that seems to engulf my being.

Before I can head upstairs to change into something suitable for such an outing, my phone trills the theme song to the Addams Family and I'm popped into Taurus-land. My metabolism is high functioning, but he's going to deal with a slightly tipsy kitty.

That's what he gets for whisking me away—again—without so much as a by-your-leave.

Obviously, he's back from his extended overseas assignment—his mission made him incommunicado for a week. He's sitting on the couch, reading, when I arrive. One would wonder why he popped me here to pretend like he doesn't know I'm here, but that's Taurus. I've learned not to question his subconscious power plays. It's a harmless ploy; he's just a lovable egomaniac. His hands obscure the cover of his book as I approach, and I wonder if he's trying to hide it from me.

Interesting. I wonder if he reads smutty stuff? I'll never stop teasing him.

I plop down on the couch, giving him a saucy grin. Between all the alcohol and struggling through making my brilliant plan for Beltane, I'm feeling invincible. A nice shag wouldn't hurt, though, so hopefully I don't look too goofy.

"I'm practicing looking aloof for a hoity-toity charity gig for my goddess, if you're wondering. Some loaded old goat is rumored to be buying imports of the extremely young, male variety. She's got me on the case."

Well, shit. That topic isn't leading to a shag.

I try not to pout as I nod. "Is that why you seem unusually taciturn?"

Since we finally did the deed, his most frequent greeting is to flip me over the back of the couch until we've screamed it out, but good. I'm not complaining; hell, I'd applaud if I could stand afterward. I'm a little disappointed that we're not doing it now.

"I'd rather not talk about it, honestly. It makes me feel as stiff as those gits' collective shirts—not in the good way." He gives me a smirk and I grin back, still tipsy enough to be loose and flirty.

I scoot a little closer, hoping that he's going to opt for flipping me over the couch.

"While I was away, I caught up on your blog. You had a mighty interesting and neurotic talk with Blondie. Given her reluctance to admit any wrongdoing, I don't blame you for telling her to fuck off. It made sense that you didn't make that entry public—not that it stopped me." He stops to preen about his technical prowess, not realizing I'd purposely allowed him access to the juicy stuff. However, as before, this topic will *also* not lead to naked time.

Fucking Rhea cockblocks me every damned time.

"Yeah, interesting is a word. Frustrating and pointless are also good ones. She glossed over her destructive behavior and acted like everything was fine. I can't force her to admit her lies, but I also can't seem to completely ditch her. I had a meeting today about a project I'm working on. It was supposed to include Lily, Sari, and Amanda. Somehow, Rhea got herself on the guest list. Since I need more people, I had to let it be. I'm not happy."

He frowns. "I saw your mate's posts, too. You're more in demand since I came out to play. Takes the term 'multi-tasker' to a whole new level—that can't be easy."

I give him an impish grin. "If you only knew."

Shaking his head, he makes a face. "I'm not sure my ego can take it. I'd wonder how often you're—never mind. I don't want to know."

My brows furrow in confusion, and I tilt my head. "I didn't mean that I'm thinking about other people when I'm with you. You're a handful, and it would be disrespectful."

He doesn't answer, so I roll onto my stomach, propping my face in my hand. The atmosphere is maudlin, and I'm not sure why. He must sense my curiosity, though, because he turns his frown into a wicked grin. Looking pointedly at his crotch, he clears his throat. "A good sight more than a handful if memory serves."

I giggle, remembering his fractured metaphor. "Indeed. Taurus in your hand, right?"

"You almost got it. A bird in your hand leads to Taurus in the bush."

"I don't think Ben Franklin would approve of your co-opting his phrase." I chuckle, glad to see him behaving more like himself.

"Do we like Taurus in the bush, pet?"

I arch my brow, shocked that the king of ego wants reassurance. *Something weird is going on.* I don't know if it's because he's read my blog or if the whole 'multi-tasking' thing makes him insecure. *Does Taurus even get insecure?* "Were the loud howling noises do not clear enough?"

Sucking in a breath, he shrugs. "I thought I stepped on your tail. How was I to know?"

I smack him playfully. "My tail wasn't sticking out and you

know it. You want to hear me say that you're good in bed? I see through you, mister."

"One 'hunk of burning clone' and I'll leave you in peace, pet." He smiles innocently and crosses his fingers over his heart.

"Not a chance. It's never going to happen." To be honest, I don't know why I refuse to call him that. It's not egregious, but it tickles the hell out of me to withhold it. I suppose it's because people don't tell Taurus 'no'.

I enjoy being one of the few who does and gets to live.

Giving me a beleaguered sigh, he eyes my body as I lounge. "You know, one of these days we might make it to bed."

I wrinkle my nose. Beds are for serious relationships. I may have taken many people to the giant bed at my house, but there was always something more about my relationship with them. I never take the casual ones there. Couches, guest rooms, pools, recliners—those are fine for the folks that are looking to have a one nighter to say they've been with me. I know he's not a one nighter, but I feel like a bed is so... permanent and I know that he's not.

I can't tell him that because I'll sound crazy.

Instead, I scoff. "Wouldn't that bed be in danger?"

"More so than that poor, abused couch? I think not."

"I've only broken a couch once, and it wasn't my fault." That's mostly true. "But I've broken quite a few beds. I'm destructive by nature, like a tornado in a can. Whoosh!" I flail my arms, hoping a little silliness will lighten the mood.

"Yet here I sit in one piece. Interesting."

Before I can catch myself, I mutter, "Give it time. I destroy everything I touch." Looking at the floor, I hope the realness of that statement won't make my eyes fill with tears.

If I'm lucky, he'll think I'm kidding.

Completely ignoring what I said, he taps my nose. "You know, I was thinking—sod off with the pokes, I think occasionally."

I play along, grateful for the distraction. Making an angelic face, I bat my lashes. "I would not say a word."

"You say that, and the tongue doesn't fall out of your mouth. Amazing." He shakes his head and shrugs, continuing. "While I was away, I got to thinking. I know little about you. I'd like to know more."

This day keeps getting weirder and weirder. Idiots this morning, no hello shag, maudlin meanderings... What is going on? Is it opposite day? Did I take the portal back to the wrong ribbon through some twist of quantum physics when I came back from hunting?

Shit. I'd better respond, or he'll think I'm nuts.

"Luckily for you, I know a lot about that subject. What would you like to know? I can talk until you interject if you don't have specific questions, but you know that."

Looking amused, he chuckles. "Are you intimating I have a tendency to interject various tidbits of myself into conversations when they're unnecessary?"

"No, I'm saying that you're not too shy to give your opinions when you so choose."

"I am an opinionated, very well-rounded and tightly compacted ass."

"None of which is objectionable." I smirk and give him a wink. "I'm not exactly known for obsequiousness myself."

Boy, is that an understatement.

I'm as outwardly extroverted as possible, and most of the people in the community—except for Sari—are very introverted. It makes for frustratingly silent meetings and fights, but I've learned to work around it. "So besides being the leader in this 'burg, I'm the shoulder to lean on. Making sure everyone is happy is important to me. I get guilted into things that I shouldn't because I feel bad if I disappoint people."

He arches a brow and grins, leaning over to rub a thumb along my jawline. "I caught that already."

I think for a moment. "Okay, but it happens everywhere. People I don't even know have always told me about their problems. It's weird. It means I attract crazies like no other. That explains my family, I guess."

"That squishy middle is more of an ocean, isn't it gorgeous?"

I wrinkle my nose and cross my arms over my chest stubbornly. "No, it's not. It's small and surrounded by a big freaking fence and a dragon and lots of stuff so no one can get in." At least, now it is, that's for sure.

He leans forward, kisses both of my eyelids, then pulls back to kiss my nose. I give him a frustrated look as my tough posture fades. "Your big cheater. You're trampling all over that tough image of mine."

"I know you better than your image, Sandwich."

I sigh dramatically, trying to diffuse the emotion of the situation. This is getting more serious than I'm comfortable with, given his lines about our relationship. "Yeah, I suppose you do."

"Does that bother you?" He gives me a curious look and I can't tell what he's thinking.

Yes! It does, dammit.

You can't be this nice. You're going to break what's left of my heart into pieces so small that I can't glue them together again. I can't have you, so I can't fall for you. I'm a complete idiot and I'm letting you lead me down a path to pain and heartbreak with a smile and a wink. I don't say that, though.

I shake my head. "Nope."

Damnit. Why am I so Goddess blessed stupid?

He gives me another intense look and I can't tell where we're going with this conversation. "How do you feel about having someone around you won't have to meditate for?"

I stuck in a deep breath and let it out slowly, being careful how I choose my words. "Relieved? I'm less forgiving of the garbage lately. I stopped feeling guilty about telling people 'no' when I needed to. I put space between me and the things that I can't deal with." Like Wilde, Rhea, and the trembling masses yearning for me to make them feel popular.

"Like you did the other day when you were texting with me after your spat with Blondie?"

When I told him about her crying therapy session, that sounded like it came straight from a twelve-step handbook, he listened. He had his own run in with that bleached bitch that precipitated mine. Despite his assertion that they had a rough conversation, she was in my house later, acting like everything was peachy keen.

She's a bi-polar Barbie right now.

"It was a terrible night. I was tired, annoyed, and then angry that she'd upset you. By the end of the day, I was ready to put a lock on my door. If I'd lost it on her when she showed up at my house today, she and I wouldn't be speaking."

His jaw drops, and he gapes at me in disbelief. "Me losing it is shocking? I don't buy that bridge. I lose it all the time. You gotta push me damned far, but I do."

"No, that's not it. For a minute, it sounded like you were saying you'd blast her because she upset me. That can't be what you meant, so never mind."

I pause, deciding how to answer this question. "I got upset because of how she behaved. She lied to me, used you, and she was selfish. She disparaged people who have done nothing but love her. She takes no responsibility for the damage she caused. Her excuse is always 'there's something wrong with me'. When she showed up today, she acted like nothing was wrong. It pissed me the fuck off."

Rhea left me so pissed and hurt that I let things happen with my other mates I shouldn't have. I had to heal those things before he got home. Trust Sari and Wilde to jump on someone who's down and keep jumping until they quit struggling.

"That's much less of a shock."

"I was mad that you poked your head out, and she immediately threw something ugly at you. That's not exactly encouraging you to hang around, is it?" I huff, not sure at this moment what part of her behavior made me angriest.

My mind hasn't wrapped around a way to communicate how upset I was. I'm terrified to reveal my biggest fear—that Taurus will say, 'fuck this' and dart back into the hole he's been in for the past few years. If that happens, Rhea will have shredded my heart, fucked over Rafe, and left me without an escape from the terror twins.

Giving me an odd look, he says, "So it was about me."

Oh, ho. More than you know, buddy, and much more than I'm going to admit. "Maybe a little."

"Ah." He looks at his hands for a moment and sighs. "Unfortunately for Blondie, she hurt me."

I shrug uncomfortably, willing to give a tiny concession so he won't look so downtrodden. "I'm protective of people I like. I don't like to see them hurt."

"I don't allow many people close enough to hurt me. Once they do, they don't get close enough to do it again—ever."

"I know how that is." I close my eyes and think about the chasm that has been growing in my family. It's widened with Wilde and Sari, but I have always blamed that situation on them. Now I see they may have manipulated Rhea and Alistair, but those two wanted it. There were no innocent parties in that mess, save Rafe and I.

We were the only true losers in that little game.

He shakes his head. "I'm not sure you can. I have nothing in me that goads me into guilt, tender feelings, or loyalty to the disloyal—you do. Once you're out of my life, that's it. The teeth-gnashing I have for the gnome is warm by comparison." His expression is glittering with ice and I almost shiver at the feel. He pulls a bag of peanut M&M's from his pocket and, as if to soften the blow, he holds out a handful from the bag. "Want one?"

I lean over and nip the lone green one out of his palm. As usual, I crack the chocolate off, lick it clean, and crunch the peanut last. "Thanks. But you're wrong, you know. My line is harder to push than yours, but people have crossed it before. There are people I will never forgive until the day I die. I won't even pretend to deal with them. You gotta earn it to live there, though."

I look at my hands, thinking of Clea and the host of people she turned against me. *Definitely on the list.* That makes me consider where the people in my life currently sit. Mating concerns aside, haven't the extended families crossed that line several times over? Why am I letting this stew instead of ridding myself of their bullshit?

"Fair enough," he says, studying my face. "My line is easier to push than yours because I have one simple rule. It's a variation of 'don't shit where you sleep'. You can gun down your mother with a street howitzer, and I'll be right there with you through it all. You can hurt yourself and others, and I'll never leave your side. But if you turn on me once—out of jealousy, petty envy, or your own neurosis—and I get hurt, that's it." He tosses another green candy at me and I catch it in my mouth, making him smile.

"I beat myself to death before I take it out on others. I don't expect others to deal with my shit. I punish myself better than anyone else could because I prefer to handle my own neuroses." I give him a crooked smile and shrug, feeling oddly melancholy.

This conversation is making me review my options. *What would happen if I severed ties? How would it affect my mate, my family members, and my community?* My biggest fear is that the ripple effect could destroy everything I've built in the Resistance. The cost to benefit ratio is running through my mind like a freight train.

"Here's the rub: I'm a cold, cruel man. I'll still chat Blondie up. With Talia and her being close, that's not something I can avoid. Hell, we might even shag one day. It's at the very least on the furthest boundaries of the realm of possibilities. But she won't ever be inside my heart again, so the past will taint everything. She'll feel it; the sensitive ones always do."

"If you're sensitive, you can always feel certain emotions. Ice is one of them."

"There's nothing I can do to change that, nor would I want to." His expression is odd again and I can't help but feel that I'm missing something important. "Do you still like me, pet? I'm a difficult bloke to know."

Pressing my lips together, I struggle to answer honestly as while avoiding revealing things I don't want to. "You aren't difficult to know. You're straightforward and on the arrogant side, but you don't play games. You're a lot less hard to get along with than you project."

That much is infinitely true. Compared to the tricksy, pitfall filled relationships that make up my current family, he's a breeze. What I don't tell him is that he's also funny and smart, warm and tender, and surprising at every turn. Telling him those things would reveal too much of what I'm feeling.

It's so precarious, the little ledge I'm standing on, hoping nothing knocks me off.

The Cat and the Bird Skirt the Rules

DELILAH

Huffing, he shakes his head. "If you could see one of the neurotic nits tie themselves up in knots dealing with me, you'd have a different opinion. I upset them without even trying." He blinks and frowns. "*Hey*. You're not exactly the tiger *you* like to project, pet. Unless you're talking Tigger."

"Not everyone knows that, Taurus. I'm careful to keep the fence up now. My people have to know that I care, or I can't lead. But they also need to know that I'm not open for business."

"Why me? Why let me see what you're hiding from your own people? I doubt it's because of my sterling reputation."

He must really want to know because he's leaning in close and crowding me a bit. I shrug in response, feeling cornered. "I don't know. Maybe because you're honest and my gut said I could trust you. Maybe you're such a big, dangerous man that you crashed through the gate. I can't figure it out." I give him a teasing grin, trying to lighten the mood a bit. "My emotions aren't an exact science. People have gotten past my boundaries before I know they're there."

The last M&M flies into the air and he goes to catch it in his mouth but misses and growls, "*Shit.*"

Completely flummoxed by that not-so-sterling example of clone coordination, I suppress a giggle. "What did you do, baby?"

He glares. "I biht mhy fuhckin tohnghue."

Trying not to burst out laughing because it will only make him angrier, I ask, "Are-are you okay? You didn't spear it, right?"

Glaring harder, he mutters, "Nohte me, ignohring you."

I purse my lips, sliding off the couch. Coming over to him, I put my hand on his jaw. "Let me see."

"Why, sho you cahn pohke iht with ah stihck?"

"No. Quit being a baby and let me see."

Sulking, he sticks his tongue out warily. I lean down, peering at it for a second before wrapping my lips around it. Sucking softly and brushing my tongue over his, I wait until I feel it tingle, then draw back and smile. "Better?"

I think he hears me, but he stares at my mouth as if he got whacked with a crowbar.

"Huh?" he finally responds.

I give him a fond smile. "I asked if it stopped hurting."

"No. Try again."

I wait for him to stick his tongue out and lower my lips to his. Slipping my tongue in to brush over his gently, I focus on the spot he bit, sending soothing tingles. I realize he's probably faking now, but I'm willing to go along. I can feel the weight of that look that I can't define. To be honest, this is a little self-serving—I'm so damned glad he's back.

He kisses me back enthusiastically and I tumble onto his lap. My hands wrap around his shoulders, holding on as the kiss deepens. He groans into my mouth and it makes everything in my stomach clench. I didn't intend to start something up, but hell and be damned if I'm not going along with it.

Taurus pulls back suddenly and surges to his feet, catching me before I fall. He sets me away from him, running a hand through his hair. "Bloody buggering hell, stop that."

I blink up at him, shocked and hurt at his words. "O-Okay."

"We're not supposed to be doing that. I decided last night."

Did he forget to inform me of some rather large change in our arrangement? Did I do something egregious, and he's cutting me off? What in the hell is going on? I feel my chest tighten and my entire body tense, on the verge of a 'Wilde' panic attack.

"See, you start the kissing and the purring and then I'm naked and pounding into you without a thought in my head, but how fucking incredible it feels." He rakes his hair again, looking agitated. "It doesn't leave much time to get to know you better. You've become important to me and I don't want you to think I'm using you just for the naked sweaties. I thought if we took a break from the snugglies, I could do that. It worked because I got you to talk by keeping the chair distance between us. But you're lolling on the couch like a hedonist and it's hard. I stayed strong until you stuck your tongue in my mouth. Then, like the typical testosterone dolt that I am, all thought of getting to know you flew right out the window. That isn't right." He takes a deep breath when he finishes his rant, crossing his arms over his chest.

Now what in the fuck do I say to that? Holy Christ.

There's so much I could say but I agreed to play by his rules—rules which he is not playing by right now—and I can't have him thinking I lied. He might get freaked out and bolt. Being important to him isn't a big deal, right? I mean, shoes are important to me. He's saying I'm good for having a friendly chat and getting him off. It's not a declaration, regardless of how goofy he sounds.

Shit. He's glaring and I think he expects me to say something. Play dumb—that'll buy time.

"Oh. I didn't mean to break your resolve. I mean, I didn't know you had... resolve." I scramble to the other end of the couch, leaving a safe distance between us. "Is this better?"

"Not exactly."

"Sometimes I forget you don't know me well enough yet. I drape over things—which makes sense with the kitty. It's not sexual all the time. It's just part of who I am now."

"What I've noticed is when you drape over me, I stop thinking with my big head and start plotting with the lower one."

I cover my mouth as I chuckle, not correcting his accurate assessment. "I wasn't trying to be tempting. I'll be good." I cross my heart and lean on my elbows, looking repentant.

He snarls, "Great. Perfect. Bloody sodding wonderful." Sitting down, arms still tight across his chest, he frowns. "Thanks for the slip of the tongue. It doesn't hurt anymore."

I frown back at him, eyes narrowed. "Now what? You're awfully grumpy, considering I'm doing what *you* wanted me to. You're welcome, by the way."

"Give me a minute; I'll calm down." He gestures crudely and growls, "Get it?"

Pressing my lips together, I nod. I'd tell him that my body is raring to go too, but he's being such a cranky dick that I don't want to.

"I tried not to be my normal hormone-driven self and take some time to get to know you. But you sucked on my tongue. This is *your* fault."

"You were pissed that you bit your tongue. I only tried to help."

"You were the hussy that sucked on my tongue! How's a smart man supposed to get blood to his head when you do that?"

"I was trying to make you feel better, you big ape!"

"You're all sexual and stuff, no matter what you're doing. It's your fault."

"Duh." I roll my eyes at him. "But I can't very well stick my fingers in your mouth, can I?"

"Oh, I'm an *ape* now, am—" He just caught that, but my question stops him in his tracks. His incredulous look almost makes me snicker. "Actually, as they're not attached to a large, unpleasant object, you can!" He stalks away from my couch, tossing himself down into the armchair.

"It seemed weird. I'm not a dentist. Using my tongue seemed more practical." I glare back, not sure why he's being so damned obstinate. I made it better, didn't I?

"This is what I get for liking someone. All this—argh. feeling. Bloody woman."

I stomp my foot, infuriated with his tantrum. What in the hell is wrong with him? "I didn't say I didn't like big apes. You called me a hussy!"

"*I sodding like hussies. Especially when you're all prickly and stompy and tramping on me, you silly nit. It's a bloody turn on!*"

My eyes narrow and I stomp over, poking him in the chest hard. "Then you shouldn't throw a damn tantrum and run away, *you ass!*"

He opens his mouth to shout back but halts, surging to his feet and grabbing me by the shoulders. "You're right."

"I know that." I push up on my toes, my eyes swirling with my beast behind them. The angry emotions of our argument were enough to wake her from her nap and she's ready to go.

"*Fuck,*" he roars.

I'm not sure if that's a suggestion or a command, but he stops yelling to tangle his fingers in my hair. Yanking my head back, he sears my mouth with a kiss that he doesn't see if I'm amenable to. I kiss him back hungrily, my hands crawling up his chest to bury in his hair. Our tongues duel roughly when I press against him from head to toe. My body flares hot and I let the growl slip from my chest.

Furious, he growls back and picks me up, using his speed to pin me against the nearest wall. He rips his mouth away from mine long enough to spear me with a turbulent gaze as he tears off my shirt. My legs slide up onto his waist, wrapping around him tightly. I pant as his hands cup my breasts and pinch my nipples. "Fuck! There's... plenty of time... to get to know me."

As soon as he feels my legs tighten on his waist, he lets me use the wall behind me to stay upright. Looking down at his shirt with a toothy grin, he gets rid of it with a thought. His hips and the wall support my weight, so his hands are free to continue teasing the sensitive buds. He watches them pucker before blowing on one. "Fuck is right."

I arch into his hands, my blunt nails raking down over his shoulders. I squirm as his cock pushes against me through our clothes. I was hungry for him and fighting has made it worse. Driven by the sting of my nails, he sinks his blunt teeth into the skin above my breast. I cry out, shivering at the teeth. He pushes me into the wall harder as he tastes one nipple, then the other. His head lifts and he growls darkly. Grabbing my waist, he turns us, shoving me so I tumble away from him.

Looking up at him from the ground, I growl. That kind of play will trigger my Beast, and he needs to be very careful here. She *loves* to be chased, even if I hate to run. I wait for him to do so, knowing I'll have to slam the cage in place internally.

But he just watches me as frees himself from his pants. His lips curl as he gestures at my remaining clothing. "Take them off or lose them," he mutters, stalking towards me predatorily.

The primal energy in the room nudges her loose and I yowl as I kick my pants off. If she weren't taking the lead in this, it might trigger some unbelievably bad things. Instead, I'm propped on my elbows and panting heavily, my veins flooded with fire. A macabre grin dances across his face as he bends over and flexes his muscles. He yanks me off the ground painfully before shoving me into the wall to press his body against mine. Grinding his cock against my stomach, he brings his fangs forward just enough to graze the skin on my chest. They move from one breast to the other and I shudder.

I can't fucking take the fangs; I'm going to lose control.

I rake the tips of my claws down his back, and he hisses in pain and pleasure. My features flicker and I rub my tummy against his shaft eagerly. She struggles with me inside, making me hiss and snarl. She can't be entirely free, so she's banging against the bars and howling up a storm. He's not mine—we can't do that. It's hard to tell a raging primal Beast 'no', but that's what I'm struggling to do while Taurus is turning my brain to gelatin.

He pulls his hips away, and the fog in my brain clears briefly. His arms lift me an inch and then he pauses. Our eyes meet, though nothing as tame as understanding passes between us. Feral and possessed, he bares his fangs at me. Without warning, he slams into me in one full thrust and roars, his demon triumphant.

My own fangs burst free and I'm unable to keep from joining the roar. My back arches and my head thumping against the wall when my body grips his cock tightly. The claws unsheathe completely and dig into his back reflexively. She's not totally unleashed, but my eyes are swirling with green and gold highlights. If he didn't expect this, he's a fool. There's only so much I can hold back when it's like this and I'm doing the best I can to keep her from tearing into what she wants.

Unconcerned, his golden eyes meet my emerald ones. Sweat trickles down his spine as he fucks me hard, slamming his fist into the wall near my head. Passion and pain cast a haze over us, giving my Beast some of what she needs. Suddenly, he sniffs the air like an animal to sense my level of desire. Satisfied, he smirks through the sharp incisors and I growl back.

My chest heaves, taking in great heaving pants as my hips buck and slam against his. Leaning down, I swirl my tongue over his shoulder, tasting his skin. I lick the sweat off, savoring the salt on my tongue. Fully unsheathed claws slide down the slick muscles of his back involuntarily and he snarls, slamming into me harder. I gasp, hoping I didn't break skin. A red mark won't get us killed, right?

Christ, I hope not.

He lowers his head and runs his tongue over all four of my fangs. I shudder, my Beast feeling accepted in a way she rarely experiences. His thrusts get rougher, harder, and faster. I shift against him, nipping his tongue with one as he kisses me. The last thread of his control snaps—I can almost hear it. His head flies back, and he roars. My fangs and claws push him over the edge, but he continues pumping into me. His hand snakes down to my clit, flicking it roughly, and my hips buck against his when my body explodes.

I can feel his grin against my shoulder as we come down. He bites me again—blunt teeth only—and my chest rumbles in pleasure. I rake a hand over his ass in retaliation, raising my emerald and gold eyes to his as I struggle to float back to the surface. He holds me close, still buried inside me, as he wobbles back to the couch. Once there, he slowly withdraws and lowers me to the cushions. As if it just occurred to him, he looks down at me as I loll there, aches and bruises forming.

I'm a pale ass bitch and I mark up good. I can't help that.

Unsure of what is going on in his head, I meet his gaze with a feline smirk. He seems perturbed and I don't know why. Picking up his pants, he puts them on and backs up a step. His eyes travel over the long welt across my chest where his fang trailed—not deep enough to draw blood, but enough to leave an angry red mark. Still silent, his hand reaches back to touch a claw mark on his back, wincing for a second. Then he just stares at me again.

Did I cross a line by scratching his back or by letting him scratch me? I don't know. I panic inside because I did it again. Not to the degree I did with Mercury or Wilde, but I let her out too much, crossed a line, and it's all ruined.

Feeling tears prick behind my eyes, I close them and pretend to get my breath back. I'm trying not to hyperventilate. It's like this wild, untamed part of me is cursed. She has to be shackled up and shunned for everyone's safety. I open my eyes when I feel his gaze change.

A wry grin is teasing his lips. He drops on the couch above my head and I stay silent, waiting. Reaching out, he grabs for my hand,

and contrary to the bestial tone of that incredible shag, he kisses the underside of my wrist gently. I try not to get my hopes up, but he seems okay, so I laugh lightly. "Bloody hell in a handbasket."

My purr kicks up once my chest loosens. I try to relax the aching and tense muscles of my frame, so I don't look as freaked out as I am. He grins at the purr, but remains eerily silent.

Deflating, I look up from under my lashes, murmuring, "Are you okay?" He has no idea what it costs me to ask or how afraid I am of the answer. I keep it all contained because I will never give a lover the ability to hurt me that way again.

He looks at me for a long minute with no expression on his face at all. "Yeah, I'm fine. It wiped me out. I feel melted."

Melted? What the hell does that mean? I arch a brow, asking carefully, "You don't look fine. Even if you are... melted?"

"Yeah, melted inside. It happens when I get that demonic during a shag. It's like a little of my soul—if I have one—burns off, gets lost, whatever."

I nod, but I have no concept of that to relate it to. I go furry and it's still me. Well, there's her, but that's part of me now. It's not as if I lose anything besides control. Getting the furry to go away is hard sometimes. She wants to stay out whenever she wants rather than go back to her spot inside. I wonder for a moment if that's because we're so separate and maybe we shouldn't be, but I don't know enough about how that stuff works to muddle it out.

"I've gotten totally feral. One night, I couldn't talk for hours. I started growling people off if they came near us, looking around, sniffing for stuff. It was like I couldn't get out of the primal."

"That's the penalty for primal pleasure," he says, still giving me that weird look.

"I get it." I don't, but at least I can relate it to something I understand. Is it possible that his demon—being a true clone—and my beast work differently? Does that mean she didn't come from the clone blood? Fuck. This water is way too deep to tread while naked.

"Then there's the other."

Other? Shit. Now what? Something is *very* wrong here and I don't know what it is. It keeps feeling like he's okay for a minute, then he lapses into brooding. This kind of bi-polar shit is when it goes badly with Wilde. Please don't let this behavior be some bull-shit that she brings out in other predators.

His eyes sweep over my form, and then he spears me with a look. "Didn't bite too hard, did I, pet? I know the human teeth hurt more."

I snort. *Man, does he not know me very well.* "Oh, no. Trust me, you can't bite too hard. Thank you for asking, though."

"Some don't much appreciate it if you don't," he mutters, shrugging.

My brows furrow. Again, with the laconic bullshit. What is *wi*th him? He's never like this. "Um. Are you *sure* you're okay?" I gesture towards his back, realizing that there are marks even if they're not bleeding. He's not like my boys—they're used to the claws.

My heart skips a beat as I wait, but he grins. "Hurts. Stings. I'll be fine." He looks over his shoulder for a moment. "Think you might have drawn blood, but you probably could have eviscerated me right then and I wouldn't have noticed."

Oh shit, this is the problem. I fucked up. It was one of his rules —no blood. Oh, bloody fucking goat balls. "I'm sorry. I'll be more careful; I promise."

He waves a hand. "Why bother? You enjoyed it, didn't you? Being that feral and wild was good, right? Sure, it would have been better were we mated and could finish the deed. We didn't do too badly for each other despite that."

What? Did I step onto Planet WTF and no one told me?

Is he making nice before Talia skewers me with a launched Bowie? I lick my lips and shrug, making light of what I'm about to say. He can't know how much this matters to me, so I gotta be cool. "I didn't want to cross any lines." I stare at my feet, suddenly engrossed in the sparkling nail polish on my toes.

He nods in understanding. "Pet, we can rip each other's spines out. As long as our blood doesn't mix and we don't bite through the skin, we're good."

Whew. "Okay."

"Kind of a shame. I think I'd like to drink from you while I'm drinking from you," he grins evilly, and I can feel my porcelain skin get paler. "But I'm bent that way."

I breathe carefully, still unsure whether this entire evening is going to get me killed. "It's not bent unless maybe I am, too. She's a big fan of feasting."

"I think we're both bent, pet." He gives me that odd look again and my stomach flip flops.

Why does he keep doing that? "That works. If I'm not the only one, then I'm cool with it." I force a grin, hoping it will cover up the nervousness still racing through my veins.

He winks. "You are *not* the only one. On that note, I've got to get out of here. I know, I know—a fuck and run. But our show will be on soon and it's my night alone with the golden one."

"It's okay; she's your mate. Go spend time with her." I have no idea what I'll do when I get home, as it's been hours since my afternoon meeting with the ladies. I'm sure the boys have sussed out where I disappeared to. "I've got some shopping to do for a ritual."

"A ritual? Shit. You left the interesting bit till last. I'll have to grill you tomorrow, pet."

He blows a kiss at me; I pretend to chomp it and then return the gesture. "Bye, baby."

I am so irrecovably screwed.

The Cat and The Artist Fret The Details

DELILAH

Rafe insisted we measure my sacred space before we went for supplies. I'm glad we did. He thought it might not be big enough for a true Beltane ceremony. He also pointed out that bringing those people into my space might leave residue or access issues I'd have to cleanse. I hadn't thought of that, either, and I sure as fuck didn't want others to know what I get up to there.

I cleared an area just south of our house that would be big enough to hold our ritual. At home, we protect my space, keep it cleansed, and it has everything we need. A new area needed more preparation to be viable. Together, we hopped the portal to buy the accouterments for performing a Beltane ceremony. I picked up extra items that newbies might not have, so they wouldn't need to touch my tools. A witch's tools are sacred and keyed to her essence. I only let my family touch them. Since we returned, I've been busy sanctifying. The space will be ready for the ceremony even if the participants aren't.

That, my friends, is the challenge. Except for Lily and Calista, none of these people are actually Wiccans. I don't have a clue what they're expecting. However, I guarantee that even the experienced ones won't expect the display once I let my magick free.

Hell, I'm not sure what to expect.

Rafe looks at me from where he's cleared the last corner and calls, "Again, I ask. Are you sure about this?"

"Nope, but it's worth a try."

"What will happen if people get disappointed by the mate they call?"

"I don't know. None of us know who our Goddess' will call, despite their claims to the contrary."

"That could be dangerous."

I sigh and walk over, looking into his eyes. "I know that, especially with people who have powers they can't control. If it goes well and they call down a Goddess, it will get intense."

He nods, his eyes dark with worry. "It could be dangerous for all involved."

I know that he's worried about me as much as I am about him. That's reasonable, honestly. "I have to do something, Rafe. You know I can't go on like this. We're headed to a complete disentanglement with our mates. The stories about unmating are all fraught with warnings about how dangerous it is. There's no way for me to control the beast inside, deal with them, and stay upright if I don't accept my full potential."

His eyes flicker, and his sadness hits me in waves. He doesn't have an escape like I do. Burying himself in the studio—painting or drawing in a multi-day frenzy—can only help him work through so much of the pain. I see his grief naked on his face before he shakes his head. "It's plain to see there's no coming back from a second set of betrayals. *Who knows what—or whom—they're doing behind our backs? Who knows what other voids we're not enough to fill?*"

I thought I was careful to make sure that he had never found out about what Rhea had said to Taurus. Wilde must have told him. Anger flows through me like lava and I grit my teeth to hold the beast in as she rattles the cage. The only reason Wilde would tell him that is to punish and hurt him—probably during a vulnerable moment. That son of a bitch. "Neither of us is enough for anyone, it seems. We're destined to be wanted but not loved like some clothing fad."

His nod is silent and I feel the pain again. Between his short-lived Victor fiasco, Wilde, and now Alistair, men have hurt him as much as women. Sari and Rhea are no small part of his damage, but oh, the men. They have broken him. That gender reversal might be unusual, but given the people involved, I know how it happened. The women want him to love and validate them, which he does as best he can. The males have far fewer self-esteem issues; therefore, they emote more outwardly, good and the bad. I don't know how he handles it. He's got the patience of a saint and the heart of a lion, I swear.

I take his hand and kiss his bruised knuckles. I'm tragically unsure whether it's from an art project or something more awful. He won't tell me if I ask. Neither of us discusses the things that happen behind closed doors. As close as we are, we have our silent shame, trapped in cages of our own making with no way to get out alive. We don't want anyone to know.

I feel my shame when Victor looks at me because he found me after one of the worst times. No one else knows about that night. I made him swear on his fangs that he would never speak of it with anyone, even Rafe. I'm no one's victim in public. I cannot be that weak and lead my people.

"Let's go inside, baby," I say softly, pushing one of his long locks off of his face. "We've got a sizable hole in our calendar without the blonde mates. It's not our day for the uglies, either."

"Speak for yourself. I've got a few hours left to myself, but I made a deal with the devil for a week in hell."

I look at him in shock, taking his hands and squeezing them. "No. You can't. *Why?*"

He shrugs. "You need space. I agreed to get it for you. Distraction works best, you know that. You're not ready to be outed. It'll be fine because the coyote will be there. It's not the same when he's not alone."

I swallow hard, instinctively reaching up to touch the tiger lily Taurus left on the porch for me this morning. I pinned it in my hair because I felt so giddy. "This is a bad idea. I don't trust him, and I don't want you hurt. We've gotten punished enough, love, but they will never believe that."

"That's true, but it'll be fine. We're on the outs with the other two and without her making it primal, there shouldn't be anything to wreck vengeance for. He'll probably be all bad poetry and that rot. I'll be fine."

I give him a serious look. "I need you to think about this. I can come if you need me, but we both know you're too stubborn to ask for help. We're too ashamed to even talk about these things with one another. We just dance around it like Fred and Ginger. Are you sure you want to be there with him without backup?"

"Stop worrying, my night bloom. You need a few days to answer your electronic dog collar without interruption." He smirks, handing me the basket of leftovers from the sacred space. "The rest of the crew have planned outings to keep them busy."

My fear tempers the excitement of being unfettered. He's offered to spend a week in the lion's den. Is he self-punishing over Rhea's comment? We do that and it's screwed up, but we hold guilt differently than most people. Our damage is very compatible; it's why we work so well together. "Are you absolutely sure? I mean, I like the idea of being free, but I'm concerned about the fallout."

"I'm a big boy, woman. Let me know if you get stuck by yourself, but otherwise, breathe easy."

Turning towards him, I push up on my toes and kiss him lightly. "You, my love, are the sunshine after the rain, you know that?"

He chuckles and ruffles my hair. "Remember that the next time I get charcoal all over the bathroom, eh?"

"It's not me you should fear, then; it's Hex." I grin and open the back door, waiting for him to follow me inside so I can make plans.

The Cat and The Bird Admit The Truth

DELILAH

I look down as Taurus slides up my body. Every inch of me is trembling from the mind-blowing orgasm we just shared. My mind is fuzzy as I sift my fingers through his hair, closing my eyes as I catch my breath.

My phone buzzed right after Rafe left for the Coyote Den. I was still fretting about him, but I wanted to see Taurus. I didn't expect to do anything besides hash out Rhea's bullshit from her phone call earlier in the day. She'd hurt both of us, but he was in Manila for some godforsaken reason. That's when I went to measure the space with Rafe to distract myself.

All of that to chat about. Yet here we are—naked and finally sated.

"Hello, pet," he murmurs as my eyes open. He brushes a fingertip over my cheekbone, then his thumb over my lips. I tore them to ribbons with my fangs. Dropping his head to rest his forehead on mine, he asks, "Are you okay? Your lip looks pretty ravaged."

I chuckle throatily. "I do it all the time. It'll heal in a few minutes if I let it." I don't mention that I only have to do that with non-mates and it hasn't been a problem for months. He doesn't need to know why I had to shred myself.

"A fact I doubly appreciate because it brought us here, but you've lost me. I thought your healing fixed things automatically, like... phhhhhhffffft." He makes a gesture like something closing and I shake my head.

"No. It took me a while to figure out I can keep things from healing *or* cause them to heal if I focus." I point to the collection of scars on my neck, shoulders, and chest. "Like these and this ugly sucker on my ribs that has to do with Wilde. I have to concentrate hard after it happens. If my brains get scrambled like now, though, it might heal before I even realize it."

He frowns. "Do you think I'm a prick if I say I don't want to hear that ponce's name while we're in, uh, couch together?"

"My bad. I didn't think about that." I stroke my palm over his chest soothingly.

"It's not like I have a right to be territorial. I'm usually not. It's..." he shrugs, and I watch a complex set of micro expressions play across his face.

Shaking my head, I put a finger to his lips. "No worries."

I have to make this easy for him. I do *not* want him to ask about the scars below my neck that I so idiotically drew his attention to. We do not need to discuss where they come from, especially not here and now.

"It's like when you're here, you're mine. This is separate from the rest of them." He casts his gaze down and shrugs. "Stupid, I know. It's the knuckle-dragger in me, I'm sure."

The grin he gives me doesn't quite reach his eyes, and I puzzle over that. Finding no answers, I kiss his cheeks, my expression soft. "You're right. It's different." I nip his earlobe lightly, ignoring his chest thumping in favor of the sentiment that makes my heart squish.

His shiver makes my lips curve up. He murmurs, "You've got a way about you, Sandwich, that I'm right fond of. When you're not being all stompy, anyway."

That jackass purposely gets me stompy, but his words make my chest ache. I am so fucking screwed. This is getting deep, and I'm in over my head. *Danger Zone, Maverick,* I tell myself. "It's all your fault, you know. You get me riled up and stuff."

Smirking, he growls playfully. "Well, yeah. You jiggle when you're stompy."

I chortle, completely at ease despite our nakedness. "You have a jiggling fetish. I think you're obsessed with boobs."

"Why wouldn't I be? I don't have any of my own, so they draw me. Besides, yours are... well, yummy comes to mind." He bobs his brows and tickles his fingers along my curves.

Swatting him playfully on his chest, I wrinkle my nose. "You tease me about liking your ass."

His eyebrows shoot to his hairline and his eyes dance with mirth. "Maybe because you can't get your mind off of it?" He shifts and rolls on his side, tossing a leg over mine and cupping my face with his hand. His eyes grow serious, and I hold my breath to wait for whatever he's going to say. "You're beautiful."

Surprised, I duck my head, eyes cast downward. "Thank you." The compliment was delivered so seriously that it makes me flush. "Sorry. Compliments fluster me."

"Do you always turn that cute pink color when you're flustered? Because if you do, I could say that much more often."

My hands fly up to cover my cheeks, and I grumble in protest. "I'm not pink."

He looks thoughtful. "No, actually, you're more of a primrose. Damien would know some rot about the exact shade, but who wants to listen to that blustering artist when they don't have to?"

I glare, trying to keep my skin from flaring any hotter than it already is. "I wasn't disputing shade, I was... Oh, forget it." He dips his head and licks from my collarbone to my neck. "Distracting me, eh?" I pretend to grouse, but he knows that makes me wriggle.

The fiend is doing it on purpose.

"Hey, I know what's good for me. My mum might have been a sterile test tube, but she raised me right." He wags his eyebrows, lips quirking.

I giggle and pinch his side. "Test-tube baby."

His confused expression tells me I should explain. Honestly, I don't think about how lacking his pop culture literacy might be. Why would Taurus care about a movie from the other side of the Rift? "There's this movie called *Bebe's Kids*, and this guy calls the horribly behaved kids test-tube babies. It's hilarious."

He frowns and narrows his eyes at me. "Are you suggesting that I'm horribly behaved?"

His scowl aims for menacing, but it falls short. I smile again, the playful atmosphere making it hard not to do so. Truthfully, how menacing can you be stark naked? "They're basically mini criminals—wrecking things and beating people up and such."

"Nothing like me at all, then." His look of innocence is so strikingly uncharacteristic that I can't help myself: I snort.

"Not even a little, Mr. Halo."

"That's me: Mr. Clean with hair."

I giggle, clutching my tummy. "Mr. Clean. Oh yeah, sure." I tug his earlobes. "You're missing something here, I think, to make that look work."

"Oh, right. Earring." Looking thoughtful, he shrugs. "I could get one, I suppose."

I try to imagine someone as sleek as Taurus getting his ear pierced. "I'd do it for you if you wanted. Before you laugh, I did it for a living in the other place. I pierced lots of people, so I know what I'm doing." He eyes me warily and I shrug. "I'm not kidding. I've pierced lots of the boys here, too. They ask me to do much more delicate things than your ears. Every one of them is unscathed. I mean, you can't tell me you haven't noticed all the metal I sport."

His eyes rake over my form, and I wonder if he's counting.

Besides the twelve in my ears, I have four others and holes where three more go when I want to put them in. "Forget it. I'm not one to follow the crowd, thanks."

"People always ask for the most dangerous thing they can think of. I have plenty in my ears, but no one has asked me to do an earring here yet."

"No one here wanted you to pierce their ears? Really?"

"Not yet. Plenty of nipples and belly buttons and cocks and tongues—no ears."

"I have no intention of getting my nipples or dick or belly button skewered." He shudders at the thought. "I'll rip myself open in a good brawl, but no dice on those."

"You didn't seem to mind any of mine," I taunt, flicking my tongue bar at him wickedly.

He gives me a look like I've lost the plot and jumped into another book. "Why in the holy *fuck* would I mind that? Between that and the distracting shinies below..."

I snort again. "Right. Did I even ask you to consider the big time shit?"

"No, you didn't."

"It takes a particular tolerance to pain to get piercings below the neck," I smirk, wiggling my lower half against his.

He shakes his head. "It's not the pain, puss. Hell, pain doesn't hurt. It's the thought of it." He grimaces. "A dick ring? Talia would cut the thing right off me—either that or laugh me out of the house."

I debate letting him in on the secret that they're not all rings and some are quite pleasurable for the ladies. *Nah. That's more than I feel like dealing with while I'm spent.* "I'll tell you a secret: I faint when I get a flu shot, but I have no problems with tats and piercings. You'd better not tell anyone." I poke his chest because I mean that.

Weakness is not for sharing in our world.

"Tell anyone you faint when you get a flu shot? I wouldn't

dream of it." He gives me the wicked grin again and I narrow my eyes. Laughing, he waves his hand before reaching up to tug his earlobe. "An earring, huh? That you put in for me?"

"I'll even use a nice clean needle because I like you so much."

"*Nice*," he huffs, almost choking. "Real cute, kitty."

I try not to smile. He's glaring at me as if he might try the pouting thing again. "Are you a hoop or stud man? Jewelry is important, you know."

He looks at me in consternation, then drawls, "You know, I have no urge to eviscerate you. You poke me with your teeny weensy little sticks. I rise to the bait like a bloody carp, and yet I have not one urge to rip your head off your neck and drink from your lifeless corpse." Rolling backward, he leans against the cushion of the couch. "How odd."

"I can guarantee I'm not nearly as fun dead. It'd be singularly disturbing if you did that in combination with the other things you like to do with me."

"Most people irritate me. I want to kill them slowly and painfully. That feeling goes away with my friends because I don't eat them. I'd go through a lot of friends if I did, wouldn't I? And I don't have a lot to start with. But with you..." He trails off, frowning, and I'm not sure what the hell just happened.

I tiptoe my fingers up his chest, not meeting his eyes because eye contact feels too intimate. "Maybe you realize that I only aggravate you because I like you." I slide my eyes up to his, then look down again when I lose my confidence.

What the hell am I thinking saying that out loud? Holy shit, I'm an idiot.

His eyes glow eerily. He rests his thumb against my lips before stroking them gently, watchful of the almost healed tears. Finally drawing away, his hand traces down my chest to my stomach in a gentle caress. His voice is the barest of whispers as he says, "I like you, too."

The Bird and The Cat Seal The Deal

DELILAH

Oh, shit. That was a bit too real. What is he playing at? It's no big deal. I like lots of things: shoes, jewelry, vodka, crazy socks... that can't mean what it felt like, right? Is he...? I mean, does he? Holy Christ, I look like a gawping moron right now.

Do something, Deli!

I press my lips together, leaning in to rest my forehead on his. My hand rests on the column of his neck and my voice is just as soft. "Good, because I kind of like you—even when you are being an irritating jackass."

Whew. That should lighten the mood enough to make me not feel like I'm—Well, I don't know how much more naked I could be, but trust me, that's how I feel.

He grins tenderly at me, lips twitching as if he's trying not to make a smart assed remark. I give him an 'I'm onto you, Mister' look and he grins more. He knows I wouldn't change a damned thing about him, even if he is a jackass. "Maybe especially when you're being a jackass."

Bursting out laughing, he squeezes me tight. "Can we talk about the 'hunk of burning clone' now?"

I give him a stubborn expression. "You will never get me to say that."

"Okay."

"I guess you'll keep trying."

"Of course." He chuckles, sitting up and putting his hands behind his neck. There are rippling muscles everywhere as he stretches. "Can I ask you something about the earring thing?"

My eyes roam over his chest, feeling the beast lick her chops internally. It's hard to focus when I'm watching that fucking ten pack move. I can't guarantee how coherent his answer is going to be. "Uh-huh."

"Bear with me." He stops as if trying to figure out how to word what he's about to say. "Hypothetically, there's a clone with only one mate and no interest in taking another."

"Well, that'd be on the nose." I sit up a little, my interest piqued.

Where is he going with this?

"However, that clone meets someone that I—he grows fond of. He likes the shagging and fighting and talking and everything else."

I eye him suspiciously. On the nose doesn't cover this little gambit, but I'll play along.

"After a long time, feelings might develop or some such rot."

Taurus never minces words. He's dancing around this, and I should understand where he's going. I'm too busy wondering why we're talking in hypotheticals because there's clearly something specific he wants to know.

"Let's say this git isn't interested or able to claim the object of his affections. But he wants there to be something between them besides a bunch of heart-shaped milk duds, green M&M's, an outfit or two, and a wilted flower. Hypothetically, would an earring be an acceptable substitute for a relationship like that? Obviously, it would be in the much distant, totally not right now, future."

That's a KO. You could knock me over with a feather. Is he saying that he wants to do something *like* mating? Like he wants me to mark him? I mean, that's a serious commitment on the clone scale of commitments. Marking is akin to an engagement. Usually it's achieved through biting but not sharing blood, but given his views, I suppose something that pierces the skin is equivalent.

I must have waited too long to answer because his eyes widen and he coughs. "Wait. *Don't answer.* Forget I said anything. I don't know what I was thinking."

Fear and hope war inside of me like feudal knights. I don't know whether I'm going to have a panic attack or smile like an idiot. Idiot might win, as I'm sure I'm making a face like a ruddy simpleton. He honestly likes me that much?

That's more than like... that's... love?

"I mean, a couple of good shags and I'm getting all touchy feely. It's ridiculous, right? Hypothetically touchy feely, I mean."

Oh, what a thin line we are treading. If he means what I think he means, this is huge. It's beyond what I would have considered as the realm of possibility with him. It's like science fiction. I hope he discussed this with Talia or she will fucking kill me. Not to mention how many problems it will cause with every branch of my family oak.

Looking inside myself for the truth, I realize this is where we've been heading for weeks. I've been slipping deeper into the emotion that I was trying desperately to not to name. But I know its name, and this is when it becomes important.

I must be ever so careful.

I give him a shy smile. "I guess it would depend."

He frowns, his expression dark. "Depend? Bloody hell, depend on *what?*"

"On whether the other person was touchy feely." That's a nice, non-committal response to this farcically vague conversation. "Hypothetically."

His face falls and disappointment flits across it. "You're right."

"They might not think it's ridiculous at all."

"Oh?" he says, tilting his head as if he's curious.

"They might have felt the same and you know, just didn't say anything."

He looks puzzled and scratches his chin. "Huh. Well, why would they do something daft like that?"

"They might have a hard time admitting stuff like that. They could be scared about feeling feely after a few amazing shags. They might even worry they didn't keep up their end of the agreement. Maybe."

"Hypothetically, if you have a hard-headed jackass that has feelings for someone and a hard-headed kitten with the same problem, they'll get nowhere if no one cops to it. In that situation, the jackass might have the same worries, you know."

I look at him in surprise—admitting fears isn't a very 'Taurus' thing to do.

"Oh, bloody buggering hell. Sod this."

That makes my fragile heart skip a beat, so I open my mouth to get a word in before he can change his mind, but I fail.

"Listen to me, Sandwich." I stop, watching him warily. "I like you—a lot. Maybe more than anyone but my golden one. I'll wear a bloody earring for you, but only for you, and only if you want me to. You don't have to decide now."

He stops, but not long enough for me to interject, so I cross my arms over my chest. "You're worried that it's too fast? Me, too. Sometimes, I worry about it so much that it claws at my gut. But when I feel, I act. That's how I am when I'm not being a royal poof. So, here's the deal: you gotta decide what you want."

I go to speak yet again, but he holds up his hand and shakes his head. "I've decided, and yeah, it'll sting a bit if you can't handle it, but it won't change my ticker. Hell, you don't even have to decide soon if you don't want to. Try it on for size in your noggin, and then let me know." He reaches over and tweaks my nose playfully, but I know there's seriousness behind it.

Instinct takes over as his words sink in. My gaze goes hazy as I pop into my mate's mind to check in with him. I'm comforted that he isn't worse for the wear yet. Rafe and I have always been this way: our inclination to share doesn't require a lengthy sit down, even for heavy topics. We're so rock solid that we simply let each other know what we're doing as a courtesy. Neither of us would ever deny the other something they truly wanted.

In the recent past, large, emotional leaps with people—like our mates—flowed through our bond because I didn't have all the blockades up. But since I've clamped down on what our current mates can access, everything with Taurus has been separate. This is not mating—more like a marking—but I have to let him know before I commit to this extremely risky idea. It's only fair, and it will protect him if anyone finds out before I see him again.

My laid back mate gives me a bit of crap about predicting it because even if he couldn't feel it in our bond, he knows me better than anyone, except possibly Victor. I huff and let him brag, noting that Vic dominated the betting pool at our house, and he finally winds down. I wrinkle my nose as our connection closes. He seemed too chipper, and it worries me he was hiding something.

I can't dive into that at the moment, though, because my lack of focus means I have a nearly vibrating clone pretending to be nonchalant as he strokes my tummy. Looking up, I give him a soft smile and reach up to touch his ear. "Do you think right side or left?"

He looks ready to preen, but holds it back, saying calmly, "I'm thinking left."

"Very rakish. You'd have to decide between hoop, barbell, or stud."

"I'm not exactly a hoop guy. I'm thinking of a stud. What's your birthstone, kitty?"

I giggle. Bad idea. "It's purple."

"Not one of those, thanks. Isn't there a stone called a cat's paw?"

"There's a tiger's eye, but they're kind of brownish. That doesn't seem like you, either. Maybe a barbell instead?"

"Has to be a stud—you know, for the studly me." He winks, and I chuckle.

"Oh, yeah, you're a real tomcat, baby," I smirk.

"Hey! It's not nice to insult your new boyfriend before you even mark him, Sandwich!"

He looks so affronted that he doesn't even register my slack jawed look.

I mean, boyfriend. Mark. Taurus. Panicking now.

What in hell's name am I going to do about the terror twins? How will I hide what they do from him? What will happen to his brother? Are we going to admit any of this in public or is this a hidden thing, like his affair with Rhea? What did I just agree to?

I need to breathe. She's sensing fear and anger—it makes her hungry. There are no food sources nearby. I have to breathe or this is going to be bad. Oh, fuck, oh fuck, oh fuck...

Drop the mask, Deli. Let some of this out by talking. Use your words or you are going to fuck everything up.

I take a deep breath, licking my lips as I visualize smoothing out my voice and loosening my gut. "I-I wasn't insulting you." The nervousness swamps me, and I babble. "Did you know a stud—or a tom—is what they call the male cats when the female is in heat? Hit that one on the nose, didn't you? Um, did you say boyfriend?"

"I have a feeling I'll be hearing all about feline matters for a while, but no, I didn't know that." He rolls his eyes, ruffling my hair. "As for the other question, I think you need your hearing checked." He whistles quietly, looking around with that faux innocent, pie-plate halo look. It's like it's bred into their DNA, I swear.

"I feel obligated to tell you that whistling never works—even for me—nor does that dented halo you keep trying to don." I huff, struggling to hide my frayed nerves.

"Oh bugger, what else are you going to call me? I'm not your mate and I'd rather you NOT call me a jackass if we ever make it out in public. 'Hunk of burning clone' notwithstanding—which you can call me *anytime*—what else is there?"

Public? Whoa. Now we're really fucking serious. Talia's going to let him strut around the community telling people he's committed to someone that isn't her?

Holy shit biscuits. I stepped in the pasture and I'm waist deep in shit.

I might give the impression that I'm not excited, but I am. Oh, boy, am I. But I have to be cautious because this is not just unlike Taurus. It's the opposite of everything he and Talia have ever stood for. I'm already emotionally decimated by people I mistakenly trusted. I ignored the warning bells about them in favor of my heart.

This has the potential for *such* amazing things, but so did splitting the atom. Look what came of that. I'm afraid of something wondrous being turned into a weapon of Deli destruction. There won't be anything left to glue together if Rafe has to mop up the tiny little pieces that were once my heart.

This is not mating, though. There's an escape hatch, right?

Marking may be more serious to him than it is to the current generation of clones, and I respect that. But mating is a whole different ball of wax. This is like wearing someone's letter jacket—an outward symbol of commitment. I'm not marrying the mercurial murderer. We're simply showing people we're an actual couple.

Except... the clones usually consider it a stepping stone to mating. I don't know what to do with that little gem of knowledge. Fuck. I wonder if he knows I know that? I look over at him and grimace. He's looking at me expectantly. What was I supposed to be thinking about?

Oh! What I'll call him. "Eventually, I'll think of a term of endearment. I'm pretty slow at the 'nickname' thing. I take forever to decide. My primary is embarrassingly good at it. It drives me crazy." That much is true. Rafe is *way* better at the nick thing than me. He rolls them off his tongue like it's nothing.

"Great, I can just imagine what ridiculousness you'll choose. I'll be some manner of posterior for sure."

"Oh, you will not!" I wrinkle my nose and swat at him. He doesn't understand how pet names work in my family. If we care about you, you get one. Once you do, we almost never use your real name again. It always takes me a while to find something that 'feels' right, and I won't do it until it's perfect.

Emotional OCD, that's me.

Before I can protest, he rises to his feet, sweeping into his arms. Swinging me around as he claims a smacking kiss, he growls. "I'm going to hold you to that, Sandwich."

"*No. Flying!*" I squeal, thumping him on the shoulder.

Sitting me down for a moment, he gives me the warmest smile I've seen yet. "Here's the deal. It's gonna be a gold stud with a precious stone. You decide what that stone will be, if you want it shaped—whatever. I'm wearing it for you, so you've got the right to decide what my mark will be. I'll get the stone tonight and you can stick me tomorrow. However, it's getting late. I'm being called and we've been ignoring it. Not to mention, I'm bloody hungry."

I heard the vibration from the pile of clothes, but I ignored it. This conversation was more important than whatever the Company wanted him to do. I mean, you can only kill someone once, right? It'll keep. "Sapphire, like our eyes. I've never been a diamond girl. I prefer stones with more flair than cache."

Taurus nods, pecking a kiss on my jaw. "Sapphire it is."

"The shape doesn't matter. Just make sure it's a nice clear cut. I trust your taste."

Sniffing haughtily, he mutters, "I should say so."

"Well, I said so; don't get huffy. Don't get over eighteen karat gold or the posts get all bendy."

"I have at least *seen* a woman before."

"Here, I thought you'd been living in a cave, thumping your chest the whole time," I drawl wryly.

He barks a laugh, his eyes twinkling. "How would I have time for the dick swinging if I did that?"

That makes me giggle until I snort, and I cover my mouth in horror. When I regain my composure, I sniff. "I like it better when it's not swinging, anyway."

"It's harder to impale yourself on me that way," he drawls, making a lewd gesture.

Not to be outdone, I reach over and give his cock a squeeze, my expression mischievous. "If not downright impossible."

Chuckling lustily, he backs me up against the wall, thrusting his hips into mine. Suddenly, he freezes. "Stop that! I'm sodding starving, damn it, and this will get us naked again."

I try to look innocent, but he seems to have forgotten that I'm still naked. I bat my lashes at him, wiggling a little.

He rolls his eyes. "Women."

I mock an exasperated face. "Clones."

His expression gets serious as he puts me down. He walks over to gather up his phone and belt. "Are you sure about this, Sandwich?"

Leaning over to pick up my clothing, I nod. Thankfully, it's not shredded tonight. I turn to look him in the eyes as I reply, "Absolutely. You?"

He arches a brow. "As it was my suggestion, I'm not likely to want to back out now—you're the chicken."

"I am not a chicken!" I huff, crossing my arms over my chest.

Liar, liar. Hell, if noses grew or pants combusted, I'd be front heavy and have a singed ass by now. I am an enormous chicken. In fact, I'm such a chicken that now that he's not touching me, I'm shaking in fear.

I'm opening myself up to the most dangerous predator I know. I'm not scared of being killed—except by heartbreak. I don't know why I trust him so quickly. It terrifies me because I didn't think I could trust anyone new after the Winter Incident. When Rhea started her campaign of betrayal, what little hope I had for healing that part of me died. Yet here I am, jumping headfirst into the fray like a methed-out lunatic.

"You were putting yourself out there and I missed it?"

Hell, no. I was following the rules; you feathered git.

"I was tip-toeing up towards it when you 'hey listen upped' me."

"The kitty was tiptoeing. My hearing's good, pet, but even I couldn't hear those footsteps."

"I was!" I wrinkle my nose. He's right, but I can't let him know that. I cross my arms over my chest and give him a defiant look. "Fine. If you want me to put it out there, then what do you have planned for my mark?"

His mouth opens and closes as he gapes at me.

Ha! Speechless Taurus. Score one for the broken kitty! "See? I can do it."

He mutters something under his breath about felines.

Cocking my head to the side, I ask, "What's that? I didn't quite catch it. I'm putting my mark on you and...?"

"Yeah—the earring. Didn't we decide that already? Taurus will be a marked puppy."

"I asked if you planned to reciprocate?" I'm treading on thin ice—what if he says no? I know that I'm damaged goods. Sari suggested that having my notch on your bedpost makes you special, even if your bedpost is mostly unmarred. Maybe he just wants my brand. Maybe—

"Hussy!" His stomach growls loudly, and he grits his teeth. Hissing, he narrows his eyes at me. "I hoped you'd want to, but I was—well, I didn't want to presume."

"Presumption unnecessary."

"You want to?" he asks carefully.

I nod, watching him as my stomach does flip-flops. *This better not blow up in my face.* "I do."

He grins, picks me up, and spins me again. "Good."

"K-keeping me in s-suspense?" I gasp. He *knows* I hate when he flies me without asking.

Damnit, I can't think.

"Oh. Well..." A frown mars his perfect features. "I have no idea. I didn't get that far."

"You can think about it. I know you're all ravenous. I'm game for whatever you—"

"A neon 'hunk of burning clone' sign on your car, maybe?"

"I take that back." My peeved expression makes him smirk and I grump, "Who the hell uses cars around you, anyway?"

"I'm teasing, love."

I mutter obscenities under my breath, finally putting on my last article of clothing.

His eyebrows hit his hairline, and he wags his finger at me. "You lick your cream with that mouth, puss?"

"I do and you of all people should know it." I smirk, recalling earlier as my eyes darken with primal heat.

"Fuck," he groans, adjusting himself and shaking his head. "Stop that. Give me the basics because I've got an idea, but I want to see if it pans out."

"What basics?"

"Do you want more jewelry? If so, what type? If not, what else would you consider?"

"What won't I do is the better question. Besides have 'hunk of burning clone' tattooed on my ass, that list is *much* shorter."

"I can't sink my fangs in your neck and roar like a mighty man, Sandwich," he grunts as he toes on his shoes. "No giggles, please. That is a very valid mental image."

My face has to be as pale as a corpse. I can feel the heat draining from me from head to foot like I'm going into rigor. Fangs. Biting. That's—that's really mating. Valid image? Is he serious? His face says he is. That's *much* bigger than I thought. I mean, I'm okay, but... but...

Get yourself together, Deli. Answer him.

"Honey, I'll do just about anything you want, like I said. If you consider jewelry, I don't wear gold—or silver or platinum only. You know I like sapphires now. If you wanted me to get stuck with something, clearly I'm not averse to the poke or the ink, but *no* burning clones."

"Then the whole deal's off, hussy!" He swats my rear and I laugh, pinching him back. "Listen, how about this? Let me think about it."

"I'm cool with that."

"I want it to be..." he stops, frowning. "I want it to be special. I hope you don't mind."

My smile widens and I whisper, "It will be because it's from you. And you'd better go eat."

"What with all your yammering, woman, it's a surprise I didn't eat *you*."

"Ooh, scary." I am *definitely* not afraid of that anymore.

"I'm not without my weapons, kitty. On that note, I'm going to get some sodding dinner."

I grin, flicking my fingers at him saucily. "Off you go then."

"You don't get away that easy." He swoops down and captures my mouth, then breaks away to leer at my dazed expression. "Much better. Later, Sandwich."

I wave, muttering something that might pass for goodnight if I was high. Once he's gone, it occurs to me I forgot to tell him about my deal this week.

What the hell am I going to do while he's off doing god knows what?

The Cat Savors the Anticipation

DELILAH

I pop back to my house with the phone app.

Calling out to see if my crew has left yet, I frown.

No answer. What the hell?

It's barely five in the evening and they never leave for outings until later. Sauntering downstairs, I find several notes on the counter and they make me smile. I do so love my family.

Delicat-

I went out with Imelda, the kids, and their girls. Lazy said he's stuck with the writer this weekend because the coyote went to the real place for some event. He thought you should know that she went with the little fire and the knife thrower. He didn't sound happy, but that's his own sodding fault. Sonny left food in the fridge for you. Aradia was fed; don't let her fool you. He gave her Omahas galore before we left. We'll be back later. Hex said everything you need is in the main bath if you go out

tonight. This means you are FREE tonight. We changed
the voicemail to 'do not disturb.'
Be careful, love.
~Victor

Circe-
Don't listen to the raging Idol. Have a good time, have a
drink; hell, have all the drinks. Get laid. Everyone needs
to let loose, especially you. The bleached boys don't know
how to have fun. Try not to look like a ragamuffin when
you do it? This one has taste.
~Philomena

Nancy-
They're all insane.
I date a riddle speaking flower dancer, so that's saying
a lot.
Have a good time, don't wrinkle the pretties, and stop
worrying about everyone but you.
The artist is fine, we're fine, and you need a few days off
the crazy train.
~Hex

I chuckle to myself, shaking my head. I have the most amazing
family. They know me like the backs of their hands. They gave me a
lovely gift and then made certain that I could enjoy it.

Feeling lighter than I have in weeks, I heat the steaks Leo left for
me to just shy of rare and grab a soda. I'm hoping this is fuel for this
evening. Taurus didn't promise that he'd call for me, but I sensed
his excitement. I can't believe he wouldn't come back right away.

I don't know what consequences my decision will bring, but I can sense that change... she's a comin'.

I'm sitting on my back veranda, sipping an exquisitely chilled martini. My young tiger is playing in the yard on the romper set I had the boys build for her.

It's been hard not obsess over what's will happen when I meet the bird again. Last night—or this morning—was unexpected. Apprehension is making my bravado flag.

I wish Philomena were here. She's the best person to have this conversation with because she pulls no punches and has zero tact. If I'm being a goddamned fool, she'll tell me straight. I need someone like that because the boys want to make me happy. They don't always give me the smack upside the head that I need when I've gone off the rails.

The Taurus phone buzzes and I frown. There's no way he's ready for me. He had to hunt and get the earring. Besides, he also had no idea what he wanted to mark me with. No way he figured all of that out in three hours.

> Birdbrain: It's a sodding mess,
> Sandwich.

> Queen Kitty: What's a mess?

Panicking, now I'm panicking. What happened? Is Talia going to kill him? Didn't he ask first? Crap, crap, crap...

> Birdbrain: I can't ask the melted Crayola
> for a favor without one, it seems.

> Queen Kitty: You asked Damien for a favor? What for?

Birdbrain: That's not important. Talia's pissed. The living room's toast and we're beat to hell.

The lack of pertinent information is making me hyperventilate. Why can't he answer a bloody question for once? No wonder Damien is beating on him.

Birdbrain: And it's HIS BLOODY FAULT!

> Queen Kitty: Talia's pissed about the mess, I suppose. Why did you and Damien get into a fight?

Birdbrain: That git can't follow the simplest of instructions and then he sodding gives me lip about it. ME!

> Queen Kitty: Does that mean that you have your mark thing?

Birdbrain: MAYBE. If he would tell me what the HELL the sodding thing DOES!

I close my eyes, unsure how to fix this situation. He's had a fight with Damien, pissed off Talia, and I'm betting it was actually his fault. But he wants me to make him feel better? I don't know. This is hard without visual cues.

> Queen Kitty: So, stop fighting with Damien, so he'll tell you how it works?

Birdbrain: *growl

> Queen Kitty: Don't growl at me, Mister. You can't do this if you don't know how it works or if you've crippled yourself to find out.

Birdbrain: Good point. See? It's good
that I rang your bell.

Queen Kitty: I am the brains of this
outfit. Make nice or whatever passes
for it.

Birdbrain: I'm looking forward to
tonight.

Queen Kitty: Me, too. Don't get beat up.

Birdbrain: Not a possibility with Crayola,
pet. Later.

Queen Kitty: Later, baby.

The Cat and Bird Are All Alone

DELILAH

One minute I'm buzzing around my room getting dressed; the next, I'm in Taurus-land.

Even though I was just there six hours ago, there's been an upgrade. The recessed doors I saw before are open and one leads to a walk-in closet. The other is definitely a bathroom, and the doorway he likes to hang in looks like it leads somewhere now. Every time I come back, he's added something new. It almost feels like as we get more serious, the space gets more defined. It's odd yet endearing.

How the fuck is he doing this?

I walk over to the closet, curious about what's in there. I don't have time to explore before my kitty senses tingle. Turning back to the doorway that I assume leads to a hallway, I see him. He takes a deep drag of his smoke as he leans against the doorframe. The light casts half his face in shadows. Dressed in form-fitting, bespoke pants and a silk shirt the color of the sky before sunrise, he strikes an impressive figure.

"Rumor has it there's a feline in here that's off her bird for me. I thought I'd drop by and see if it's true."

My eyes dance. *Playing, are we? I can do that.*

I drop onto the couch, clad in satin pajamas and smelling of jasmine. I didn't know when he'd call, but I spent a *long* time making certain that I wouldn't look like a hobo when he did. "I am fond of this annoying, knuckle-dragging clone who shows up occasionally."

Taking another drag, he acts like he's pondering my response. "That's a shame. I'm sure I don't fit that bill, so you must not be the kitty that's all squishy towards me. Guess I'll go find the right room." He pushes off the doorframe and turns to go, calling over his shoulder. "That's unfortunate, though, as you're the one in my heart."

Crap. He's going to make me say things—things I can't take back, things that blur the muddied lines we've been crossing for weeks. *What do I do?* I press my lips together and sigh, warring with myself before blurting, "Wait! You fit the bill. In a lot of ways."

Taurus pauses in the doorway. He looks over his shoulder, arching an eyebrow. His eyes practically glow as he studies me. "Do I? Isn't that interesting? Maybe you're the right puss, after all?" Turning slowly, a warm smile tugs at his features as he takes a step into the room.

Damn him. I settling back on my haunches and he rounds the end of the couch. I give him a shy smile. "I think I might be."

Oh, please. Please let that be the end of the tests tonight.

"It would do my heart good to hear that, as it's quite fallen for you." He grins boyishly and winks, crouching down in front of me. "I'm not copping to the annoying and knuckle-dragging part."

When he grins like that, I swear to hell and everything evil; I feel like I'm going to melt. It's oh-so-very-dangerous, and I'm slowly sinking into the pit of no return. "Of course not. It would shatter that image of yours." My hand comes up to cup his cheek and I rub my thumb over the prominent bone structure. "That's okay, though, because it's endearing when you're big and bad."

Taurus presses his cheek into my hand and closes his eyes. "Good thing I'm that way by nature." His eyes open and he pins me with a sincere look. "I missed you."

I beam—no way to stop it. *Damn, I'm in so goddamned much trouble.* "I missed you, too, baby."

Moving to sit on a free cushion of the couch, he runs a hand down my leg. "Sorry I'm late. My dinner was harder to corner than I thought he'd be."

"I can keep myself occupied occasionally." He does *not* know I flitted around my house like a teenager, swapping clothes, hair, and makeup until I almost collapsed. I ended up crossing the portal to hunt so I could calm my nerves. Of course, the added benefit to that was I could ensure that she doesn't cross a line when we do this if I'm fed.

"I killed two birds with one stone—dinner and one of Talia's targets. Bastard was one of those magnate types that buy zoo animals, starve them near to death, and let rich 'hunter' types shoot them for sport."

I growl, the Beast affronted. "I don't like hunters, and I sure as fuck don't like people that abuse animals. Unless the hunter is me and the prey is entirely different."

He shakes his head as if discarding the ill effects of his work. "I put him in one of his own cages and used the cattle prod on him for a while. Then I had a couple of Company chums teach him what real animals can do—the long, bloody, hard way. It took longer than I expected, especially with my other errands. But you're here now and my world is right again."

I scoot over to lay my head on his shoulder. "It's better when I'm here with you." I kick up a purr, wanting to soothe the distaste radiating from him.

He relaxes into the purr, smiling again. I think he's smiled more in the past ten minutes than ever before. Stroking my hair, he looks down at me with a mischievous glint in his eye. "How was your day after you went home, Sandwich? Anything interesting happen?"

The subject change whizzes past me and I scramble to catch up. "Not bad. I came home to an empty house, which is unusual. The notes informed me where they'd all gone, including that Sari and Rhea went to an event on the other side of the portal. I ate and relaxed for a bit, but then Sari started texting me. I guess Rhea's being... interesting. I got annoyed afterwards and took my new bike to the other side for a hunt. Then you texted, and I got dressed for when you called."

"You and the gnome theorizing scares the fashionable pants right off me. I'm glad it was nothing traumatic, though."

"All I can say is 'godspeed' to Talia. Although, the pants part isn't necessarily a bad thing."

Chuckling, he kisses my forehead. "There's that one-track mind of yours." He pauses. "I wondered about Blondie today. She didn't chat me up—despite being with the ladies—so I figured she conned some other hapless victim into giving her a fix."

"I didn't hear from her and I figure it was their trip. I'm glad to have those two out of my hair for a bit, honestly. It explains why Alistair asked Rafe if he could come stay with us while Rhea sorts things out last week. Rafe was a surprised by that."

"He's staying with you for a while?" Taurus' expression darkens and I wonder if we're about to have the talk about his 'brother'.

"Not right now. Rafe's not home and the rest of my family are off having some sort of party night. He stays with us a lot, though, so it seemed like a silly ass question. No one's ever asked before. They just show up."

"Blondie must have gotten her bi-yearly fill-up of Taurus because she's not knocking my door down. Good thing, too, as I was feeling like a used tissue." He shakes his head, making a face.

I sigh. *No way to avoid this shit now.*

"Sari's theory is that she's jealous. All her shit started after I blogged about you meeting with me. Sari and Talia will probably get an earful this weekend."

"She got jealous when I agreed to help you out?"

I scoff. "You don't pay attention, buddy. I thought you caught up on the blog."

He exhales slowly, rolling his eyes back in his head. "Haven't you figured it out yet, Sandwich? I'm only interested in you. The rest can go hang. If I see something on that blog that doesn't have your name on it, I don't bother with it."

I rub my cheek on his shoulder. "This didn't have my name on it, but it was about my household. Rhea said even responded to it, so I thought you'd pay attention."

"Things were so much simpler when I was off on my own with my woman," he mumbles.

I blink, suddenly feeling very uneasy. This shit is why the concept of marking him is scary. I smack his arm playfully, trying to combat my fear. "You're a big boy. You can fend off the masses."

"The problem is that I don't want to fend them off—I want to annihilate."

"That's no skin off my ass."

His smirk is evil. "Do I have to tell you why I'm falling for you again?"

"You're a dangerous influence, Mister."

"I rarely annihilate the people I love." His chest puffs out and he huffs. "Correction: evil influence."

"There go the feathers." I tickle his tummy, feeling lighter. I'm semi-ignoring the love comment. It was flip, right? He meant that like—oh hell, I don't know what he meant and I'm too chicken to ask.

He grabs my hand and brings it to his lips, nipping my knuckles. I wiggle, and he sucks a finger into his mouth. "Mmm...tasty."

His phone vibrates, and he pauses for a moment, snarling when he looks at it. "There goes thinking Blondie won't try to chat me up today. She's on the other side with the gnome and my goddess.

She's supposed to be having fun with her friends, but she's texting me."

I can only imagine how angry he is that she's giving a longtime friend like Talia half of her attention so she can text him. They must have gone drinking. Rhea gets very flirty when she drinks. Since she doesn't do it often, she loses her judgment pretty early on.

He snorts, looking at the phone as texts continue to come in. "Apparently, I need Viagra to keep it up." Grinning wickedly, he deadpans, "Remind me to turn you over and see if that's what's stamped on your ass."

I giggle. "Last I checked, they stamp Viagra on a lot of things, but not my ass."

His lips curve before he glares at the phone again. "If you hadn't specifically told me you were keeping this quiet, I'd let her know what I find."

Snickering, I pretend to turn so he can look, hoping to calm him down. His arms wrap around me as he tucks me back into his lap, smiling fondly. "You're all the incentive I need to stand to attention, pet. That wild streak is better than chemical substitutes by a good bit."

I grin, my nose wrinkling as I feel a flush creeping up my neck. I squeeze him hard. "The bonus for you is that I don't have any weird side effects like male PMS."

Arching a brow, he shakes his head. "I wouldn't be so sure about that, kitty. You should have seen the blow out with that portal popping prat I live with."

"It turned out alright, though, didn't it?"

"That it did, baby."

I kiss his nose. I'm a little disappointed that it seems like we won't get to do the marking, but I enjoy spending time with him. Having this weekend to come and go as I please with him is amazing. I'm going to cherish every second, no matter what we're doing.

"Speaking of not telling anyone, I was reading your blog while I waited for my dinner to be alone. You told the gnome about us? I didn't expect that."

"I told her because she was in a snit. Rhea acting weird at the get together and she couldn't understand why. Sari got paranoid, which is what started the texting. I probably shouldn't have." I shift, realizing something and feeling guilty. "Rhea was being bitchy and Sari wanted to slap her around. She might have told her about us to hurt her. That's probably why you just got hit with that Viagra crap."

"What exactly does the little snot know? I hope it doesn't open a can of worms for the golden one. Talia won't take any shit about us, that I can promise you."

"Only that we slept together." I shrug, picking at the non-existent lint on his shirt. Keeping these secrets was draining and Sari caught me in a hyper moment after I fed. The truth popped out. But I'd have to explain this after his mark, anyway.

Best to get them ready now. Right?

"I don't recall the sleeping part. So you weren't large with the 'I like him' bit." His expression shifts and I can't read what he's thinking.

I snort. "Sari knows I wouldn't be sleeping with you if I didn't like you. I may get around, but I don't just let everyone have a ride. I have too many crazies as it is."

"She didn't give you shit about me? I worry about that, Sandwich."

Ha. You and me both. My admission alone is likely to put Rafe in some tricky situations, especially since she left him home alone with Wilde. He hasn't answered since I asked if he was okay with the marking earlier today. That worries me. Neither Sari nor Wilde has tried to chastise me since and that is fucking sus, bitches.

"She teased me, but it's good natured so far." I'm minimizing the impact because I'm certain more serious repercussions are yet to come. "She did the same thing when I started seeing Wilde and Alistair. It's one of the few times she acts girly."

That part is true. She's weirdly girly about Rafe, too, but I don't know if that's an affect. Sari is a hotbed of tiny neuroses are not at all hard to manipulate if need be, so I'm not sending up the flag yet.

"Thank Hell that it's not me. Blondie's bad enough, but I'd never fuck that therapist's wet dream."

I giggle. "I'm sure Sari feels the same way, darling. She's definitely not angling for you."

Yet. Give it a chance.

The Cat and The Bird Talk It Out

DELILAH

Her intense hatred of Talia and Taurus will fade when she finds out that he's not banging me as a distraction. That's exactly what happened with Alistair. Sari knew Rhea and Alistair for years without getting physically involved with them. The second we started dating; she was there like someone used a dog whistle.

Sari will never admit it, but she's no different from Rhea. She's more outwardly aggressive and vindictive, but not different. It will gall her to no end to find out Taurus has feelings for me. Her backward, treacherous pursuit of him will begin immediately. I promise you that. It's another reason I was so close-lipped about our relationship.

"You have no idea how happy I am about that. The way she was pushing Wilde on Talia way back when made me angry. It went nowhere because even though Talia was interested, she didn't want to deal with the gnome."

She should never, ever go there. I want to scream that at the top of my lungs, but I can't. I'd have to explain why, and I can't do that. I can't share my shame with another human being. I nod, giving him a weak smile. "Yeah, I heard about that. Kitties have good ears."

He throws up his hands, nearly knocking me off balance, and I blink at him. "Bloody hell, you lot talk too sodding much! It's like a soap opera if everyone was on crack."

"Everybody tells me everything—or they used to, I guess. Exhibit A proving I'm out of the loop is your phone that's still going off." I point to the couch arm where he'd laid it after the last round of her nonsense. Shaking my head, I sigh. "Sari and Talia almost certainly don't know that she's ringing you. In the other place, everyone's on their damned phone all the time. It would never occur to them she's dinging your bell in the Rift."

Reaching over, he picks it up and growls in disgust. "Rhea's trying *so* hard right now. She's telling me how much she likes when I'm bad. It's like she wants me to sext her while she's with my bloody primary!"

I roll my eyes hard enough to send them into the back of my head. Muttering something thoroughly foul under my breath, I try not to lose my temper. *Of-fucking-course she's doing this while the others are around.* It makes her feel like 'bad girl' to be doing naughty things they don't know about. She probably ripped it straight out of a scene from some romance novel she's read.

"If I were interested, I could have her flipped like a pancake and spread eagle in a couple of sentences. But she tells people I'm the bad guy. I wonder if I ever get to play the good guy," he muses absently. His expression is melancholy, and it breaks my heart.

I bite my tongue as my anger builds. Rhea's lies, her treatment of her mates, and the way she's using him is unconscionable. "I'm being quiet, so I don't say something nasty. Don't think I'm not listening."

His brow furrows. "Nasty to me?"

"No. You're a good guy, even if you like to pretend you're not. I'm being bitchy about her. I'm so tired of her bullshit."

The phone buzzes again and my body tenses, my anger peaking

to the point of the beast lifting her head. I'm going to murder Rhea, mate or not.

"God, this is pathetic," he sighs, looking at the phone. "Do you know what's funny?"

Nothing. Not one goddamned thing about this is even remotely funny, but I sigh. "That's she may not only be texting with you to get her fix. Meanwhile, she's probably pretending it's her mom on the phone. Some Resistance people bring their tech with them, and Caesar made it work. It's helpful for those that go back and forth a lot. The Company isn't the only ones with working cells here."

"I didn't know that, so that's not what I meant. Though, that makes it surprising that you didn't have one before the one I requisitioned for you. Is Blondie trying to shag all their gits? Why not fuck her mates?"

"No one in my family carries one except Philomena. I mean, I guess I do NOW. We decided that with so many people after us, we didn't want an electronic dog collar. We have a house phone with voicemail. That's enough. We refused to get tethered to phones." I pause for a moment. "I don't know what the Duchess uses hers for, but it's never in public. There's a strict rule about technology interrupting family time, so it's not an issue."

He looks surprised again, and I shrug. "I was tied to my phone on the other side. That's not what life is about here. When I moved here, I gave out an email and the landline to my 'old life' family and friends. No one asks questions anymore, so they might think I'm hiding from the law. As for Rhea's mates, she hasn't asked about Rafe lately, thank Christ. Is she trying to get a leg up on Constantine and Mayhem? Almost certainly."

"Anyone bad enough for this destructive bent of hers?"

My anger swells and she's rattling at the bars, eager to rip and tear. I snort and roll to my feet, knowing that pacing will keep the Beast at bay. "It's not possible. With her self-esteem and guilt, they'd have to sate the need to punish herself. Between Constantine, you, and Mayhem? Only you—hands down—no matter what Belle says about Mayhem."

"Why me?"

His eyes follow my path as I prowl. I wish I had something to smash or destroy or squash flat. My fury feels impotent, and I can't quell the roiling primal inside of me. I look over at him, my eyes swirling with emerald as I fight the change.

"What the bloody hell did I ever do to anyone that I'm this thing that's scorned and shit? I keep to my primary and stay away from all this drama. Yet Crackerjack's jonesing for a fuck from the monster and everyone knows. Christ."

The hurt tone in his voice makes my anger dissipate like mist. I shake my head, my crimson curls tumbling out of the loose pins I'd put in. Walking over to cup his face in my palms, I give him a soft smile. "You did nothing wrong. I don't know what the bloody hell is wrong with her. I know what's right with you, and it's a lot more than you like people to know about. Don't let her drag you into her neuroses. Her upsetting you is starting to mightily piss me off."

Letting go of him as my body tenses again, I move to prowl when the red rage comes back just as easily. I have to burn off this negative energy and keep her in place.

He grabs my arm before I can get far, holding on. "Don't. I'm letting her get to me. I'm confused and probably a good sight more sensitive about it than I should be. But it's my dick she's after and that makes me cranky."

I give him a stubborn look. "I still don't like it."

"When I asked if you knew what was funny, I was going to explain that my intention tonight was about as far removed from this scenario as you can imagine." His lips tilt into a crooked grin. "I wanted you naked, so I show you just how important you are to me. As it stands, I'm closer to seeing her bare assed than you. That bugs the hell out of me."

I give him a feline grin, my Beast distracted by her other favorite 'f' word. "That can be rearranged."

Striding over to him, I pluck the phone from his hands and toss it onto an armchair where we can't hear it vibrate. He eyes the satin appreciatively, as if seeing the whole look I'd put together—minus the hair—for the first time. "Nice digs, Sandwich. I can't believe that I missed it when you got here."

I flush and he apparates what looks to be a large peacock feather. He waves the feather back and forth as I look at him in confusion. "About this. After being late and having a thrown in the living room, I couldn't bloody get the details out of fur face. I don't know how it's supposed to work. He promised Talia that he'd..."

Before he can finish, the California surfer-looking muse appears, walking out of a small portal. He looks a little worse for the wear in the facial department. They must have really had a bitching fight. No wonder Talia threw a fit. She's at that event with the trio of morons, and these two have torn her house to shreds while fighting.

"Hi." I wave at the monster I've only seen a few times before. I'm so focused on about this whole marking thing: I don't question his arrival, his appearance, or his bruises.

Taurus growls, looking like a child that's had its toy taken away. He glares at the monster like he's going to kill him on the spot.

Damien chuckles and winks at me, clearly amused by the situation. His eyes roam over my skin with interest, and Taurus narrows his gaze. Talia is golden brown and I'm Gothically porcelain, so I'm a complete dichotomy to what he's used to.

Artists notice that type of thing.

"Okay, cub, you put that on your skin, diddle with its size and placement—it's voice and touch activated. You get it right where you want it and then say the magic word. Poof! Then it..." He looks at me for a moment, studying my reaction. "Honestly, it burns itself into your skin. I've been told it hurts like a royal bitch, but it doesn't hurt for more than a moment or two."

Obviously proud of his accomplishment, Damien finishes with a flourish and stands back with a contented sigh. He either doesn't see or is choosing to ignore the narrowed glare on Taurus' face as he looks at me expectantly.

Burns? Hell, I can do burns. I can do much worse than that without batting a lash. Wilde had a candle phase a month ago, and I learned to deal with heat quietly. "I'm sure I'll survive. You'd amazed at what I can withstand pain-wise."

Please don't let them ask questions about it.

Taurus reaches up and plays with my hair idly, and it soothes me. "I'm not thrilled about that bit, regardless of what you're comfortable with, Sandwich. Are you sure?"

Damien waves his hand dismissively. "She's sure, asshole. She's burnt amber, isn't she?"

I blink. "What he said." It makes no sense to me, but I assume Damien sees the world in colors. They must denote emotions to him.

Taurus rolls his eyes. "Okay, so we go with that. Now, do I need to get the pliers to drag the 'magic' words out of you, or are you going to willingly burden us with your stunning intellect?"

"Oh, sure," the muse says as if he's forgotten. His smile grows suspiciously wide and his eyes twinkle merrily.

For the first time, I notice his shirt isn't a shirt. The wild patterns on it swirl and spin and change colors chaotically, as if reflecting the mood of its wearer. I assume it is his pelt when he's in his monster state, so that's interesting.

Taurus lets out a growl of frustration when no answer comes. I lick my lips, trying not to choke on the testosterone level in the room. I'm pretty certain that the only reason he isn't strangling Damien is that I'm on his lap. I lean back against the clone, kicking up a silent purr to soothe him.

"If you want it smaller or larger, you have to fucking say

'smaller' and 'larger', man—ain't that the coolest? It works with 'bigger' and 'littler', too. When you get it in place and you're ready to do the deed, say this—it's more a phrase than a word, but after I spoke to Dickhead, I was inspired. So, the foxy feline has to say 'hunk of burning clone' and *presto*! Sizzle city, marked mostly mate." Damien laughs again as he watches Taurus. He crosses his arms over his chest, lips moving as he silently counts down from five.

Precisely at one, Taurus roars. "What?!"

My eyes narrow and glitter menacingly at the muse. Is he fucking kidding? He's getting him riled up again, and I just got him calm.

Taurus gapes at his housemate before he turns to me, looking frantic. "No bloody way I told him to do that, Sandwich!" He snarls at Damien. "You son of a bitch! I'm going to kill you! Sod the golden goddess' dictates!"

The muse holds up his hands, laughing so hard his face is red—or persimmon, he'd probably say. "Oh, *fuck*, man. That was *priceless*. Between the pouty pussy and the dark cloud of stupid, I'm dying here." Chest heaving, he hiccups a cough and tries to calm himself down. "Okay, so I lied. Play not slay, man." He eyes me and thumbs a finger at Taurus. "No sense of humor. I swear."

I ponder whether I should laugh or help Taurus smack him around. "Imagine that! You did that on purpose, so I'm sure his anger is a *huge* surprise." I roll my eyes and mutter under my breath. "Men. Clones. Muses. Whatever."

Still chuckling, he looks to the ominously silent and glowering Taurus. As if he was waiting for the attention, Taurus picks me up and sits me aside. He stands up slowly and walks over to Damien, grabbing him by the shirt. Growling, his demon face drops as he gets in his face. "What. Is. The. Word?"

Too amused with himself to take offense, Damien wipes a tear of mirth from his eye. He's got all the concern of someone who isn't being held off the ground by a murderous clone. "You really need to lighten up, dude." He looks at me and shakes his head. "You *sure* you want to be burdened with this gob?"

I roll my eyes *again*, thinking I might strain an eye muscle if they don't stop. "Guys, I am suffocating on the testosterone here. Can we put them away for a few?" They don't move and I sigh. "Don't ask questions when you know the answer, Rainbow Brute."

Taurus shakes him so hard his teeth rattle together, not that it seems to dent the muse any. Finally, Damien relents with a chuckle. "Bond. Not James, of course, but that's it. Bond."

The clone holding him smirks intently. He snarls, "Say goodbye to the nice and more-patient-than-we-deserve lady, idiot."

Damien grins winningly and waves cheerily at me. "See ya around, babe."

I swat Taurus on the arm. "Would you put him down? He's being annoying, but no need for the caveman gig. Sheesh."

Taurus turns and looks at me, his eyes glowing. "Sure. Right now, in fact." With that, he walks over to toss the muse from the room and slams the door closed behind him.

I sigh, giving him a reproving look. "Didn't we talk about abusing people that are doing you a favor?"

"That wasn't abuse, kitty. That was us on a good day." He grins wickedly and slowly opens his shirt to show me the multi-colored bruises from his pecs down. "This was abuse. Though, I'd feel better about my aches if that one at least showed his wounds like a real man. He goes from one form to another and pphftt, he's right as rain. He was more broken this morning, I can assure you."

"I'd fix yours if you weren't such a big man who won't let me." I stand, running my fingers over him gently.

"I'd rather you do this." He kisses me forcefully, thrusting his tongue in my mouth to rub it against mine.

I murmur low in my throat, kissing him back hungrily. I try to be aware of his bruises, but *this* is what I've been waiting for all day.

Moaning low in his throat, he thrusts his hips towards me and draws back to rest his forehead on mine. "Talk about curing what ails you."

My hands slide down his back, resting on his hips as he presses close. I give him an impish grin. "It does? A kiss?"

"It's not the kiss, love, it's you." Grinning tenderly, he lowers his lips to my neck and nibbles. When he lifts his head, he looks at the feather on the couch and then at me. "About that thing."

"How could I forget after all the ruckus?"

He dips his head and grins sheepishly. "Sorry about that. I don't think you've met Damien before."

"I haven't really *met* him—only sort of. To get to the party Talia was going to have for you, my people formed a caravan. Heather won a weekend with him in an art contest. He was along for the road trip with her. During one stop, he caught me in an incriminating position, but it definitely did not count as 'meeting' him."

"What position would that be?" He arches a brow and I flush, unsure he'll want to hear this blast from the past.

"Naked." I flick my eyes down. I'm not ashamed, but I don't want to make a big deal out of it. He looks at me and I can feel the burning stare as he waits for me to expound. I drop to the couch, tugging him down with me. "Not just naked, more like in the middle of something. My fault—it was a public place."

He growls, then sighs. "He saw you getting fucked. That lucky bastard. Maybe I will kill him when I get home."

"It was in a hot tub; no need to kill him. Besides, you get to do it, not see it. You got the better end of the bargain, I'd say."

His eyes roll to the ceiling, and he nods. "Hell, fuck, yeah." His expression gets melancholy. "You know, I'm a little surprised that you don't despise me. You had to have heard an earful before we met up on that dark street."

"I did."

"I must have seemed like an ogre. Even to my own eyes, I seem like an ass, given what I've read about myself and I *know* me."

"I usually figure that the story is always somewhere in the middle of what I'm told, so I make my own judgments about people based on my experience. Otherwise, I sure as hell never would have talked with Rhea." I shrug, leaving it at that. Rhea was *not* immediately accepted into our community and I'm the one who did a lot of campaigning for people to let her in.

Good job, moron.

The Bird Gets Serious

DELILAH

"You really disliked her for a long time, I hear."

I frown. "Who said that?"

"You did. What part of I don't talk to anyone else did you miss?" He tweaks my nose playfully and I roll my eyes.

"I disliked how she treated people. A lot of it was over—you know what, I'm not even going to say it because it's getting redundant."

"From where I'm sitting, baby, it's all redundant with her—cyclical even."

"One of these days I'll listen to—" I stop mid-sentence as his hands move over me pleasantly. "Distraction is always the best way to get my attention."

"Give a woman what she wants, is my motto. Agreement and gropes are usually right up there."

"When I'm in the mood, I can go for both."

His hands wander more, making me wriggle, and he grins wolfishly. "Is the mood striking you now, pet?"

"Every time you're around, it nearly bashes me in the head." I scoot closer, eager to run my palms over his chest, his abs—anywhere I can touch.

"I can't tell you how grateful I am." He yanks me onto his lap.

I'm definitely ready to pretend no one else exists for a while. I flick a nail over his nipple, scratching it through his shirt as I squirm against his hands. Leaning in, I catch his lower lip in between my teeth, tugging on it playfully. His hand wraps around the back of my neck, holding me to him. His tongue slips between my lips, stroking against mine, and I nip at it.

I growl softly as his hands slide underneath the fabric of my tank to roam over my back, scratching with blunt nails.

"Baby, you feel good." He lifts his hips to rub them against mine and I chuckle throatily.

I lick from his collarbone to his ear, sucking on the spot behind his lobe gently. "You taste delicious." I'm careful not to bite too hard, but I raise a mark as I smooth my hands over his shoulders.

He growls in pleasure. Driven by emotions and desire, he bites my shoulder, then licks it to soothe. "Ditto," he mumbles. His hands move to squeeze my ass, and I rock against him.

Working the buttons on his shirt, I let out a soft groan when I get my hands on bare skin. My fingers move over his abs, dipping into his belly button before I lick the rim of his ear. This is kinda fun, snogging before the fireworks. It's very couple-y, you know.

He leans up so I can push the shirt over his shoulders and off. Once his skin is bared, he tugs the hem of my tank up and tosses it. Meeting my eyes, he murmurs, "You really are beautiful, Deli, and I'm one lucky bloke to get to see you smile once in a while."

I feel the flush creep up the back of my neck. "You always make me smile." Brushing my knuckles over his jaw, I whisper, "I can't say that for many people, you know."

He grins wryly before tweaking my nipples, making me jump. "I know. Lately, it's even less and I'm sorry about that. It's not my fault, but I'm sorry it's been so dramatic. When I coax a smile out of you, I feel better about myself. Odd, isn't it?"

"Not so odd. At least, not any more than it makes me feel better when you ask me to come curl up and purr on you."

Blinking, he looks surprised. "I love when you do that, kitty. You get cozy and warm, draping over me, then that soft rumble kicks in. It's like you're caressing my body from the inside. It's a good thing."

"I know. It's comfy." I smile shyly and shrug, as few people appreciate me for comfort and closeness.

He takes my chin between two fingers and raises it to catch my eyes. "What you did just then melts me. I doubt I'd be able to kill things if you used that on me too often."

I look up through my lashes. "If I shrug at you?"

"No, it's those brief glimpses of the soft center. The occasional blush or touch of shyness—even the kitty tiptoeing you did yesterday. Mixed in with the whole of it—" He rubs his hand over his chest. "I'm not used to it—it moves me."

"You have plenty of hidden facets that are endearing, too. Besides, you wouldn't get the glimpses of the squishy side if I didn't adore you so darned much."

He stops ogling my breasts when my words catch his attention. "A-ha. You adore me."

Giving him a look like he's gone daft, I nod. "Hell, yes, I do. There's no way that you didn't."

"That's news to me, kitty. Last I heard, you 'liked' me." He frowns, looking like he's going to pout again.

I look confused. "I said that to yank your chain. Baby, if I only liked you, why would I be letting you brand yourself on me? It's bloody ridiculous how head over heels I am for you. I assumed you knew."

He literally beams. Taurus smiling like the sun just shined on him is something that I never thought I'd see, but that's what it looks like. "Besides the 'bloody ridiculous' bit, the rest sounds right nice."

Suddenly, he sets me aside and practically bounces off the

couch. Reaching into a drawer by the mini-bar, he grabs a lighter and lights candles I didn't even notice. Once they're all flickering, he switches off the lights. Standing in the middle of the room, he pins me with his gaze as he slowly unbuckles his belt. "You love me, Deli loves me, the Sandwich loves me." He tosses his belt and undoes the top button on his pants, prowling slowly towards me.

"Rub it in," I grumble, watching him with a teasing glint in my eyes. "I'm never going to live saying that down, am I?"-

He gives me a supremely smug look, unzipping his pants as he goes. "Technically, you said 'adore', not love, but I inferred." His pants drop and he steps out of them, kicking them out of his way. Naked, hard, and tight, he's shadowed in the candlelight as he watches me. "I wouldn't mind hearing the 'L' word, though."

He runs a hand from his pecs down to his crotch. "If I'm a good boy, will you tell me? I'm fairly sure I can be good, though I've not tried it recently. Yeah, I'm sure I can. How hard can it be?" He looks serious for a moment, as if considering.

My mind boggles, trying to figure out which statement to reply to. I open my mouth, stop, then start again, and finally, I chuckle. "It looks hard, but I'm sure you can be a good boy. I don't know you'd look anything like yourself, but you could do it if you wanted to."

His cock twitches under my gaze, and his expression goes from teasing to hungry. He takes a step towards the couch as he holds up his hand. "I'll be a choirboy right until I spontaneously combust—albeit for all of five seconds—if you say it for me." His eyes reflect the light of a dozen flames as their shadows slide over him. He takes another step, flashing a fang at me playfully.

Christ in a cartoon. Somewhere in me, I knew that this night was going to make everything real. We're going to cross lines that I never considered crossing, and there's no return from a night like tonight. Can I do this? Can I walk into a room without a door and hope to come out alive? Once I say what he wants, once it's out loud and in the universe, I can't take it back.

It exists. It consumes. It can destroy me. Goddess help me if it blows up in my face, but I can do it.

"Come here," I whisper softly, holding my arms out.

All I had to do was ask. He's in my arms before my heart beats again. Studying my face as if to memorize it, his eyes roam before coming to rest on mine. His voice is husky, as if he's overcoming something caught in his throat to speak. "I'm here, baby. I'm not going anywhere."

My hands smooth down his face to his shoulders, smiling tenderly as I study his features. Stretching up, I press a kiss to his forehead, one on each cheek, and then on his chin. I speak in a low, velvety voice that I only seem to conjure when I'm in the bedroom. "I know. And I love you."

There it is. The world hasn't come crashing down, but we're alone. No one else can hear, and that is keeping me from shaking from head to toe.

He bobs his head, accepting my words. Leaning closer to me, he dips his head and brushes the barest of kisses across my lips. "I love you, too."

My arms creep up around him, squeezing tightly. I push up to kiss his lips, my tongue tracing the lower one before darting back into my mouth. "Good."

"I think you're right," he mumbles against my skin as he buries his face in my breasts. "I think I've got a tit fetish." As if to prove it, he lowers his head to a taut peak and sucks hard.

I groan softly as my back arches. "Not that it was a complaint, mind you."

"Scratch that. I've got a 'you' fetish."

My grin widens and I slide my hands down his back, resting them in the dip of his spine. "I'm surely not complaining about that."

His arm reaches down to pick up the feather he dropped when he fought with Damien. He eyes me intently, slowly lowering the soft colorful barb to my cheek, brushing the most sensitive filaments over my skin. "I want you to wear my mark, love." Tickling under my chin, he inches downward. The feather dances over my bare skin, making me shiver.

I suck in a breath as it tickles over me. I want more and so does she, but there is only so much truth I can deal out in one day. I'm sure that etiquette dictates that I keep that tidbit to myself—that and my lack of a death wish at the hands of flying swords. "I want to."

The iridescent blue eye winks up at me as he strokes my breasts with its soft barbs. Over and over, he coasts over my nipples until they throb. Only then does he trace my ribs and glide over my abdomen. His eyes burn like the sun as he watches the long, luxurious trail. I'm right on the edge of screaming when he asks, "Where do you think, love?"

I blink the lust haze out of my eyes, trying to come up with a better answer than 'any fucking where that gets me fucked immediately'. Drawing in a breath, I let it out slowly while my heart races. "It depends on what kind of visibility you want—whether people can see it when I'm not naked."

Oh, I'm being so cautious with that statement. Was I asking if he wants people to know about this? Yes. I can stay hidden, but it will hurt. I have to prepare myself for the sting that would come with it. I'm just going to rip the band-aid off and see if I bleed.

"How about this? I'll let you put it anywhere you want, even on your fetish." There's the brave kitty from days of yore: push the decision to him, make him tell me he that we're real. He has to admit it to me if I'm becoming a shadow sidepiece that gets loved only if no one's around.

That gambit doesn't seem to bother him. In fact, he seems pleased. He grins wolfishly, flittering the plumage over my thighs before pulling it away to trace down to my foot and back. "I have half a mind to put it in the middle of your forehead, you little minx."

The Cat Fears Discovery

DELILAH

Did he figure out that I'm testing him? I hope not.

My weak little hummingbird heart can't take another sadist. I may dance on ledges in clubs and run with the big dogs physically, but emotionally, I'm an amputee. "You could, but it wouldn't match everything. That would throw my whole sense of style off. But I'm sure you'd get a kick out of me explaining to everyone in the universe how it got there."

I said 'everyone in the universe.' *That means in public, you demonic jackass. Come on, say something.*

He chuckles deeply, giving in to temptation enough to bite at the tip of my nipple. He might be too distracted by my nakedness to catch my desperation. "I would, hussy, so watch the sass." The feather glides over the inside of my knee and moves upwards teasingly. "But I may have a better idea."

Squirming at tickles, I ask, "You do?" I'd sass more, but he's distracting the hell out of me with the feather.

"Mmm hmm, I do. If you give me a few moments, love, I'll show you." His hips rub against my thigh with fantastic friction, making me whimper. He doesn't have a lot of control left because his eyes are swirling gold as he watches me. Nipping my neck, he grins as I try to tug him up with my hands. Finally, he moves the plumage upwards, stopping at my left breast. Closing his eyes, he listens for my erratic heartbeat.

Once pinpointed, he lays the feather down, the colorful and unmistakable eye directly over my heart. The plumage curves along the topside of my left breast in a graceful arch as the quill disappears into the shadows of the curve of my hip. When he finishes, the tentative placement, he looks up at me questioningly.

"I can shrink it if it's too big, love. It's a rather large feather." His voice is husky as he murmurs, "Or we could move it?"

I look down at it and then up at him. I'm filled with more emotion that I can comfortably verbalize, so I say, "I think it's perfect where it is. The size is fine if you like it." I don't tell him it's bigger than the tattoo his brother had inked on my stomach. Point of fact, it's bigger than any mark anyone put on me. I grin nervously. "It's dramatic—like you."

He knows I have to consciously allow regular tattoos to stay on my body. They're harder to heal than bite marks. The one I had removed after the mess with Mercury came back the next day and I ended up having to push the ink out of my body. However, the one Alistair got me seems to fade on its own. I don't know if my healing is getting strong or if my magick knows that our ties with them are dying. I don't even want to consider what it would take to get this sucker off.

"There's that sass again, missy. It's a good thing I love you." He drops a kiss to my lips, then eyes the feather judiciously. "It's a bit too large, I think. Even if we're going for dramatic, we can still lose a bit of overkill. Do you want to see how it works?"

The magick user in me is excited to see Muse magic, but I'm so overcome by the emotions that the words get stuck. Instead, I nod at him with a shy smile.

"Smaller." The feather glows for a moment, then shrinks about ten percent, leaving the quill to end right at the curve of my hip.

Curving around my breast, the eye stayed exactly where it was placed, as if it knew that was the focal point.

"Ooooh," I say, biting my lip. The tint of childish glee twinkling out of my eyes makes him laugh, and I shrug. I'm always captivated by magickal items, and this is no exception.

"You like that, huh?" Taurus studies the placement thoughtfully. He seems to be oblivious to the fact that as he gets closer to marking me, his hips are rubbing against me more persistently. "Do you want to try?"

I shake my head. "It might be a fun toy, but I like it where it is." My hand reaches up to brush a lock of hair off his forehead affectionately.

He looks thrilled with that response. "Good, because there's another surprise. Damien forgot to mention it when I—ahem—saw him out."

I tilt my head, looking curious. "Oh?"

That one brief word stands for so much. My entire body tenses as I brace for some caveat that makes this not as important as it feels. I guess my other mates really broke me. I'm sitting here, waiting for the sword to drop and slice off my head.

Leaning over, he whispers in my ear. "Say 'stick'."

I look down at the feather, murmuring, "Stick."

The feather glows and gives off a faint flowery odor. Taurus grins from ear to ear, then reaches out to nudge it with his finger. It's stuck to me like glue. He looks at me with a wicked grin, his expression asking if I understand.

I blink. "What did you do?"

Levering himself up, he purposely lets his eyes go golden. His hand tangles in my hair and in a voice almost lost to need, he explains, "It's stuck to you until we make it permanent. We're going to do this together."

With that, he lets go of his tightly leashed control and captures my lips, allowing his tongue to play with mine as his fingers stroke over me. I moan as his fingers make my entire body shiver, my legs sawing against his. Pressing against him as our bodies move, I feel the fire spread through me like a flower blossoming. This is the point of no return and I hope I can control her well enough to enjoy this. A tightening of muscles has his hips nudging my thighs apart. Pulling my arms over my head, he pins them there.

He breaks the kiss on a ragged sigh and raises his head, spearing me with demon eyes full of lust and animalistic joy. "We're going to fly, love."

With that, he thrusts inside of me, and a growl rumbles out of my chest. My body surges up to his and my thighs framing his hips. Eyes flashing emerald flecked with gold, I lick my chops when the beast emerges. He shudders and his hips slam against mine in quick, hard strokes. Gold eyes glare down at me intently as if he's stalking prey and I rumble back, letting him know it will be a fight.

My control is better, but she is howling like a hellcat to get all the way out. His demon just challenged her, and she senses an equal. She *wants* him and she can't have him. This might get ugly.

"I want to claim you as we come, love." His pace picks up and my claws tear down his back, marking his skin.

She tests the cage—the word 'claim' sending her into overdrive —and I struggle internally. I don't want this to get ruined, but I fear I won't be able to hold her. I snarl up at him, my body aching with each jarring thrust. My features shift—I can't help it—and it's all I can do to keep her from breaking loose entirely.

A long, low growl slips past his lips. "Mine. Mine. Mine. Mine!"

The growl turns into a roar from the depths of his being. His hands pressing my wrists deep into the cushions above my head, but I keep my eyes on his, letting him fight his own battles. The full demon visage emerges on a bellow of volcanic emotion, and it almost looks like he's going to bury his fangs in my neck. She hits the cage door hard inside of me, desperate to answer the call. I fight to free a hand, praying this will keep her satisfied before she causes a diplomatic nightmare.

My back arches off the couch and I work to keep my fangs far from the skin where they're itching to tear into. "Yours," a voice that is entirely Beast growls. With another moan, my body shakes, raking my claws over his back hard enough to hurt when I fall over the edge.

"Mine. You're mine." Each 'mine' is a brutal thrust, and he finally throws his head back to let out one last roar. "*Bond!*"

A fierce, yowling cry echoes out of my throat as the feather sears its way into my skin. On instinct, my hand snakes up to the appointed ear. Chest heaving for breaths and squeezing him tight enough to break something, I pierce the lobe with a claw. I can only hope that the tiny trickle of blood will sate the beast. Sex and pain are making her rage to bite and tear, and I'm not sure that I can hold her much longer.

My skin is sizzling with the heat of the feather searing its way onto me, and I'm shaking with the force of our shared climax. My entire being feels like it's coursing with magick and beast and lust, and I've never felt this way before. With one last bellow, he collapses on top of me.

Limbs drape over him and my throat feels deliciously raw from the screaming. My breath comes in shallow pants and my eyes slip closed, savoring the emotions rocketing around inside me. The beast seems mollified by the piercing—though I broke my clean needle promise—so I relax. I've won this round, despite the hard-fought battle.

Taurus stirs on top of me. His features slide back to human as we tremble together. Looking down at my chest, he seems to realize that part of him is lying on top of my new mark. He pushes up to make sure he's not hurting me and his eyes meet mine. Once he sees my sated smile, he grins broadly. Untwining our nearly broken fingers, he wipes a sweaty lock of hair off my forehead. He leans down and kisses me gently. "I love you, Sand-wich. Mine." As an afterthought, he licks my collarbone playfully.

I trail bruised fingers up his sides, schooling the wince off of my face. "I love you, too, baby. Yours."

"Tired?"

"A little." I flush, not telling that the most exhausting part was fighting off a hungry, possessive hellcat that wanted to drink him deep.

"Sod that. All you had to do was lie there and get a little singed. I did all the work." I smack him playfully and he frowns. "It didn't hurt too much, did it?"

"Nah, only for a few seconds. Besides, I did more than lay there, you ape."

He growls, nipping my shoulder. "Minx."

I wrap around him, nuzzling my nose across his collarbone as a soft purr kicks up in my chest. The Beast has faded, the fire in my veins has faded, and I'm feeling victorious. "You're going to put the stud you brought in soon. I don't want it closing up."

Yawning loudly, he looks at the clock. "Minx, you did it to me again. A nice, clean needle, my round, compact ass."

I give him an innocent look. "What did I do?"

He points out the window. "Oh, look. It's sunrise."

"I'll be damned."

"No doubt both of us will be, love. It's a good thing that I still have... Oh, what's that now? Two full hours before work."

"You could have told me. You called me here late. I don't have any responsibilities this weekend, so it doesn't matter if I sleep in."

"I did nothing I didn't want to do, now did I?"

"I didn't say you did."

"Yeah, I noticed you're slippery that way. I gotta watch what I say around you."

I snort, smacking his aforementioned compact rear end. "I'm tricky that way."

"That you are, pet. That you are."

The look of satisfaction on his face makes my eyes sparkle and I give him another squeeze because he looks so cu—manly and attractive. My expression is bright as my hand rubs his over his abs.

"Hey, lady, do you know you've got a peacock on your chest?" He smirks, mocking a terrible American accent.

I blink, pretending to be clueless. "Oh, my goddess, no! Get it off! Get it off!"

Laughing crazily, he pushes away from me to get a good look at the mark. All the color drains out of his face and he gasps. "Bloody buggering hell, do you *see* that?"

I look down. "It's hard not to."

"What did that pea brain Picasso say it was? A tattoo, right?"

"Yeah?" I give him a confused look, suddenly feeling very wary.

His eyes drop to my chest and he reaches out a hand to run a finger over the eye. Drawing back as if it stung him, he frowns. "Then explain to me why the bloody thing is moving. Sandwich, it looks as real as when I was holding it!"

My eyes narrow. "It's moving?" I squint down at myself, fatigue making me loopy. "That's nifty! Look at it!"

"Let me try something." Leaning over, he blows gently across my breastbone. The feather stirs gently, as if on a light breeze. "Did you feel that?"

My nose twitches and I mutter, "It tickles."

He reaches out again, stroking the eye with a thumb. "And that?"

I shift, feeling that in a part of me that does *not* need be re-awakened. "Uh-huh."

He backs over to the edge of the couch. "From here, it's not as noticeable. I doubt I could see it if I weren't straining, and I've got rather good eyes. The color and detail are bloody amazing."

"It's not so bad right now."

"Well, there's no breeze. You'd better hope that's just an 'us' thing, beautiful, or you're going to have a *hell* of a time explaining it to people."

I snort. "A harder time than when I grew fangs and a tail?"

"Point taken." He tilts his head, studying me. "Come to think of it, you kind of look like the cat that ate the peacock—all but for a single feather."

Laughing softly, I lick my lips. "Are you disappointed I missed something?"

"Bloody right!" He eyes me as if he's found a new toy. "Kiss me."

Pulling his face to mine, I kiss him, feeling languid and relaxed. Groaning, he reaches down to stroke his thumb across the eye of the peacock feather, massaging it slowly. My eyes pop open and I squirm, feeling it all over my body. The room fills with the scent of desire, both of our bodies responding to it.

He draws back abruptly, staring at me with wild eyes. "Bloody hell, I *like* this thing."

"Damn." I whistle low.

"I guess this means I *won't* be killing Damien. It also explains his behavior yesterday, the sneaky rotter."

I chuckle. "No wonder he was so damned amused. Bastard."

"Sodding muse." He sighs and shakes his head. "Balls. I'm going to buy him a present and I wasn't going to Canada until November."

"Why Canada? What's up there besides hockey, Mounties, and bad beer?"

"Maple syrup. He loves the stuff. It's a sickness, I'm sure. He can tell which jars are from which tree; it's freaky."

"He's as picky about syrup as I am about booze."

"Idiot thinks he's a connoisseur. He threw a bottle at me once because it was of inferior quality."

I burst out laughing. "No way."

He frowns, looking as if he might pout. "You love me for my cheap laughs. I'm onto you kitten!"

"I love you for the cheap sex, too. Give me some credit." I bob my brows, propping myself up on my elbows.

"Now, now, love muffin. We can't have the ego go 'pop', can we?"

"Baby, nothing could put a dent in *that* behemoth."

"I'll give you that," he smirks.

I squeeze him tightly, murmuring, "Though the freebie hugs and squishy stuff aren't so bad, either."

"Tsk, tsk. What would the people in our world think if they ever found out that a) I was capable of that rot, and b) that's why you loved me? Talk about your definition of apocalypse."

"The Apocalypse is guaranteed once people find out anyway," I grin, ruffling his hair.

"Blondie will have an aneurism."

A low snarl escapes before I can stop it and I mutter, "That's enough to make me preemptively stomp."

He eyes me curiously, and I sigh. It's hard to explain where I am with the people in my life right now. I love my mates, even when they're slicing me to the bone. I can't just cut them out, but I don't know what to do with them. Realistically, you can stop loving someone—I just don't know how.

His eyes light up. "*Wait.* Stomp for me, baby? Imagine I got that neon 'hunk of burning clone' sign attached to your car."

Giving him a dirty look, I shake my head. "That would earn you a beating."

"Will you please *stomp* for your irritating jackass that melts you with his kindness?"

I get up, giving him a fond but exasperated look. Making a production of it, I stomp around the room like a great big idgit. "Are you happy now?"

"*It does*! The bloody feather shivers when you do that, like you're standing on a moving train! It's trembling from your jiggle, baby."

"Oh, *great*. Now I have plumage? Could I *be* more confusing?" Scowling, I stomp over to him in a faux huff.

"It's not noticeable unless you pay attention," he says. "I doubt a human would see. To them, you'd probably just have a huge peacock's feather over your left tit. Who's saying what they'd think?" He looks like he's going to pout, and it melts the starch right out of me.

"Fuck 'em. I don't care what they—or anyone—thinks. I like it." I cross my arms over my chest, irritated at the thought of someone telling me what I can or can't do.

"You sure? I could get Damien to tell me how to take it off or stop it from doing that."

"I was teasing you, baby. No need to fret."

Shrugging nervously, he tries to play it off. "It's new for me."

I drop onto his lap and smile. "I was sure when you put it on, and I'm sure now. That won't change."

Hugging me tightly, he murmurs, "I love you for that, though. It'll probably cause a head butt or two."

That is an understatement the likes of which have never been seen, but I'll let it go with that.

"So, I've got to go. I have to spend some time at work today—right before I die. I'm not as young and spry as some kitties I know." He kisses me softly. "Is this the part where I tell you I may like you a little?"

"It's also where I say I might like you, even if you're an ass."

"Riiiight. I remember this part. I bray, you hiss, and b-i-n-g-o was his name-o." He laughs, reaching over to pinch my bum.

"Today, I think I'll do this." I lean in and kiss him, then take a deep breath for courage before saying, "I love you."

"Damn. That's only today's treatment? I could bloody well get used to that."

He takes me in his arms and places me gently back on the couch. Smoothing my hair, he gets down on a knee in front of me. "I love you, too, beautiful. See you soon."

Watching him leave, I sigh. Once he's gone, I gather up my

forgone clothing. I may be the biggest idiot alive, but today, I'm a happy idiot.

Hopefully, it lasts.

The Socialite Gets The Dirt

PHILOMENA

"These diva-tinis are beyond the beyond, darling," I croon as I stretch out on the lounge chair. It's unseasonably warm, and I feel like I've melted. I hope to hell that I don't have unsightly chair marks when I get up. As much as I adore these boys, their housemates' style in interior design is lacking and they don't seem to have control over it.

Surprising to hear from me, I'm sure.

Chatting up the internet isn't exactly my thing. I don't even use social media sites. It's tacky, and I don't need the approval of the trembling masses to validate myself. I catch a lot of grief from those bottle-headed boobs and their equally sex-crazed mates, but if you want the real brains of the operation, you're looking at her. I might be drunk ninety percent of the time, but I'm a fucking android, people. It's in my programming, not my bloodstream. My mental capacity isn't even the teensiest bit affected, regardless of what I consume.

Idiots—poorly dressed idiots—but I digress.

The lazy painter is somewhere in the house with the hipster blogger. I'm in the same city, but we're not in the same zip code because I haven't seen him since we got here. I hitched a ride with him because he was heading to the same place. The conversation was about as scintillating as listening to C-SPAN, but he mentioned keeping my ears open for issues. I don't know what the hell that's supposed to mean. They're all screaming, sexed-up dimwits.

How am I supposed to know what's worrisome and what's part of the game?

He seems to think I will, though. The request doesn't surprise me; I've known something bad was going on since Victor disappeared with the cat. Our prickly maker won't talk about it, and since he usually can't keep his trap shut even to eat, I assume it's at the kitty's request.

"Duchess P, you're thinking way too hard. Did you mix downers with uppers again? You know, that just makes us normal."

My boys—Janus and Roman—are similarly toasty. They're comfortable on their own chairs, sipping the pink drinks and sunning in front of the pool. I'm not sure what decides the weather in the Rift, but I'll take sunny and warm in late March any day of the week.

Believe me when I tell you this because the other morons that live here don't. There is nothing going on between me and the dancing duo. They're screwing each other, but not me. All those bleach heads giggle and gossip, but my boys and I are strictly sane fashionistas floating in a pool of nymphomaniacs with bad closets. Who has time for all the mess involved in anything else? I'd spill my drink, have to share my Xanax...

You can see the reasons for my distaste, yes?

"I did not. I'm contemplating the time it will take me to completely replace the clothes in your family's closets to make them remotely presentable. Also, my drink is now empty."

Roman chuckles and moves to refill my glass. Meanwhile, Janus launches into a lengthy speech on respecting other people's boundaries—something I truly could not care less about. People see me in public with these fashion challenged twits. Does he not realize that?

I'm not actually doing that, by the way. His family's wardrobe tragedy is his problem. I am, however, mentally cataloguing—which goes quickly for an android—the anomalies in my family dynamic in the past six to eight months. Once I finish, I can extrapolate a likely scenario to explain the recent changes to everyone's behavior, including the addition of the Designer Assassin.

Frowning, I realize something. There seem to be more controversies and contusions that I wrote off without the context the lounger's request now gives me.

Troublesome. I will discuss this with Siren and Sandrine when I return home. The three of us will decide what to do. You can't trust the men—they're too easily swayed by their libidos. The kitty will lie like a Wall Street banker in a congressional hearing if she thinks we've figured out her dirty little secret.

The question is: how bad is it?

It's obvious that the bimbo and her subbie mate have been sidelined. The whispers say it was because of betrayal. It would have to be really fucking bad for the cat to close the doors.

The bigger question is: what have the dog and the fluffy writer been up to?

Janus finally stops rambling about personal space and people's privacy, so I let it fly. "That's all fascinating, darling, but what I'm interested in is the dirt. We can make kissy faces at not nosing into other's peoples' business, but as beautiful as our faces are, it's not what we do. Something stinks in the garden, my flouncy friends, and we are more than fashionably late to the party. What in the Dolce and Gabbana is going on around here?"

They look at one another—a sly, knowing look—and what passes for my blood boils. They have been holding out on me.

Unacceptable.

I stand, my posture regal. My Versace sunglasses are positioned low enough for my Streep in Prada glare to pin them. "Emotions cause wrinkles, boys. Stop pussyfooting around the smoking hole in the ground and make with the information."

As if by magic, their chairs scoot closer, drinks get poured, and I return to my chaise to listen. There is much to be done and I hope I am not too late to salvage the wreckage.

The Cat And Bird Are Unaware

DELILAH

I ended up staying on the couch because I was too tired to move. When I woke, I found a photograph propped against the candle that burned all night while we talked, laughed, loved, fussed, and soothed.

He probably wanted to see me when he left, but was afraid to wake me. As much as I swagger about my youth, we've pulled a lot of all-nighters lately. I'm glad he let me snooze so I can be awake this evening.

The picture—a puppy and a kitten romping together in the tall grass on a sunny spring day—made me smile softly. *Talk about your reputation destroyers for both of us.* As much as that stuff makes my heart ache, neither of us wants a reputation for being squishy and cute.

Feeling grimy, I use the bird phone to go home and shower. The spray coasts over me as I try to think of how I can top that gift. It hits me as I'm washing the shampoo out of my hair and I end up almost drowning myself. After I get out of the shower, I hunt down my phone, looking for the references I need.

Calling Hex home to help me with it, I grit my teeth as he

shows with Chaos in tow. Oh, how I *hate* her family. Chaos isn't that bad once you learn to translate her nonsensical ramblings. But the people she lives with are Sari sycophants and I'm in no mood for that. Once Hex finishes, I extricate myself from playing a game of melt the army men with Chaos. Grabbing a drink, I head upstairs to make sure I look presentable.

Deciding what I'm wearing is good enough, I zap myself back to Taurus-land. His scent says he's here, but I doubt he's awake. He would have greeted me by now. I was gone a couple of hours, and he didn't leave any sign of when he'd be back.

Hopefully, he's not grumpy.

I tiptoe up to the couch and peep over the back, a mischievous grin on my face. Holding the sleek stuffed panther to my chest, I tug its tail. The vibration makes a soft purring sound. He'd *never* get caught dead with something so cute,. Regardless, I turn it over and inspect the hand embroidered peacock's feather stretching over its torso and belly. Attached to its neck is a ribbon with a small piece of parchment on it, which says '*So I'm here when I'm not*'.

Hex did amazing work on this bad boy.

I carefully place it on his chest, grinning as I watch him sleep. As if sensing me, he cracks an eye open only to come face to face with the cat. "*Arrrgghhhh!*"

He jumps up in surprise and gives me a wild-eyed look, making me shriek. "Dammit, don't do that!"

"*Me?*" He clutches his chest as he heaves in a lungful of oxygen. "You scared me witless with that, uh, present? You got me a present?" Tilting his head, he looks down at the stuffed cat. "You got me a 'you' substitute."

I shrug, not wanting to make a big deal out of it since he seems so flummoxed. "It's nothing. I was out, and I saw it."

Again, with the lies. This emotional wasteland is making me a big, hairy liar all the time. It's not like I got him an engagement ring; it's a toy.

Sheesh, Deli, woman up.

I stop berating myself when he picks it up off the floor with a boyish grin and runs his fingers over the embroidery.

"You saw it with this mysteriously specific design?" He stops and holds it up to his ear, as if just noticing the vibration. "It's purring!" His expression turns delighted as he looks at me.

"You pull its tail."

He pulls it again, looking at it with amazement. Suddenly, he realizes that he's holding a stuffed animal like an old friend. He looks at me, then purposely around the empty room, as if someone will see him. "If anyone ever found out I was holding this, I'd have to immediately kill myself. But I love it."

"I won't tell; cross my heart."

"It's a little you," he says, looking less like a lethal killer than a little kid.

Dropping onto the couch, I tuck my feet under me and smile fondly. "That's what I was hoping."

He sits down next to me, his head resting on the cushion as he looks over at me. His eyes are tired, but his expression is serious. "God, I missed you today."

I reach over to run my hand over his cheek. "I missed you, too, baby. Have a hard day?"

"It's me—how I am. I get knackered and I stop functioning. I may as well not even bother with the bleeding commute to work. I couldn't do a fucking thing as tired as I was." I run my fingers through his hair lightly and he continues, "I thought about Blondie a bit because I'm a masochistic fuck. I remembered a lot, which pissed me off and turned me on because damn, some of that shit was hot."

I blink, willing my hand to keep going as I'm the last person who should have a gripe about having other lovers. But somehow—here and now—that stings. My free hand rubs over my heart absently and I stay quiet, unsure what to say. *Why does it feel like I took a cannonball in the chest? Is there something I'm not doing right?* I am so screwed up by all this damned Wilde bullshit; I would have questioned none of this before.

"I've concluded that Blondie is the *most* two-faced person I know, or she's out of her bloody mind."

"I have no idea which is true. I thought I knew her, but I guess I was wrong. She has a lot of problems." I whisper for fear I'll let it slip how tenuous my emotional state is right now.

"I've known her a while; Talia has known her longer than that. Though, if you saw everything I did, you'd laugh at the pattern of behavior. I forgot I started her on her sexual quest."

I shrug. "Maybe that's why you're such an important conquest."

"I saw some blogs back then, with the gnome giving Blondie advice on how to get me in the sack."

"Did she give her the 'every guy likes to fuck, give him the chance' lecture? I have names for all of Sari's stock speeches."

"It would be *so* much easier if I could eat them."

"The problem is they've been feeding each other's dysfunction for years now. There's no stopping that train."

"You know what? This is bloody ridiculous—all of it. They deserve each other. They're happy in their misery and probably wouldn't recognize a healthy relationship if it bit them on their asses. Though, one would wonder how healthy that brand of relationship would be."

I snort, not because he's been funny, but being bitten on the ass started the *most* fucked up relationship that I've ever been in. He does not know how ironic that is. If he knew Wilde had started that way, he'd laugh me out of the room. I sigh. "It wouldn't be very healthy. Trust me on that one."

Looking worn out and upset, he reaches for his present and pulls its tail as he wraps his arms around it unconsciously. "Do I even want to ask?"

I chuckle. "The first time Wilde bit me was on the ass."

"He claimed your ass? What a wanker."

"Not claimed, but marked, I guess? I got him drunk, so that excuses it a little." I give him a half smile.

If I could turn back time, oh boy, would Cher and I do things differently...

"You mention your relationship with Wilde a lot. What's so different for you than for Blondie with that ponce?"

I shrug. "I mean, I think it goes back to that bite. Wilde bit me the first time we slept together. Back then, he didn't even bite Sari. He sure as fuck hadn't bitten Rhea. He treated her like his Lady Fair because that's what she lived through with him: a romance novel. He's always called me his Darkness—which is the part of him that Rhea couldn't touch. I'm a bad, rude girl. I guess it made her feel like I'm closer to him? I don't know; it's stupid. She doesn't want what I have and trust me, I'd give it to her, but she couldn't handle it."

I pause, shocked that I said what I did. Clamping my mouth shut before something else gets out, I panic.

Holy Hell in a handbasket, someone gag me. My mouth's run off on its own.

"If I wasn't in such a foul mood, this would be roughly akin to a poorly written Greek tragedy."

More like a tragedy re-told by the Marquis de Sade, but okay. "I guess so. She's definitely made Wilde her Helen of Troy."

"I think part of my bloody problem with Blondie is that I can't wrap my mind around wanting to be something that you're not. She's not a dark force like me, Talia, or Sari. She has a dark side, but that's not her driving force."

I notice he left me out and perhaps he's mistaken the chewy center for a rainbow of light. He'll learn eventually, but now's not the time to correct him. "She wants to run with the crowd, not get left on the porch getting the vapors."

"That explains my problem with it. Joining is not my middle name."

I snort. "Me, neither. I lead the crowd, not follow it."

He looks at me for a moment as if assessing me. "You know, it occurs to me I have yet to receive any kind of welcome at all from you tonight, love. Sick of me already, are you?"

"No, I'm not tired of you in the least; don't be so prickly."

"Prickly? Me? What would make you think a character like me would get prickly?"

"I have *no* idea," I snort, then kiss his nose. "Did I forget to tell you how glad I was to see you?"

"I'm still having some insecurity about us, kitty, and the lack of sleep is making it worse. I think I'm bigger a poof than normal." He draws me closer and mutters something under his breath that even I strain to hear with enhanced hearing.

"What was that?"

"I said I love you. Damn, woman, you deaf?" He gives me a petulant look, shrugging as if he doesn't care.

"Nope. I enjoy hearing it intelligibly. Love you, too, baby."

He exhales and grins a crooked grin at me, shifting me on his lap to get closer. "How can you be so not insecure about us?"

I have *no* answer for that. I'm a mess of insecurities, lies, half-truths, fears, broken wings, and scars inside. I can't say that because it lets the full on crazy out. He didn't sign up for that, and I'm not comfortable enough to share it. I wrap myself around him, purring softly as I rub my cheek on his. "Because I know I love you and because my gut says it's right. I trust my instincts—or I try to."

I mean that. I'm following my gut despite the firm and loud protests in my head.

A warm grin spreads across his face slowly as he nods. "You know what? Sometimes, it really is that simple. Thanks, love."

"No problem. I'm a fount of knowledge, you know."

"We're founts of something, you and me, but somehow I don't think knowledge is our strong suit."

"Evil. Got a streak a mile wide."

He eyes the feather and smirks. "Not quite a mile, but close enough to be seen."

I chuckle throatily and arch my back, my eyes darkening. "You got that right."

His hands bury in my hair and he tugs my head back, nipping his way down my neck. Eyes lift to mine, swirling gold as he puts shaky hands on my hips. He draws a deep breath before murmuring, "Your mark; your man."

"My man," I echo, my voice husky as my hands slide to his hair. I'm enjoying nipping along the fragile skin of his neck. I know his rules and that's going nowhere fast, but Christ, a girl gets to dream, right?

A slow smile tugs at the corners of his mouth and his right hand moves up from my hip to run the length of the feather teasingly. I squirm as his fingers strum the tattoo, grinning at his enthusiasm. He touches his lips to mine and the emotion of the moment overwhelms me. "Mine. Yours. Together."

The Cat Knows This Is Big

DELILAH

His voice is a ragged whisper as he sups at my lips, each kiss a little longer and a little more intense than the one before. The sensations his hands on the feather cause make my hips rock against his. I groan as all the feelings and emotions inside me—all the hidden fears and thoughts and love—funnel out into our embrace, making me cling to him tightly.

I can't say everything I need to say because I can't feel everything I feel. It's not okay to betray everyone for these feelings or to lie to him about what he's done to me. But I am and there's nothing I can do about it—he's hooked me. Maybe it was because I'm hurt and vulnerable; maybe it was because I've always wanted him.

Maybe it's just him.

Pushing my hair out of my face, he murmurs against my lips in a ragged voice, "I need you." His hands caress the skin under my shirt before gathering it and lifting it up. "I want you." He waits while I raise my arms, dropping a licking kiss to the underside of a nearby appendage. "I love you."

Oh, lord. This feels so serious.

My heart flutters and I look up from under my lashes, feeling his hands roam over me. I'm naked from the waist up, which means he can genuinely appreciate his mark on me. He leans forward to run his tongue over the eye of the feather, right over my heart. I can feel it in my toes—that tattoo is hellaciously potent.

"I want to bury myself in you, baby, and feel you squeeze me."

Then there's that mouth. I draw in a shuddering breath as he kisses the mark, my hips jerking automatically. I swallow hard. "I want you so much. I love you," I whimper, surprised at the fierceness of the emotions flowing through me. My fingers slide down his chest, blunt nails scratching as I try to keep my world from tilting off its axis.

He sucks in a breath as my nails tease him, then he lunges from the couch. Wrapping an arm around my back to hold me tightly, he moves with clone speed. His mouth sears mine as we slam up against the wall, and he cups my ass in his hands. "Naked. Now."

I nod, my breath catching as I fumble with my pants. Pushing and kicking at them as best I can, I growl. When I'm finally free, I lift my legs, wrapping them around his waist to wriggle against him. His groan makes me feel supremely feminine. A muscular arm lifts me higher so he can reach his buckle and zipper. It takes some doing, but he gets his pants undone and down, stepping out of them quickly.

"Gotta love that clone dexterity," I mutter, and he grimaces as our bodies press intimately. Turning with his back to the wall and he leans into it, settling me firmly on his hips.

I'm not sure I can wait much longer.

"Christ, you feel good."

I hiss, scratching along his shoulders as he moves against me. My whole body clamors for him so hungrily that it's overwhelming. I gaze into his eyes, squeezing my thighs around his hips and moving more insistently. I can feel the beast uncoiling and I'm ready to stop thinking.

He moans, his eyes closing as he tightens his grip on me.

Nipping and sucking at my throat, his free hand cups a breast and he opens his eyes to mine. Our bodies align, almost joined, but his pause seems important. I look at him, my pulse racing in fear. As we gaze into each other's eyes, my name—my actual name—is a growl on his lips before he thrusts into me. Flexing a hand on my hip to push me down onto him, he moans against my ear. "Bloody... God, don't move—not yet."

I tense up, trying to fight the natural instincts to move and bend and purr and howl. He pushes off the wall and staggers to the couch, dropping us onto it in a way that makes my inner wild side slam against the bars in a rage. She wants out, and she wants it now. Until a few months ago, sex had never been so complex. It was never a fight for survival and dominance over me.

Until a few weeks ago, I wasn't having sex with Taurus.

All she wants is what she believes is rightfully hers. I keep fighting inside as the need courses through my veins like hot lava. My hands shake a little as I hold on to his shoulders, throbbing as he fills me. Licking my lips, I take purposefully even breaths, biting my lip to hold myself together. "It's so... I feel..."

His hands dance up my abdomen, kneading my breasts, pulling at my nipples, scratching and rubbing along his mark on me. Even he seems to struggle mightily for control. Spearing me with golden eyes, he growls low. "It feels good together."

Fingertips skating over the new mark make me tremble. "Love this," I murmur, hips wriggling impatiently.

"God, yes." His hips thrust again, and he moans as I grind against him, eliciting a shiver that I can feel run down his frame. "I know," he growls as his hips buck faster and harder "... you don't have your spurs tonight, love," his fangs lower and he drags them across my feather almost snapping my control right there "... but I'll whicker for you, if you ride me at a gallop."

I growl low at his words, feeling the burn of the beast clawing her way out. As amazing as this is, I don't know how much time I have left before the struggle becomes a losing battle. Raking my claws down his chest, my eyes flash as my spine rolls fluidly, bending unnaturally as my movements speed up.

His eyes widen in surprise, and a choked roar rips from his throat. "*Christ.*" He stops to kiss me with brutal force, then tears his mouth off mine to stare into my eyes. His eyes gleam hotly and his earring flashes in the soft glow from the lamp. "I. Love. You." Cupping my face in his hands, his hips rock against me hard and fast, repeating himself as we move in unison.

I suck in harsh pants, my body gripping him tightly in every downstroke. My eyes swirl with color when my head falls back. I let my lower body do all the work as I raise and lower over him roughly. My nails scratch over his abs, leaving bright red raised furrows on the sculpted muscles. I reply to every chanted profession in the deep, rough voice of my primal side.

This is ruining me and I have no intention of stopping it.

A keening cry escapes from his chest as he loses control, his grinding thrusts reaching a fever pitch. His head falls back as he roars my name when he explodes. I shriek as my orgasm rips through me like a wildfire, searing my insides. Whimpering and moaning his name, my eyes roll back in my head while I shudder from head to toe.

Taurus strokes the eye of the feather with one hand, a satiated and sloppy grin on his face as I tremble. His touch softens, then finally falls away entirely when I finally collapse against him. Eyes closed, he runs a spent arm up and down my spine lazily. "I have to tell you, love. This may be the shortest relationship a clone ever had, because I think you killed me."

I rub my face on his shoulder, purring softly as he strokes me. "Mmm... now I gotta bring you back or something," I mumble raspily. "I don't think I'd like you dead very much."

His chuckle is gravelly. "Oh, I don't know. I'd probably be easier to put up with that way. The sex would undoubtedly go downhill, though."

"Less mouthy," I ponder, "but that could be a drawback, too."

I chuckle at his expression and qualify. "However, you're not that hard to put up with now."

He quirks a brow and rubs his chin over my cheek. "You're only saying that because I make you scream."

Ha. If only he knew what hard to put up with means. Christ, it's hard having a secret shame to remind you of your failures.

I give him a small grin, hoping to chase away the dark with a little lighthearted banter. "True. But you're good for other stuff, too." I'm sprawled so comfortably on his lap that I never want to move.

"Blasphemy," he teases. "I am not."

"You are, too, you big blowhard." I chuckle softly. Tweaking his nipple playfully, I feel cozy and warm again.

He looks thoughtful. "Actually, I think I'll stick around. I'm not ready to kick it yet. Though, if you ever fuck me like that again, it may not be up to me."

"I was only doing what you said."

He laughs and rolls his eyes. "Oh sure, the *one* time you listen to me and it gives me cardiac arrest."

Giggling, I poke his chest. "Be careful what you wish for, Mr. Weak Heart."

Clutching his chest dramatically, he moans. "Death by sperm donation. Hell of an obituary."

I snort. "Yet another thing I'd never live down."

His brow arches. "Bloody hell, that would sure twist a lot of knickers, wouldn't it? People pointing and whispering. 'She's the one that offed that Taurus git. Fucked him to his happies and popped his ticker. Can you believe it?' You'd be a gossip sensation."

I roll my eyes. "Man, the crazies would line up at the damned door. I'd never be able to sleep again."

"I'd wager one or two would spring for a medal."

"Oh, wait. That already happens." His snark makes me smile and I shrug. "Possibly."

Giving me a stern look, he muses. "The golden goddess may take some issue with it, though."

"I think she'd definitely take issue with me—a pointy one. It's a good thing you survived, I suppose."

Eyes alight with fondness, he chuckles. "I suppose." He flops sideways on the couch, pulling me with him.

I curl around him, purring softly because I know it makes him melty.

He gives me a smirk and murmurs, "You know, you've already totally mushed out on me about everything else: falling for me, wearing my mark. Would one teeny tiny little 'hunk of burning clone, yeah, baby' really kill you?"

"Yes. It will kill me dead." I grin.

He grumbles good-naturedly. "Yeah, well, can't have that. It'd break my heart. You know, if I had one."

I roll my eyes and pinch his rear. "Don't be silly. You know you have a heart."

"Shhhhh. Bloody hell, woman, I have a reputation to uphold here." He winks and kisses my nose.

"Cause sooooooooooo many people can hear us here."

"Fine, if the walls don't have ears, then I'm officially changing my name to Adonis. You can call me Don."

"If you think I'm calling you the blond Adonis, you are nuts, buster. Your ego is massive enough as it is."

"*Oh, come on.* I don't get 'hunk of burning clone.' You're killing me."

"Mmm. So sad."

"Now I don't get blonde Adonis? How bloody fair is *that*?"

"Your life is so unfair." I giggle and smirk at him.

"Don't you giggle at me, missy. You're one step away."

"One step from what? You're naked and not very threatening."

"From going over my lap for a spanking, which I can do as I am, minx!"

I pretend to gasp for effect, hoping that some trick of my

mind doesn't flash me back to bad things if we're headed for this kind of play. I've been okay with others, but it would be now that I'd have some PTSD-like meltdown, wouldn't it? Ruined things are a specialty of mine of late. "Oh no! Not that!"

"*That's it.*" He laughs, grabs me and sits up, draping me across his lap and swatting my bare ass once as if warning me. "Do you take it back?"

Okay. Good so far. Fun, but no freak out. "Hey! And... no."

He rubs his hand over my light red skin, then swats me again, harder this time. "Take it back."

"No." My grin is impish, but I can see and feel where this is going. If we stay playful, I think I'm okay. I can't let anything too serious or too emotional slide in or we'll have problems.

"Take it back," he growls low and I chuckle throatily.

This has possibilities.

We're completely wiped. It's late, and I don't have to be home soon. No one's waiting, but I don't make a point of that because Talia is waiting for him.

It's a pisser, but I can lie here after he goes, soak in his scent, and pretend, right?

I am the most fucked up, sad, broken toy in the box. If anyone knew how royally buggered my headspace has become, they'd all run. My firmest foundations are shaken, my strongest beliefs challenged, and all the while, I'm trying like hell to survive what amounts to emotional rendition from someone I love. My brow furrows, and I'm glad that he can't see my face when I'm lying on his chest.

The turmoil inside of me must be written all over it.

His voice interrupts my dark thoughts. "Want to use me as a very manly pillow, love?"

I blink. *How do I answer that without becoming the Blonde Backbiter?* I paste a smile on my face and curl closer, buying a little time to dig through my neuroses. "Mmm. Sounds good to me." I purr softly, distracting him from the small spots of tension in my frame as I wonder what exactly this means.

"Hey. Wait a bloody second—I've been had."

Holy hell. Who told him what? Did someone tattle on something I wasn't ready to share yet? Did I say something? Christ. I have to play it cool. "I mean, yeah, twice. Wasn't that the point?"

He narrows his eyes and glares at me. "No," he frowns. "Yes. No." Shaking his head, he takes a deep breath, presumably to calm himself. "The point is, you said I'm like every other clone out there —or person out there, not sure really, as I'm still fuzzy. You were supposed to get punished."

"I said you had the same fetish as every other male. I don't know how much it counts, given what we were doing when I was taunting you."

Looking like he's fighting a yawn and losing the battle with being indignant, he sighs. "You're right, love. I'm like everyone else; you win."

No shit on that one, buddy. I'm wondering when every surprise topic will stop making me feel like I'm tap-dancing on a minefield. *Am I ever going to share it all with him? Is it ever not going to feel precarious? I don't know.* We have some serious fundamental differences in what is acceptable and not. The only people I've ever truly given everything to are my mates, and that also has not worked out for me. I don't know how eager I am to open that door again. "It's no fun if you agree."

He presses a gentle kiss on my forehead. "Recap the evening, love. I've been fucked, conversed with intelligently and saucily, fucked again, and it's after three am. I'm too bloody pleased with myself and you to be contrary." He arches a brow as he looks down at me. "Besides, I'm one of the few people on the planet who knows what an amazing a person you are, so forgive me if I'm secure in myself enough to say that I'm not like everyone else. I'm luckier."

Ouch. That one got me right in the ticker.

While it's not unpleasant or hurtful, it's enough emotion to be scary and makes me a little sad at the same time. He wouldn't feel so lucky if I bared it all. He'd run like I had set him on fire and I'd be alone again. Not literally, but between the shared pain of me and my primary, we're marooned on an island with no visible way off. There are too many spider webs holding us in place. It's a prison of our own making.

Okay, that's too serious again.

"Point taken, smooth talker." I look up, my eyes sparkling.

"I did *really* enjoy that spanking."

Shit. We're skating on thin ice. The S&M I was into with Alistair was only okay because he prefers being on the bottom—no flashback triggers there. "You would."

"I don't recall you complaining, either."

I chuckle. "You're right." This time.

He mutters to himself, scratching his chest idly. "Remind me tomorrow to chisel in stone that you said that, kitty. I don't know about you, but I'm wiped."

"Me, too," I yawn, preparing myself for when he's gone. It feels empty and alone. I'm such a sad sack about all this. I could paint my face up and write an emo song.

"Are you going to get some sleep?"

I nod. "For sure."

"God, I don't want to move. Maybe I'll crash here for tonight."

He can't see my expression and hopefully he hasn't noticed that I'm not breathing. Stay here? He always goes home. I'm second and that's what I signed up for. Sleeping here is intimate. I swallow hard and whisper, "It definitely wouldn't bother me. You make a good manly pillow."

Keep cool. Keep being casual, like it's no big deal. You fill beds with ten plus people and not all of them are special that way, right? It's become a status symbol to sleep in the enormous bed. How can sleeping together for four hours be special?

You're over-reacting, Deli. Calm yourself.

Closing his eyes, he tightens his hold on me and I try to relax more against him. "Maybe for a little while. I love you, kitty."

My voice is whisper soft as I reply. "I love you, too, baby." I smile sleepily, drifting already as I snuggle into his arms.

He reaches over the back of the couch and blindly gropes for a light blanket to pull over our naked bodies. I fall asleep not long after, the long day forcing my troubled mind into submission as I shut down.

Tomorrow may hold more answers.

The Artist Gets Caught

RAFE

I feel like I'm going to die right here on the floor of the bedroom. Despite my aches and pains, I can't call her because I reassured her leaving me here would be okay. She needs the time to herself with someone who's going to be good to her. Unfortunately, I also can't let the others know because the cat will get word.

Worse, someone will find out what's been going on behind closed doors.

There has to be something I can do, though, because I need help. I was wrong about the coyote keeping Wilde in check—she was away all weekend with the firestarter and the knife tosser. No one told me I'd be left me alone with him after he found out where my primary was. Of course, he took out his frustration on me; I was convenient and I'll heal.

It's become a recurring theme between these two.

Normally, I could depend on Sari to temper his ire a bit. She's not much better, but she hasn't reached full strength with her animal mutation yet. It makes her less wild and slightly more restrained. The two of them have amped up their game since the cat and I mated with Flame and Alistair, and it's getting dangerous. Most visits start out with one of them bitching about it having to share us. After the addition of her coyote and Wilde's demon, the constant jealousy lead me to believe that they'd finally calm down because they had something the others didn't.

Until they figured out what was going on with our other mates and now, it's become less a pleasure dungeon and more a torture one.

It's not an actual dungeon, but the room where we used to play is much more twisted than it used to be. We can't make them happy because we are *not* enough to distract their neuroses. Despite what Sari and Wilde preach, they would be happier if *all* their varied lovers were only in interested in them. That's not how it's supposed to work and it's causing a shit ton of grief amongst the family.

So far this weekend, Wilde has been exacting his revenge for everything that bothers him. From my relationship with Alistair to his fear of the agent stealing the cat to his trust issues, it all fell to my feet. His frustration at my refusal to answer questions about where the cat is hiding fueled two days of sheer insanity. I could have broken free before now if I truly wanted to—clone strength is no joke—but... then he would have hunted my primary down.

We're both trying to protect one another while keeping this fucking mess a secret—but that can't last forever.

I'm a flexible clone, and I enjoy a slice of pain with my pleasure. My kind lives a dangerous life at the Company and were trained to withstand an enormous amount of pain. I don't partake in that anymore, but a little rough and tumble is fun. However, if there was any pleasure in this, it was all his. Wilde's various methods weren't intended to drive me wild—no, there made me submit.

Honestly, I'm amazed I'm still upright and the fact that I drove myself home after freeing my limbs is terrifying.

But I couldn't stomach another night. I had to feign weakness and promise I could get the cat to heal me. He bought it, but only because he wanted me to continue 'playing'. For all his insecurities,

Wilde doesn't assume that anyone would want to leave when he's in his 'demon-mode'. In fact, the cat did such a good job of convincing him that his demon was an acceptable part of him. He assumes everyone loves that wanker's twisted desires.

Trust me, this is not *what we envisioned when we encouraged him to embrace his inner dark side.*

The irony is that I have to hide all of this. I'm too sore to move and I might have a few joints out of whack from hanging. Without my primary, I'm not sure I can hide this if someone tries to help. The bruising is obvious, so—

"What in the name of Tom Ford and Coco Chanel happened to *you?*"

Jesus Christ. How in the hell did the boozy bint know I left, much less get back here without a car?

I rub my temples gingerly. I can't deal with her attitude when I'm worried that I might pass out. That's the *last* thing I need her to see. "Bit of a rough night. We get a bit carried away when we're having fun." I leer at her, hoping that referencing my sex life will send her straight to the liquor cabinet while I figure out what to do.

She snorts. "Pull on the other one—I don't want to end up lopsided."

I arch a brow, not up for protesting more. She doesn't give in at first and I lean against the doorframe with a groan. This stand-off can't go much longer or I'm going to tip over.

"You look beaten to within an inch of losing consciousness. By your lack of horror, it was not something new. When confronted, you're a shitty liar, so don't bother. I'm going to carry you to the bathroom and prop you up. We'll get you clean and then to bed— where you will stay all of this evening and most of tomorrow—so you can heal before the kitty gets back."

Blinking, I tilt my head in confusion. This is a side of Philomena I've never seen before.

Bossy, yes, bitchy, yes, but this? It's weird.

"Siren and I will take turns bringing in food, art supplies, applying poultices from the cat's cabinets, and watching the clone healing to ensure that you don't need a proper doctor. Do *not* fight me on this or I will sedate you. My boys dropped the four-one-one on me when I pigeon-holed them this morning. I know what you two have been hiding."

Her glower makes me shiver, as if she's going to finish the job Wilde started. "Look, we can't..."

"Put a sock in it. If you won't defend yourself, I can't force you to. But I can damn sure let the rest of the family know. We'll see where it goes from there."

With that, she hefts me up on her shoulder and carries me into the bathroom, slamming the door behind us.

I guess we're done talking.

The Bird Wants, More, More, More

❦

DELILAH

Morning Gorgeous,

Had to get to work and didn't want to wake you. I'll find you later.

Last night was.... amazing. No, fantastic. No, mind-blowing. No. Life changing, beautiful, hot, wonderful, sexy as fuck ... nice.

Bugger that.

I don't care if I sound like a prat.

It was bloody incredible. I'm hard again thinking about you marking me as your own and I won't deny it.

I love you.

Dragging myself away sucks, and not in the good way.

Think of me, kitty, because I sodding know I'll be thinking about you.

Taurus

After reading his note this morning, I cleaned up the mess we left before heading home. I only spent a few moments there—enough to get clean and grab a snack before I popped back to the secret place via his magic app thingy. Rather than exploring any of the doorways, I sat down with my book and promptly fell asleep.

Being up all night several nights in a row will make anyone exhausted.

When I wake up, I stretch my limbs and arch my back until I hear the vertebrae pop. Wrinkling my nose, I grumble when I feel the crease of my book left on my cheek. A familiar scent catches my nose and a grin curls my lips.

He thinks he's being sneaky, but I'll teach him.

I pretend to not notice his presence, adjusting the blanket and settling in with my book. A disappointed harrumph sounds from behind me. I hear him walk past the door again, as if he's waiting for me to notice him. Feeling his annoyance makes it so hard not to giggle. He finally strides into the room and I close my eyes, singsonging, "I can smell you."

Taurus peeps over the back of the couch. "You need to stop bloody doing that."

I giggle, my expression mischievous as I make no promises. "How was I supposed to know that you didn't sense that I was lying in wait?"

He rolls his eyes and huffs. "Did you get the letter I left for you, love?"

Giving him a soft smile, I nod. "I did. You were right: it was incredible, amazing, and indescribable."

His chest puffs, and he struts around the couch. "Glad I satisfied."

I drape my legs over the back of the couch, reclining against the arm. "How was your morning?"

He flexes his neck, stretching out tense muscles. "Busy. But I couldn't stop myself from coming to see you. I hoped you'd be here."

I hold my hands out. "I'm glad you did. Do want me to help get that tension out?"

Taking my hand, he flips it over to kiss the underside of my wrist. "Nah, kitty, I'm good. I just had a couple of negotiations flare up. I'll be alright."

"You look all tense and stuff, so I offered."

"I am tense, but shockingly, not in a foul mood." He grins, the heat in his eyes unmistakable. "I doubt much could stomp on my parade today, love." Dropping onto the couch next to me, he leans back into the cushions and pulls me close. "That's the reason I wanted to speak to you."

Seriously, he has to cut it out with the heart stopping pronouncements.

He acts like he's the one with the bad ticker. Every damned time we do this 'let's talk' dance, I expect to get kicked in the teeth. It feels like a piece of my soul dies each time.

Have I simply moved from one prison to another?

I don't say any of those things, though. I look up and smile, keeping my fear cloaked. "What's on your mind, baby?"

"I don't want you to take heat because I'm sniffing around you, kitty."

"I won't be able to avoid that, but I'm not worried because I don't care what everyone thinks." I tilt my head, not sure how to reassure him without lying my ass off. He's right to worry and it *will* be a problem on many levels, but he doesn't need to know that. I can take care of myself—probably. "Rhea is the only person who might throw a public fit. Things have been so bad with her lately, though, that I don't care if she does. But if the rest fall in line, she'll follow the crowd. "

"It's an interesting geometric shape we've got going on. You and the gnome are mates, yet you hate Belle. She's tight with the gnome, and I hate the gnome. I love you and you love me, but the gnome is tight with you. Oh, and everyone is confused about what Blondie's doing. Yet, you're all supposed to be family. It boggles the mind."

I sigh. He doesn't even know the half of it. "I have a lot of difficult baggage; that's true."

"In all fairness, I should warn you that if you get hurt, I'm not sure I can be cavalier about it. Even if the small witted Belle tries to take you on—despite knowing you can handle it—I won't be able to take it lying down. I get evil when one of mine is threatened."

Oh, boy. What's going to happen when Wilde gets bored with torturing my primary for a few days and I end up bearing the brunt?

Most of the time, I can heal myself, but not if my emotional state gets too bad. When that happens, I lose the ability to multifocus and bad things come to light. "I appreciate you wanting to protect me. Sometimes that will be a struggle and you might have to rein in your fury if I ask."

"Actually, I usually just kill the opposition. Rules be damned." He grumbles, "I can't help it, minx. My bloody heart is all involved and shit."

Touched beyond my ability to express, I lean up and press a kiss to his jaw. Reaching around to stroke my fingers over his earring, I say softly, "I know, and I love your involved, yet weak ticker."

Suddenly, he curses and smacks his forehead. "Me and my big bloody mouth. Now, if something happens, you won't tell me because I might go all rampage. Bloody buggering hell."

"Not necessarily. I suck at hiding things when I'm really upset."

That's the truth. I'm good at hiding problems when they don't directly connect to the situation at hand, like with Wilde. When

I'm with Taurus, it's separate in this weird wormhole we're calling home. That makes it easier to disconnect from the problems connected to my other home. The fear gets in sometimes, but only if I face a trigger or a threat to this brief escape.

Pointing his finger at me, he gives me a stern look. "You better not, missy."

"Even if I pretend, it eventually gets dragged out of me. It's not always worth the effort." That's only partly true. I've made the boys go through some obnoxious machinations to get my problems out of me in the past. But I don't know that he needs to worry about that yet.

Rubbing his earring, he murmurs, "Don't feel you have to hold back on me if something is upsetting you."

Crap. Now I'll have to lie or—

"I vow that I'll always think before plunging my hand into someone's chest and ripping out their rotten, shriveled little heart." He gives me an angelic grin, and I snort.

"How very romantic of you."

"You knew what you were getting into when you hailed me, love. I'm not exactly house broken." He tilts his head, looking curious. "My dark side doesn't bother you, does it?" His expression is concerned, though he's asking a bit late in the game. When I don't answer right away, his eyes slide down to the feather on my chest. "I suppose if it did, you'd not be wearing that."

His smug grin is contagious, and I nod as if he's completed a hard task well.

"See? I *can* learn."

"I knew you could." I give him a crooked grin. "Your darkness isn't an issue. We've talked about it, and it didn't seem to bother me, did it?"

"You about repetitive positive reinforcement, right?" I nod and he continues, "You have to remember something when you get annoyed at my occasional lapse in confidence. The only other person—outside my primary—that I've ever liked just chased me down for all my nasty, dark habits while cursing me behind my back for them."

"Baby, I'm not annoyed. It makes me want to coddle and reassure you."

His brows furrow as he frowns. "You know, I think you like when I'm a little unsure. Not because I'm unsure, but I because you *enjoy* being squishy with me."

I scowl. "I do not."

"Oh, no? What if I tell you I've got an enormous hole in my chest from the hurt others have showed off on me and only your purrs make it feel better? Do you think you'd climb up on my lap and give me some puss?"

Shit. He called my bluff. Do I move because he might tell the truth or stay out because I'm being obstinate? Dammit, there's no upside. I scoot onto his lap, positively glowering now. "That's cheating."

He wraps his arms around me and rubs his cheek on mine. "Well, yeah. Dark side."

"You are a bad, rude man, but you're my bad, rude man. That makes it okay." I sigh as if it's the most trying thing in the world.

Leaning into my ear, he whispers, "In case I haven't told you today, I love you."

The scowl fades and I feel a warmth spread through me. "I love you, too, baby."

He looks pensive. "Not to change the subject, but I never talked to you about those blogs posts you pointed out to me after my Rio trip. You know, the ones you said I should read to see your mate and his male mates interact? I thank you ever so for it because the goddess thought it was hot."

I blink. He turns on a dime sometimes. "It's a brave another world since you've been in seclusion. Love is love, you know?"

Giving me a sideways glance, he nods. "Some of it was right illuminating."

I arch a brow, waiting for him to elaborate. *Was that a*

euphemism for hot as fucking hell? I don't expect *him* to say that because he got weirded out by the clones having relationships with one another. I wonder if he's changed his tune, now that he's seen that it's not about the face, but the person behind it.

That's remarkably interesting.

"When you've never given much thought to something, and it's dropped in your lap, it's hard to get your mind around it. But when you see the effect it has on your mate—which was violently pleasant—you're bound to get bonked by the light bulb. But some stories were better than others."

Uh-huh. "Really?"

"Writing style lends more to the story than voice. I still don't grasp the love your male mates seem to have for each other, but the physical? I can appreciate that. I told Talia that I'd keep her updated on new chapters in the boys' forays. If you'd give me a heads up, I'd appreciate it."

I chuckle. He definitely does not understand if that's what he wants. With Alistair off limits and Wilde off the deep end, Rafe won't be having any fun escapades. Losing Alistair hurts the worst for him because it's not Alistair's fault that his woman has wronged us. It's also not like he's putting a stop to it, either. It's a terrible choice and an unfair situation.

Wilde, however, is a whole other melon to smash.

He shifts under me, looking uncomfortable. "Not that it affected me, mind you. It's not for me."

I don't know what's going through his head, but involving Rafe with anyone else is not a good plan. He's so broken that I can feel it reverberating through our bond. Rafe does casual fine, so that's not the issue. History has shown that no one who's been with him can allow it to stay that way. He's so easy to fall for, so easy to be with, that you can't help but love him. I don't even think the Big Bad could withstand it; Rafe could melt a glacier.

"Of course not, dear."

"Right." He nods, as if reassuring himself, and I suppress the urge to chuckle.

"Tell me about style. Rafe's a talented writer, but art is his most comfortable tool for expression. Wilde thinks he's a Pulitzer winner, and he's only so-so. Alistair is...well, writing is less his gift than talking. More than likely, you're reading something one of the guys has transcribed to their mates except for the two-bit Tolstoy."

"The way you write about your mate and his partner is opposite of the way the gnome writes about them. It's so dissimilar that it seems like Rafe's a different person. I find it hard to get a bead on the git, to be honest, because I feel like he's got a split personality."

I snort. "Yeah, I get that a lot. Rafe is many things and adapts to what the person he's with needs. He's hard to pigeon-hole because of that. However, Sari tends to..."

"... not comprehend the full capacity of the English language?" He winces, looking sheepish. "Sorry."

"No, it's not that. She gets finite ideas of who people are in her head. It doesn't matter if they reflect on what that person is actually like. You wouldn't be the first person to say when she's blogging about the guys' escapades that her characterization of my mate —or Alistair or me—is skewed."

"Sod her. When you describe Alistair and Rafe, it's not bad. When he's with Wilde, I want to bloody heave."

"Because it's Wilde, or because it's so emotional?" I'm digging deep, but honestly, who doesn't want someone impartial talking to them about their writing? I'm no *professional* blogger like Wilde fancies himself to be, but I like to write. My chronicling of our families has been a labor of love. It's interesting to hear a contrasting point of view.

Plus, it's distracting him from topics that make me squirm.

"It was the overabundance of flowery and pedantic emoting from Rafe that boggled the mind. He didn't act that way with my —with Alistair."

I snort softly. Guess it was hard to digest the end of that

sentence being 'my brother.' It's a misnomer, but it makes me giggle that he almost said it. "Alistair and Rafe's love is more primal. Things with Wilde are on the squishy side. because Rafe likes to make his mates happy. He's softer with Wilde because he likes it that way."

What Wilde likes now is pain. Inflicting it, to be specific. Emotionally, physically, spiritually—whatever he can do to twist the knife via his demon. He acts as if the rest of us don't have something dark lurking inside us we learn to control.

"I don't fully understand the love because I don't see myself falling for a man the way I've fallen for a couple of stubborn, irritating females. I understand wanting to give people you love what they want, though. The physical, however, is hot as fuck."

He doesn't know the half of it; he hasn't been there *live*. "You don't fall for a *man*; you lust over someone, and you get physical. Eventually, you spend time together. Maybe bad things happen and you support one another. Boom—you've fallen for someone you didn't intend to and hey, looky there, it's not a lady."

Taurus gives me a look that says my explanation of how people figure out they might have other desires is insulting. "I read those stories with Talia. For the first time, I had the thought that there might be drawbacks to being me."

Gasping dramatically, I put a hand to my chest. "Drawbacks to being you? Never."

"No sass from you, missy, or I'll eat you!"

"Oh, no, please don't!"

I know where this is going, and it's a welcome distraction from weighty thoughts. Ignoring those things has definitely worked out for me in the past, right?

I'll never learn, but at least I'll die satisfied.

The Artist Prevents An Intervention

RAFE

"You can't let them beat the living hell out of you anytime they feel like it, you git."

Hex looks at me like I've lost my mind, and I know it's hard to comprehend. The cat and I have allowed something egregious to go on because we want the people we love to come back. We keep wishing that they will revert to the people we feel in love with, but they haven't.

"I know you're worried. I get it; I would be if any of you were in this situation."

Our split from the coyote and the writer would affect more than just the cat and I. Hex has a relationship with that crazy ass droid, Chaos. He could be in a spot if that hillbilly twat bulldogs for the coyote. The same goes for the bitch and her fairy twins. The family is entwined with the Coyote Den enough that disaster looms if we make rash decisions.

"We've got your back, you bleached idiot. None of us will let you guys go into that hellhole alone. I don't care how much you love those lunatics; it's not happening." Philomena gives me a look as if the discussion has ended and I should nod my head like a good boy.

"Ratchet it back, designer dictator. We're grown-ups who make grown up decisions. You can't put a moratorium on our liaisons. If you think I'm being a stubborn jackass, imagine what the kitty's going to say when she hears."

"Our lovely Juliet is going to get her own intervention, long hair. It's unacceptable to think that what you went through this weekend is happening to her," Leo says, glaring at me angrily.

"I don't have to think about it; I've seen it and worse." Victor finally speaks, having watched in unusual silence as the rest of our household went on the offensive. "You think the git's been hurt? For what I saw, I should have put that frilly asshat in the ground. She wouldn't let me. She begged, pleaded, and cried as best she could in the state she was in. Then she swore me to secrecy on our bond."

His eyes cut to me at that statement, as only a clone would understand the complexity of that relationship. The claiming bond is sacred. Blood and ancient magic ties oaths on it. He hasn't caught fire for talking about it, so maybe that was Company bullshit.

It would be like those fuckers to teach us some fabricated mumbo jumbo that to keep us in line.

"Victor, you're talking about it now, so—" Hex starts.

"I didn't tell you. You found out on your own—a loophole, I suppose. I still feel itchy all over." He shrugs and lights a smoke, walking out onto the porch with his back to us. "I guess that keeps me from burning up inside or whatever the hell is going to happen."

I rub my temples. "Guys, this is ridiculous. The more you push, the more she'll resist. I've been taking the brunt of his abuse to spare her, and I'll keep doing that. My healing will take care of it. I'll be fine."

"Horseshit!"

I blink. Sandrine was just more forceful than I've ever heard her. Her arms are crossed, and her eyes are on fire. Siren is flanking her, looking equally pissed. Christ, the cat and I have graduated to one of the abused kids Siren defends.

We really have lost our footing.

"I love you all, and the cat loves you more. The best thing you can do is to get her to admit that we might have to let go of more than Rhea and Alistair." I feel a bit of a tug inside on that statement, rubbing my hand over my chest absently. "Showing her that there are better things out there than their painful games will help, too."

Philomena stops sipping her martini as if dumbstruck and narrows her eyes at me. "The pernicious prick. You let her get knee deep in with the most dangerous person in Mr. Roger's Neighborhood, so she'll let go of the others when it's time. You, lazy, are a sneaky son of a bitch. You don't think they will stop, and you want her to be ready to let go. Chanel, in a teacup, you're diabolical."

I shrug, not meeting anyone's eyes as I feel their judgment. My mate did most of this on her own before that plan occurred to me. "Losing four mates will be a blow. Mating is permanent for clones, so it's going to ache every day, all the time when they're gone. Who can blame me for wanting to help her curb that pain with a distraction?"

"You will ache. You will pine. You will be alone in that." Siren speaks softly, her black eyes glittering with menace. "You do not deserve that, nor does she. We can make them suffer."

I shake my head and sigh. "Trust me, I considered that option. It's an unbreakable bond, Siren. They will open the gates and let their pain through to us."

"Then what do we do?" asks Hex, looking angry that he feels helpless.

Join the club, brother. Knowledge does not always make things better. You're all part of a big, ugly secret and a puzzle that cannot be solved yet. "We survive. We let her find our way out of the darkness. She always does—that you can take to the bank."

Philomena snorts. "Until then, we drink?"

"I'm all for that," I mutter, hobbling into the living room. "Leo, find us some food and grog, matey."

He snorts and rolls his eyes. "Lucky for all of you, I'm an impeccable host. Reprobates."

The Bird Has a Crisis of Faith

"So much for your theory—doing it more did not lessen the need," Taurus drawls sarcastically.

"I thought it would," I mumble. My eyes light on him as a wicked smirk curls my lips. I lean down on my elbows, crawling forward.

Uh oh. He's not looking at me. It's serious time.

"When is this going to let up? I mean, I was a bloody monster that time."

I frown, not understanding why he's so upset. "When is what going to let up?" My eyes flash as I scent my way up his leg, prowling still as I come out of the ferocity of our coupling. "You know I like a little fang in my thang."

He groans at the pun, and I drop kisses lightly on his abdomen. His pulse kicks under my lips and I nip him lightly. "This sodding scream of want I can't get free of. No matter how many times I take you, it doesn't go away." He lowers his arm and looks down at me, his gaze tortured. "I almost bled you this time. Christ, Deli, I was so goddamn close."

That admission makes everything go still inside of me. I quietly pull back, stopping my playful touches. I've been studiously ignoring the screaming ache of blunt teeth marks, the howl of unfinished business from my beast, and the fangs that are still dropped in my mouth. She noticed the wave of primal energy.

I can't fuck this up.

Tilting my head so my hair falls over my shoulder, I shrug. "I don't know how to respond to that." I scramble down the couch, tucking my knees up as I look at him with an unsure expression.

"I'm losing it with you." He rolls to his feet and dresses in hurried motions.

Ouch. That hurts.

Perhaps my cool disregard wasn't enough to keep his morality at bay. My heart is full of fear and pain, so I sit my chin on my knees and watch him silently. This might be the moment I lose the buoy that is keeping me from sinking.

Dressed now, he crosses the room to the curtained bay window and pulls it open to stare out into the sky. Without looking at me, he murmurs, "I love you."

I know that, but as I've asked my other mates, will it be enough? Will temptation make it so hard that he gives up? Everyone gives up on me. Am I like a flower that if you hold me too tightly, you crush me?

"I love you, too," I reply softly, my eyes roaming over him from behind. I have nothing else to say to comfort him.

He's going to break my heart; I can feel it.

"You're consuming me. I didn't think I had this in me because I've always been a one-woman man, you know?"

If he's trying to explain why he's leaving, he doesn't have to do this. He needs to rip the Band-Aid off. I'll leave the place where I feel safe for the first time in months behind, but I won't accept it unless he says it. "Yes, I do."

"Last night was," his voice breaks, "... special to me. Once we marked each other, I thought the things I've been feeling would go away. I thought they'd lessen enough that I could look at you without feeling myself inside you so keenly that I groaned with it." He turns his head to spear me with a deep blue stare. "That's how it is every time—more since I put the mark on you."

My eyelids fluttering as he mentions the mark. I feel it tickle against my skin and I know how he feels. She wants him with a drive that I've never felt before. I've only been with him a short time, but she's determined to make him her own. This is wild calling to wild and begging to be free. I don't know how I'm going to keep her satisfied, honestly. Maybe it's better if he gives me the boot. "I know."

Turning away again, he continues in a raspy voice. "It's not just the sex. It would be easier if it were, I expect. I keep seeing myself doing the most poof-like, asinine things to get you to smile at me. That isn't normal for me. I know you don't enjoy getting stompy, so I beg you to do it for me so it's not so bad for you. How big of an ass am I?"

My lips quirk and the heaviness of the situation fades for a moment. "Poofy things?"

He snorts derisively. "Surely you don't think I normally act like a drama queen with the goddess, do you? She'd kick my ass or have me committed."

I give him a rueful grin. Honestly, I thought this was normal for him. "Aw, now you're going to make me say that you're not really an ass, but I like to poke at you?"

Looking at me seriously, he shrugs. "But I am."

"An ass? No, you're not. Even if you were, you're my ass, and I like you." That is true—too much, in fact.

His grin is haunting. "Yeah, well, that's rather the problem, as I like you, too. Do you want to know what the best time of the day is —outside of being inside you?"

"When?"

"The very first time you crawl up into my lap because before that, it's like the sun hasn't shown yet. Then you do, and it does.

How fucking pathetic is that?" He snorts and throws himself down into a chair.

I arch a brow. "Not so pathetic from this end. Maybe not looking at it from your big bad image, but no one else has to know that, do they?"

"It would facilitate a sundry of community murders, so I suppose that would be a bad thing."

"I hate trying to get bloodstains out of the greenery."

"See, it's not so bad right now. The craving for you has ebbed. This is good, but when we're doing what we did... Do you realize that I've never made love to you?"

"I don't know. You were tender the other night." I give him a soft smile, trying to calm the fluttering of my heart and the fear churning in my stomach. Why is he drawing this out so much?

"I've been *not* animalistic all of one time, but that's it. Look at your shoulder, love. Look at what I did."

I push the hair off my shoulder and shrug again. Who does he think he's dealing with? Bites are part and parcel for me. "And?"

He frowns. "You think I'm being ridiculous?"

No, I think you're trying to break up with me and holding it together is getting hard.

"No, I don't. I didn't mind that. I mean, it felt..." I squirm in my seat, studying my toes intently, finally saying, "I don't want you to do something you don't want to."

"The problem is that I want to." Grinning ruefully at me, he shrugs a shoulder. "Want isn't the problem. I could all but taste your blood on my tongue, love. That coppery, hot, bitter redness coating my tongue and soothing my stomach is all I think about."

My eyes lose focus for a moment as he speaks, my nose twitching. The Beast rumbles eagerly inside of me at the image. "Um, okay. If I can make it easier for you, let me know."

He grins at my expression. "Do you see my problem?" Sighing, he purses his lips. "I didn't mean to make you feel bad, pet. I'm just confused."

"You didn't make me feel bad—kind of helpless, maybe? I don't know what to say or do to make you feel better." Also, like I have to be super careful what I say or do because this feels like a minefield of epic proportions.

His eyes cut to mine, looking regretful. "I'm sorry."

"It's okay. I'm not upset." I'm confused, concerned, and cautious, but none of those are upset. Is he going to stop coming here or put crazy restrictions on us? Will he disappear and leave me alone? I don't know what he's trying to tell me except that he wants to bite me and can't because of his 'code'.

The fucking 'code'—how I hate that old guard shit.

It's as complex as the shit with the loonies wanting to share but being incapable of sharing. Why can't people be happy? Accept what you can have, treasure it, and learn to be happy with what's in front of you. Sure, the beast *wants* to claim him, but it will not happen. Since reason isn't one of her strong suits. I have to figure it out. Does that mean I shouldn't love every minute I'm with him? No. It means that life is what it is—nothing more, and nothing less. Suddenly, I realize that he's talking again, and I tune back in. Shit. I hope I didn't miss something important.

"I've got things to work out. I wanted our marks to be enough because it goes against everything in me to take another mate. Then we're doing our thing and I can taste you on my tongue. I don't want to just drink you; I want to drain you completely and give you back my own." As is quickly becoming a habit, he rubs the sapphire in his ear while he broods.

A zing of surprise paired with a shudder runs through me. That doesn't sound like he just wants to bite me. It sounds like he wants to—Does he want to mate with me? I let a deep breath out slowly, trying to calm myself down. I'm jumping to conclusions high enough to breach the caped hero territory. I can't get worked up. This is most likely going to end in me being killed in the morning, so to speak.

"Baby, whatever you decide, I'm behind."

There. I got words out. Good job, Deli.

His eyes narrow, and he growls low. "Hell help me, I want to have you do the same fucking thing to me. I want your fangs in me—taking my blood, drinking me down."

At that statement, my eyes fly up to meet his. My heart is hammering like a hummingbird in flight. His gaze is so fierce that I can feel the heat on my skin. "I want to." It slips out before I can catch it, and I lick my lips, waiting to lose an appendage.

His gaze goes fuzzy for a moment, and he shifts uncomfortably in his seat. Leaping to his feet, he shakes his head and snarls. "Shit. I'm the poster child for anti-angst, sweaty, naked fun, but I'm turning this into a bloody soap opera."

"You aren't!" I protest quickly—maybe too much so—because he whips his head around to look at me. "I love you. I'm okay with whatever decision you make. Please don't worry."

Please, please don't get upset.

I can't lose another person who wormed their way into my heart—not right now. It's the height of selfishness, but I need him. More than I want to, more than I should, and even with the limitations we have, he's the most stable thing in my life right now.

"I need to think, pet. I need time to work it out in my head. It's killing me. This want for something that goes against what I believe in. Apparently, I'm the biggest prat in the world." He looks disgusted with himself, pulling a smoke out of his pocket and heading for the window again.

I snort. "Trust me, you're not."

"I also want you to understand that this has *nothing* to do with your choices, but I'm not sure I can share a family tree with branches I'd like to burn. Do you understand?"

Speaking of the actual biggest prat in the world, here comes Wilde to ruin yet another chance at happiness. He isn't even here, and he's wrecking me emotionally. Jesus, isn't that branch of the family the gift that keeps on giving? He and Sari are akin to a dead animal you can't find that stinks up your entire house. I nod, letting out a slow breath. "I do."

"And Talia? She's more of a forest fire type of woman."

"I accept that. There are complications to a family as big as mine. I'm struggling with mates that have lost their minds and I still don't know how to reconcile that problem. Everyone doesn't have to play in the same sandbox."

He whips around, eyes blazing and face serious. "Never speak of this place like that again. It means more to me than that."

I blanch. "I meant you don't have to associate with people you don't like. I sure as hell don't associate with those inbred hicks in Texas. Dollars to donuts, a mating happened that I was never told about."

His expression is sheepish, then incredulous, and then returns to normal. I guess he didn't know that mates could operate in that fashion. I have no answer for him. "Sorry, I misunderstood what you were saying. That's a good policy, though, as family reunions would be a *bitch*."

"Truthfully? I doubt it could make anything worse."

"I wonder how much potato salad it would take to drown the gnome," he muses.

"I *hate* potato salad."

He grins. "I despise the stuff. Full of coincidences, aren't we, kitty?"

"That's me. An enigma wrapped in a riddle wrapped in—well, usually, leather."

His hand reaches out to me as he barks a laugh. "Come here, kitty."

I crawl over to curl up in his lap with a sigh. This makes all this hard stuff better. It shouldn't since we're in a giant mess, but his touch makes me calm and helps me find my center. The only person who's ever been able to do that as easily as he is Rafe.

It's odd.

He strokes his hands down my spine idly and then murmurs, "I promise you I'm going to figure out what I'm comfortable with. I'm sorry I'm such a prude."

Is he? I'm not sure you can be sorry about such a firmly held belief system. It's intrinsic to who Taurus is. However, let's be honest: this *entire* situation goes against everything everyone who has ever met Taurus thinks he believes in. The very room we're in, the things we've shared, and the marks we placed violate the image he and Talia have crafted for years. There'll be hell to pay when people find out, but that's neither here nor there.

"You are not a prude. Besides, it's not like I didn't know who you were and how you felt when I put a mark on you, is it?" I reach up and rub the earring lightly, reminding him I accept him as is. I may have to struggle with myself and my feral nature, but I respect his convictions.

"I suppose it'd be easier if I bit you and got it done with it." His head turns at my words and he frowns. "This is enough for you? Because it's not enough for me. I'm happy, miserable, and everything in between—all because of my sodding values."

Okay, I've clearly caused both a crisis of conscience and a complete world view meltdown.

Before we met in that park, I would have categorized Taurus as the least likely person to evolve. I didn't set out to make him change or alter his core beliefs. I don't even know if I want to be responsible for that. I don't want this if it's going to screw everything up. I don't even know how to figure out if it will screw everything up.

This fucking sucks. What do I do?

I turn my hand to stroke his cheek gently, trying to ease some of the pressure he's putting on himself. "Baby, I'll take anything you have to give. I don't want to ask for something that you're not comfortable giving." Taurus rests his head against mine and I feel his body relax. Giving him the space to figure out what he wants and how he wants seems to have diffused the situation.

Since I'm on a roll, I decide to be honest. "I enjoy seeing the earring. Would I like to sink my teeth in and drink you deep while you're pounding inside me? Oh yeah, absolutely, but not if it's going to be a problem. You are what is important to me." I look into his eyes, my expression earnest.

His fangs drop, and he growls, shifting under me. "*That* was not nice."

I wince, feeling the response to my words under my ass. "Oops. I'm sorry. I get carried away."

His eyebrow arches and he scans my face to look for a sign that I was purposefully taunting him. I shrug and give him a sheepish look, feeling badly that I riled him up while he's having a crisis of faith.

When he's satisfied, he nods. "I appreciate your candor, even if it's going to make it hell when I leave."

"I can move if it will help."

He shakes his head. "In a second. I want to hold you for a little longer."

I smile and lay my head on his shoulder. "That is always okay."

"I was toying with the idea of getting a tattoo."

I'm getting used to his abrupt changes of subject, so I follow along. "What kind?"

"I asked Damien to work up one like yours for me. I like the idea of a peacock with its tail draping down instead of up, but with one tail feather missing."

I can't help it; I beam. "That'd be neat!"

"If I do, would you put it on me?" He tilts his head, looking nervous.

"I'd love to." Who wouldn't? The last time we placed a Damien tattoo ended well for both of us. How can I resist literally branding him with a reminder of me?

He grins boyishly and bobs his head as if I've done him a huge favor. "Thanks." Sighing, he kisses the top of my head. "I really need to get out of here. I have lots of unpleasantness to deal with tonight."

"Okay, love." I don't tell him that tonight is the last night that I'm completely unfettered. Our three days are up. Lucky for me, it's at the time that we've stepped into a vast spiderweb of problems.

Lifting me as if I weigh nothing, he sits me on the couch and kneels next to it. "I love you, Deli."

"I love you very much." I brush a strand of hair off his forehead, wanting to sigh with the ache of knowing that our weekend is over.

"See you later, maybe?" His gaze is hopeful, and I don't know what to say. I have no idea what fresh hell I'll find at home and he's trying to make a big decision.

"Give me a ring."

No promises, but I didn't close the door, either. Good job, Deli.

Kissing me gently, he gets to his feet. "Later."

"Later, love." I murmur, watching him go. Once he's out the door, I gather up the stay-cation bag I'd hidden under the couch and straighten up.

It's time to go home to Kansas, Dorothy.

The Goddess Has Her Say

TALIA

"Talia, you're doing it again."

I blink and the blade in my hand halts.

Damn.

She's right; I am doing it again. There's no imminent battle coming, but I can sense the turmoil in my mate as he finishes the last job of the day before heading home.

"It's nothing, Theodora. Taurus is..." What do I say? He's battling himself, but I can't share why.

When the Company created the original community in the Rift, it was made up of their operatives and their staff. It was a small group with a set of beliefs that stemmed from the lore handed down by the original clones. It expanded to include a more diverse set of people, and even though we won the Battle of Blood and Steel, that victory was too late. Everything had changed and the original occupants were no longer comfortable in our home. We withdrew from the giant orgy full of whackos that took over.

That, it seems, is no longer an option.

Taurus answered her call because she intrigued him. Ever since, it's been a whirlwind of fights, broken furniture, lacerations I can't explain, and moods so black that he damn near fills our house with a bevy of emotions that choke me. But there's also been this boyish excitement and joy that he hadn't shown in so long... the spark socializing gives him that it doesn't give me.

I was a touch empathetic before I moved into the Rift. As it always does, the Rift magnified my small gift, making me a full-blown empath. Besides what I feel from our mating, I feel everything from everyone. It began when I moved here, long before the cat stepped through her first portal. I've learned to shield, block, and divert the overload to save my sanity. However, when Taurus is so over the top with his emotions, I can't keep them from slamming into me.

Right now, he's overflowing with big feelings and has no idea how to handle them.

Between his confusion about what he feels for her, our shared rage at the twits we considered family, and that toxic gnome's family, our house has been teeming with emotions to the point of bursting. I'm lucky my head doesn't split open daily.

This new set of desires is making him feel guilty; I know it. It's driving him to question the very foundations of our beliefs and that's eating him up inside. When he consulted me about doing a marking, I knew it wouldn't be enough.

Taurus is the original predator. Alistair may have come first in line in terms of creation, but Taurus is only one of his brothers that still lives the life they created him for. He's a killer, a mercenary, and a predator first and foremost.

That part of him has found its match in someone else, and he's consumed with guilt over it.

Don't mistake me—I am his primary mate. The bond between Taurus and me is deeper than the strands of the universe they pull the clones from. I may work in the Company's operations department, but I am also a hunter. I have a dark side that I hide. Unlike the cat, I don't share it with the public. People see my blades and my leather, and they stay away. I prefer it that way. He did, too, until her.

Satan help us, he wants to mate with her.

He's in love, and he's so conflicted. This is completely out of his wheelhouse. He's never considered a mate besides me. That was almost hard wired into his DNA. But for the first time, he loves someone besides me. It's just our bad luck that it's a half-cat, half-woman who's mated to a small army of people we hate and lives with a fleet of people we've never met. Who the hell else she's got ties with, I don't know, but I guarantee it is bigger than either of us knows.

This 'suburb' of the Rift is *much* more populated than the Company knows. It's a city of its own and Deli is the Queen of their universe. Maybe of *the* Universe, as some of these people I've never even heard of. I can't even assess the danger of interacting with them because there are so many unknowns. Threat assessment is my specialty, and I'm stymied.

I have to do it, though, because I can feel his need thrumming through our bond and he's almost home.

"Talia, you haven't answered me."

I sigh and look at the perfectly coiffed and comfortable Theodora. Her head is tilted in concern. "There's been a lot of change lately, Theodora. I think we're getting ready to see even bigger changes yet. The bird has lost his mind."

"Is this a bad thing, Talia?"

Hell, if I know Theodora. Maybe. Probably. Almost certainly. "I don't know. He's coming home to ask me something important, and I am not sure how I feel about it."

"Does it make you angry or hurt your feelings?"

"No, it doesn't." I'm surprised to discover that, as I say it out loud. I'm not angry or hurt that he loves her or even that he wants to mate with her. Mating for clones has always been the equivalent of a magical marriage. It's bigger, more dangerous, and more permanent, but marriage is the closest thing humans have to it. "It makes me worried—for him, for us, for our life."

"Will it change that much?"

Notice how she never asks what it is. Theodora is so proper that if I did not tell her, she assumes it's not her business. "Yes. I think it will change everything."

"I see." She tilts her head again. "If it does not make you unhappy and is not a direct threat, but it will make Taurus happy, then it seems worth the risk. That is an assessment based on very little knowledge of the situation, I admit."

She's right. However, she's thinking with logic only, as androids do. I'm considering the emotional fallout. I don't know enough about Deli to form a complete picture. I know what I've seen as I keep a side eye on the community and what I saw at her house.

The most telling thing I know is that my mate is head over in heels in love with her. In fact, he is so in love with her he is standing on our front porch, smoking and pacing and talking to himself like a lunatic.

Our neighbors are going to have a fit.

"Let me go see if I can unruffle his feathers, Theodora. You and Damien may want to find somewhere else to be while Taurus and I have this discussion."

She nods, rising gracefully and heading for their rooms. "I agree. We shall find a suitable engagement to give you privacy. Contact us if you need help."

I smile and nod, grateful for her thoughtful behavior. "I will let you know when we have decided, Theodora. As it affects our family, we will discuss it once we know for sure."

"Of course."

I sigh, shoring up my shields because I can feel the frenetic, confused energy bouncing off the front door. I know this one's going to be a doozy.

Once more into the breach...

The Cat Leans On The Artist

The weekend away was a poor plan.

Too many plates were balanced precariously, and I knew everything could come crashing down—which it did. I sat through the family intervention—a silent, angry dinner—and now, I am stepping out of the shower before I have a few hours of downtime with Rafe. He looks ragged, but my housemates told me it was much worse when he got home.

Add guilt to the top of my list of recent failures.

The clone in question is drying his hair while giving me a rueful look. "I tried to tell them you wouldn't take well to being ambushed like that."

"I didn't, but it doesn't make them wrong. We have to decide eventually. You can't take the brunt of their punishments forever. One day, he'll go too far and we both know it."

Plopping down on the bed next to me, he sighs, "This time was bad, love."

For Rafe to admit that, it had to be nearly intolerable. "I won't ask, but if you want to talk, we can. Come here." Reaching over to the table, I click on the TV. I flip through the movies, looking for one of our favorites that isn't emotionally tied to someone. "Let's find some hooch, watch movies, and you can paint my toes."

He snorts. "Making me feel better includes manual labor, eh?"

I run my fingers over the long, shiny French braid his hair is tied back in. "This is pretty. I'd offer to run my fingers through your hair because you like it, but I don't want to take it down. Who did this?"

"The bitch did." He smiles and rolls to his feet to locate the mani-pedi kit. Bringing it over to the bed, he places it nearby before sitting down next to me.

"You let her touch you?"

"She didn't give me much of a choice."

Huh. "Well, it looks lovely. I like it."

We curl up in the pillows of the gigantic bed, content to decompress in the waning light of the afternoon. The movie rolls on and we laugh—something that's been in way too short of supply lately. Leo drops in with food and drinks, hanging out for a few as the pirates clash on the cliffs.

One movie ends and we turn on the next, the atmosphere cozy and calm. I've missed this. He picks up the kit and position me with my foot in his lap, working on my toes. He's just as proficient an artist with nail polish and brushes as he is his paints, so his choice of decoration is elaborate and beautiful.

"You'll get a call before the night's over," Rafe murmurs, working on my middle toe with a flourish.

I tilt my head, wrinkling my nose. "I doubt it. Taurus said he has to think. When someone like him wants to stop and think about things, our little *affaire à retenir* is kaput. It's a shame; I feel a kinship with him I haven't felt with anyone before. I think it's because of the beast."

His brow arches as he looks at the quivering feather on my chest. "I dub thee, Queen of the Understatement, my Night Bloom. You dove into the deep end of the ocean without a life vest. It won't be easy to swim away."

I close my eyes as he works quietly, painting miniature Van Goghs on each toe after the base coat dries. He's right and I know it. When Taurus breaks it off, I'm going to be raw and bleeding inside for a long time. Sighing, I rub my chest as I consider it. Hell, we may have to wall off from everyone. I may not survive unless I stop letting everyone in until I heal. "If he hotfoots it, I'm going to have issues—a lot of them. Perhaps volumes."

"Uh-huh." He starts with the pinky toe on my left foot, working quickly. "Maybe that's not what's going to happen, though."

I blink. "What do you mean?"

"I doubt the git's ever had this thought before in his life, and he voiced it out loud. Words have power, my love. Saying it out loud makes it real. I don't think he would have said it unless he was testing your reaction. It's a matter of clearing the channels and reconciling desire with core beliefs now. This feels more like a when' not an if."

Feeling like a cannonball hit me in the chest, I take a deep breath and try not to panic. "Do you really think so?"

"Yup." He looks up, his expression serious. "I'm okay with you being happy. I'm always okay with that."

He's not happy, though, and Taurus is demanding about my time. I can't imagine it would get less so if we mated. "What about you?"

"I'm fine. I have art, friends, and you. Troubles don't last forever. I'm a simple clone, love."

"That is an act. You are more complex than you let on."

"Perhaps," he says, sipping his merlot. "But I adjust to change well; I always have. We'll be okay."

"What do I do, Rafe? I'm scared."

His hand reaches up, cupping my jaw as he looks at me. "When we met, you ruled this place with the aplomb of badass bitch who made no apologies for who she was—not even to the judgy over-lords of the Cabal. All the pain and betrayal made you retreat into a scared, self-doubting shadow of the woman I fell for. I will always love you, no matter what facet is showing, but I know you miss being the real you."

I can't look at him as I contemplate that because I know that he's one hundred percent right. I *have* let them fill me with self-doubt and fear that I never used to let get the best of me.

"What do you do with the asshole who is luring that woman out of hiding? You decide to be strong, bold, and brave; be the *queen* you always have been and always will be."

I chuckle. "Man, aren't you a feminine product commercial tonight."

"*In vino veritas*, my Night Bloom." He smiles and pours me another glass.

"Are you sure about this?"

"I have been since the day we met." He kisses my forehead, and I feel comforted. "Trust your gut. It worked for us, eh?"

"That it did, baby. That it did."

The Cat And The Bird Parlay

DELILAH

I wake up, looking around wildly. I am not... *damn* him. I'm here with no warning again. "Taurus?"

The room is dark, and he's back lit by moonlight on his pale skin. He looks like a paranormal romance novel cover again. Bastard. He's doing that on purpose, so my brain short circuits. "I've thought about it. I haven't thought of anything else since I left you. It's lame, but it's true."

I blink myself awake, trying to follow his conversation in my hazy state. I don't sleep a lot because of nightmares, but when I do, it's pretty damn deep. I usually need several hits of caffeine or morning sex to have such a serious conversation.

"The irony is that my biggest concern was Talia's reaction. It was surprising to find out that she's confident enough in us to know that she can't be replaced. She thinks you'd make a colorful addition to our family. My primary actually said that she knows you make me happy, which goes a long way with her. She even said that she respects you enough to trust you with me. Talia's done her best to protect me—albeit mostly from myself—from all the back-biting bints with attitude problems."

Looking confused—as Talia and I have met a grand total of four times—I nod, waiting for the punchline.

"She seems to believe that you'd do the same, regardless of what toes you'd have to step on. I don't know how she got the opinion that I need protection." He frowns, looking irritated.

"You don't, but I think she knows I'd do it if I thought you needed it." I've protected more than either of them knows for weeks. Keeping everything quiet and low key with him was not just to make him comfortable; it was to make I sure I didn't set off panic alarms around the community.

The legend of Taurus and Talia is a boogeyman story now; I had to keep people from panicking.

"Anyway, my goddess accepts any decision I make. What I don't know is... how does this type of thing work with your people? Are they okay with it?"

I chuckle. He really does not know how families work here. I might be the only one who even informs my mates of my intent with shit like this. "Rafe told me this evening that he knew this was where we were going. He didn't know why he felt that way or when it would happen, but he knew it would. He would never stand in the way of something that might make me happy."

Taurus looks confused. "Rafe knew we would... What?"

"When I told him about the marking—I asked him before I said yes. He said that's when he knew that we'd end up here, eventually."

"That's who you were talking to! I didn't think to clarify then." He snaps his fingers and studies me closely. "Are you sure that he doesn't mind? I'm not the easiest clone to be with because I don't play well with others. As your primary mate, though, I will always treat him with respect. If I ever meet the bugg—uh, bloke."

"Because all the other clones I've mated with are so easy to deal with."

"I'm usually *much* less 'angsty soap opera' than the rest of those rotters."

"He's too laid back to worry about that. From the beginning, Rafe has always shared me. He trusts me to do what makes me happy, and that's what makes him happy. I do the same with him. We're extremely secure about our relationship—Taurus and Pisces fit together like puzzle pieces."

He snorts at the Zodiac reference, and I wince. He's going to have a *really* hard time with my magick. The Universe has far more options than he's been taught and I'm fairly certain that I'm going to rock his world after the Beltane ceremony if he thinks astrology is hoodoo.

Wait until he finds out that everything he was taught is fluffy garbage exists.

I realize that I've tuned out on him again, and curse mentally. I have to stop doing that.

"...that brings me to problem number two."

I sigh, knowing that I can't rewind to problem one now. Hopefully, it's not actually a problem. "What is that?"

"I'm *not* laid back. I love and trust you. I want you to be happy. But I can be a jealous sod. I got that way with Talia in the past, and we went rounds over it. I haven't felt that with you yet, but we've been shut up in our own world. It may not be a problem because I know that you already have several mates, but I don't know. I just want to be honest about it." He turns to look out at the moon, almost as if he can't say that to my face.

Although, maybe he simply enjoys looking dramatic. Either is a valid possibility.

Shaking my head to clear it of that nonsense, I consider what he said. I can't decide whether to be offended that he might not be jealous or worried that he might be too jealous. Finally, I settle on cautiously neutral. "I don't mind possessive, though I rarely experience it when it's actually about me. I've dealt with jealousy before. If you're honest about it, you'd have the advantage over others."

"You've seen the chest thumping and dick swinging, though, not as bad as it can be. The one thing I can assure you about is that if I have a problem, I'll let you know. I don't play games like that." Done posing for the moment, he pads over to the couch and sits next to me.

"That's a lot less likely to turn rotten, so I can deal with it."

"I play *some* games, but not those kinds." His grin turns into a frown suddenly. "You sound like you're already decided, kitty."

Shit. I do, right?

I had that long conversation with Rafe and found my Zen in it. I'm probably being too easily convinced. "I told you earlier that whatever your decision was, I'd go with it. I let you mark me, so it's not a surprise that I'd go a step further, is it? I love you and you're mine. This would underline that in big, bold ink."

"What do *you* want is the real question? You keep saying that you'll go along with me, but I don't want a kitty on a leash. I want to know if you want this."

My eyes narrow and I dig deep, finding the girl Rafe, and I discussed. "I don't follow; I lead. I told you what I'd like to do, and I meant it. I do nothing this permanent if I don't want to. But I didn't want to put pressure on you because you were so conflicted." I do lots of other things under duress, but nothing like this.

Mating is not something that you let peer pressure decide for you; I learned that the hard way.

His brows furrow. "Telling me what you want is not the same as pressuring me. I know the difference, so I want you to tell me what you need without worrying about that, okay?"

My eyes widen and I feel the panic setting in. This is scary and I haven't been the sassy, confident vixen in a while. I'm having trouble keeping her from taking off at a gallop. "I was being careful. I'm gun-shy about emotional commitment after a few missteps."

"Fair enough. The recent past has scarred both of us in ways that don't heal quickly. I'm suffering, so I can imagine you are as well. Gun-shy is a good word for it." He pauses and holds up two fingers, looking apologetic. "Two more things, but they are important."

"Okay," I say, feeling the tough girl edge away again. It'd be awful helpful of the beast inside of me to help tie her down while I deal with Taurus. The slumbering predator huffs what might be a laugh and I groan. I'm on my own until I get to the bloody shit.

Great.

"One of them is more to let you into my head, so buckle your seatbelt and take your Dramamine," he says, winking.

I pretend to brace myself against the couch. "I'm ready."

"In my mind, this place where we meet is separate—disconnected from everything else. When you come here, I don't see the marks on you, other than mine and Rafe's. It's like they disappear. Maybe that's why I don't have the jealousy and rot with the others. I don't see them."

That little tidbit is interesting, but I don't think I should tell him it's not a trick of his imagination. He can't see my marks, bruises, or scrapes because of the glamours. Some of it is visual, and some are via auditory cues I've implanted during phone conversations. He hasn't a clue I'm using magick and neuro-linguistic programming to cover up everything that would make him upset.

Taurus gestures to the surrounding room. "This is our oasis—a quiet place beyond all the shit. It relaxes and comforts me even when you're not here."

I didn't know he came here when I'm not here. I've only done that a few times while waiting for him. But he's been escaping to our place just to hang out. "I understand."

"When you're here with me, you're mine — all mine and I'm all yours. The others don't factor in. It might change for me after I drink from you. My sense of honor prevents me from blocking this place from your Rafe or my Talia. I'm not saying they'd want to intrude, but I'm honor bound if they do. Does that make sense?"

Honor bound. Have we stepped into the Wayback Machine and gone to the middle ages?

I consider asking, but he's clearly serious about this. That is doing nothing for my nervous tummy. "I wouldn't want you to keep the family out if they wanted to be here."

"Nor would I, but Rafe is the only mate that I feel comfortable having here."

"I wouldn't expect to bring extended family here," I say, giving him a wry look.

"I'm not entirely sure who've you have taken to you. There was a fucking army on your lawn that night. But someone like the boozy socialite—Philomena, isn't it? She'd be fine. In fact, I'd kind of like to meet her. I think we'd be aces, pet."

"Philomena is rather bossy and arrogant, so probably." I chuckle. They'd get along about as well as anyone can get along with Philomena. "The people who are actually mine—not necessarily through mating—are Rafe, Hex, Leo, Philomena, Siren, and Sandrine. Caesar and Victor live with us now, but they're—well, they're mine now."

"Damien or Theodora may drop by from time to time." He waits for a response and when I seem okay, he continues. "Rafe's like me, I know, but Leo, Hex, and the rest are droids?"

"Yup. Hex is all Eighties punk rock, but don't let it fool you—he's the major domo of our house. Leo's laid back and casual unless you mess with his kitchen. You've heard of Philomena, our swilling socialite. Siren is an elegant hunter with ethics much like Talia's and Sandrine is tough, fun, and surprising at every turn. She has a *huge* genetically engineered spider named Buzz that she's not allowed to have out around me. Lily's droid, Mercury, bio-engineered that beast and I'm lucky I can sleep at night just knowing that he exists."

"Leo reminds me of my brother—not Alistair, but Trey. That bastard could cook. The only thing I never understood about Trey was why he hated wearing clothes. He almost never put them on. Thinking of him cooking bacon gives me the wiggins. Of course, there was also that incident with the vacuum cleaner, but I digress.”

I snort. The image is perfect. “My guys stay clothed now if there are guests around. Rafe and I...not so much.”

His eyes gleam. “That works for me.” As if he just realized he said that out loud, he clears his throat. “Moving on.”

I giggle, pursing my lips in amusement.

“Immediate family’s fine, but not extended family. I would kill Wilde and even Alistair if they tried to come here.”

“I wouldn’t invite them here, baby. I get enough of their garbage everywhere else. If anyone ever says I invited them, they’re lying.”

“Okay. But um...” He stops for a moment, looking at his hands as if he’s nervous. “You wouldn’t mind me meeting your family?”

Mind? Hell, I figured we would hide in the shadows for all time. He’s nuts. “Of course not!”

“I have to ask this, but don’t get mad. Do you want me to socialize with your crew—the extendeds and such?”

I frown, tilting my head. Why would I get mad about that? It’s a valid question. “What do you mean, do I want you to?”

“I’m nervous. You’ve got this complex world with an excellent information network, and I’m not sure you’ve got room to squeeze me in.”

“Oh!” I beam and scoot closer to him. “It’s an enormous world, but there’s always room for someone I love. Anyone who doesn’t like it can shove it.”

The Cat Negotiates Further

✦

DELILAH

"Are you sure?"

Is he kidding? I'm the gal that I can't cut out people who are abusing me.

"Once you're mine, you're automatically included in anything you want to be in. I'm being vague about that because I don't know what will happen or what you'd want to be in on. But you're always invited."

He tilts his head. "So if I want to show up at a shindig at your house, I'm invited."

"You are always invited—to anything, anywhere."

"As is my family, I assume. Theodora's never really been out and about. Since Donatella made her for Talia, she only stayed at the house or covering for Talia at work. Being a Talia droid made her different from every other droid out there, and she's always worried that it would freak people out."

"My door's always open; in fact, it's never locked. Family is family, love. Rafe's birthday is in May and we'll probably have a big shindig—we always do."

"By the by, did anyone tell you that no one let *me* know about

Theodora? I found out by coming home from a gig to see Talia on the couch, knocking it with Damien."

I cover my mouth. "*No way.*"

"Obviously, it wasn't Talia. But imagine my surprise when she yanked me off Damien's bloody body and tossed me through a wall. Talia's strong—my blood's helped there—but she's not that strong. Then Talia stormed in, mad as a wet hen, because other than injuries—it was a colossal mess. The goddess gets irritated when her house gets mussed. And somehow, it was all my fault."

"I can't imagine how." I give him a wry look.

"So I didn't stop to sense for her before I opened up a can of English whipass on Damien. That doesn't mean that I should clean it up myself."

"We had a big ass fight like that in our house. When he first came home, Hex used to turn Leo off and hide him in a closet. Caesar thought it was funny to program the early droids like Leo to hate clones. Victor got revenge by programming Hex to do the opposite... and he showed him where they hid their power switches. Hex would be all 'Oh, he's sleeping downstairs' and I'd find Leo the next day in a damned closet. It blew up big time after a while."

He bursts out laughing, leaning back in his seat. "That's hysterical. Who knew the toaster, and the traitor had such good senses of humor?"

"Luckily, by the time Rafe came to live with us, Hex was over that. Leo had also gotten over his daddy issues about Victor and things worked out okay."

Taurus frowns, shaking his head. "My head is spinning, love. There's so much history that I don't know."

"After Rafe, I never had a problem with my people joining our family. My boys accepted that I'm kind of a softie and take in strays all the time." I look at him, watching his face. "Was that an overload of information?"

"A little," he admits. "I think I'll restrict my reindeer games to you, your immediate family, and mine for a while—maybe forever." He shivers, as if dreading the amount of people he might have to interact with.

"It's your choice, baby. If you want to come to parties or go out, I'll be there. Even if I have to smack someone around for getting fresh—which is probable—I'm happy to have you around whenever you want to be."

Practically beaming, he nods. "That's why it's a good idea if I stay close for a good long while. You're so insane over me you're likely to kill someone if they try me."

I narrow my eyes and growl. "More like maim. Killing community members is counterproductive, as you said."

"Aww, baby, are you being protective?"

"Always."

"I'm touched, kitty—more than you know." He sighs and pauses for a moment. "That's most of my issues, but there's one left."

I arch a brow, still growling a bit at the idea of bints pawing at him. "What is it?"

"Can I call you warrior princess, baby?" His eyes dance and he squeezes me tight. "Uh...obviously, that's not the issue."

I snort. "You can call me anything you want except cute."

"My little warrior princess," he says, looking delighted before he leers at me. "Well, that blows it. You are cute."

I give him a dirty look, my eyes narrowing as I plot a painful punishment for that statement.

"*Especially* when you get that evil gleam in your eyes, like when you think of someone knocking me around in public." He nods as he looks at me, grinning. "Just like that."

"That or laying hands on you. I'd probably growl at that, too." I wrinkle my nose, not intending to admit that.

He blinks at me as if he hasn't heard correctly. "Huh?"

"I didn't say that it made sense," I mutter peevishly.

I'd prefer he leave this alone because I don't even understand why I feel this way.

His chest puffs, preening like he's going to spread the tail feathers all the hell over me. "Are you saying you'd be jealous? You're kidding me, right? You? *Jealous*?"

"No. Possessive." It escapes my mouth, and I curse silently. That was *not* something I wanted him to know.

"How long have you been feeling that way about me, kitty?"

The whole bloody time, you great ninny. I clamp my mouth shut until the urge to scream that at him dies. "I just would be. It's not a big deal." I cross my arms over my chest, looking aggravated.

"That was not an answer to my question."

"Fine," I huff, blowing hair out of my eyes. "Recently, I think. Probably since the feather." I rub my fingers over the spines of the feather, my expression troubled as I feel it ache a little.

"You weren't feeling possessive when Blondie was chatting me up the other day, were you? You were mad she lied to you."

"I was mad as hell that she lied to me." I retort, feeling cornered. I'm troubled that this is the first time I've realized that I feel this way and frustrated that I blurted it out.

"Were you feeling that way when you thought I'd fucked her?" He tilts his head, looking curious, and I don't know how to answer him.

Yeah, that hurt like hell. But it's not my place to cast stones when I live in a glass house, now is it?

"I was because I got the feeling that she was trying to do it before I did. I felt like it was a competition. That annoyed me."

His lips curl. "It was—you won."

"You know what I mean."

"I know, kitty, but I'm putting a happier spin on it. A first prize Taurus is a good thing, right?"

I lean up to kiss him lightly. "You are a wonderful prize, though I wouldn't use that terminology on someone I care about."

Drawing me into his arms, he murmurs, "Thanks, love. You're a bloody excellent prize yourself." Switching gears, he gives me a supremely arrogant smirk. "Now, let me see if I get this right. With this newly found possessiveness you've got going on, I'll need clarification on the rules. Does that mean you'll be snatching bits bald if they try to cozy up to my lower half? More importantly, does that mean I get to vice that versa?"

"You will never fucking let me live this down." I put my face in my hands, completely chagrined. How could be such a fool?

"I'm surprised, love—pleasantly, but still."

"Even I get possessive sometimes. I think it's the primal part of me because I've never felt it as strongly as I do now. The stronger she gets, the stronger those urges are."

"And we both know I bring out the primal in you." He looks me in the eye. "Can I be honest?"

"It seems like you're the only one who can anymore."

He smiles at that, leaning forward to put his forehead on mine. "It makes me tingly to think of you loving me enough that you don't want to share me. Thank you for telling me."

Boy, that feels serious.

Despite the lighthearted tone of this conversation, the significance of that admission doesn't escape me. It delineates the chasm between our belief systems, and I'm not sure if it's actually a good thing. I don't know why the beast is so attached to him, but she gets fierce about it.

Maybe it's because she can stretch her legs when we hunt and run?

"You're special," I say softly. "When people are special to me, I'm protective and possessive. Despite my ability to share without qualm, I still get the 'mine' feeling like anyone else. I'm a greedy bitch because a lot of things are mine." Well, they were at one point. I suppose now I can't say I know what's mine or everyone's. Honestly, do I even want what I'd previously claimed anymore?

"As in, I'm yours and everyone else should keep their hands off?"

I squirm. I'm very uncomfortable with this part of me. I don't like to discuss it because it's antithetical to my beliefs. "Yeah, sort of."

Shooting to his feet, he picks me up and spins us around in a circle. His smile is wide as he twirls us around gleefully.

I shriek, surprised as hell, so I thump his shoulders hard. "We've discussed this flying thing!"

He sits me on my feet and pulls me to his chest. Kissing me quickly, he runs a finger down my jaw. "Baby, in my entire life, I've only loved one woman besides you. You have nothing to worry about—no one else can have me. In case you missed it, I'm kind of stuck on the faithful gig. I don't expect reciprocation, but just because I've taken you doesn't mean that I'm going to become a gigolo." His arms squeeze me to him tightly, and I squeak again. "I started falling for you faster than you know, and I love you even more for telling me that."

"I didn't think you were going to strut out around, pimping yourself out. I'm worried about people's inability to allow me to have anything to myself. It might make me a little growly, that's all."

"Thanks ever so for *that* imagery, but you can get growly all you want, baby. I have one last thing to ask you before I have to get some sleep. It's late again and tomorrow I have at least thirteen hours of bullshit to deal with at work. Do you realize that since I fell for you, I haven't gotten a single full night's sleep?"

"You can tell me to shut up anytime, silly. We don't have to be up so late every night."

"No, actually, I can't. You've worked yourself into me, baby, like an addiction that I crave feeding."

I try not to look pleased, but fail miserably.

"I love you, Sandwich."

"I love you, too, baby."

"My last concern is Blondie. I'm worried about her reaction if we mate. We might have gotten away with the marking by banking on her following the crowd, but this is bigger than that. You told me what her issue is with me and mating with you means that we're going to hit that button hard. I'm afraid Talia's friendship with her will suffer. Hell, I'm even worried about what she'll do to you when she finds out."

"She'll go with the crowd—at least in public. Sari will make a show of being okay with it and Rhea will follow her lead. That doesn't mean they won't be awful behind the scenes, but they won't come at us publicly. And Rhea has *never* confronted anyone on her issues with them, so her friendship with Talia will be fine. Fake, but fine."

"Christ, do you even have to tell them?"

"I'll have to mention it at some point. You know that as mates —even less than perfect ones—they're owed that much."

"Balls," he grumbles petulantly.

"Sari's been a good girl so far."

But Wilde has not been a good boy.

He plops down on the couch, pulls me down, and buries his face in my stomach. "That's terrifying." Holding onto my pant legs as he leans into me, I can see that he's having a hard time trying to reconcile what is right with what would be easier.

I whisper softly, "I love you, Taurus. None of the other people can change that. You don't need to worry about them. I know there's been a lot of hard shit lately, but I promise you I'm here to stay."

He blinks owlishly as he looks up at me. "What did you call me?"

"What did I call you?" I echo, giving him a puzzled look.

"My name. What did you call me?"

"Tau-rus," I repeat slowly, wondering what the hell is up with him.

"Do you know that it's the first time in—I don't know how

long—that you've called me that? It's the first time you've said 'I love you, Taurus' period."

His expression is so serious that I try to muddle out why I haven't. I haven't purposefully avoided his name or anything.

"Not counting mumbling shit while we're going at it, of course. But actually saying it out loud? That's the first time. I worried maybe you had forgotten who I was." He doesn't look at me, clearly embarrassed to admit that it bothered him.

I shake my head vehemently. I know exactly who he is and what I say to him. I consider everything carefully to ensure that I don't fuck it all up. "I could never forget you."

"With my wee insecurity about us, you not calling me Taurus was plaguing me. I don't know why, but hearing you say it like that makes us more serious. You can't walk up to Rafe and say, 'I love you, Taurus' without him giving you a strange look."

Hell, he'd look at me funny if I said it to Taurus directly in front of him. My family is so used to using nicknames I couldn't tell you the last time I said that to Rafe like that, either. I wonder if that's bothered anyone else. "I didn't mean for you to feel that way. I know exactly who you are." I smile softly, turning his face back to mine.

"You said the exact right thing, minx. I'm not saying I'm completely secure yet, but I'm better than I was. I can deal with the rest of my worries now." His posture relaxes as he tugs me closer.

I reach over and pull his hand to the feather. "This is you. I can't forget who you are because you're here all the time to remind me."

"You're right—mine." His grin widens as he strokes the feather gently. "However, no more telling me about the wacky stuff the others are into. Half of me wants to heave and half is genuinely curious if you liked it."

I smile, ruffling his hair fondly. "No more wild tales unless pertinent to the topic at hand."

"A bloke gets unsettled, wondering about that shit."

Oh, he will not let this go. I'm going to address it right now. "I didn't enjoy everything I've ever been asked to try. Sometimes there were fun kinks, of course. Some things I enjoyed with certain people and not others. But lately, it's...not been fun." I tread carefully, knowing that if I don't, it will open the door to questions I don't want to answer.

"You didn't enjoy all of it? I suppose that's good to know. It makes me feel less...prudish."

"I mean, I'll try just about anything once. But I didn't enjoy having to...come up with more outrageous things like it was a competition? That shit takes the fun right out of being naughty."

"I can't help but think I'm at the tip of a very difficult iceberg." His brows furrow and he looks melancholy, as if he's worried that he won't be enough.

Lord knows I know how that feels.

"Taurus, you have nothing to worry about. There are things you do with me that none of the others do: hunting is a prime example."

He gives me a flabbergasted look. "You're mated to other clones, though. Obviously, I don't mean Wilde, but what about my brother, Rafe, or even that asshole Victor?"

"None of the clones that live in the Rift hunt anymore. You and I can run and hunt and feed our primal sides. It's a gift that no one else can give me."

"We can train and spar, too. That's when the real fun starts: grand theft, targets, chasing down the wicked."

"See? Rafe and Victor will spar with me, but they won't go at me for real and they *definitely* won't do any of that."

"There are a couple of baubles in museums around the world I'd like to pick up, not to mention that you haven't lived until you've switched the Egyptian mummies and the Incan mummies without security going off." He bobs his brows playfully and I can tell that he's feeling better.

"I have a cat suit like on the TV show," I grin excitedly, trying not to look like I'm geeking out as hard as I am.

"Oh, Christ, you want me because I'm bad." Rolling his eyes, he puts a hand over his heart as if he's struggling not to have palpitations.

I swat him firmly. "You know better. I like you for a lot of reasons and bad isn't one of them."

"I know why you like—love me. I can do wicked with a grin and a wink. Not much affects me if I get caught because all I do is hunt, fight, and irritate people all day long. I also love you so much that sometimes I can't get two words together for the lump in my throat when I look at you. And I'm not ashamed to tell you about it, either."

"That about covers it, yeah." I duck my head, feeling shy as there's an enormous lump forming in my throat now.

"I love you for similar reasons, so we don't have a problem. Plus, the stompy and jiggly bits are nice."

I snort. "Uh-huh."

He tips my chin up and gives me a long, slow kiss. I wrap my arms around him tightly, feeling the emotion inside me well up. He pulls back eventually, resting his forehead on mine. "That's why I want to mate with you the old-fashioned way. I'm sick of restrictions; I won't have them with you. Do you understand?"

My voice is soft as I look at him, emotions choking me. "Yes."

"You're still along for the ride?"

"I am."

He looks at the ornate clock on the wall—a recent addition—and sighs. "Then when it's not four a.m., you and I are going to see about a peacock, a bloodletting, and a nice, long drink."

"Oh, goody!"

He looks me in the eye, hands cupping my cheeks. "I will drain you, kitty. I'm not doing this halfway. By the time we're through, we'll be lightheaded, and neither of us will know whose blood is in whom. I damn well better not grow a tail."

Giggling, I shrug. "I don't think you will." Of course, I never thought I would grow a tail, so I'm not sure I can promise that. "It will pop out when you bite. I won't be able to stop it. I don't think you've seen what happens when I let her fully out, so don't, um, be too shocked."

I don't say that lightly.

The first time she popped out, people were intrigued and enchanted. That didn't last. The discomfort that I feel about her because of Wilde makes me overly sensitive about letting people see the full monte. She has no patience for those who don't appreciate her, and I don't have a lot of self-esteem left in that arena. It's why I started on the journey that led me to him. I wanted to know how this happened so I could reverse it. I haven't ever told anyone that, though, and I don't plan on telling him now.

"The last time I yanked it, I got a fun response. I'm looking forward to it."

"You didn't get half of it," I chuckle throatily.

"Oh, but I will." His smirk makes me wriggle, and he laughs. "Are you sleeping here or are you heading home?"

I blink. "I hadn't thought about it."

"Well, if I go now, I can get three hours of sleep before my thirteen-hour day."

"Then you should go get some sleep. Keep your strength up." I give him a playful grin, masking the fact that I hadn't considered being mated to someone who won't spend a large part of their nights and days with me. Or how I will manage splitting my time with people who expect us all to sleep in a kitty pile.

"I'm out of here. I love you." He leans down and kisses me lightly.

"I love you, Taurus."

"Do you have things going on tomorrow during the day?"

"In the morning, probably. I have a ritual to organize."

"Oh, good. I might actually get some work done rather than pop in here to be with you. I've got a death at one that might run a little while, so I may not you until later in the afternoon. You will see me, though. I promise that."

"Okay, baby. Sleep well."

"Night, love."

With that, he disappears. I look around, trying to figure out what I've gotten myself into and how it's going to change my life.

I guess it couldn't make it worse, that's for damned sure.

The Family Gets The Scoop

RAFE

"Where did you hear this, Philomena?"

Her eyes narrow as she glares at us. "Where do you bleached numbskulls think I heard it from? The glittery grapevine is always on the case."

Leo's expression turns troubled as he leans against the counter. "They've already started building?"

Philomena nods grimly. "Yes, and it will be completed in a matter of days. Mayhem enlisted some old Company friends, unknown to us, to help with construction. They kept it hidden by choosing a location just inside our bubble, near the bridge to the Cabal Quarter. Not many people live out there."

She takes a slow sip of her martini, her focus unwavering. "My boys are ecstatic, despite the place looking like a total dive."

A thought crosses my mind. "The cat's going to be furious when she finds out."

Philomena lets out a heavy sigh. "Oh, she already knows. It was the coyote and her bulldog who arranged all of this behind every-one's backs. They didn't even tell their own families. And they didn't waste any time - everything has been in the works for weeks now thanks to their deep pockets and connections." Her lips curl into a sneer. "But of course, the glamor guys are thrilled - it's right up their alley."

Hex slams his fist down on the counter, seething with disgust. "That pathetic waste of space from the south. She's always starting trouble. Now I understand what Chaos was ranting about - singing about bottles and cans, empty chairs and empty tables, rebels and rogues. It's been like she's watching *Les Miserables* on repeat."

"The real issue here," Sandrine drawls, "is that this dog is furious that one of her pack has gone to the enemy. So she's sending a clear warning: if anyone crosses her, she'll unleash hell."

"They're trying to establish their business in our community without even consulting the council," I grit my teeth in frustration. "Taking over land they claim is public domain. It doesn't matter if it's true or not. They've built their building there and are now posting their 'rules' for everyone to follow as if they have the authority. And appointing trailer trash as their bouncer? It's like saying they have a pet shark in their pool, but inviting people over for a swim." My braid whips around as I shake my head.

"That was precisely their intention," Siren interjects from behind us. "They want to assert dominance, knowing our leader is preoccupied. And they plan to use brute force to enforce their own set of rules, causing conflict within the community. There can't be two sets of regulations for members to abide by. It's a small-scale revolution."

"Fuck this. Why can't these pathetic assholes just shut the hell up and leave well enough alone?" Hex's face twists with disgust as he struggles with his girlfriend's crazy family, causing chaos in their lives.

"Listen up, minions," Philomena slams her glass onto the counter. "This is not a war zone. It's a damn karaoke bar. Our beloved droid bartenders are here for one thing: fun. They don't give a damn about our petty dramas, parties or designer clothes. And for once, we need to let them do their job without interfering.

Because if we don't, things will go to shit real quick. So instead of plotting like children, let's agree to keep our families out of this mess. The cat and librarian can deal with their own problems while we handle ours."

She's right, but it won't be easy.

The cat is seething with anger and betrayal, but she'll have to put that aside for now. If I can redirect her focus towards taking down the arrogant peacock in their midst, maybe she'll see it as a challenge rather than a burden. And hopefully, the clueless bimbo from the backwoods will get bored and stop meddling in our affairs like she always does.

I sigh and look over at my family. "Someone get the straws because I am *not* going to be the one to break this news."

The Coyote Is Building A Zoo

SARI

There's trouble afoot. I can *smell* it.

Since the literal incarnation of my spirit animal manifested, I can smell everything. This is different, though. Our nearest and dearest are drifting away, and I have to stop it. Wilde's tried his best to provide discouragement, but it hasn't worked.

It's time for mama to take over.

You're probably wondering why I want to keep people from being happy, aren't you? You can wonder all you like; it doesn't bother me. It's incorrect, but people are always assigning inaccurate motives to my actions. No one ever understands how I—how we—work. It's the curse of being the 'misunderstood rebel' that I've dealt with my entire life.

Everything—and I mean everything—I do is to protect the people I love, even if it's from themselves. They don't always comprehend what I'm doing, and that causes a lot of dust-ups, but I don't worry about it.

When the Cabal left after the Conflict, Wilde and I were adrift. We switched sides to help them and got our reward, but they all peaced out. It was a domino effect. Talia's family went into exile. The other leaders went back to the other side. The Resistance disappeared, and the few semi-permanent residents we knew weren't enough to keep us occupied.

We could spend more time in the other place and for a while, we did. I got the brilliant idea to hang out in Bytes 'N Chips, hoping that some of the hidden rebels would come there. Good thing I did, because that's where we met Deli and her boys. Back then, it was her, Leo, and Hex. She was head over heels for Victor— who could blame her—but Donatella was still around.

I called around to some of my Cabal friendly folks that left, and we built a bar down the street from the Cabal Quarter. We called it Dirty Deeds, and it was a new place for everyone to play. Well, everyone that was cool, of course.

DD was invite-only and the hottest ticket in town.

I had people; Deli had people. We were a natural match in terms of leaders who didn't want to be leaders. Wilde enjoyed her constant challenging of his strict behavioral norms, and I liked how free spirited she was. We ruled the roost at my little venture until the bar exploded in the middle of the night. Faulty gas line, they said, but I've never believed that. I think the Company got involved because we were taking away from Bytes 'N Chips' recruiting capabilities with our private venue.

In the meantime, Deli had met and mated with Rafe. That meant Wilde was a lot more comfortable asking if I minded if he courted her. She was so different from 'tomboy' me and his 'Lady Fair' Rhea. Deli was bad to the bone, and he liked she made him stretch his boundaries. Once she had a mate, he didn't worry about upsetting me.

Wilde and I have always understood one another's needs.

After a short, but adorable courtship full of dates, flowers, and taking drives in the country—all that rot he loves so much—not only did he end up mating with Deli, but I got involved with Rafe. I've loved that clone from the beginning, you know. He may be lazy and loungy, but he's a stallion in the sack and makes my heart do girly flip flops. I haven't ever been able to figure out why, but he does. I ended up mating with him just as quickly as Wilde did with Deli.

Deli finally invited us to join the Resistance community after we mated. I had no idea how many people lived there full time. We met all the families, and I saw Heaven for the first time. Her family kept growing, and they made new droids for all the members and new recruits. There were droves of people to play with in her hidden corner of our world.

Tension flared with Rhea and Alistair after we started spending more time where they couldn't find us. The drama stayed in the background at first because I didn't *tell* our new mates. They didn't need to know that our other loves were demanding we mate with them now—even though Rhea had insisted she and Alistair would never mate with others. That was Talia's influence, but once Rhea saw Deli horning in with Wilde, she had a conversion of beliefs.

We did it because we loved them. It wasn't enough, though.

Rhea wanted more of our time, more of us, and to read about fewer adventures with the other two. It was hard to explain that because Deli, Wilde, and I were writers, we had to tell our stories in the blogs. It wasn't our fault she didn't like to write, and couldn't play the same way. She was constantly miserable, and we fought all the time about where Wilde and I were spending our time.

Finally, I went to Dels with my hat in hand. I begged for her to invite Rhea into the Resistance despite being droid-less. That was the only requirement to be part of the Resistance and though it was reasonable, I had to get Rhea off my back. In retrospect, it was one of the dumbest ideas I've ever had, and I've done some dumb shit in my lifetime.

After a week on pins and needles as Deli, Lily, and Dona discussed her inclusion, I went out and bought one of those stupid robot dogs. I gave it to Rhea as a present and went back to Deli to plead again. I knew it was a cheap trick. I was playing on her heart strings for someone that made her uncomfortable. I gave her my personal guarantee that none of the bad behavior they'd seen from Rhea at Dirty Deeds would happen here.

I shouldn't have given that guarantee.

I've known Rhea for a long time in the other place. She's not evil, but she has *issues* from her childhood. Her worst behavior stems from being adopted—inferiority issues from her non-adopted brother and her adoptive father. The same issues eventually crop up no matter where Brenda is, and even I can't control them.

Shit, my bad. That was probably confusing.

Most of us take on alternative names for our new lives in the Rift. Talia's the only person I've ever known who uses the same name on both sides. Brenda is Rhea's Earth name and mine's Priya. Deli swears her actual name is Delilah, but I'm not so sure. She's not semi-permanent, though, so I suppose it doesn't matter what her Earth name was, huh?

I digress. It happens.

Rhea always comes in like a meek little rabbit, but this time, she hit like a wrecking ball. Within a month, Deli was dating Alistair. Rhea started seeing Rafe, and *boom*! Somehow, they're mated. Then she pushes on this family mating thing and I'm like...*whoa*.

Mating involves sex, blood, forever—involving all four of us means Rhea would have to take part. I'm cool with an occasional dip in the female pool and Wilde was absolutely in love with Rafe. But Rhea was never—and I mean *never*—comfortable with homosexuality if wasn't packaged in a fluffy friend to take shopping.

It was amazing to watch as an outsider observer. She got Alistair involved with both Rafe and Wilde in a short timeframe. I remember wondering what in the hell books she read about this at her bookstore. Rhea does nothing new without research. I would have bet my last quarter that she and Alistair had a stack of erotica and a browser full of slash fiction that she used to get them ready.

I figured Deli would have more sense than fall for it and believe me; I *tried* to warn her. The kitty didn't listen, and neither did her mate. I tried to stop the train by booking a trip with Wilde, Alistair, Rhea, and I to the other side for a sci-fi convention. I figured Rhea would lose her momentum and I could prevent it from going any further.

All I accomplished with that gambit was the four of us mating. I'm still not sure how it happened, but I *know* tequila was involved. Deli and Rafe got *pissed* that we did it without telling them, especially because they had planned something similar with Rhea and now I'd cut them off.

I can't win for losing, right? That's the story of my life.

My attempt to help blew up in my face for *months*. I can't help but think it lead to Deli inviting the head fucking dictator of the Cabal back into our world. I mean, what in the actual fuck was she *thinking*? Of all people, Talia and Taurus are the most rigid, least free loving, and most judgmental of *all* that wretched group. Wilde and I only joined their side in the Conflict because they were *obviously* winning, and I wanted some of that clone magick shit as a reward.

Queen D brought back the Terror Twins with her tête-à-tête with Taurus and then she hid it for weeks. Hell, I only found out once she'd posted enough blog info to guess. I still haven't figured out why the hell she tapped him. She told us it was for a project, but I doubt it. What the hell does that blowhard know she couldn't find online? The girl's a literal genius.

What could he possibly be teaching her?

It might have to do with the hellcat she grew at Christmas. I thought she and Wilde had that fixed after the big night. He's been walking around with his cockneyed demon loose more than ever, and I figured they tamed one another. Our reindeer games get a lot rougher now and that makes us both happy, especially since my pup showed up.

The mystery of 'why' is unimportant, though. The important

thing is that since that blasted bird showed up, Rhea's in psycho mode and Deli's completely MIA. She keeps insisting that nothing is going on. Normally—given Taurus' ideas on life, love, and limb removal—I'd believe her.

Except...something has set Rhea in overdrive. All she seems to want to do if screw Taurus instead of crying about how mean he is. Except...Deli has been MIA, and when she's not, she's distant. Except...Deli won't talk about Taurus like she did with Alistair. Except...I don't trust Taurus or Talia as far as I could throw them.

Something stinks in Deli-land—I need to find it and throw it out. Deli's brilliant, but she's oh-so-easily distracted. It used to be by sex. Wilde tried that, and he's tried pushing the protective button.

It's not working.

I'm going to push her anger button. Belle and I have a plan that will have her so distracted that she'll abandon whatever bullshit she has going on with Taurus to attack us. Our friends in the community will jump in to defend us and there will be a big ass schism over who's right and wrong. She won't have time for Taurus, and eventually, he'll get bored and leave. With him gone, Deli will have time for her mates and though we're all dysfunctional, we can go back to normal.

It's a perfect plan and I have the *perfect* way to execute it. We will hit her in public, where she can't stop us without looking like a dictator.

See? Like I told you, everything I've done in the past and everything I do now is to protect those I love.

I can't figure out why people don't understand that.

The Gates Are Open At The Zoo

I grin as I walk through town placing the flyers in every mailbox at every house in the Resistance Quarter. This is going to ruffle feathers when the right people see it, but Belle and I decided it has to be a direct hit. Deli won't turn away from her new toy if we don't aim right for her heart.

This place is the thing she's so damn proud of and it's a vulnerable target. Fucking with the landscape here in ways she can't control or decry for lack of proof will help me regain control of her. Once I get her in line, the rest of her family will follow suit without a fight.

I desperately need to get them back in our lives; the others simply don't compare.

Belle and her family are great when I want to wage war, but they simply lack the emotional capacity and attention span to be constant playmates. Rhea and Alistair are obviously too eager to be loved; they'll sell us out for a butt plug. The kitty and her ilk are the most intelligent, feisty, and adventurous folks in the Rift right now. Losing them to our shitty arch nemesis is a blow, but I can fix it.

After all, Taurus and Talia are about as interesting as vanilla yogurt on beige khakis. They only want to diddle each other and that leaves big gaping holes—see what I did there—in the cat's kink profile.

I know... I sound like I'm scheming against someone I don't like, but that's not the case. Wilde and I love our mates, though some more than others. Obviously, my attachment to Rafe and Wilde's to Deli supersede everything. Though Wilde is pretty fond of the lazy artist, too. I just see Dels as more of my sister and the whole mating thing required something I knew she'd enjoy. It's not like we ever have to do it again now.

My punky bulldog-esque friend has mentioned a couple of times that attitude might fuck things up, but I don't think so. Deli loves the people she loves and asks for almost nothing. She won't demand things I don't offer, and even if she does, I'll just be demure. She'll tire of asking over time and the whole 'female mate' thing will disappear.

I'm smart as hell when I want to be. It's why I always win.

"Are you sure we're not missing anyone?"

I squint, looking over at Belle with an eye roll. "The community is a big fucking circle, B."

"Yeah, but... it feels like we're missing something."

Tilting my head, I think about it before snapping my finger. "Shit, we have to do the Cabal Quarter, too. A few people still live there."

"Good call, S. You always get what I'm saying."

I wait until she spaces out again and sigh. She's just not always the most connected person. It's not satisfying to spend time with someone who's only really alive when they're going to war.

At least, not for me.

I hold the paper out in front of me, grinning as I read it again.

COME ONE, COME ALL!

THE COYOTE DEN AND THE RANCH INVITE YOU TO THEIR NEW JOINT VENTURE:

'THE ZOO' WILL BE OPEN TO THE PUBLIC ON MARCH 31ST. JOIN US FOR DRINKS, FOOD, AND DEVIANT FUN AT THE NEWEST PARTY PLACE IN THE RIFT.

THE ZOO IS A FULL SERVICE KARAOKE BAR HOSTED BY OUR RESIDENT BROADWAY BABIES, ROMAN AND JANUS.

ANYTHING GOES AT THE ZOO.

NOTHING IS TOO WILD, TOO SCANDALOUS, OR TOO DEVIANT BECAUSE YOU AND ME, BABY, ARE NOTHING BUT MAMMALS.

SEX, DRUGS, BOOZE, AND VIOLENCE ARE NOT ONLY ALLOWED, BUT *HIGHLY ENCOURAGED*.

BE WHO YOU ARE—*NOT WHO THEY EXPECT YOU TO BE*— AT THE ZOO.
NOTE: BEWARE OF THE BOUNCER. BELLE IS ITCHING TO BUST SOME HEAD IF YOU ARE A BUZZKILL TO US OR OUR PATRONS.

HER RULE IS *LAW* IN THE ZOO, AND YOU'D BETTER BELIEVE SHE'LL BE ENFORCING IT.

The Cat Vents Her Fury

DELILAH

How *dare* they? How *fucking* dare they?

I'm so furious that I'm vibrating with rage. My beast is howling inside, slamming against her cage to get out and take care of our threat. I can't let her, even though the betrayal and rage are coursing through my veins like venom.

Sari's last den of inequity got blown to smithereens. She had nowhere to go and no one to play with. After the strings I pulled to get her in my community, after allowing her asshole friends in, she does *this*?

Fuck them. No, they'd like that too much. Un-fuck them.

Sari and the twittering bint from the boonies not only built a business in *my* community without so much as a by-your-leave to Lily or me, but they released a nasty blog post about the 'rules' for visiting their stupid bar. Rules they *know* that violate our community charter. Rules that are geared toward Belle being able to bully and abuse anyone she likes if she or Sari feel they have been wronged.

I am livid in ways mere human words cannot describe. The

world should *bleed* from my anger. Mountains should shake and thunder should clap down from the sky in a rain of fire—because I have been betrayed *again.*

None of that will happen.

I can't rip, shred, and tear through the world to mete out my justice because I am a leader. Lily and I are not a council of despots like the Cabal; we do not rule with fear and anger. We have a town charter, a set of rules that all members must abide by or face justice from the will of the people. Their violations will be dealt with, but we must deal with them with through fairness, grace, and reasonable restrictions.

That's all moot, though, because the goddamned place *opens tonight.*

Poor Hex must have drawn the short straw because he stayed far away as he relayed the news yesterday. He behaved much less aggressively than was his norm when he took me to the site of the bar. He tried to keep me from busting through the door and tearing the place apart by reasoning with me. He was successful, but when I returned home, the first thing I did was beam myself out. I have to find my center, so I can handle Sari and her erstwhile pet with aplomb and diplomacy.

My sacred space would help me do that if I weren't filled with a need for blood vengeance. I don't need the calm tranquility of nature right now; I need a partner in blood and pain. Taurus has away for a week and I was already going insane before this stunt. We decided on the mating question and he immediately gets called away for a long mission.

Of course, all this shit happened while he was gone.

Pacing back and forth, I look around. He's done some work again. There's another door way between the wall with the closet and the one with the bathroom that leads to what looks like a staircase. I keep waiting for him to take me on a tour, but it hasn't come up. I may have to take it upon myself.

I feel the hairs on the back of my neck raise and turn my head to look at the doorway to the hall. He's leaning against the door-jamb, watching me pace. A warm smile reflects happiness at seeing me here after our separation. I push everything away inside, not wanting to cheat myself of a lovely moment with him. "Hi, baby."

He grins wider. "Hello, beautiful." Pushing off the wall, he walks up behind me and drops a kiss on the back of my neck. "How was your week, love?"

"Best left undiscussed," I mutter. "How was work?"

Arching a brow, he senses that I'm not in the mood and shrugs. "Not bad. It was like running at ninety miles an hour when everyone around you was driving beaters, though. It gets like that for me when I have to work in a team. I'm used to just eat—er, dealing with those who annoy me in a different way, but I can't when it's agents. I almost snatched a vile bint in admin bald today. That was a good time."

I ponder that, thinking about the usefulness of his ability to dispatch with his enemies. I could use a few hedges pruned right now.

"Are you lining up victims in your head, pet?"

Wrinkling my nose, I shake my head. "They would violate your rules. It wouldn't help to line them up."

"Then put your pointies away because I've brought someone with me, kitty. He might take offense to your wild side when you turn around and meet him."

I blink, putting a hand to my face; I didn't realize that I had fanged out. I close my eyes, soothing her with reassuring words until I can feel the cat fade. "Okay, I'm ready."

As if by magick, he leans over and picks up a wee little cage. Inside is a very tiny, remarkably irritated looking peacock.

Putting my hand over my mouth to cover the giggles, I gape at it. All my anger melts away in child-like glee. "Is that a Damien creation?"

"It is. Imagine my surprise when he hung this little screamer from my bedpost this morning in Havana." Holding up the cage—

which was roughly a three inches by three inches—he peers inside at the indignant fowl.

"He is hysterical." My lips quirk as I imagine that scene.

"Damien definitely has a sense of humor you want to stick a stake in."

"Good thing I didn't bring my baby today. I thought about bringing her."

That much is true. My tiger familiar, Aradia, can sometimes soothe the ragged edges of my anger. My beast understands her, and since the transformation, we can communicate via the Beast. It feels like a fairy tale, but her growls sound like words in my head. She's going to make a fantastic hunting partner once I'm comfortable enough to really get out.

"Your... baby?"

His confused expression makes me smile. Though my household is used to Aradia—who Preston kindly rescued from an abusive home-brewed zoo belonging to hillbillies—Taurus is not. She was a birthday present I would have never asked for—because she's endangered—but love with all my heart. Aradia lives in a pampered, loving home, so I feel like I've made a difference. I haven't introduced her before because she was tied into my relationship with Alistair, so it felt wrong. Now that Alistair is all but gone, it feels okay to do so.

"Pick up the cage and hold it high above your head. Trust me."

-He eyes me warily, but lays the tiny birdcage in his palm and lifts his arm up. "Tell me no one's around the corner with a bloody cell, waiting to post a picture of Taurus the git."

"Nope." I push the button on the bird phone and a piercing whistle echoes through the mic.

His hypersensitive hearing must have hated that noise because he shouts, "Bugger, woman! Ever heard of a concept called *warning*?"

I watch as my ten-month-old 'baby' bounds in, dragging her blanket in her teeth as she leaps onto the couch. I scratch behind her ears, knowing that Aradia doesn't know that she's not a five-pound cub anymore but the size of a Great Dane. "Aradia, darling, Uncle Leo's putting you on a diet. No more Omaha filets for snacks." I ruffle her fur again and look over at him. "This is my baby. I forgot to mention her when we discussed family."

His mouth drops open and a shriek of fury—a wee little shriek from a wee little bird—comes from the cage above his head. "It's a bloody tiger. It's a white bloody tiger." He frowns, as if ready to give me a lecture on owning endangered wild animals, and I cut him off.

"Preston—that's Michaela's droid—found her in a half-assed hillbilly zoo as a cub. He decided she was the best birthday present I'd ever get. I know she's endangered, but they were treating her badly. Once I met her, I wasn't sending her back until she was healed and...well, she's safe now that she's mine."

"We could always dye her, I suppose."

"Dye her? She's beautiful!" I give him a peeved look, scratching the head of my regal looking familiar, as if he insulted me personally.

His brow arches. "Do you know how much fun it is to hunt with a real predator?"

I nod. "We ran together a little after you and I met. I haven't had time lately, but we're very in sync because she's my familiar. I thought you'd like to meet her. I forgot her the last time I came here, and I felt bad."

His eyes gleam. "Why am I not surprised that she's the size of an SUV?"

"Because everyone in my house spoils the bloody bejesus out of her?" I snort. "She's the baby of the house in every sense of the word."

He eyes her for a moment. "She's beautiful, right enough—like her mamma." His hand stretches out, but he pulls it back, eyeing her teeth as she yawns. "Can I touch her? She won't rip my arm off or anything, will she?"

"Keep that up, buster, and I'll think you have a crush on me." I look up at him and shake my head. "Of course not. She's a hunter, but she's a lady. Hold your hand out first; she'll smell me on you. She's friendly as long as she knows people."

"Do you think I've forgotten how to properly meet a lady?" His hand goes out to the enormous cat, knuckles up as he waits for the tiger to initiate interest.

"Given our introduction..." I chuckle. "Her claws are trimmed. Not so that she can't use them, only enough to keep her from shredding everyone unintentionally."

Taurus stands perfectly still for her, though his eyes glow. He reaches out to speak into my mind quietly so he doesn't startle Aradia. ~ *It's a good bit more than a crush, love.* ~

I watch as my baby sniffs and pokes at his hand, her powder blue eyes looking up at him shrewdly. After a minute, she butts her head against his hand and a soft rumbling sound escapes her throat. "There you go. She doesn't think you are food."

Grinning mischievously, he bobs his head at me. His hand scratches behind the tiger's ears as he talks to her. "What's your name, beauty? What did your mama call you?"

"Aradia." I grin as she licks his hand and nuzzles his fingers. "Looky there, she likes you." I stroke the tiger's flank gently, listening to her rumble.

"Aradia, aren't you just the lady?" He gives her a rough caress on the head, and she plays back, pretending to growl playfully.

His expression is boyishly happy as she butts him with her forehead, and he chuckles. "Women fall for me. What can I say?"

I roll my eyes. "You go, Casanova."

His smirk widens at my remark. "Tell it to the judge, baby. You're positively smitten, and this beautiful, amazing girl is just as susceptible to the flattery as you were." A squawk distracts him and he chuckles. "Uh, pet? Do you have somewhere I can put this little guy without him becoming a morsel?"

I look down at Aradia, staring into her eyes for a moment.

"Down." The tiger ambles across the room, laying her head on her paws as she curls up on the rug. "Now stay, my darling. Be a good girl." Looking over at him, I grin. "You can put the peahen down."

"I'll have you know that *you're* the peahen, pet. That's the cock's mate." He tries not to smirk again but fails. I snort and he winks. Putting the birdcage on the table, he comes closer to me. "You're a feisty one today."

"I am at that, my love." That was *not* true when he came in, but it sure as hell is now. Seeing his acceptance of another major part of my life eased my worry about making the enormous commitment. It also lessened the ache from the loss of my old life. Losing the good parts of life with my other mates has plagued me since everything was upended. His love has a watering can for my soul, slowly nurturing the fragile seed back to life.

"Does that mean you're not in the mood for a cuddle?"

"I am. Are you offering, big bad?"

He opens his arms and smiles tenderly at me. "Always, baby." I crawl into his arms and curl around him, rubbing my cheek on his shoulder. "I saw a blog post from the gnome today and thought I'd ask about it. It seems pointed at a specific person, but it doesn't mention names. It's not about me, is it?"

"No. She's still in the dark about most of this. You must watch threads I'm purposely ignoring. It's probably about me."

"At least she's not waving that flag. I made the mistake of reading that series with Wilde and Amanda on his blog—the 'bringing you death' rot. I nearly heaved on my tablet. People say that I'm a drama queen, but pulling the ribbon out of his hair and declaring that he wants to take revenge is ridiculous. Then saying that because she wants to die, he'll help her? Pure drivel and an excuse to abuse a woman."

"So you don't want to read about Wilde beating the hell out of Amanda to feed her masochism and his sadism, either? Shocking."

Today was a shit show on multiple levels, which is why the bar hit me like a crowbar. Since I've been MIA, not only has Sari been plotting this idiotic bar and having Wilde beat the crap out of my mate, she's been hanging around Amanda a lot. Apparently, Amanda didn't go through her 'my life is pain' emo stage in high school. She's apparently questioning her existence through a series of 'quests' that she's doing with various people.

I'm not joking; she seems to think she's fucking Odysseus.

-After the first post, I tuned out. I have enough actual pain and genuine drama in my life; I don't need to manufacture it, for Christ's sakes. However, it does *not* surprise me that Wilde's part in this epic load of bullshit is to get physical with her. That seems to be his oeuvre, now.

"Fighting or sparring are different. Beating on a woman for the hell of it makes me want to bash his face in. I can't imagine what's going through all of their minds, using that as an outlet. What if it triggers someone's PTSD? I know I don't know a damned thing about most people's dead life on the other side, and I'll bet they don't, either. It's sick."

I duck my head, pursing my lips together. He doesn't know what kind of silken webs can keep someone in that kind of relationship, despite how strong they are on the outside. I don't think Amanda has nearly the issues that Rafe and I do with Wilde, but I can't comment on her allowing him to hurt her. I'd be a hypocrite.

This bullshit with Amanda and Wilde working out their 'demons' together started right after I spent the weekend with Taurus. I'm hoping that it's not because of me, but because Sari and Amanda are insane. Wilde lost his mind a long time ago, so he's just in it for the sadism. I've avoided participation in her quests by being unavailable, but I won't be able to avoid it forever. If Taurus thinks that's the worst it will be before it ends, he doesn't know Wilde like I do.

"It's a little dark for the funnies, isn't it? Aren't we supposed to be lighter than the ugly place you ladies hail from?"

"I thought so. Amanda's been working through issues with this —or so I hear. Sari jumped on because she loves angst, but I also think she and Wilde are using it to work through their Rhea issues." And maybe me, who knows?

Shaking his head, he shrugs and lets go of me, walking over to the table to look at the bird. "It's not my place to judge. Sorry." He kneels with his back to me and staring into the tiny peacock's cage. The tiny avian is ruffled and angry, twittering at the top of his lungs now. It sounds like he's getting bitched out in pea-cockney.

"That shit's not my bag. I've stayed out of their garbage on purpose this time." His brow arches as I snark and I clear my throat. "I'm sure someone will come to me for some kind of psychobabble eventually, but I want no part of this stage." I have my own problems with that family and maybe, just maybe, it's nice to not be the one getting their ass kicked.

"They'd be coming to the right source, I expect." He pokes a finger at the strutting and puffed fowl. "Hey now, you'll not be going on me until you calm yourself, you little git."

"If you want me to calm it, I will." I tilt my head, giving him an angelic smile. "I've been told I have a way with cantankerous fowl."

The bird spits at him—no mistaking it—causing Taurus to grouse. He looks over his shoulder. "You think a purr might help? This one's in a pisser of a mood."

"Hand it over, darling."

Taurus cocks a brow at the cage, as if deciding it might not be the best idea to throw it. He picks it up by the golden floss at the ring and hands it over gently. "Best of luck; that one's incorrigible."

I smile mysteriously, opening the cage door and holding my hand out. The bird puffs up and gives me a supremely annoyed look. I make a soft, rolling, cooing sound in my throat and its head tilts. Prancing a bit, it finally hops into my hand. I keep cooing softly, one finger smoothing its ruffled feathers gently. Looking up, I shrug. "I'm good with animals."

Taurus watches as we interact with a narrowed gaze. "Especially peacocks, apparently." He looks at the bird wryly and shakes his head. "Brother, don't I know it."

I give him an amused glance, still petting the bird until he seems to calm down. Once calm, I set him up on my shoulder, his tail draping down my back. "It's all in the attitude."

Grumbling under his breath about him having plenty of attitude, he snorts. "Yeah, well. You stroke my feathers just right, so I can relate."

"Admitting you have feathers now?"

He growls low in his throat. "Metaphorically. Minx."

"I love when you talk yourself into losing an argument."

Puffing up himself, he grumbles, "Hussy. I have no idea what you're talking about, I'm sure." He points to the bird. "Are you going to help me place him or what?"

"Don't you have to lose some clothes? I mean, he makes a kick ass shoulder ornament and I look like a multi-cultural Boudicca, but you can't put him on until you're bare."

"You just like seeing me strip for you, admit it," he preens, looking more and more like the smug bird on my shoulder.

"I'm sure I have no idea what you're talking about."

His whisper is low and full of mirth. "That doesn't work for you, either." Eyes gleaming, he unbuttons his shirt—button by slow button—as his eyes scorch my skin. Sliding out of it with a ripple of tendon and tight muscle, he drapes it over a nearby chair. "Perhaps lower?" The light in his eyes says he isn't talking about a tattoo, that's for sure.

Licking my lips, I nod. "Couldn't hurt, could it?"

With a feral grin, he reaches for his belt buckle, unhooking it and pulling it from its loops. Moving with liquid grace, he slides the button on his slacks free, then lowers the zipper click by timeless click.

Now he's messing with me. Honestly? I'm fine with it. He's gorgeous to look at—all clones are—but Taurus is built differently. Maybe it's the training, working out, and fighting for work that makes him so much more predatory looking. My primal side finds it imminently delectable. A low rumble forms in my chest, and every nerve in my body tingles.

His pants fall to the floor at his feet and he steps out of them, slowly twisting the muscles in his body to bend down with lithe grace. He picks them up, still eying me intently. With a flick of his wrist, they fall on top of his shirt. Standing naked with his legs parted slightly, he smirks at me as I watch him.

"You uh, um, want to?" I gesture up to the peacock, which nips my finger. "Now?" I can't help the squirming in my seat because he smells amazing, and she's taken notice.

He chuckles low in his throat and drawls, "That caused the strip tease—or did I misinterpret your interest?"

DELILAH

"Huh?" I give him a dazed look.

His eyes glow, flickers of yellow dancing in them hotly. "The tattoo, love. Remember? That *is* why you wanted me naked, right?" He takes one slow step towards me, muscles sliding under tight skin.

"Uh, yes. The tattoo."

"I mean, it's not like you have any other ideas." He takes another step towards me, searing me with his eyes. Once he's standing in front of me, an unholy smile tilts his lips. Cocking his head at me, he asks again. "Did you, love?"

"Uh. No." I shake my head. "Just putting this on." I've become a functional mute. I don't remember what I should say, wanted to say, or even what I am supposed to be doing.

Damned beast. Damned fire in my veins that's making my head fuzzy.

"Well, then, nothing else to do but get it on."

I blink, once again distracted by his innuendo. "Do you know where you—any ideas?"

Taurus chuckles darkly and holds out his arms, tightening his ab muscles to taunt me. "You tell me, love of mine. If you were a peacock, where would you want to be on my body?"

He's definitely fucking with me. I can't peel my eyes away and I can't think. "If I were a...? Uh, you could put it near where mine is... or your shoulder blade... or your tummy." I lean forward and inhale his scent deeply, my eyes closing.

Keeping his features impassive must be hard, but he's doing it. I don't know how he's so damned calm. "Good ideas, all. Maybe you should hold him against me to see where it looks good."

I stand, grateful for the movement because it might help me wrangle the Beast inside me. Walking around him slowly, I hold the bird up to his shoulder blade for a moment and consider. "Hm."

He cranes his neck to watch, obviously amused by the thoughtful expression on my face. I mean, it *is* permanent. I should be thorough, right? Focusing on the tattoo is helping me clear my lust fogged brain, so I'm going to keep doing it.

Two can play at his little game.

"Yes, dear?"

"Just pondering." I smile, circling back to his front and holding the bird up to his pectoral, studying. Lowering it a bit to above his abs, I make the feathers drape down over his tummy and hip. That's pretty, but I pretend to consider it further because I can.

He groans as my fingers whisk over him, and I hide my smile. "I'm wondering how much you're enjoying my restraint." He looks down at himself, growling. "Or lack thereof."

"I want to make sure it looks good." I tilt my head, studying him again before nodding. "Yeah, that looks good."

His eyes roam over the graceful curve of the bird's tail, the calm serenity of it in my hands, and the proud tilt of its head. He grins at me, and the similarities are hard to ignore. "Smaller or larger?" he whispers.

"He looks good like this, unless you think it's too big."

Peering down at the plumage, he looks at the colorful cascade over the side of his stomach and hip. "I like it. It's a definite statement and I'm into statements." His eyes cut up to the top of the feather peeping from the neckline of my tank top.

"I'm aware. So do I say...?"

"Ah, like before? No, it's a different word this time." He rolls his eyes. "Damien was feeling whimsical and ironic. The temperamental blighter. I'll spell it and then you say it."

I nod, preparing for something completely infuriating.

"K - I - T - T - Y."

"Oh! He is so cute." I smile and grip the bird despite its squawks. "Are you ready?"

His eyes are golden embers as they burn into mine. "Forever."

I smile softly as I murmur, "Kitty."

The bird in my hand glows bright blue and green, its tail trilling as the magicks take hold. Its head raises in prideful indignation as it's drawn into his skin. The pain of the marking has to be racing through him because he snarls, locking his muscles in place. In a moment it's done, and he releases the breath he sucked in. He glances down at the bird and then back up at me. "Well?"

I clap my hands. "It looks wonderful." I trail my fingers over it lightly, feeling the feathers of the tiny bird in wonderment.

Surprised, he jerks, learning the nifty little thing that happens to me when the feather gets touched. You feel it everywhere, and I mean everywhere. "Uh. I see he left in that nifty bonus."

I smirk. "It would seem so."

He nods, then runs a deliberate thumb over my mark to wipe the smirk from my face. "The touch thing is hot." I shiver and he steps closer, rubbing the eye of the feather harder. When he's within a hair's breadth, he stops, murmuring, "I'm naked."

"I noticed," I reply, scratching blunt nails over the bird to feel him shudder.

"You're not."

"I can be."

"Good idea." His smile turns evil as I shiver. "Unless you'd rather play canasta."

I raise my arms to help him, shaking my head. "No canasta."

With a tug, he has it over my head and his right hand rubs the leather of her feather, playing with it until he feels me squirm. "Pants, too, beautiful."

I flick the buttons of my cutoffs, letting them fall to the floor. My whole body trembles as he toys with the feather. He takes a moment to look down at me in appreciation, then grabs my hips and pulls me to him. His arms hold me against him as we back toward the couch.

Tumbling together, his hands roam wildly along my skin. Our lips meet in a hungry kiss and we shift to our sides, legs twining together. I moan low, my hands skating down his back and over his ass. He inhales, breathing in the scent of my arousal that is pulsing in the air like magick. Our kiss intensifies until it becomes a brand and we tremble as one.

"If we..." he growls out roughly. "Baby, if we do this, we will mate tonight. Do you understand?"

I nod, digging my nails into the bird as our bodies press together. "Yes."

His hips buck and golden eyes find mine, his expression wild and hungry. With a twist of his torso, he's on top of me, chest heaving as his eyes ask me a silent question. I nod emphatically, feeling the beast ready to be free for the first time in weeks.

"Now, now... please."

His cock fills me with a slamming motion and my nails sliding into claws as they dig in. His growl is primal, features shifted as we move, lust driving his thrusts harder. The heat building up in my body overwhelms the logical part of my brain. She bursts free, and I'm too lost in the coupling to note whether he's noticed my fangs and features shift.

My eyes are completely feline, emerald and gold swirling in them as She floods my form. His growls are low and dark as I scratch and snarl. I'm going to lose control, but he speaks, and I have to shake my head to comprehend.

« *Je vous veux. Je vous voudrai toujours.* » He rumbles phrases in French and emotions swamp me, knowing that he learned it for me. « *J'ai besoin de vous. J'aurai besoin toujours de vous. Je t'aime. Je vous aimerai toujours.* »

The declaration melts my heart, and despite the beast's dominance, the need for him thrums in me from head to toe. The primal, the emotion, the lust, and the hunger: it's all fueling me as our bodies move in unison.

« *Je vous réclame. Vous êtes les miens.* »

Even the beast acknowledges the love flowing through us as I look into his eyes, feeling my orgasm speeding toward me like a freight train. He snarls, his eyes dropping to my throat to watch my hammering pulse. Moving with speed only a clone can, he buries his fangs in my skin and the world shatters around me. My claws slash down his back as the magick of mating propels us to come together. Drinking hungrily, he clutches me as if I'll disappear. I moan low, aftershocks fluttering through me from the pull in my veins. The sparkling sensation of blood loss tweaks at my consciousness and I shudder, euphoria setting in.

At that moment, he instinctively knows that I'm fading. He stops drawing little by little—ever careful of that line between pleasure and danger—to lift his head. "Deli, love. I've drained you. You need to drink now."

Giving him a drunken smile, I lick my four pointed fangs in a supremely feline manner. I pull his head down, a low growl rumbling out of my chest. The beast practically roars her claim, "Mine!"

It's a fight to not to tear in ferociously. She is hungry for someone that accepts her, and that's made her starving for him. His taste dances on my tongue like fine scotch—mellow and rich. At the edge of my consciousness, I feel my tail pop out, marking the last piece of her taking the reins. It strokes up and down his lacerated back soothingly as I drink. Our bodies are still shivering, wave after wave hitting us as this moment stretches into eons.

Suddenly, something inside me clicks into place.

Our auras show up in bright colors as we mix and meld and mate. I feel so much that my nerves spark like they are on fire. The heady floating feeling fades as she feasts, and I realize that we're edging toward that line of danger again. Finally, I let go, licking his wound so it will close, but stay scarred. Whispering his name, I look into his eyes, feeling his demon and my Beast gazing at one another from within.

He collapses on top of me while my tail strokes gently and a calming purr kicks up in my chest. Coasting down together, the intensity of our mating slowly subsides as we lie together and catch our breath. His hand reaches out to caress my feather and I purr louder, the touch making my skin hum again.

"Nice appendage, love," he murmurs hoarsely, tilting his cheek into the fur as it passes his face.

I smile, waiting to see if any of this has thrown him off. I don't know if the trouble that started with others will begin when he sees the changes that happen after the Beast takes control.

"I'm dead, right? No, wait. This isn't hell, so I can't be dead."

Chuckling, I shake my head. "Not dead."

Looking pensive for a moment, he grins. "I thought I might feel guilty."

I tilt my head. "You did?"

He looks embarrassed. "Well, yeah. I'm rather surprised at how *not* guilty I'm feel. I feel like everything is right inside of me." He ducks his head and looks away. "It's nothing. Probably exsanguination induced delusions or whatever."

My expression softens, and I pull his face back to look into his eyes. "No, I feel the same way. I've never — I mean, not so much before—and it's tingly everywhere." Now it's my turn to feel awkward, and I look away.

A fingertip to my chin raises my gaze to his to see the honesty and emotion in his eyes. "It was a first for me, Deli. The first time I've bled anyone that much without intending them dead; hell, the first time I've been bled that much. Is that what you're trying to say? Because I'm tingling, too, and it's a new to me. I'd like to know it's not just me."

I nod, my eyes wide. "I've never drank that much while intimate—not even close. Nor has anyone drank that much from me. It's like I can feel you in every corner of my body; my head's buzzing."

He chuckles deeply, stroking the feather again. "What can I say, baby? I'm positively intoxicating." Snickering, he wags his eyebrows dramatically before giving me a serious blue stare. He drops a kiss on my lips and murmurs, "I love you, Deli."

"I love you, Taurus." I smile, my eyes twinkling. "Your chest thumping is back, so you must feel stronger."

He closes his eyes, and rolls onto his back, sliding an arm around me to snuggle me cozily. "I'm feeling bloody incredible. It's like I'm inside your skin or you're inside mine." Blinking, he turns to me as if he's getting panicked. "You've, uh... never that much? Maybe I shouldn't have?"

I arch a brow, not following his logic. "Why not?"

"It's just—maybe you didn't really want to. I did and maybe you felt obligated..."

Snorting, I shake my head firmly. That's too silly to even consider. She has wanted to tear into him from the moment we got intimate and I've been straining at the chains to keep her back for weeks.

"You didn't?"

"I took what I wanted. She was so hungry that I couldn't stop. She wanted to drink you deep, baby."

"Why was that? Because I'd drained you so far?"

"I don't think so. I've felt all, um, hungry and stuff like that before—with you." I bite my lip, not knowing how much I should admit to. It's been an ache for so long, but what if it weirds him out?

"What do you mean, before?" He rubs his thumb over my lower lip lightly, making sure I'm looking at him.

"I think I could have—no, probably would have—done it like that even if I'd gone first." I squirm, feeling so emotionally exposed that I'm having trouble.

"Are you saying you wanted to drain me from the beginning, love?"

"You make her... me... hungry. I told you that. It's like I need all of you."

"She, um, didn't want me dead, right?"

"Of course not, you overstuffed turkey!" I huff, giving him a salty look.

"Good. Back to this drinking thing, then. I may tease, but it means a lot. I'm gratef—no, I feel... I'm not sure how to put it. It's like you chose me when you chose me."

My lips curl. "Yeah, it is, isn't it?"

"I did, too," he whispers.

My tail brushes over his face. "You know, this doesn't pop out for just anyone. I have to get completely lost in her. And, um, to let her out—all the way out—I have to really trust the person."

"Those control issues are coming right along," he chuckles. His expression gets curious as he looks at the appendage. "It doesn't come out every time you get—intimate? I'd think with the biting that she busts out all the time."

I shake my head. "No. I don't let her run completely free much at all anymore."

"Why not? I mean, I assume it's a primal blood thing. They bleed you; you grow."

This requires me to avoid specifics or I'll have to admit things I am not ready to discuss. "I haven't figured that out yet. The tail pops out when she's close to getting out—but only if she's super ramped up. If it doesn't come out, the spot burns at the base of my spine, but stays put."

He laughs, looking delighted. "Good to know that our initial meeting didn't ruin it for me. I like when you give me tail."

"It's not mating specifically, I know that. It hasn't popped out with most people. In fact, there's only four people who have seen it." That part is true. I've never let her out that far with Wilde. The trust isn't there, and he's made a mess enough with the fangs, much less the rest of her. I'm not free with him—not at all.

His features flash and fangs drop instantly. "I don't want to know who. So, help me if that poetic prat or my brother have, don't tell me."

I blink. *Whoops. Hit a minefield.* "Okay, I won't."

"Bloody hell, that's worse, isn't it?" He snarls, his temper flaring, and he growls low. "*Mine.*"

I hold him tightly as his wrath boils up. "Yours." I kick up a purr, stroking my fingers over his arms. The purr calms him, so I keep it up, murmuring, "Always yours."

Once he's back, he grumbles. "Well, shit. That wasn't exactly enlightened, was it? Bugger."

"No worries."

Giving me a guilty look, he sighs again. "I don't want to be the prat that gets all psycho-stalker because you have a past. And a present."

I reach up and cup his cheek. "I wanted you to know that it's special. It wasn't fair to bring up the others. Don't worry."

He nods, then looks at me earnestly. "I won't sleep with Blondie."

"Where did *that* come from?" I give him a look as if he's jumped the track.

"I told you once that it was within the realm of possibility. I wanted you to know it's not anymore. But it's, uh, not..."

"You don't have to do that for me. I mean, if you wanted..." I look away, feeling guilty that I can't offer him the same pledge. For once, I feel bad that my lifestyle may cause him a lot of pain. I'm not ashamed of who I am, but feeling selfish.

"Do you want me to?"

"No, but I don't have the right to expect—I mean, pot-kettle-black. It's not fair for me to ask that." Fairness is important to me. It balances my world, my chi, my life. I can't ask things of him that I can't reciprocate.

It violates every part of who I am to do so.

He looks down at me. "I told you once that I was a one-woman man in my heart. It turns out I was wrong. I'm not going to fuck Blondie. Not because you asked me not to, but because you'd hurt if I did. It's not remotely important enough for me to risk your feelings." He shrugs. "What can I say? I'm a two-woman man. Think of it as—a wedding present."

I smile softly, tweaking his nose. "You are as soft as a teddy bear inside. You know that, right? Maybe it's deep down under your skin, but it's there."

"*Take that back*!" Lunging for me, he causes us to roll off the couch and land with a thud on the floor. He tickles me as I try to get away. "Take it back, hussy. I don't have the strength to spank you tonight!"

"Nope. Nyah, nyah, nyah."

Pinching, tickling, and squirming, he laughs as I try to fight back with girly slaps. Finally, he slams his mouth down on mine, kissing me deeply. All the fight drains out of me and I melt into him, my hands sliding over his chest.

When he lifts his head, he murmurs, "I have a favor to ask, though. I'd thank you ever so if you could do something about the slices on my back?"

I give him a sheepish grin, though somewhere inside she's eying him with a satisfied look. Closing my eyes, I lay my hands over his shoulders, letting the tingling energy build in my palms. He's had my blood recently, so this should work without a lot of effort. I feel the skin sparking under my touch as I slide my fingers down the scratches gently. "It should only take a few more seconds because you had my blood."

"I wouldn't mind you going back over that hungry detail for me again, either." He grins. "Not that I'd push."

I swat his rear. "You're lucky I love you. Otherwise, I'd have to beat you for being an ass."

Growling, he jumps up and storms to the window. "I changed my mind. I'm going to go shag Blondie six ways to Sunday and then kill some kiddies as an appetizer. Stupid sodding French learning poof."

His outburst surprises me, but I shrug nonchalantly. I'm not letting a pouty clone ruin our time. "Then I guess I can't tell you about the hungry stuff."

He stomps over, his expression petulant. "What about the hungry stuff?"

Holding my hand up, I wait for him to help me up. He looks like he's warring with himself, but he tugs me up and tumbles us to the couch again. I grin victoriously, reaching up to cup his jaw. "You make me all wild and primal. I feel like I need to drink deep every time so I can feel every part of you."

"Would it *kill* you to mention that I learned sodding *French*?" he grumbles.

"It was romantic and hot and all the other adjectives I'd use will make you huffy."

"Hot isn't bad." He gives me a shy grin. "I did okay? I mean, was it right and all?"

"Yes, and it was all dark and growly, which is sexy."

He laughs, and I give him a puzzled look.

What is with the bi-polar clone thing? Do they all lose their crackers when they mate with me?

"I mated with you today."

"Yes, you did."

"And if I'm not mistaken, you mated with me."

"Uh-huh."

"What is today, minx?"

Son of a bitch. "April first. Oh, bloody hell."

"Irony's a straight bitch."

"We probably shouldn't tell anyone, huh?" I ask, edging right along a ledge that I hope I don't fall from.

"Tell anyone you like. I'm not the one that's going to take the heat—though I should warn you. You get prickly when people pick at me. You might be a veritable porcupine by the time it gets around."

"Well, they should be smarter than to poke at my mate—or more full of holes. One or the other."

"Fuck, I love you, minx."

"I fucking love you, too, baby."

I hope it's enough to stop the train that's headed right for us when everyone finds out what just happened.

Pre-order Book Two in Rise of the Resistance now!

World & Pronunciation Guide

CHARACTERS, PETS, & CREATIONS

Delilah Lenore O'Hara (dee LIE luh Len ORE OH Hair-uh) numbered as x1501; human—maybe. Lived in Rift for two years, born in an Earth town called Whistler's Hollow. Thirty-five years old, lives in the Resistance Quarter in a house called The Maison with her family of clones and droids including: Rafe, Victor, Caesar, Hex, Sandrine, Siren, Philomena. She is mated to Wilde, Sari, Rafe, Alistair, and Rhea. Rafe is her primary mate. She is one of the current Resistance leaders and mayor of the quarter with Lily. She has a pet white tiger named Aradia given to her by Preston for her birthday this past year.

Nicknames: The Cat, Nightbloom, Sandwich, Peach, Deli, Delicat, Twinkles, Darkness, Kitten, Queen D, Darkness, Nancy, Juliet,

Donatella (don UH tell UH) numbered x098; human; living in Rift three and a half years. Leader of the Resistance during the Conflict, creator of droids. Lived in Down Under house with Victor and Caesar until she met James. She left the Rift with James and his droid Lucinda to live on Earth, abandoning Victor and Caesar to live with their family friends at the Maison.

Nicknames: Dona

Rhea (Ree-UH) numbered x256; human—maybe? Living in the Rift for four years in Cabal Quarter. Mated to Alistair, one of the original three brothers, and close friend of Talia from life on the other side of the portal. She lives in The Firehouse with Alistair and eventually mated with Sari, Wilde, Deli, and Rafe. She has a robotic dog she used to get into the Resistance.

Nicknames: Flame, Blondie, Lady Fair,

Rafe (Ray-F) numbered 086; clone; former operative. Clone won in a contest by Dona that fell for Delilah and became her primary mate. Mated to Sari, Wilde, Alistair, and Rhea. Artistic and known for being languid. Lives in The Maison with Deli, Hex, Sandrine, Siren, Leo, Philomena, Caesar, and Victor.

Nicknames: The Artist, The Lounger, The Stoat, Royalty, Ennobled One,

Caesar (see ZAR) numbered A001; droid. First droid created by Victor and Donatella and leaders of the Resistance in the Conflict. One of the creators of almost all droids, and a submissive. Was involved with Lucinda until she moved with Donatella and James to the other side of the portal. Likes to be on a leash. Changes his hair color frequently.

Nicknames: Puppy

Victor (Vik-tor) numbered 020; clone. Former mate of Donatella and part of the Resistance in Conflict. Lived in Down Under house with Caesar and Dona until she left for the other side with James. Lives in The Maison with Caesar along with Deli's family now. Has a deep history with Deli and Rafe. Secondary father of all droids with Caesar.

Nicknames: Vic, Fangy, Pops

Alistair (Al-is-TARE) numbered 001; clone and one of the three original brothers. Lives in Firehouse with Rhea and was a big part of the Cabal side in the Conflict. Former operative for Company. Mated to Rhea, Sari, Deli, Wilde, and Rafe. Very close with Deli at the moment because of craziness. Loves her beast.
Nicknames:

Sari (sar-EE) numbered x260; human—maybe? Lives in Coyote Den with Wilde, Janus, Roman, and Calista. Mated to Wilde, Rhea, Deli, Rafe, and Alistair. She was a defector from the Resistance in Conflict and helped Cabal win the war. Turned to Resistance again after Cabal abandoned Rift. Convinced Deli to allow her to join their town based on her former droid turned clone, Wilde. Has a coyote mutation and is torturing people now.
Nicknames: Coyote, Gnome,

Roman (Roh-man) numbered as A201; droid. Partners with Janus and lives in Coyote Den with Sari, Wilde, Calista, and Janus. Rumored to be involved with Philomena in a threesome.
Nicknames:

Janus (Jan-us) numbered A202; droid. Partners with Roman and lives in Coyote Den with Sari, Wilde, Calista, and Roman. Rumored to be involved with Philomena in a threesome.
Nicknames:

Philomena (fill OH main uh) numbered A200; droid. Lives in The Maison with Deli, Hex, Rafe, Leo, Sandrine, Siren, Caesar, and Victor. Drunken pill popper but cares about her family. Rumored to be in a threesome with Roman and Janus. Fashion hound and elitist.
Nicknames: The Bitch, Duchess P

Wilde (why uhld) numbered 056; was a droid and turned into a clone by The Company after he and Sari betrayed the Resistance. Blogger and intellectual snob. Mated with Rhea, Sari, Rafe, Alistair, and Deli. Lives in Coyote Den with Sari, Calista, Janus, and Roman. Was a sweet romantic, but recent events have him allowing the suppressed demon inside free and he is using it to punish those who upset him—including Deli and Rafe

Nicknames: the Blogger,

Sandrine (san-DREEN) numbered A124; droid. Created for Leo as a companion by Vic and Caesar. Has a panel in back that keeps Buzz, a genetically mutated spider, in it. Kicks ass and takes names. Lives at Maison with Caesar, Victor, Deli, Rafe, Leo, Hex, Siren, and Philomena. Helps care for the animals, including Aradia and Mercury's giant bugs.

Nicknames:

Leonidas (Lee-oh-nye-dis) numbered A096; droid. First droid created for Deli. Lives in Maison with Deli, Rafe, Hex, Victor, Caesar, Philomena, Siren, and Sandrine. Dates Sandrine. Chef of the household. Very easy going. Loves pulling pranks with the other earliest droids.

Nicknames: Leo, Romeo, Nuts and Bolts,

Hex (HehX) numbered A100; droid. Dates from Belle's family. Punk rocker ala Billy Idol. Lives in Maison with Deli, Rafe, Leo, Victor, Caesar, Philomena, Siren, and Sandrine. Martha Stewart of the house, runs and decorates everything. Wears frilly aprons and combat boots. Second droid Deli ordered.

Nicknames: Punk, Rocker, Sid

Theodora (thee OH door uh) numbered A 050; Droid. Created by Dona to help Talia when she was ill and couldn't work. No one knew she'd been shot, but Theodora is the only droid to be modeled after a person, not a clone template. She looks exactly like Talia, but is the polar opposite in personality. Involved with Damien and they all live in the Homestead house with Talia, Taurus, and the hellhounds.

Nicknames: The Lady, T, Theo,

Damien (day ME en) numbered M001; muse. The only muse known to exist. Appeared to Talia one day and has lived with her since. He and Taurus fight constantly. He talks in riddles and visual images, making it hard to understand him. He has various forms, can hop portals of his own, and has a monstrous form he rarely shows. He is an artist and has muse magic that no one understands. He is partners with Theodora.

Nicknames: Melted Crayon, Crayola, Monster,

Belle numbered X300; human; living in Rift for three years; Cabal Quarter home called The Shop that mostly goes unused for their home on Earth called The Ranch; joined the Resistance after Sari pressured her to be let in; she ordered Chaos first, then Veruca. Functions as Sari's bully.

Nicknames: The Bulldog,

Mayhem numbered 045; clone given to Belle during Conflict; mechanic; edgy rocker look; only mated to Belle; friendly with Sari's family; Deli thinks he's sent out to seduce people to get them to like Belle; supposedly closed to Michaela;

Nicknames:

Chaos numbered A215; droid; speaks in riddles; looney tunes; dances and sings; prophecy is supposed gift; dating Hex

Nicknames:

Veruca numbered A255; droid; created for Belle to shift into a wolf; edgy punk; not dating anyonel friends with Calista

Nicknames:

Cruise numbered ;clone; mated to one of the original Cabal members; left the Rift to become an A-List celebs after the Conflict

Shea numbered A116; created for Tamara after Resistance formed; lives at Tropical House; family in house Manuel, Grayson, and Derek; casual lover of Deli; also has ties to Black Rose Family

Manuel numbered 092; broken out of Company program without permission; claims to be mated with Tamara; lives in Tropical House; family in house are Derek, Tamara, Shea, and Grayson; ties to Black Rose Family

Tamara numbered X1601; human from Earth; chef; lives in Tropical House; family in house with Grayson, Shea, Derek, and Manuel; ties to Black Rose Family

Amanda numbered x1753; human; lives with Constantine; member of Widow's Peak Family; closest to Sari;
Nicknames:

Constantine numbered A120; lived here six months with Amanda in Widow's Peak Family; close with Deli; one of her non-mate lovers;
Nicknames:
Lily numbered x471; lives with Mercury; favors droids; semi-involved with Rafe; part of Captain's Ship family; co-mayor of Resistance with Deli
Nicknames:

Mercury numbered A097; droid; quirky and odd; makes genetically altered bugs; likes role play; lives with Lily in Captain's

ship family; involved with Deli as non-mate lover; hurt her when beast came out; voyeur and loves to take pics/video
Nicknames: Captain

Aradia Deli's white bengal tiger; rescued from a bad circus by Preston and given to her for her birthday

Twist Deli's all black ferret produced when she dressed as a pirate for a movie opening night with Mercury

Tweedle a ghost that lives with Lily and Mercury

LIST OF FAMILY NAMES, HOUSES, AND MEMBERS

The Maison Family: Delilah, Rafe, Leo, Hex, Sandrine, Siren, Philomena, Victor, Caesar, Aradia and Twist

The Homestead Family: Taurus, Talia, Theodora, and Damien, and the Hellhounds

The Den Family: Sari, Wilde, Calista, Roman, and Janus

The Firehouse Family: Rhea, Alistair, and Priscilla

The Ranch Family: Belle, Mayhem, Chaos, and Veruca

The Down Under Family: Dona, Lucinda, and James

The Captain's Ship Family: Lily, Mercury, and Tweedle

The Widow's Peak Family: Amanda and Constantine

The Tropical Family: Tamara, Shea, Manuel, Grayson, and Derek

The Black Rose Family: Rita, Wally, and JJ

The Gearhead Family: Michaela, Preston, Aramis, Kane, and Shane

The Library Family: Dahlia, Mack, and Rupert

The Tech Family: Heather and Chance

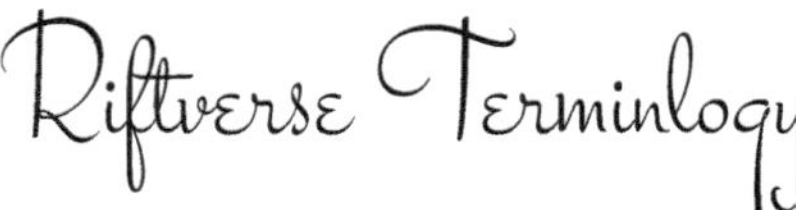

Riftverse Terminlogy

Warning, this list has potential spoilers

Clone- created from DNA and modified through trade secrets involving quantum physics, wormholes, and the Company scientists.

Android/Droid- am artificially intelligent creation that is technologically advanced far beyond human capabilities including bodily functions, charging, and sentience. Created by Donatella, Victor, and Caesar prior to the Conflict and continually improved upon by a team of their creations.

The Rift- A pocket dimension that the Company HQ and staff, along with humans of the Cabal and Resistance live in.

Bytes 'N Chips- A dive bar used for one of the portals to The Rift as well as a frequent recruiting location.

Dirty Deeds- A bar created by Sari that was the location of unspeakable debauchery. How it was destroyed is unsubstantiated.

The Maison- Delilah's enormous home. It is the epicenter of Resistance activity.

The Cabal- A human governing body put in place by the Company to keep the human inhabitants in line.

The Resistance- Originally, the rebels and droids that fought the Cabal/Company in the Conflict. Currently, the inhabitants of Deli's hidden city.

Claiming/Marking- A ritual involving biting that is akin to engagement for clones and some droids.

Mating- A ritual like marriage that involves biting, claiming, blood exchange, and marking.

Apparate/Disapparate- A form of travel used by some clones and magicks users that is similar to teleportation.

Sacred Space- The anointed space a magick user keeps to perform rituals and spells. Only Deli has one.

The Zoo- The new karaoke bar Sari and Belle opened without permission.

The Company- A mysterious organization that created The Rift, runs the secret Project Reality, and maintains surveillance on the inhabitants of The Rift. Allegedly, they are a private mercenary organization with no ties to any government, criminals, or other governing bodies that operate as both white and black hats if you can afford them.

Familiar- An animal that facilitates magick for an extranormal, also serves as a companion and protector.

The Beast- The name for the sentient panther shifter inside of the Delilah.

Demon- All of the clones are created with one based on their template and the droids are also programmed with one if it suits their template.

Template- The base appearance and personality of the droid/clone. These were decided by the scientists of the Company and mirror a cast of individuals they cloned/passed through the wormholes.

Oversight- The individual that runs the Company. He/She is unknown to those without Alpha Level Clearance.

Clearance Level- Those involved with the Company have clearance levels for access to information and systems. It is based on the Greek alphabet with Alpha being the highest level with the least individuals.

The Conflict- The war between the droids and the clones (Resistance and Cabal) that resulted from the caste system the Cabal created.

The Battle of Blood and Steel- The final battle of the Conflict prior to peace talks.

The Creation- This refers to the process of the creating the first three clones and the subsequent process refinement.

Other Place/Side/Real World- Earth, circa now-ish

Project Reality- The name for the experiment the Company is running that contains the inhabitants of The Rift. They are unaware.

Portal- The pathway to The Rift from Earth. The main one is located in Bytes 'N Chips, but there are more throughout Earth. Those who can apparate do not always use them.

Reviews, Print, and Merchandise

If you have enjoyed this story, please review it.
It helps other readers find my work,
which helps me as an indie author.

Thank you!

Reviews for this shot are appreciated on the following platforms

TikTok
Instagram
Facebook

To purchase print copies or merchandise, go to The Worlds of Cassandra Featherstone

Sneak Peek: Veiled Flame

LOSER

Kat

The little blue icon on my app has been glaring at me all day, but I'm too damn nervous to open it. Everyone at Woodlawn High has been buzzing all day with their notifications and the squeals of joy and moans of despair were too much for me to take. My anxiety is through the roof—this is the moment I've been waiting for since middle school, but I can't seem to force myself to bite the billet and check.

Maybe it's because I don't have the support system most of my classmates have?

That's probably true, given I've always been a loner and I don't fit into any specific 'caste' here. It's hard to make friends when you get shuffled from foster home to foster home over the years. I've rarely stayed anywhere long enough to make a friend, much less a group of them.

I'm not delinquent or anything—the families I've been placed with just return me like a pair of pants that doesn't fit after a year or so. The caseworkers click their tongues sympathetically and hunt down a new placement, but I've never been given a reason *why* people don't want me around. One lady said I must be born under a bad sign and hell if I knew what that meant other than I'm not good enough to keep around.

It would be different, almost understandable, if I misbehaved or got bad grades. But I don't—I'm always in the top five percent of my class and I do everything I'm asked. I don't even lord my smarts over the other kids or adults. Being presentable and unassuming was something I adapted long ago to improve my probability of staying in a home long term.

Unfortunately, it never worked and though I should be a shoo-in for scholarships and acceptances galore, I can't bring myself to be rejected yet again.

So I wait for the last bell of the day, slinging my bag over my shoulder and trudging home to the latest in my temporary housing. I can't even contemplate looking at the possible heartache waiting for me in the college application system WHS insisted we use. The fear is too great and despite knowing I'll be on my own for good at the end of this year, I'm unable to risk the pain.

I hate being this way.

My court mandated therapist says it's some sort of attachment disorder that's common in foster kids, but I think that's bullshit. The problem isn't *me* not forming attachments; it's asshole adults not forming one to me. Being left at a safe haven in a fucking basket as a baby wasn't because *I* did anything wrong—again, fucking adults couldn't handle their commitments.

As usual, I arrive home to an empty house. There are two other kids who live here—Bryce and Blake—but they're at football practice. Of course, the Jamesons *love* them; they get to strut around at games because their strays are the stars of the team. I'm not mistreated, but I'm definitely an afterthought. Both of my 'parents' are still at work, so I drop my bag on the couch and head for the kitchen to get a snack:

Don't get me wrong. I *could* have been placed in far worse homes than any of the seven I've been in since elementary school. None of the ex-fosters starved, beat, molested, or abused me. They were all decent folks with jobs and houses that weren't hellholes, but they never liked me.

I have no idea why. I tried to be everything they wanted.

But when the end of each school year came, I was handed in like a textbook and off I went to some group home until the next contestant stepped up. It baffled everyone, not just me, but that's what happened every single time.

Sighing, I pull some fruit out of the fridge and grab a soda. I have homework to do and if I want to have time to work on my stories, I'll need to get it done before the house is full of people at dinner time. Bryce and Blake will have gotten messages about their applications, too, and I'd bet my pinkie toe those idiots got into some big sports school. Brett and Allison will be oozing happiness for them and I don't know if I'll be able to keep food down if I have to admit my failure when they ask.

Being eighteen sucks ass.

After I grab my books and tablet, I head down to the den. I have to give my current parents credit; they set up a very nice workspace for us to study in the converted basement. By the time they took me in, the Jamesons created a cozy room down here where the three of us could relax and do our work for school without being interrupted. It might have been more for the boys than me, but I appreciated it all the same. Desks, a couch, big chairs, and bookshelves fill the space, making it almost seem like our mini-library. They even put a small fridge for drinks and snacks in case we had to be up late to cram.

It's my favorite place in the entire house and I spend most of my time here.

I sink into the huge armchair, putting my drink and snack on the side table. It only takes a few minutes to arrange myself in the soft cushions and I pause to tug my headphones out of my pocket. Music always soothes my jagged edges and I need it to stay focused on the bullshit AP Calculus I need to keep my average up in. My course load is heavy, but I applied to tough colleges. I wouldn't have a chance to get in, especially on a scholarship, if I wasn't taking equally challenging classes in comparison to all the prep school kids.

As always, the sounds of Vivaldi carry me away as I scrawl equations on my screen and before long, thoughts of the blue notification completely fade away.

"Kat!"

The shouts barely register as I continue working on the problem set, gnawing on my lower lip in concentration.

"Jesus fuck, where is she? I could eat a hippo!"

"Kat!"

Thumping followed by what could pass for a stampede of elephants jerks me out of my math filled trance when Bryce and Blake come down the stairs. They smell as bad as the aforementioned pachyderm's cage, so they must have rushed home right after practice. The blond twins glare at me as if I'm the offending element despite being sweaty and covered in dirt and grass stains.

This doesn't bode well.

Usually, they're tired and hungry after practices so I'm used to cranky ass boys, but tonight, there's a light to their faces. That had to mean they've gotten their letters and dinner will be a gush fest in honor of their perfection. I'm going to need all of my strength to fake smile and nod as Brett and Allison fawn over them.

I don't begrudge them their success—not really. They work hard and play even harder on the field. It's not their fault they're the American dream teens and I'm the nerdy basement troll no one wants. But it's awfully hard living in the shadow of their bright light, especially when I'm no less intelligent or talented.

"I'm finishing the AP Calc, guys. What do you want?"

They roll their eyes at me before Blake scoffs. "It's not due until Monday. You're so hyper."

Duh. I take anxiety meds, douchebag; of course I'm 'hyper.'

"I can only be who I am, Blake." That earns me a snort from Bryce and I know it's because he thinks that's the problem. "Is dinner ready?"

"Almost. Get upstairs and set the table so we can shower—Brett's orders." Blake grins smugly.

The two of them seem to always arrange it so chores get passed to me for some half-assed reason and this is no exception. Sighing, I put my stuff aside, fully intending to hide down here after the dinner mess is cleaned up. Likely by me, but like I said, I could definitely live in worse foster homes so I let it go. Doing some chores isn't worth risking the group home for the last few months of my high school career.

They take off running up the stairs and I wait for them to disappear before I follow suit. My phone is tucked in my pocket and I feel like it's a stone of shame I have to bear. I know once the adults make over the twins' success, they will remember me, and I'll be forced to find out what disappointment lies in wait for me. The dread weighs on me, but I head into the sunny kitchen and pick up the pre-prepared pile of plates, silverware, and napkins on the counter.

Allison looks up from the stove and gives me a half-smile, nodding as I take the dishes into the dining room. Like I said, no one is mean or horrid, they just seem...obligated. After a while, it makes it hard to waste time trying to be bright and sunny. Being reserved makes it a hell of a lot easier not to feel rebuffed when they don't pay attention to you regardless.

"Make sure you include champagne glasses for your dad and I!" she calls from the other room.

The twins definitely got acceptance somewhere big. Brett must have gotten the bubbly on the way home.

Once I set the table, I return to help Allison bring out the roast and sides. I'm a little amazed at her efficiency when it comes to getting the housework done while working full time, but I suppose it's something people with real parents get taught as they grow up. My home life has been so fractured that I haven't learned how to cook more than very basic shit from YouTube videos. That may be a problem after graduation, but I've never felt comfortable enough to ask Allison if she'd teach me. I'm sure she would try, but it doesn't feel right.

"How was school, Kat?"

I look over my shoulder, seeing Brett in the entry to the dining room. He's already changed from work and smiling, but I see the distraction in his eyes. He's waiting for the boys to come down. "It was fine. I've got a Calc test at the end of the week. I'll be studying a lot to get ready."

"Good, good. No matter what happens with applications, keeping your grades up will ensure no one pulls any offers," he says.

Those words aren't for me. They are for the two wet haired boys who just appeared behind him.

"Kat's too much of a geek to ever let her grades slip, Dad," Blake says as he pushes past his brother and drops into his usual chair at the table. "Grab me a Powerade since you're in the kitchen, mouse!"

Both Brett and Bryce stare at me and I turn around, heading to the fridge despite the fact that I was *not* closer than the other twin. Out of habit, I take two of the drinks and a soda for myself. I've been here long enough to know Bryce will send me back to get him one as well. It would feel like typical sibling stuff, but for some reason, I just *know* they do it to fuck with me. I have no idea why I feel that way, but trusting my gut has been the one thing that helped me get through all the upheaval in my life over the years. It's a good gauge for knowing when I'll get booted or if people are being earnest in their reactions.

The therapist says that's some sort of trauma induced early trigger warning shit, by the way.

After I hand out the drinks, I sit down on my side of the table and we wait for Allison to come out. Brett is at his seat at the far end of the table and the twins are punching each other as they look at something on their phones. I know where this is all going but I drop my gaze to the table, swallowing the coppery taste of fear as it courses through my body.

I'm going to be exposed and there's nothing I can do to stop it.

Read the first three episodes free on Kindle Vella: https://www.amazon.com/kindle-vella/story/B0BSTMB1X3

Sneak Peek: Bloodthirsty

QUEEN BEE

They dim the lights in the club, and the spots click on as the curtain slides open.

It's a full house tonight in the little burlesque club off the Rue Pierre Montaine.

Chez Arc En Ciel is not well known compared to the *Moulin Rouge* or *Le Lido*, but the wealthy from both sides of the Seine gather here for shows four nights a week. If you pass the various layers of security checks to even be permitted to book a reservation, you also have to be able to afford the two thousand Euro per guest cover charge. If you don't eat or drink anything, that's all it will cost; however, that would get you blacklisted.

Intro music pumps through the speakers and I stand on my mark in the opening position. My cane is resting on the wooden boards of the stage by my front foot as I pretend to lean on it. Roars of applause echo through the room as our troupe of dancers catch the lights, sequins sparkling like diamonds when the stage lights rise. We're dressed in pinstriped black pant suits and fedoras to match the big band style opening to the song. As soon as the horn-filled intro finishes, the dance begins.

I follow the routine with precision, snapping and popping my hips to the beat as we spread out across the stage. You wouldn't know by the fake smile on my face that I'm scanning the crowd. Two fan kicks later, I've rotated past the proscenium, and I think I've found my mark. Twirling, I stop in the place I need to be for the bridge, singing along as if my life depends on it. It might, to be honest, because I need to sell my cover tonight, so no one notices me.

The Guillotine moves in the shadows, but tonight, she's in the spotlight.

My ass shakes as I dance my way through the song, swinging the prop cane I'd replaced with one of my design. You wouldn't know by looking at it, but it's not the painted balsa the other dancers have for a very specific reason. I need it to complete the mission that forced me to spend two months in Paris working my way into this job at *Chez Arc En Ciel*. If I can't strike tonight, the surveillance, counterintelligence, and time spent building this cover are wasted because my mark is leaving for Asia tomorrow.

Tonight, the Cobra dies for his sins.

The break of the song slows the music and the dancers pour into the crowd to wiggle around the rich assholes. It's choreographed, but it's also to advertise each girl for private dances in the lounges upstairs. We're not strippers—not that there's a damned thing wrong with a woman using her body to support herself—but we do bare more skin in the closed rooms. The *laissez-faire* attitude of the owners means as long as we kick them thirty percent of the fees for those dances, they don't care what any of the girls do in the rooms. I'd find it sleazy, but the girls who work here are highly skilled performers who choose to make thousands of dollars a night rather than peanuts in some ballet troupe or chorus line.

By the time I've flirted my way to the VIP tables, the Cobra is staring intently at all of us. Spotlights pin each one of us on the floor at the bass hits, and I swivel my hips as my free hand slides down to the secret spot on my jacket. In unison, we tear the jackets off to reveal rhinestone studded bras with straps crisscrossing our waists like shibari ropes. A lift of the fedora and pop of my hip, along with the beat, draws the fierce-looking brawler's eyes directly to me. I pout prettily and stalk towards his table with the swagger of a tiny dicked asshole that owns a monster truck.

His thin lips pull back over the famed curving fangs he had implanted. Dark, glittering eyes follow every move I make as I approach, and I pretend to whip my hair from side to side as I check for his guards. They're here somewhere, but I need them to be far away so I can beat my escape before they notice. When I get within inches, I tap his leg with my cane and spin around to shake my ass in his face. The grunt of approval makes me want to heave, but I turn, holding onto the prop with both hands. My feet click on the floor in a soft shoe step as I make 'fuck me' eyes at the dirty bastard. He leans back, his pants tented as he gestures towards his lap.

Fucking gross.

I don't care about his weapons trade or what happens when people get the shit he moves. I have no clue why I have to take him out. The reason they have sentenced him to death isn't part of my contract, and I'm nothing if not a dispassionate observer of the darkest parts of human desires. Twelve years at *l'Academie* ensured I care very little about anything that isn't directly related to my ability to complete my jobs.

Sighing, I dance closer and drop onto his rather unimpressive erection and wiggle. There's plenty of cloth between us to prevent him from doing anything I'd make a scene over, so I focus on the task at hand. I slip the cane behind his head, resting the wood against his neck as I tug him forward. The move reads as playfully bringing his face to my breasts, but at the last second, I click the release built into the custom weapon. One end slides open to reveal the razor sharp garotte and before he can say a word, I yank it through.

Faint gurgling is the only noise besides the end of the song, and I carefully slide the sides of the cane together. Climbing off the nasty fucker, I put my hands on his cheeks so I can pretend to flirt with him while I arrange the head so it looks as if he's leaning back in the booth. It needs to look realistic to allow me to return to the stage with the others. When I have it settled, I back away from the booth, blowing fake kisses as I walk backwards through the crowd. I almost collide with a dark-haired guy with his collar pulled high as I head for the stage, and I roll my eyes. Whatever celeb that is trying to keep their face away from the paps is doing a shitty job of it.

The entire troupe takes a few bows and shuffles off of stage left to the wings. I exhale a sigh of relief when the next group enters on the opposite side. I haven't heard shouting yet, so I don't think the Cobra's men realize he's down. Now I take this emetic pill, have a vomiting episode, and I'll get sent home.

That's when Arabella Montaigne, the burlesque dancer, will cease to exist, and Remy Arsine Benoit will re-emerge.

I smile to myself as I chew on the tablet that will have me retching my guts out in a few moments. This is a more complex extermination than I usually prefer, and I can't leave my normal calling card behind. The Cobra's head had to remain in the booth rather than get delivered to his home in a basket.

Such a shame, that. I quite enjoy the reactions my little gifts engender when they're discovered.

Walking into the dressing room, I carefully strip my costume off, putting all the pieces in my bag. Every item in the locker room that belongs to gets placed in the duffel carefully as I wait for the effects to hit me. It won't do to leave loose ends, even if my prints have never touched a single surface in this place. My gut rolls and I turn, facing one of the other dancers as the vomit finally comes. Gracelia screams like she's being skinned when I hurl on her and it's everything I can do *not* to smirk through the chunks.

"*C'est la merde!*" she shouts, running for the showers as if she's on fire.

It takes less than a minute for the owner to send me home for the night. I walk out the back door of the building with everything just as the sirens scream.

Perfect timing, as always.

I jump into the first cab I can hail, directing him to the *Hôtel de Crillon*. Their suites are the ritziest in Paris, and it's my go-to hideout when I'm here. I used to only stay in the Bernstein Suite, but some rich fuckwad purchased it six months ago. If I could track them down and beat the hell out of them, I would, but I booked my schedule until late 2025. Assassins with my skill set and accuracy are getting harder to find. They forced the old guard into retirement because they refuse to adapt to the digital age. Too many cameras, crime labs, and hackers running about to do everything Cold War style.

The future of murder for hire is millennial, people. We're old enough to be stable, but young enough to be agile with new technology. Plus, most of them are broke AF from crooked ass student loans.

It's not an issue I have, but I've been in the business since I hit double digits. You don't survive *l'Academie des Invisibles* if you haven't killed someone before the end of primary school. It's unheard of.

I was eight the first time I used the weapon that would become my signature.

Shivering, I tap on the window of the cab and bitch the driver out. He's taking a longer route than necessary to raise my fare, and I'll have his guts for garters if he doesn't knock it the fuck off. A string of curses in French erupt from him when I voice the accusation, and I slam my palm on the window with enough force to crack the plexiglass barrier. He almost drives into another car, but when he regains control, he makes the requested adjustments to our route.

We arrived at the front entrance after a few more arguments and a traffic jam around the *Champs*. I throw the euros at him in disgust, memorizing the medallion number for later. He's not worth my time, but I have quite a few contacts who might be interested in blackmailing a cabbie in town. Getaway cars are cliche in the crime world now. Most ne'er-do-wells like myself find greater comfort in anonymous taxis or ride-share accounts hacked through the deep web accessed on burner phones. If your ride doesn't know you're a villain, there's no one to flip if law enforcement comes looking.

I never look the same for any job—ever.

I will not use Arabella Montaigne as a cover in the future, and once I move to the location of my next job, I'll ensure that she meets with a terrible fate. It's a lot more work to slowly kill off my alters once I've used them, but it's also why I've never even come close to being caught. The dancer with long wavy red hair, freckles, and big green eyes will never grace the streets of Paris again after I hop a plane. She will, however, get a minor story in the paper and an obituary when I decide how she tragically dies.

The Guillotine will rise from her ashes and be reborn.

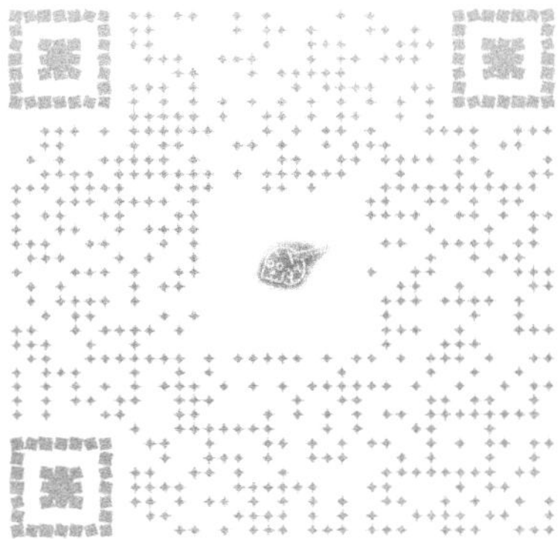

Sneak Peek: Come Out & Prey

JUST A GIRL

Delores

Sighing, I look around my bedroom at the posters and decorations covering my walls. My obsession with pop music, musical theater, and high school rom-coms sickens my parents. They would prefer me to be into heavy metal and horror movies like the other kids my age.

Being the only child in a family as prominent as mine is difficult when you don't fit the mold. My parents—like their parents and all my friends' parents—are apex predators. Preds rule our world, and the division between us and prey is so severe that we regulate them to a completely different echelon of society. Prey shifters are weak and beneath our lofty abilities. The ruling class of elite predator families stretches back generations, and they've evolved into a bunch of assholes who only care about succession and greed.

My animal has not manifested yet, but it will soon enough. Luckily for me, none of my friends have manifested their inner animals, either. I'm part of the in-crowd at school, and my boyfriend, Todd, is the most popular guy in my class. While he and I aren't officially engaged yet, we've talked about it enough that I know it's only a matter of time before he puts a ring on my finger. I should be on top of the world, but I can't help but feel like my life just doesn't fit me the way it's supposed to.

Every teenager wishes their life was different, but I dream of becoming an entirely different person. Not inside, mind, because I'm pretty comfortable with who I am. I don't want to be part of this legacy, this society, or even this family. They are all focused on competing to be the richest, the deadliest, or the most powerful, and I want no part of it.

I walked over to my closet and pulled out the outfit that I had chosen for my tour of Apex Academy. My mother hired her personal designers to create a custom school uniform for today and expects me to present the 'appropriate' image of the sole heir to a Council seat.

I hate having to pretend to be like them because I'm nothing like them.

Regardless, I pull on the short, pink pleated skirt, three quarter length sleeve blouse, knee socks, and Mary Janes that comprise the uniform for my exclusive private high school. Since I'm using a 'college visit' day to tour the Academy, I'm expected to represent Shifter Secondary as well.

Shifter Secondary is the most exclusive high school for unmanifested shifter teens on the East Coast. Unfortunately for me, it was not my parents' first choice for my education. They hoped I'd follow in their footsteps by choosing to force my animal to emerge early. If I had done that, I could have attended *Apex Academy Lower School.*

I didn't have the stomach to use my body in that manner at fourteen.

Their heirs followed my lead, which made my mother and father furious and their hoity-toity council colleagues angry. My closest friends, the Heathers, also refused to force their animals to emerge, as did Todd and his friends. That was the first time the adults in our circle decided I was a bad influence. After that, I had to toe the line at every turn, ensuring that I followed all the strict rules and regulations that govern the heirs to council seats.

Everywhere I went, I had to dress in a manner befitting the next Drew to sit at the table. They forced me to take dance lessons, piano lessons, diction lessons, and other more humiliating tutorials to prepare for the day that I became a true predator. In our society, teenagers have no say in how we prepare for our animals to emerge.

Your parents make all the decisions, choose your friends, choose your mates, and decide every detail of your life down to what you eat every single day. At least, that's how it is in my family, because my mother is from the old world.

She came over from Slovenia when she was incredibly young and met my father on the society fundraiser circuit. Her idea of preparing her daughter for the future involves lessons in makeup, clothing, jewelry, and on how to keep your mate satisfied. Lucille is completely unconcerned about whether I end up happy, only that I attend to my council seat and my husband's *needs.*

Once I get dressed, I grab my vintage Vuitton bag and peek at the mirror for a last check before I head downstairs. I tuck my perfectly highlighted blonde tresses behind my ears, and the smokey eye and winged liner are on point with this year's fashion trends. I apply a quick swipe of cherry red lip gloss and open my mouth, inspecting my teeth to make sure they are pearly white. Even though once I develop threatening incisors or sharp fangs, something will inevitably cover them in blood, my parents want my smile to look like a toothpaste commercial.

It's all such utter bullshit.

I take a deep breath and turn on my heel, heading for the door. I can already hear my parents yelling in a Scotch and vodka induced rage in the drawing room. It's only eleven thirty in the morning, for Hera's sake.

Lucille and Bruno don't fuck around with cocktail hour. They are nicely sauced by ten a.m. every day, without exception. I can't remember a time when my parents didn't get drunk off their asses at an event or party, much less in our 'home'. They liquor up and fight until they part for the day, and then start again once they arrive home from their daily commitments.

I brace for the barrage of criticism my mother will subject me to when I cross the threshold. Closing my eyes, I whisper words of encouragement to myself via lyrics to some of my favorite songs, desperately trying to hype myself up before she can tear me down.

"Delores! I hear you breathing at the top of the stairs, darling. Come down this instant and let your father and I inspect your presentation."

My mother's purr *sounds* friendly, but believe me, it's not. I roll my eyes as I make my way down the stairs, knowing my mother won't hesitate to send one of the staff if I don't acquiesce to her command. Most of their staff would gleefully jizz themselves with being chosen to drag me downstairs for inspection.

At this time of day, the only servant in the drawing room will be Matilda—my ex-nanny turned personal assistant—and that request would test her loyalties. As the only person in my household who has my back, I don't want to put her in that position, so I answer. "Yes, Lucille. I'm on my way."

I'm not allowed to refer to her as 'mother' because it makes her feel old. 'Lucille' is always what I've called the woman who supposedly gave birth to me. I'd be tempted to disbelieve we shared any DNA at all if it weren't for our similar bone structure. She's about as nurturing as a rattlesnake, and if it weren't for Matilda, I might have died as a child. If the kitchen staff whispers are accurate, I have to accept that my mother neglected to feed me much of the time.

"You coddle her far too much, Lucille," my father growls. "As the heir to our family seat, Delores will come without being instructed to do so. We will not tolerate her insolence after her animal emerges. She will behave as I command or suffer the consequences."

The last of Bruno's rant echoes off the marble walls of the foyer as I step onto the hideously expensive, endangered teak floor. Schooling my features into the mask of indifference I wear whenever I have to deal with them, I enter their den of drunken fights with my spine steeled for an emotional assault.

"I apologize for my tardiness, Father. I only wished to perfect the image I will present during my tour of Apex Academy. I realize it is imperative I impress the Headmistress and her staff."

The humanoid features of his face shift seamlessly, and the hungry crocodile inside of him gives me a toothy smirk. "You will impress them, daughter, or so help me... I'll send you to Bloodstone Isle."

My stomach drops like a stone as I barely suppress a shiver.

Bloodstone Isle is a reformatory school. It's surrounded by spells and enchantments to prevent students from escaping—a feat that has only happened once in its one thousand years of existence. The most feared cat group in the shifter world—the Khan ambush —runs the school, and they're rumored to consume errant students when the Council allows it.

It's the threat both rich and poor shifter parents used to keep their children in line. Wealthy parents like mine use it as a method of controlling any heirs that refuse to conform to the rigid structure of our society. Predators don't value the lives of those who are weak, and they label heirs who refuse to take their rightful place at the top of the food chain weak. Everyone knows Bloodstone is full of criminals, miscreants, and psychos, and even they don't seem to survive.

Bloodstone is a death sentence—pure and simple.

"Y-yes, Father. I understand," I croak out. As if the pressure of touring my new school isn't enough, now I worry the Dean will relay something to my parents that gets me shipped off to Death Island.

"Bruno, darling, if you scare her, she'll frown. That causes wrinkles. Delores, chin up and smile for us."

Swallowing the lump in my throat, I flash my mother my brightest smile. Her blood-red lips curve, and her leopard fangs burst free as she all but purrs. "I will not have you sullying the family name, Delores. It's bad enough that your education gave you ideas about your value beyond breeding stock. You will take the seat on the Council when it is time, but the husband we select will control the business—as nature intended. Do you hear me?"

My eyes narrow briefly, and for what is possibly the millionth time this week alone, I nod at my mother to appease her temper. "Yes, Lucille."

"Excellent!" The leopard fades as she claps her hands. "Matilda!"

The tiny woman steps up, her eyes wide behind her glasses. She's a pred, but the smaller size of hawk shifters puts her in the servant class. I believe she genuinely lives in fear of one or both of my parents deciding to eat her. "Yes, madam?"

"Fetch Bruiser. He will accompany Delores to the academy for her tour. Tell him to take the Escalade—it won't do for her to arrive in a tiny car—it will draw attention to her extra weight. We must make an impression."

Matilda nods, and I feel the fear radiating from her, and I don't blame her. Bruiser is one of my parents' bodyguards and our frequent chauffeur. He's a Komodo dragon shifter and the house staff are terrified of him. It's hard not to be, given that he prefers to play with his food, then eat it after it's dead. The kitchen crew believes he 'handled' the gardener that looked too long at my mother when I was ten. He disappeared without a trace.

Once Matilda scurries away, I watch my parents drink and bicker about their plans for the day. Bruno is going golfing with a congressman, and Lucille is going to the spa. We all know that both outings will include stops at the homes of their current pieces of ass for a quickie, but no one talks about it. The appearance of the loving couple has to be maintained, although neither of them has slept in the same room since I was a baby.

They don't give a damn about fidelity; I learned that at an early age. Children often discover things they shouldn't because of adults discount their ability to understand the conversations happening around them.

I stopped keeping track of who they're boning long ago, because I'd need an assistant to keep the affairs straight.

While my parents' marriage is a sham, I remind myself that my boyfriend, Todd, isn't like them. Yes, his parents only own half the live entertainment industry, but my father allows me to see Todd. The other parents will force the Heathers to accept an arranged betrothal, and I'm grateful I'm lucky enough to have found the perfect match on my own as my high school sweetheart.

"Delores, Bruiser is ready to escort you to Apex. He's pulling the car around now," the hawk shifter says softly.

Snapping out of my reverie, I smile at the trembling woman. Bruiser must have scared the living hell out of her. For no other reason than it amused him, I'm sure. He's as much a brute as his name implies, and I don't look forward to riding alone to the academy with him.

Something about that shifter gives me the creeps...

About Cassandra Featherstone

Cassandra Featherstone has channeled her lifelong passion for writing into a flourishing career, a journey that started when she first grasped a pencil as a gifted child with ADHD.

Her debut novel, born during the solitude of COVID lockdown in March 2020, draws on a tapestry of personal encounters and insights that resonate deeply with her readers.

An international bestseller, Cassandra has topped Amazon charts in categories such as LGBT Anthologies, LGBTQ+ Mystery, and Bisexual Romance, among others. Her works navigate the complexities of bullying, PTSD, body dysmorphia, mental health struggles, personal reinvention, and the empowerment of claiming one's own space. Importantly, Cassandra offers a thoughtful and respectful portrayal of LGBTQIA+ relationships, subtly reflecting her own connection with the community through her narratives.

Her literary repertoire spans sci-fi fantasy, urban fantasy, paranormal, and comedic genres in academy whychoose settings, with a strong commitment to portraying consensual, safe, and accurately depicted BDSM and kink lifestyles. Her books are an invitation to explore transformative stories that are both inclusive and engaging.

Often affectionately called 'The Muppet' for her wacky theater kid personality, she resides in the Midwest with her tech-savvy husband, their creatively inclined college student, a literary-minded dog, and four scheming cats.

READ MORE AT CASSANDRA'S WEBSITE OR HER FACEBOOK PAGE. SIGN UP FOR EXCLUSIVE CONTENT AND UPDATES HERE.

FIND HER ON ANY OF THE SOCIAL MEDIA BELOW AS SHE *LOVES* TO CHAT AND *NEVER* SLEEPS!

Also by Cassandra Featherstone

THE MISFIT PROTECTION PROGRAM SERIES

Road to the Hollow

Return to the Hollow

Home to the Hollow

Rejected in the Hollow

Revealed in the Hollow

Healing in the Hollow

Revenge in the Hollow

AUDIO OF THE MISFIT PROTECTION PROGRAM SERIES

Road to the Hollow

APEX ACADEMY CAPERS

Come Out and Prey

Let Us Prey

In Prey We Trust

Oh Holy Spite (3.5 novella)

Eat. Prey. Love.

Prey It Ain't So (4.5 novel)

Prey It By Ear

AUDIO OF THE APEX ACADEMY CAPERS SERIES

Come Out & Prey

Let Us Prey

In Prey We Trust

TRANSLATIONS OF THE APEX ACADEMY CAPERS SERIES

Come Out & Prey (German)

Let Us Prey (German)

In Prey Trust (German)

DISCORDIA UNIVERSITY

Veiled Flame (Book One)

Quiet Burn (Book Two)

Zero Spark (Book Three)

Hell for the Holidays (Crossover Holiday w/ SSU & FA)

Obsidian Inferno (Book Four)

AUDIO OF THE DISCORDIA UNIVERSITY SERIES

Veiled Flame (Book One)

Quiet Burn (Book Two)

SECRETS OF STATE U

Blood on the Ice (Book One)

Suspicions on the Stage (Book Two)

Fatality on the Field (Book Three)

FAETAL ATTRACTION

Hell on Wheels (Book One)

Jammer in the Box (Book Two)

Ghosting the Pack (Book Three)

F.E.A.R. ACADEMY

Failed State (Book One)

Trigger Protocol (Book Two)

VILLAINS & VIXENS

Bloodthirsty (Book One)

Ruthless (Book Two)

Wicked (Book Three)

AUDIO OF THE VILLAINS & VIXENS SERIES

Bloodthirsty

Ruthless

TRIANGLES & TRIBULATIONS

Hoist the Flag (PQ)

Yo-Ho Holes (Book One)

CHILDREN OF THE MOON-
WITH SERENITY RAYNE

New Moon Rising (Book One)

Waxing Crescent (Book Two)

Waxing Gibbous (Book Three)

Samhain Secrets (Novella 3.5)

Full Moon (Book Four)

Waning Gibbous (Book Five)

Waning Crescent (Book Six)

RISE OF THE RESISTANCE

Ream Exclusive Prequels

Hooked on a Feline (Book One)

Peacock Me Like A Hurricane

Love The Way You Lion (Book Three)

TBA Title (Book Four)

REAM SERIALS

Secrets of State U

Discordia University

Faetal Attraction

Rise of the Resistance

F.E.A.R. Academy

ANTHOLOGIES

Unwritten

Shifters Unleashed

Jingle My Balls

Love is in the Air

Silent Night

Snowed In

All Hallows Eve